A Place to Find Love

Front Porch Promises

Book 7

By

Merrillee Whren

Merrillee Whren
http://www.merrilleewhren.com/

A Place to Find Love/ Merrillee Whren
ISBN 978-1-944773-16-8

Rejoice always, pray continually, give thanks in all circumstances; for this is God's will for you in Christ Jesus.

—1 Thessalonians 5:16-18 NIV

CHAPTER ONE

Home is where the heart is. The amateurish cross stitch, surrounded by a dark wooden frame, stared back at Whitney Hamilton as she stood in the kitchen of her childhood home. But this home was more like a prison than a place where her heart resided. Recent events had broken, crushed, and turned her heart inside out.

Her small hometown of Pineydale, Tennessee, held little welcome, even though she'd returned over a year ago to help care for her ailing father. Now he was gone, leaving a void in her and her mother's lives. Coming back home had been almost as traumatic as losing her father. The whole town knew her misdeeds. Despite her wish to restore her reputation, she doubted that could happen. She had more enemies than friends in this town.

While Whitney stood there still gazing at the cross stitch, her mother sashayed into the room, her slim figure and blond hair belying her age of seventy-five. "Do you remember when you made that?"

Whitney turned and tried to smile. "Yeah. I was nine and determined to make something for your birthday."

Eileen Hamilton clasped her hands in front of her. "And I love it so much. You were such a strong-minded child."

Whitney didn't think she had that particular characteristic. She'd never stood up for herself against her parents. She'd knuckled under to their demands at every turn. Her life looked like that cross stitch. Graceless. Floundering. Inept.

Whitney glanced toward the front room. "Lila will be here any minute to pick you up. Are you ready?"

Eileen smoothed her multicolored knit top over her well-creased navy pants. "I just have to get my purse."

Just at that moment the doorbell rang. "You get your purse. I'll answer the door."

Worry over her mother filling her thoughts, Whitney rushed to the front door. "Hi, Lila. Come on in."

Lila's wrinkled face crinkled in a smile. "Hello, Whitney. Is your mother ready?"

"She's getting her purse."

"How is she today?" A blast of hot, humid early summer air accompanied Lila as she stepped into the house.

"Okay, I guess." Whitney shrugged, quickly closing the door. "I never know when she'll suddenly do or say something very odd. Y'all are so nice to deal with her forgetfulness in your bridge group. And thank you so much for driving. I just don't trust her to drive anymore."

"I understand." Lila nodded. "She's our friend, and we want to help her."

"Thank you for being such good friends."

"Whitney, I can't find my purse." Eileen's voice sounded from the kitchen.

"I'd better help her." With a sigh, Whitney traipsed back to the kitchen, where she found her mother searching through all the cabinets.

"I just don't know where I put it." She turned to Whitney.

"Did you check in the refrigerator?" Whitney raised her eyebrows.

"Don't be silly. Why would it be there?"

Whitney refrained from reminding her mother that they had found the purse there the last time she had lost it. "Well, check anyway."

Eileen tugged on the refrigerator door. No purse. "See. I told you it wasn't there."

"You're right." Whitney spun around. "Do you remember where you had it last?"

"Here in the kitchen."

"Where have you looked?"

Distress accentuated the wrinkles on her mother's flushed face, suddenly making her look her age. "Everywhere."

Whitney took a calming breath. She had to contain her frustration. Getting rattled would only further her mother's agitation. This kind of thing was becoming a daily occurrence, so Whitney had to learn to deal with it. "It has to be here somewhere."

"Then why can't I find it?"

"Is your cell phone in your purse?"

"I think so."

"Let me call your phone. Then maybe we can figure out where the purse is." Whitney pulled her phone from the pocket of her white skimmers and tapped in her mother's number.

Moments later, the muted sound of the generic ringtone on her mother's phone emanated from a corner of the kitchen. Whitney followed the sound until she faced the old-fashioned wooden bread box sitting on the counter next to the refrigerator. She lifted the lid and found a gray leather purse. She plucked it from the box and held it up.

Her mother grabbed for it and removed the phone from the little side pocket and shut it off. "Silly me, I put it in the bread box. I must've done that when I was making my toast this morning. The bread was lying on the counter, while my purse was in the box."

"It appears that way." Smiling even though she didn't feel like it, Whitney motioned toward the front room. "You've kept Lila waiting long enough. You'd better be on your way."

With a nod, Eileen scurried toward the entry way as the purse dangled from her arm. "Lila, I'm so sorry to keep you waiting. I accidentally put my purse in the bread box."

"You have a bread box?"

Eileen nodded as she followed Lila to the front door. "It was my mother's, and I still use it."

"How wonderful." Lila held open the door, then turned back to Whitney with a knowing smile. "Have a good day. I'll have her back home by three."

"Enjoy your card game." As the door slammed shut, Whitney sank to the couch with a heavy sigh.

Would her meeting with Mary Cunningham be a blessing or a reminder of Jimmy, Mary's older son, the guy she'd loved since elementary school? But Whitney couldn't let old heartaches get in the way of helping her mother. Her mother was the only family left and the only person who loved her. No aunts, no uncles, no cousins, no grandparents.

Alone in the world. That phrase described her.

Whitney bowed her head for a moment. She wanted to pray, but she had drifted so far from God that she wasn't sure He wanted to hear from her. Although she'd attended church every Sunday—when not traveling—since she'd returned to Pineydale, a year's time sitting in a pew had done nothing to bring her closer to God. She'd been going through the motions for her mother.

Whitney glanced across the room.

Be joyful always. Pray continually. 1 Thessalonians 5:16–17. Another one of her clumsy cross stitch attempts mocked her, its message going right to the heart of her troubled thoughts. The year of the cross stitch. That was Whitney's fourth grade year. There were probably at least a couple dozen more somewhere in this house, some framed, some left in a drawer, never to see the light of day.

That year was the same year Jimmy Cunningham had captured her heart. He was the cutest nine-year-old boy in Pineydale Elementary. Not then, but years later that love had brought her pain and a major disagreement with her parents. Thinking about that lost love was futile, but she couldn't stop the memories from sneaking into her thoughts and making her miserable.

Whitney stood, releasing a loud rush of air. She could do this. Her peace of mind depended on it. As she tried to formulate her plea to Mary, Whitney paced the room. The request was a long shot, but one she had to take. The sound of a closing car door made her stop in her tracks. The time was here—the time to make her case.

The doorbell rang, and Whitney took a calming breath as she turned the knob. The door swung open, and the woman Whitney had wished for a mother-in-law smiled. Her snow-white hair stood in sharp contrast to her smooth, wrinkle-free complexion. Her blue eyes always held a welcome, despite the messy history Whitney had with her son.

"Hi, Whitney."

"Hello, Mrs. Cunningham. Thanks for coming to talk to me." Whitney motioned to the interior of the house as she towered over the older woman. "Please come in and have a seat."

"Thanks, but please call me Mary. We've known each other too long for you to be so formal."

"Okay." Whitney fixed a smile on her face. "May I get you something to drink?"

"Some sweet tea would be wonderful, if you have it." Mary took a seat on the rolled-arm couch with the floral print fabric that had graced the living room since Whitney's high school days.

"Sure. I've got sweet tea." Whitney hurried to the kitchen, eager to get away from memories of sitting on that couch with Jimmy. Would Mary's presence constantly remind her of him? Whitney could only hope not.

In minutes Whitney returned to the living room with a tray containing two glasses filled with sweet tea and a small plate of mini chess pies. She set them on the coffee table. "Some treats to go with your tea."

"Oh, I wasn't expecting food, too." Mary reached for her tea. "Did you make the pies?"

Whitney took a sip of her tea, then set the glass on the nearby coaster. "Actually, I helped my mother make them."

"How is Eileen doing these days? I know from experience that losing a spouse is difficult." Mary's eyes brimmed with sympathy.

Whitney clasped her hands in her lap. The time had come for the truth, the truth she'd been trying to deny for weeks. "That's why I asked you to come over."

Cocking her head, Mary eyed Whitney. "So what's this all about?"

Whitney lowered her gaze as she shook her head, then finally looked up at Mary. "Since Daddy died, Mom's been increasingly forgetful and confused. I'm really worried about her, especially when I go away on business trips."

"Has she seen a doctor?" Mary knit her eyebrows.

Sighing, Whitney shook her head. "She doesn't think there's anything wrong. To her it's what she calls her 'senior moments.' But everyone around her knows that it's more than that. She's at her bridge group right now, and they all recognize it. She gets confused and can't follow directions. That's why I had to help her make the pies."

"So what can I do to help?" Concern emanated from Mary's eyes.

"As you know, I have to travel frequently for my job."

Mary nodded. "Yes, I remember how much Jimmy hated that traveling when he worked for his uncle Graham."

The mention of Jimmy's name made Whitney feel as though her heart had been put through a wringer. She had to get over it. He was married and had a child. He was never going to love her again. She had thrown away that chance years ago.

Whitney couldn't bring a smile to her lips. Instead, she stared at the glass of tea in her hand. "Anyway, I'm increasingly worried when I have to go out of town that Mom may do something to put herself in danger. I was hoping you might consider being her live-in nurse."

Mary reached over and touched Whitney's arm. "Whitney, I understand your concern, but that just isn't possible."

Whitney looked up, meeting Mary's gaze. "I'll pay you twice what you're getting at the hospital."

Mary shook her head. "It's not the money. I'm only working part time, but on the days I don't work, I watch my grandchildren."

Whitney's heart sank. "I didn't realize. What am I going to do? Graham has this big trip planned for August. I'll be gone almost a month?"

"So you think your mom's memory is getting that bad?"

Pressing her lips together, Whitney nodded. "I don't trust her to be alone anymore. I'm even worried when I'm at work right here in town. I just can't go away without someone here."

"How long has this been going on?" Concern knit Mary's brow.

"It's gotten worse since Daddy died, or maybe I just didn't notice because I was so concerned with his health and didn't pay enough attention to my mom." Whitney clasped her hands in front of her in a prayerful pose. "I have to find some help before that trip."

"Is your mother on board with this?"

Whitney sighed. "I haven't mentioned it to her. I wanted to see what you said. I know she would be comfortable with you. That's why I asked."

Mary patted Whitney's arm again. "I'm sorry I can't help you, but I think you should let your mother in on your thoughts about this."

Whitney took a sip of her tea, knowing her mother probably wouldn't like the idea. "I suppose."

"In the meantime I'll try to think of someone who could fill that role for you. We should pray about it."

"Thanks for your time." Whitney picked at an imaginary piece of lint on her pants. Pray. Yeah, that was what she should do, but did God want to hear from a woman who had tried to steal another woman's husband? If only she could have a tenth of her mother's faith or a tenth of Mary's faith. If only she could snatch back time and have a do-over. If only she could move forward without a mountain of regret filling her mind.

If only.

Wishing for the impossible would get her nowhere. She had to face reality and deal with it.

"Whitney, would you like me to pray?"

Unable to speak past the lump in her throat, Whitney stared at this kindhearted woman and nodded.

Mary held out her hands, and Whitney took hold as if doing so would pull her out of her doubts and fears. As Mary bowed her head, Whitney followed suit as she closed her eyes.

"Dear Lord, thank You for hearing our prayer. We know You are the almighty God who can grant our requests. Today I pray that You would guide Whitney in helping her mother. Give Whitney wisdom, and please provide a caregiver. We pray in the name of Jesus. Amen."

Whitney raised her head, feeling closer to God than she had in years. Mary's simple prayer gave Whitney hope. "Thank you so much."

"You're welcome. Now we'll see how God will work this out for you." Mary squeezed one of Whitney's hands. "I'll keep praying, and you do the same."

Whitney nodded. "You've made me feel like things aren't hopeless."

"They aren't. God is there for you to lean on. In the

meantime, make sure your mother sees her doctor, and make sure she signs a living will and medical power of attorney, if she hasn't already done so."

"I think she has those because we got them when Daddy was sick, but I'll check to be sure. Thanks for your advice and help."

Mary stood. "Now I'd better get going. Thanks for the refreshments."

Whitney hugged Mary, then stood on the front porch as Mary moseyed to her car. With a wave, she slid in and drove away. Whitney didn't know how long this hopeful feeling would last. Maybe until she broached the subject of a live-in companion to her mother.

***

"Are you out of your mind?"

"No. I know exactly what I'm doing?" Jeremy Cunningham stared at his brother, Jimmy, who sat on the sofa next to his wife, Kelsey, in their mother's living room. Jeremy wondered whether he could convince his brother that this was a good opportunity. "I'm taking the job you didn't want."

Jimmy leaned forward, an incredulous expression on his face. "How could you think of working for Uncle Graham? He's an unrelenting and demanding boss."

"Just because you didn't love the business world doesn't mean I won't."

"What about the painting business?"

"Janelle's going to handle that."

Jimmy flashed an angry look at Janelle, the older of his sisters, before he focused his attention back on Jeremy.

"You mean you two have known about this and didn't say anything to me until today?"

Jeremy wouldn't let Jimmy lay on the guilt. "Nothing was settled with Uncle Graham until late yesterday, and I wasn't going to say anything to you until Janelle and I had a chance to work things out."

"So how's Janelle going to run the company? Does she plan to drag her kids to work?"

"Jimmy, you have no need to talk like I'm not in the room." Janelle stood with her hands on her hips. "The kids are both in school this year, and they can go to the after school program on the days that Mom can't watch them."

Jimmy sat there stone faced as he glanced around the room. "Did everyone know about this except me?"

"I didn't know." Kelsey leaned closer and kissed his cheek.

Jimmy smiled at her. She could always make him smile. He should be thankful for Uncle Graham's demands as a boss. Without them Jimmy would never have married Kelsey. Jeremy would like to point that out, but now probably wasn't a good time. Jimmy's abrupt departure from that job was off limits for discussion at the family gatherings.

"Just be happy for me." Jeremy gave his brother a challenging look.

Jimmy shook his head. "I don't know. I'd like to be, but that job was nothing but a headache. The guy that took my place is already gone after less than a year on the job. What does that tell you?"

"Uncle Graham just hasn't found the right person for that position. Until now." Jeremy's gaze never wavered as he stared Jimmy down.

"And that's you?"

"Got that right." Jeremy surveyed his family all decked out in their red, white, and blue for the Fourth of July. He looked each person in the eyes. "I'm going to see the world on Uncle Graham's dime."

"How do you figure?" Jimmy asked.

Jeremy waved a hand in the air. "I'll get to go on all those business trips you hated. I'm ready. I've never been anywhere. Do you realize I've never been out of the state of Tennessee except over the state line into Bristol, Virginia, and when we've gone to Grandfather Mountain over in North Carolina for the Scottish games?"

Jimmy shook his head. "I never considered all that traveling much of a perk."

"Well, I do. Got my passport and everything."

Jimmy chuckled. "You don't need a passport to go to Atlanta."

"Who says I'm going to Atlanta. How about Europe?"

A buzz of voices filled the room as Jeremy's family took in his statement.

"Why are you going to Europe?" Jimmy frowned.

"Uncle Graham is expanding. He plans to do business with companies in Germany, Belgium, and The Netherlands." Jeremy took in the surprised expressions.

"Wow! I've always wanted to go to Europe." Jenna, his younger sister, clapped Jeremy on the shoulder. "Now my little brother gets to go. Can you fit me into your suitcase?"

Everyone laughed except Jimmy. He still didn't look happy. "What about the marriage clause in your employee agreement?"

"Talked Uncle Graham out of that one." Jeremy

grinned. Maybe that fact would convince Jimmy that his little brother wasn't a pushover.

"How did you manage that?"

"I think he finally realized it wasn't effective, even though he had good intentions." Jeremy raised his eyebrows as he looked at his brother. "Besides, Uncle Graham did you a favor with that requirement."

"He sure did." Kelsey scooted closer to Jimmy and leaned in for another kiss.

Laughter filtered through the room as Jeremy gave his sister-in-law a high five. "He'd still be a lonely bachelor, wishing he hadn't let you get away, if it weren't for Uncle Graham."

Jimmy held his hands up in surrender. "Okay. I'll admit you're right. Kelsey's the best thing that ever happened to me, along with little Jaime here."

Jimmy reached down and rocked the baby carrier sitting at his feet. Jeremy took in the scene with a touch of envy. Jimmy was happier than he'd ever been. His life was settled with a pretty wife, a baby boy, and a thriving business. Despite the pinch of envy, Jeremy wasn't ready to settle down. He didn't want his brother's life. Jeremy wanted to travel and find his own place in the world. He wouldn't let his older brother's worries change that.

Jeremy wanted a chance to step out from under his brother's shadow and be his own man. While he'd been growing up, Jeremy had listened to teachers, coaches, and well-meaning people in town talk about Jimmy's accomplishments in sports, school, and church. Even the two misspent years that had cost Jimmy his college scholarship hadn't seemed to diminish his status in the community. Sure the debacle with Whitney had caused a stir and made him the subject of the town's gossips, but Jeremy only saw it as making Jimmy more legendary.

Jeremy had *only* been Jimmy's little brother to everyone in this town. He wanted success at this job to change that.

"Good to see you figured that out. Uncle Graham isn't all that bad." Continuing to eye his brother, Jeremy crossed his arms as he leaned against the doorjamb.

Jimmy stared back. "What about riding in the Pan-Massachusetts Challenge? How can you do that when you've just started a new job?"

Jeremy grinned. "I told Uncle Graham about that, and he understands, especially since Mitch is riding. He wants to use the team for a little marketing."

"Great." Jimmy frowned. "Uncle Graham's sticking his nose into our stuff again."

Jeremy waved a hand at Jimmy. "Be glad. He's sponsoring the team and paying for transportation and lodging."

"Since when? First I've heard of it."

"I thought Mitch would've mentioned it to you."

Jimmy shrugged. "Guess he was waiting for the right time to let us know that his dad is trying to run our lives again."

"Just look at the good side of it." Jeremy gave his brother an annoyed look.

"What about Whitney Hamilton?"

"What about her?"

"Won't you have to work with her?" Jimmy asked.

"Your tumultuous history with her doesn't affect me. I never saw her once during any of my interviews."

"Well, don't be surprised if she turns out to be a thorn

in your side."

"Okay, boys. I've let you have your say. Now it's my turn." Mary Cunningham stepped between her sons. "Since you're talking about Whitney, I have something to say about her."

Jeremy took in the surprised looks on his siblings' faces. What could his mother possibly have to say about Whitney?

"Earlier this week, I visited with Whitney." Mary held up a hand. "And before you say anything, I want you to hear me out. Don't interrupt me."

Although the silence in the room showed the respect Jeremy and his siblings had for their mother, the stunned expressions said a lot about Whitney's bad history with the Cunninghams. A burst of laughter from his nieces and nephews, who played outside under the supervision of his mom's distant cousin Carla, seemed loud in the quiet.

Mary glanced toward the window that looked out on the backyard. "I've invited Whitney and her mother to join us over at Aunt Charlotte's to watch the Fourth of July parade this afternoon."

Jeremy didn't miss the frown on Jimmy's face, but he didn't say anything. Jeremy never had much interaction with Whitney, other than the few times she'd been his babysitter when he'd been in first or second grade. She was six years older and had dated Jimmy throughout high school. Tall, blond, and blue-eyed, she'd been voted prettiest by her classmates. She and Jimmy had been homecoming queen and king. Everyone had thought they were destined to be together, but their relationship derailed when her parents sent her away to college in Georgia.

Jeremy had been sixteen when that whole mess with

Jimmy, their cousin Mitch, and Whitney went down. She left town after that and never came back until her daddy got sick. Jeremy had no idea why his mom would be having a conversation with Whitney.

Mary motioned toward the window. "You've met Carla, my cousin's daughter. She has come to town to help Whitney with her mother, and we need your help to make that happen."

Jimmy raised his hand like a school child. "Is it okay if I ask a question?"

A little smile curving her lips, Mary shook her head. "When I'm done, if you still have questions, you can ask. Whitney asked me if I could be a live-in companion for her mother. I told her I couldn't because I'm watching my grandchildren."

"Why does she need a companion for her mother?" Janelle asked.

Mary eyed her older daughter. "Believe me, if you just wait until I'm finished, I'm sure I'll answer all your questions."

Janelle looked contrite as Mary continued. "Whitney believes her mother has developed dementia and is afraid to leave Eileen home alone. Whitney travels extensively for work and worries that Eileen wouldn't be safe by herself."

"I bet she'll be on one of those European trips you're so excited about, Jeremy. I knew she'd be a thorn in your side."

"Jimmy, we don't need any comments from you." Mary stared pointedly at her older son. "So I've been praying about this, and God provided. Carla needs work, and this is a perfect opportunity for her. Whitney's pretty sure her mother won't agree to this arrangement unless she thinks it's her idea and believes she's the one who is helping Carla, not the other way around."

"So how are we supposed help?" Janelle asked.

Frowning, Mary shook her head. "You children are certainly impatient. I'm getting to that. I want you to be very, I mean very, welcoming to Eileen and Whitney. We'll not only be watching the parade, but we'll be eating supper at Charlotte's and then going to see the fireworks at the country club."

"And in case you didn't know it, Uncle Graham has paid for the fireworks out of his own pocket for years." Jeremy didn't know why he felt the need to defend his new boss.

His mom's chastening expression made him wish he hadn't opened his mouth. He shrunk back into the doorway and pressed his lips together. He didn't need to say another thing.

Mary cleared her throat. "Now that I have the floor again, I'll continue. Please do whatever you can to bring Eileen and Carla together. We're going to mention how her job fell through and that she can't stay with me long term because of her pet allergies. We would like Eileen to consider taking Carla in. So whatever you can do to move the discussion in that direction will help. And the main reason I mentioned this is because I want you to be *extra, extra* nice to Whitney and her mother. Is everyone on the same page with this?"

Digesting his mother's command, Jeremy watched the reaction of his siblings and their spouses and wondered whether Eileen would see through this crazy scheme. Did he dare mention his doubts? His mom was all revved up about her plan, so they'd better go along with it. He loved his mom. He wouldn't trade her for the world. But did anyone in the family, besides him, see how Mary loved to direct lives as much as Uncle Graham?

CHAPTER TWO

"Mom, are you ready?" Whitney poked her head around the doorframe of her mother's bedroom.

"Give me a minute, Melissa."

Whitney sighed, not bothering to correct her mother. Whitney didn't know why her mother occasionally called her Melissa, but it had started when Whitney noticed the signs of dementia. She hoped her mother didn't do that while they were out today.

"Okay, I'll be in the kitchen." Whitney slipped on the blue sandals that matched the blue in her silky sleeveless red, white, and blue top. She stuck her phone in the pocket of her white shorts.

"All ready."

Whitney turned at the sound of her mother's voice. "You look wonderful and ready to show off your patriotic colors."

Eileen glanced down at the blue shirt decorated with red and white stars. "I always save this for the Fourth of July."

"Let's head to Charlotte's. We don't want to miss the start of the parade."

"This will be a fun day. I haven't had a visit with Charlotte in a while. I just didn't feel like visiting after your daddy died." Eileen grabbed her purse.

"I know what you mean." Whitney breathed a sigh of relief when they didn't have to search for the purse. She locked the front door while her mother waited on the porch. "I'm ready for some fun, too."

Whitney smiled as she walked with her mother down the street. The hot, humid air of the preceding days had given way to a cooler, drier day. The pleasant weather and the short walk to Charlotte's would do them both good. Whitney usually worked out in the gym at the country club early in the mornings before work when she was in town, but it was nice just to stroll for a change.

As they moseyed along, Eileen recalled several Independence Day celebrations, including the time Whitney had decorated her bike for the parade and wound up falling off it and breaking her arm. "Your daddy was so upset. He felt responsible. He was such a good man."

"He was." Whitney gave her mother's shoulders a hug. "He would want us to enjoy this day."

"And we will." Her mother smiled, gazing up at Whitney.

Thankful that her mother appeared to be less confused today, Whitney smiled back. It was a good day, if a good day meant facing her old love, his wife, and new baby. Could she pass that test? The last time she'd had a real conversation with Jimmy she'd made a complete fool of herself. Ever since, she'd tried her best to avoid him.

A nod or a quick hello at church was the only thing she'd exchanged with him in over a year, except when he'd offered his condolences at her daddy's funeral. On that occasion, she'd been too overcome with grief over the loss of her father to think about her feelings for Jimmy. But today was different. There was nothing to distract her from the man she had wronged by trying to please her parents.

Thankfully, she'd been busy with work and taking care of her parents during this last year. Her social life didn't exist. There had been little chance to run into Jimmy, other than at church. Today she had to deal with her guilt and embarrassment. She doubted Jimmy had told anyone about his last day working for Graham Cunningham, or maybe she was only hoping that was the case.

She shouldn't be worrying about Jimmy. She needed to concentrate on getting her mother to agree to a live-in companion. Whitney looked forward to having someone else in the house besides her mother to talk to. Carla was perfect. The two of them had hit it off as soon as they'd met last week. With Carla in the house, Whitney could have peace of mind while she was at work.

"There's certainly a crowd at Charlotte's." Eileen's brow wrinkled with worry. "I'm just not used to crowds anymore."

"It's mostly people you know." Whitney took in the gathering that filled the wide front porch of the historic four-square house and spilled into the yard under the huge mimosa tree with the delightful smell coming from its pink blossoms.

Eileen stopped at the corner and gazed up at Whitney. "I know, but sometimes I get confused and forget who people are. It makes me nervous."

"I'll be right there with you." Whitney gave her mom a hug. Was she actually recognizing that her forgetfulness was more than just a senior moment?

As they reached Charlotte's front walk, Mary raced down the steps to greet them. "Eileen, Whitney. I'm so glad you made it. Come join the festivities."

"It's so good to see you." Eileen hugged Mary. "It's been too long since we've visited."

"I know." Mary smiled as she escorted Eileen up the front steps.

Whitney hung back as she took in the congenial greeting between her mother and Mary Cunningham. The two women had never been very close. They knew each other from church, but they didn't socialize on a regular basis, at least in the year Whitney had been back, and certainly not when she had been in high school. What had changed in the years she had lived in Atlanta?

With that question plaguing her thoughts, Whitney surveyed the porch until her gaze landed on Jimmy. He stood next to his wife as he held their baby boy, who was barely six weeks old. Whitney's heart twisted. She had wanted to be the mother of his children, but she was just plain stupid to keep pining over him. Should she bite the bullet and make pleasant conversation with him and his wife?

Was avoiding them a possible option? Although the porch was large, they would be hard to ignore. She might as well get it over with. She was no coward. Taking a deep breath, she squared her shoulders and climbed the steps.

"Whitney, it's so good to see you." Charlotte opened her arms for a hug. "You need to come by and visit and bring your mother."

Whitney wrapped her arms around the older woman, then stepped back. "Thanks for the warm welcome. I have to admit I've let work derail my social life."

"You can't let work take over your life." Charlotte wagged a finger at Whitney. "How's your mother doing?"

Whitney wished she knew how to answer that. "Better

in some ways. Not so good in others. But then you know what it's like to lose a spouse of many years."

"It's hard, but it does get better." Charlotte glanced toward Eileen. "I should've called on your mom, but I didn't know if she felt up to having company."

"She's ready. She just started playing with her bridge group again, so I think she'd like to have visitors."

"That's good," Charlotte said.

Whitney lowered her gaze. Did she dare mention her mom's forgetfulness to Charlotte? Whitney let out a little sigh. "I have to let you know that Mom's getting forgetful. I fear she may have dementia."

Charlotte placed a hand over her heart. "I'm so sorry to hear this. I'll keep her in my prayers."

"I know you will." Whitney knew one thing for certain. When Charlotte said she would pray, she would.

Charlotte motioned to the rest of her guests. "Now you go and join the young people. You don't need to be hanging around with this old lady."

"Charlotte, you're forever young." Whitney smiled, then gave Charlotte a hug.

"Off with you." Charlotte waved Whitney away.

Whitney turned and came face to face with Jimmy's older sister. "Hi, Janelle."

Janelle smiled, but her eyes hardly held a welcome. "I hear you're going to be working with my little brother."

Whitney hoped the shock didn't show on her face. "Jeremy?"

Janelle nodded. "You look surprised. Didn't you know he took Jimmy's old position?"

"I didn't." Whitney wondered how this had happened without her knowing about it.

"He seems pretty excited. I hope it works out better for him than it did for Jimmy."

Trying to smile, Whitney wondered whether that was some kind of warning. This whole conversation reminded her of her foolishness. "Me, too. Graham's a tough but fair boss."

"That's what Jeremy says, but Jimmy isn't convinced. He doesn't think Jeremy is making a wise decision. What do you think?"

Wow! Whitney didn't know where to start with that question, but she had to come up with something. "Jimmy had his differences with Graham, but Jeremy might be the perfect fit for the job."

"That's what Jeremy thinks."

Jeremy. Had she even seen him since she'd come back to town? If she had, she probably didn't recognize him. He'd been a gangly teenager with pimples, thick-rimmed glasses, and a bad haircut when she'd left a little over eight years ago. Now that she thought about it, he had to be at least six years younger than Jimmy. That would make him twenty-four—way too young to handle that position. But she wasn't going to say that to Janelle.

What was Graham thinking? That he could train and manipulate a younger man? Graham was putting a lot of responsibility on Jeremy's shoulders. Things had been going very well at work, so her best bet was to keep her opinions to herself. The less she said the better. She had said some things to Jimmy that she'd like to have back. Words that should never have left her mouth.

"Maybe he's right. Only time will tell. I look forward to working with him." At least she hoped that was true. Would Jeremy's presence remind her of Jimmy? She cringed at the thought.

"Well, I certainly hope it turns out better for Jeremy than it did for Jimmy, except he did get Kelsey out of it. She makes him a contented man. They're perfect for each other." Janelle glanced in Jimmy's direction. "Have you seen that cute little boy of theirs?"

"Not up close." Whitney fabricated a smile, wondering whether Janelle was rubbing it in, letting Whitney know that Jimmy was happy without her. That was silly. Why would anyone think Whitney still had a thing for Jimmy? They would be just as crazy as she was after all these years for letting one man keep her from moving on with her life.

"You'll have to say hi."

Before Whitney could respond, Mitch Cunningham and his wife, Amanda, who was Kelsey's sister, arrived with their infant son, Logan. The two boy cousins were born just hours apart on the same day in May.

As Mitch looked Whitney's way, he couldn't hide his surprise. "Hey, Whitney."

"Hi, Mitch, Amanda." Whitney peered at the sleeping infant in the carrier. "Logan looks just like his daddy."

Amanda smiled. "That's what everyone says. I do all the work, and the kid looks like him."

"Thems the breaks." Mitch chuckled and looked down at his wife as he pulled her close. "What brings you to this gathering, Whitney?"

"Mary and Charlotte invited my mom and me so we can watch the parade."

Mitch nodded. "It's good to see your mom getting out."

Whitney thought about the loss of her dad and her mom's problems, her lips quivering as she managed to hold a smile in place. No mention that it was good to see her. She shouldn't be offended. Neither Mitch nor Jimmy had any reason to be glad to see her. She had caused a rift between them that had lasted years. They appeared to have put that behind them, maybe because they had married sisters.

"It's nice to see you. I better check on my mom before the parade starts." Turning her back on Mitch, Whitney searched the porch for her mom.

Whitney's stomach sank when she spied her mom talking with Mary, who was showing off her latest grandchild, Jaimie, Jimmy and Kelsey's little boy. Jimmy stood there bouncing his son in his arms as Eileen looked on, completely enthralled with the cooing baby boy, no sign of the disdain she'd had for Jimmy when he hadn't lived up to her expectations while he'd been dating Whitney. Eileen was most likely happy that Jimmy had married someone else, not Whitney.

The time had come to face old wounds and bury them for good.

As Whitney approached, her mother caught Whitney's eye and waved her over. "Whitney, come see this precious baby."

Whitney trained her eyes on the infant, not daring to look at either Jimmy or Kelsey. Just like Mitch's little boy, Jimmy's baby looked just like his dad. "He certainly is precious."

"Thanks." Kelsey's voice penetrated the fog of Whitney's discomfort.

Wishing she were someplace else, Whitney forced herself to look the other woman in the eye. "I can't believe you and Amanda had your babies on the same day. That's amazing."

"My dad says we wanted to make it easy on him. Now he only has to remember one birthday." Kelsey reached for her son, and Jimmy placed the baby in her arms.

"How are you?" Jimmy asked as Eileen moved away to talk with a woman she knew from the ladies circle at church. "And how's your mom doing since your daddy's passing?"

Whitney was struck by the sincerity in his voice. He really wanted to know and didn't seem to mind that she was there, unlike his sister. "Mom's okay, but her health isn't the best these days. Daddy's death has taken a toll on her. My work is going well, and I hear that Jeremy's taking your old job."

Jimmy raised his eyebrows, his forehead wrinkling. "That's what he tells me. Be good to my little brother."

Was that some kind of warning? Whitney nodded, trying not to let her agitation show. "Chances are we won't see much of each other. After you left, I didn't work with the guy who replaced you. I concentrated on making our online presence as user friendly and up to date as possible. My work with operations and sales has been limited."

"Speaking of Jeremy, here he is." Jimmy motioned behind Whitney.

She turned, and her heart went into her throat. He wasn't that gangly, pimply-faced kid anymore. The resemblance between the brothers was striking. Both tall with dark-brown hair, they could almost be identical twins, except Jeremy's eyes were blue like a cloudless sky, while Jimmy's were gray. How was she going to work with Jeremy and not be reminded of Jimmy? Jeremy's broad shoulders filled out his red, white, and blue striped polo shirt. Those blue eyes made him even better looking than his brother, if that was possible.

She remembered Jeremy, but not *this* Jeremy. This Jeremy with the twinkling blue eyes that used to be hidden behind nerdy glasses didn't resemble the kid she had once babysat. His grin made her heart trip. What was she thinking? This was Jimmy's little brother. He was at least six years her junior. She gave herself a mental shake. Her reaction was only an appreciation for a good-looking man. That was all.

"Hello, Whitney." He extended his hand. "I guess you've heard I've taken a job with my uncle Graham."

"I have. Congratulations!" Shaking his hand, Whitney hoped she sounded sincere. She really was happy for him, but working with him would only remind her of decisions she deeply regretted, even though Jimmy appeared to have put that incident behind him. Why couldn't she?

"So I'll see you on Monday."

"Be prepared to work like you've never worked before. Your uncle Graham is a taskmaster, but then I'm sure Jimmy has mentioned that." Whitney hoped Jeremy's work wouldn't intersect with hers.

"He did, but I'm prepared." Jeremy turned at the boom of a base drum and the clickety-clack of snare drums. "Sounds like the parade is almost here. I want a front-row seat for the kids' parade. That's the best part." Jeremy glanced back at Whitney. "You want me to get you a seat?"

Whitney had no idea how to turn down this invitation. "I need to get my mom."

"Great." Jeremy motioned toward the front yard. "Get your mom, and I'll get the chairs. Meet you in the front row."

Whitney wondered if Jeremy had been too young to remember what had transpired between his brother and her. Jeremy had been in high school, not too young to have heard the gossip. She should take it as a good sign that she wasn't a pariah in his eyes. Or maybe he was only trying to have a good relationship with a coworker. She didn't need to analyze. She just needed to find her mother.

"Whitney." Eileen charged toward her daughter. "The start of the parade's almost here."

"Yes, it is, and Jeremy has been kind enough to get us chairs so we have a front-row seat." Whitney slipped her arm through her mother's and pointed toward the stretch of grass between the sidewalk and the curb.

"What a thoughtful thing to do."

"Yes, it is." Whitney guided her mother toward the spot where Jeremy was helping Carla set up multicolored webbed lawn chairs.

Jeremy looked up as Carla sat in the chair next to him. He motioned to the two chairs next to Carla. "Mrs. Hamilton, why don't you sit next to Carla. She's my mom's distant cousin."

"Thank you, Jeremy. You're such a gentleman." Eileen lowered herself into the lawn chair. "I'm glad to meet you, Carla. Are you just visiting?"

"I came here because I thought I had a job lined up, but that fell through. I can't move back home because my folks have sold their home and bought an RV and are traveling the country. So I was going to stay with Mary, but I'm allergic to cats. And she has two cats."

"I didn't know Mary had cats. Are you staying there now?" Eileen asked.

"Yes, but I've got to find someplace else soon. I'm

sneezing and wheezing all the time."

Eileen frowned. "That's terrible. Did you know about the cats before you came?"

Carla shook her head. "Mary hasn't had them long. They were strays that showed up at her door, so she took them in."

"Well, she could give the cats to someone else."

Carla shook her head. "I wouldn't want her to give up her pets."

Whitney took in the conversation and hoped it would lead where they had planned. Jeremy must've been assigned to get Carla and Eileen together. Whitney glanced toward the end where Jeremy sat. He gave her a subtle wink as he tilted his head her way. She made a slight nod.

The drum cadence grew louder, and Eileen sat forward in her chair. "The parade is here."

Whitney smiled as she reached over and squeezed her mom's hand. Her mom was as excited as a kid. Her conversation with Carla floated away with the notes of "Stars and Stripes Forever."

"I love this song." Eileen clapped her hands to the music. "It's been a while since I've watched the parade."

"It's a lively patriotic song." Whitney glanced at Jeremy and Carla, but they were caught up in the parade. So she might as well sit back and enjoy it, too.

The high school band led the parade, followed by the mayor, who rode in a red convertible decked out with flags. Next came a couple of Girl Scout and Boy Scout troops carrying flags as they marched down the street. Floats from various businesses and civic organizations, along with more convertibles and pickup trucks displaying advertisements, proceeded down the street.

"There's Amanda's sports car, advertising Mitch's garage. Bobby is having the time of his life driving that car. But I bet it's killing him to drive it at that slow speed." Jeremy chuckled.

"Is that little Bobby Ferguson?" Whitney craned her neck to see. "He was maybe nine or ten the last time I remember seeing him."

"What can I say? You're getting old, Whitney." Jeremy laced his fingers behind his head as he looked straight ahead.

"And you're still wet behind the ears." Whitney glared at Jeremy. His statement created a pounding in her brain like the sound of the bass drum in the band. *You're old. You're old. You're old.* The cadence didn't stop.

Jeremy's mouth curved in a smug smile as he turned her way. "Oooh, I think I hit a nerve."

Whitney didn't say anything, just smiled back, even though she had the urge to cover her ears to drown out the nonexistent sound. This town was making her crazy.

She wished she could retract her comment. Her response only played into Jeremy's thoughts about her. She was old in his eyes. In Atlanta she was a young woman on the go with an upwardly mobile job and a great social life. But here in Pineydale, the young women who'd stayed here after high school had gotten married almost as soon as they received their diplomas. By all accounts, Whitney was probably considered an old maid. Her friends who had gone to college had never moved back to Pineydale. They'd moved on to bigger and better places, as she had. But she'd come back for her parents.

She was stuck here. The women her age in Pineydale were married and had at least two kids. The only bright spot about living in this town was a good job and being here to make sure her mother had the care she needed. Otherwise, the place held no welcome. She was grateful for business trips that took her away, but even those held a disadvantage. She had to find help for her mother.

"Here comes your new boss." Eileen motioned toward the street.

Graham Cunningham stood through the sunroof of a white SUV with flags waving from the windows and red, white, and blue streamers trailing from the antenna and door handles. He threw candy and waved to the crowd as he went by.

Jeremy chuckled as he nodded. "That's my uncle Graham. He loves to be the center of attention. That's why he's doing this instead of hiring some kid to do it. I'm surprised he's never run for mayor."

"He's been too busy with his company."

Whitney turned at the sound of her mother's voice and smiled. Sometimes her mother seemed like her old self, but other times this brilliant woman who had been a college professor seemed like a lost child.

Whitney patted her mother's hand where it lay on the arm of the lawn chair. "Maybe after he retires, he'll run for mayor."

"Doesn't sound like much of a retirement to me," Jeremy said.

"You ought to know your uncle Graham. Do you think he really wants to retire?" Whitney picked up a piece of the hard candy from the ground and unwrapped it as she stared at Jeremy. "That's why he hired you, so you could learn the business and take over. Maybe he'll have you running his political campaign as well."

Jeremy shook his head as he made a face. "You certainly have a vivid imagination."

"That's what makes me good at my job."

"In a few days, I'll get to see you in action."

Whitney hoped not. She wanted Jeremy in a completely different part of the office. The less interaction with him, the less he would remind her of the foolish statements she'd made to his brother. "Don't count on it. You'll be too busy jumping to your uncle's commands."

"I'm ready for the challenge." Jeremy held her gaze.

The challenge would be hers. The challenge not to let his presence play havoc with her peace of mind. She would deal with it. She popped the candy into her mouth.

"Here come the kids." Jeremy stood and waved as his nieces and nephews pedaled by.

The older ones rode their bikes, while Jeremy's brothers-in-law pulled the little ones in wagons decorated with red, white, and blue streamers. Broad smiles on their faces, the kids waved at Jeremy as they went by. Mary and her daughters joined the spectators at the curb as they cheered on their children.

Whitney stood there alone in a crowd. Conversation buzzed around her, but she wasn't part of it. The joy on the faces of the people in the crowd eluded her. She might as well be one of the clowns in the parade with a painted happy face while sadness lay underneath the makeup. She wasn't sure what had stripped the happiness from her life. Maybe it was an accumulation of events. Could she ever get it back?

As the clowns threw out the last of the candy and disappeared down the street, folks gathered up the lawn chairs and headed for the backyard.

"Would you like me to carry your chair around to the back, Mrs. Hamilton?" Jeremy put his hand on the back of Eileen's chair.

Eileen smiled up at him as Whitney helped her mother up. "Thank you. That would be wonderful. You are such a gentleman. And please call me Eileen."

"Yes, ma'am." Jeremy picked up his chair as well as Eileen's.

Her mother had called Jeremy a gentleman for the second time. Whitney couldn't get over how her mother had taken to him. Why hadn't she been that kind to Jimmy all those years ago? Whitney shoved the question away. Dwelling on old hurts would accomplish nothing.

Charlotte's backyard was ready for a patriotic party. Red, white, and blue tablecloths covered tables scattered across the lawn. Jeremy deposited the lawn chairs in the shade near the back of the house, where several more chairs sat in a broad semicircle.

"Does this suit?" Jeremy looked over at Eileen.

"It's just fine." Eileen patted him on the arm. "Thank you."

"With that mission accomplished, I'm going to test my skill at cornhole." Jeremy grinned as he sauntered away.

"He should be a nice young man to work with."

"I don't know that we'll work together that much."

Jeremy was nice enough, but he would be a constant reminder of her loss. The less she saw of him, the better off she would be.

"I think I'll go watch the cornhole tournament."

Whitney stared at her mother. "I had no idea you were interested in cornhole competition."

"I've never watched it before. It'll be something new."

Eileen marched across the yard, leaving Whitney standing there with her mouth open.

"Did you and your mother enjoy the parade?" Mary stopped beside Whitney as she held a big stack of plastic cups.

"We did. Could I help you with those?"

"No, thanks. I've got this." Mary waved her free hand. "Did Jeremy introduce your mother to Carla?"

Whitney nodded as she accompanied Mary to the table where she deposited the cups. "He did, but the parade cut short their conversation. So nothing ever came of it. Do you think I should suggest Carla stay with us?"

"I'd let the day play out first."

"I suppose."

A shout of triumph came from the area of the yard where the cornhole competition was in full swing.

"That sounds like my younger son. He puts his whole heart into whatever he's doing. And look who's right there cheering him on. Your mother."

Whitney gazed across the yard to the spot where her mother stood clapping her hands. "I don't recognize my mother today."

"Is that a good thing or a bad thing?"

"I think it's good. She's really enjoying herself, but it would certainly ease my mind if I knew I had someone to be with her when I'm not around."

"We'll get there. And you should join your mother. You might enjoy a little cornhole. And Carla's there, too. Maybe you can get that needed conversation going again."

"Yeah. I should go over there, even though I'm not much interested in cornhole."

As Whitney drew close to the game, Jeremy glanced

her way. "Hey, Whitney, you going to try your hand at cornhole?"

Not if I can help it. That was what she should have said, but one word came out of her mouth. "Sure."

"Great! You can be on my team."

Whitney let out a sick little laugh. "You won't think so after you see me play."

"You can't be that bad." Jeremy handed her a couple of beanbags.

"Oh yes, I can." She fingered the blue denim cloth.

"Let's see what you've got." Jeremy grinned at her.

Whitney focused her attention on the round hole in the wooden platform. How hard could it be to put the beanbag in that hole? She tossed the beanbag. It flew through the air and landed with a smack on the wooden platform, then slid onto the grass with a soft plunk. "Well, that wasn't so good, but I warned you."

Jeremy retrieved her beanbag and handed it to her. "I could give you some pointers."

Refusing to meet his gaze, Whitney fiddled with the beanbag. "That's okay. I knew cornhole wasn't my game. I'll watch."

"You can't quit in the middle of the game."

Still not looking at him, Whitney blew out a puff of air. "Okay. If you want to lose."

"I have confidence that you'll do better this next time. Watch me." Jeremy stepped up to the line and tossed the beanbag. It slid into the hole, and he turned to her with a smile. "See how it's done."

Unable to speak, Whitney nodded as she swallowed hard. Every time she looked at Jeremy, she saw Jimmy and remembered the smile that had made her heart pitter-patter and the kisses that had curled her toes. She had to believe that eventually Jeremy wouldn't turn her thoughts to Jimmy. Her sanity depended on it.

With Eileen cheering them on, Whitney and Jeremy managed to eke out a victory over Carla and her partner, Owen, who apparently worked for the painting company that Jeremy was abandoning for the chance to work for his uncle. When Jeremy held up a hand for a high five, Whitney slapped it and hoped this would be the end of cornhole.

"Thanks for being my partner. You're a quick study. We'll have to do this again sometime."

Not on my agenda. Whitney gritted her teeth in order not to let the words out of her mouth. She didn't want to hang around with Jeremy or play cornhole.

As Whitney looked around, Charlotte appeared on the steps leading down from her back door. She rang a big bell, and everyone stopped what they were doing and looked her way. *Literally saved by the bell.* Whitney breathed a sigh of relief that she didn't have to do a three-legged race or some other not-so-fun activity.

"Thanks to everyone who has come to share the day with me." She motioned toward the two large tables laden with food. "We're going to have Graham say a blessing for our meal. Then the parents with little ones will go first. Then the folks over sixty. Then the rest of you can fight over what's left."

A chuckle rolled through the crowd as Graham joined Charlotte on the steps. "First, I want to thank Charlotte for her hospitality and everyone who prepared food. Now let's thank God for our blessings."

After the prayer, Jeremy took charge and escorted

Eileen to the spot in line where the over-sixty crowd had lined up according to Charlotte's instructions, while Whitney traipsed along beside him. Why had her mother taken to Jeremy? Maybe she remembered him as the crazy little boy who couldn't sit still in church or the bespectacled preteen who had ridden his bike across their lawn when he delivered papers.

And Whitney couldn't believe all the memories of Jeremy that bombarded her mind.

Eileen slipped into line behind Graham and his wife, Donna. "Thank you, Jeremy, for being so helpful."

"I see you've been getting acquainted with Whitney. I like your teamwork." Graham extended his hand to Jeremy. "I'm announcing some big plans on Monday when we get back to work."

"Sounds good." Jeremy nodded. "I'm ready to get started."

Whitney just stood by and took in the conversation. What would those big plans mean for her? For Jeremy? For her peace of mind?

Whitney managed to get through the meal with her mother tagging along with Jeremy like he was her long-lost son. And he was more than polite as he indulged the older woman who had practically adopted him. Whitney wished her mother would adopt Carla, but that didn't seem to be happening.

"Are you finished? Would you like me to take your plates to the trash?" Jeremy picked up his plate.

Before Whitney could answer, Eileen handed Jeremy her plate. "That would be wonderful. Thanks."

Whitney silently handed hers over as Jeremy cleared the table and sauntered off to the trash bin.

"Did you go to school with Jeremy?" Eileen wrinkled her brow, as if trying to figure out the answer to her own question.

Whitney shook her head, wondering whether her mother had any idea that Jeremy was Jimmy's brother. "No, Mom. Jeremy was several years behind me in school."

"Oh. He seems so familiar."

Sadness settled around Whitney's heart. What had seemed like a good day for her mother suddenly disintegrated with that one sentence. Whitney forced herself to smile, when all she really wanted to do was cry. This wasn't fair. Nothing was fair about her life here in Pineydale. When she'd been in Atlanta, Pineydale had been far, far from her thoughts.

Waving one arm above her head, Carla loped across the lawn. "Hey, Whitney. Jeremy says you and your mom should ride with us to the country club for the fireworks. Okay?"

Whitney waved in return. "Mom, what do you think? Are you up for fireworks?"

Eileen nodded. "What would the Fourth of July be without them?"

"Sure. Let's go." Whitney guided her mom across the yard until they stood next to Carla.

Carla smiled. "I'll show you where Jeremy parked. He's loading lawn chairs into his SUV."

As they approached, Jeremy glanced up and closed the hatch on his vehicle. "All set for a trip to the country club?"

"I am. I'm looking forward to fireworks." Eileen smiled up at Jeremy.

Jeremy opened the front passenger door for Eileen. "You get to ride shotgun."

Eileen allowed Jeremy to assist her as she climbed into the front seat. "When Whitney was young, she was so excited when she was finally old enough to ride in the front seat."

Wishing her mother wouldn't reminisce, Whitney scooted into the back with Carla. "I was actually more excited when I got my driver's license."

"Yes, you were. And now you've seen the world."

"Not the whole world."

"But enough of it." Eileen turned toward the backseat. "I'm glad you're home now."

"Me, too." Whitney forced the words from her mouth. They weren't an outright lie. She was glad to be here to help her mother, but being back in Pineydale didn't bring much joy.

After they arrived at the country club, they set their chairs near the little lake that formed one of the water hazards on the golf course. The sun hovered low in the sky as a myriad of pinks, oranges, and yellows colored the clouds in an ever-changing kaleidoscope. Conversation buzzed around Whitney, but she didn't feel much like talking.

Her mom and Carla chatted quietly, while Jeremy had abandoned his chair to play with his sisters' kids. Just like Jimmy, Jeremy loved kids. Whitney didn't want to think about Jimmy or Jeremy, but there she was thinking about both of them. She could hardly wait until the fireworks were over and she could go home.

"We have plenty of extra room, and we don't have any pets to make you wheeze. Carla, do you think you'd like to stay at our house?" Eileen's question came out of nowhere.

Carla leaned forward in her chair and slipped a glance at Whitney. "That would be a lifesaver for me until I can get a job."

Eileen turned. "Whitney, what do you think?"

"I think that's a spectacular idea." Whitney nodded as she smiled at Carla.

Eileen slapped her hands on the arms of her chair. "Then it's settled. You can start tonight, if you'd like."

"That would be great. I'll have to tell Jeremy to drive by his mom's so I can pick up my things after the fireworks." Carla hopped up from her chair and hurried to where Jeremy played tag with a group of kids.

After Carla finished talking to Jeremy, he glanced at Whitney with a knowing look. She gave him a subtle nod as a world of worry sloughed away like the sun slowly sinking below the horizon.

For the first time in a long time, Whitney felt as though God was listening as the crowd oohed and aahed over the beauty of the fireworks. She had hope for tomorrow, even though tomorrow held more unknowns than the rockets that flared into the air and burst into dozens of unexpected patterns.

Whitney grabbed on to the beauty of an answered prayer and held it close to her heart. Having a caregiver for her mother would make the other unknowns bearable. She could face whatever the days ahead brought as long as her mother was safe.

CHAPTER THREE

Adrenaline had Jeremy's nerves standing at attention like soldiers on review. He took a deep breath and tried to push aside Jimmy's negative comments about this work situation. A private meeting with Uncle Graham on the first day of the job didn't mean problems lay ahead. He could tackle any task his uncle put out there. This was only a welcome-to-the-job chat.

He told himself that as he knocked on the office door and squared his shoulders. He remembered the job interview and how Uncle Graham had been friendly and welcoming. Why should anything have changed? But Jimmy's unfavorable experience floated at the back of Jeremy's mind.

"Come in." Uncle Graham's voice sounded from the other side of the door.

Jeremy turned the knob and let the door swing open. "Good morning, Uncle Graham."

"Good morning, and a good morning it is having you here." Graham shook Jeremy's hand.

"Thanks." Relishing his uncle's greeting, Jeremy took the seat his uncle indicated.

His thick graying hair and trim figure gave Graham an air of authority as he sat behind his desk and leaned forward. "Since we're business colleagues, you don't have to call me Uncle Graham. Just Graham."

"Yes, sir." Jeremy nodded, his stomach swirling with nervous energy despite the cordial conversation.

Graham nodded. "I'm sure your mama taught you to say *yes, sir* and *yes, ma'am*."

"She did."

"It's not necessary here."

Shaking his head, Jeremy chuckled. "Old habits die hard. I'm sure you'll hear a few yes sirs along the way."

"I understand." Graham eyed Jeremy. "I also want you to understand the job situation here."

"Sure. I'm ready to get started."

"Good, but I've had some changes in my thinking."

A bad premonition raced through Jeremy's thoughts. "Okay."

Graham rubbed his chin, then rose to look out the window. An uncomfortable feeling snaked its way up Jeremy's spine. Was he going to be fired before he even started? No. His uncle wasn't that unfeeling, and he'd said he was glad Jeremy was here.

Graham suddenly turned. "I've had a discussion with Alec, and he has agreed to take over most of my responsibilities here in Pineydale. I've hired a young man from Johnson City to run things over there."

Jeremy bobbed his head in agreement, his thoughts swirling like water down a drain. Alec was Graham's younger son, the one who should have that job. But what was left for Jeremy to do—empty the trash cans?

"Now I know you're wondering how this affects you, since I originally hired you to learn the ropes here and do what Alec is now planning to do."

Jeremy nodded again, feeling like a bobblehead. He wasn't sure what to say, so he remained silent.

"I learned my lesson with your brother. I handled that all wrong."

Wow! Uncle Graham admitting that he was wrong. A first? "But it all worked out in the end because he learned this business wasn't for him, and he's doing well with his woodworking shop."

"He does love creating excellent cabinetry and furniture." Jeremy wondered when his uncle would get to the point.

"I've seen that." Graham nodded, a contorted expression on his face. "I was truly sorry to see him leave here, but I forced his hand. And he didn't back down. I admired that."

Anxiety knotted Jeremy's stomach. "So what does this mean for me?"

"You know during your interview I mentioned expanding the business internationally." Graham stepped around the desk and sat on the edge. "And I had intended for Alec to do that expansion, but he has a young family and doesn't want to be away from home for long periods of time. I understand that now because of Jimmy."

Jeremy didn't know all the details of why Jimmy had suddenly quit working for Uncle Graham, but here was a clue. Jimmy had married in haste to please Uncle Graham, but no one except immediate family knew the whole story. Sometimes Jeremy still couldn't believe Jimmy had married Kelsey to help her hide the fact that she was pregnant with another man's child, a child she eventually had lost in a miscarriage.

Despite the crazy beginning to their marriage, Jimmy and Kelsey had fallen in love and now had a little boy of their own. Even though Jeremy saw how God could somehow take the messes humans made of their lives and turn them into something good, Jeremy was happy he didn't have to jump through Uncle Graham's marriage hoop. But Jeremy had no doubt there would be other hoops to jump through.

"That still doesn't tell me where I stand in all of this."

"Do you have your passport?"

Jeremy nodded, a touch of excitement at the thought of seeing the world. "Expedited just like you said."

"Great." Graham gave him a thumbs-up sign. "You're going to be using it in a few weeks, and you'll be working with Whitney on the international front."

Whitney. Jimmy had warned Jeremy about her presence, but she'd been cordial and not overbearing on the Fourth of July. And she definitely cared about her mother. Was being teamed with her a good thing or a disaster in the making? Would he find out why everyone still considered her a pariah? He knew the bad feelings between Jimmy, Mitch, and Whitney, but that was ancient history.

"I thought she did all the IT stuff. That's not my area of expertise." Jeremy wasn't sure where his expertise lay, but certainly not IT.

"Yeah, she does, but I want her to work with you and show you how things run around here and take that plan to partner with groups in Europe." Graham cleared his throat. "I don't mean this to put you down, but you're fresh out of college and have a lot to learn, and Whitney can teach you a lot. She's business savvy, and she can speak four languages besides English."

"That will definitely be helpful with international business talks." Four languages! And he spoke one. English with a pronounced southern accent. Now that he thought about it, even though Whitney had grown up in Pineydale, she only had a hint of an accent, probably because she'd learned her speech patterns from parents who hadn't grown up in the south. Would she make him feel like a hick from the sticks?

"My thinking exactly." Graham looked at the expensive watch on his arm. "Whitney will be here in a minute."

"Great." *Maybe.* He hated the negative thoughts running through his mind. *Don't be surprised if she turns out to be a thorn in your side.* Jimmy's words clung there like the unsightly peeling paint on the houses he'd renovated.

A knock sounded on the open door. Jeremy turned. Whitney stood there in a charcoal-gray suit and a bright-red blouse, her blond hair pulled back from her face in some kind of braided updo that made her look businesslike yet feminine. He jumped out of his chair as if he'd been shocked.

"Good morning, Graham, Jeremy."

"Come in, Whitney." Graham waved her into the room.

Jeremy didn't know why she made him nervous, but this wasn't the Whitney from the Fourth of July, who had been dressed in patriotic clothes and handled her mother with kid gloves. She looked almost as intimidating as Uncle Graham. She was tall to begin with, and her heels made her even taller. Jeremy found himself standing eye to eye with her even though he was a couple of inches over six feet.

"Whitney, have a seat." Jeremy motioned to the chair he'd been sitting in.

She smiled at him. "Thanks."

Jeremy grabbed another chair from the nearby corner and placed it next to hers. He breathed a sigh of relief when she returned his smile and sat in the chair as Graham settled behind his desk.

"Now that I've got both of you here, I'd like to put forth my plans." Graham leaned back in his chair and steepled his hands while he rested his elbows on the arms of the chair. He looked at Whitney. "First, I want you to take Jeremy to lunch at the country club today and get him signed up for a membership."

Country club. Membership. Lunch. Those hoops of Uncle Graham's were getting more constricting and numerous. Jeremy wanted to know what purpose this membership would serve, but he was afraid to ask.

"Sure. No problem." Whitney nodded.

"Do you have a set of golf clubs?" Graham looked directly at Jeremy.

Golf clubs? Jeremy saw where this was headed, and he didn't like it. He'd hacked around with an old set of clubs his dad had picked up at a yard sale years ago, but Jeremy hadn't touched a golf club since his freshman year in high school. He'd run cross-country in the fall, sat on the bench most of the time for basketball, and played baseball in the spring. Golf was not his sport.

"I don't own clubs."

Graham eyed him. "So you're not a golfer?"

"Sorry, sir. I'm not." There was that *sir* again. Would he ever get used to calling him Graham?

"Whitney here will make you a golfer. She's got a good game."

Jeremy just smiled. It was the only thing he could do. He had to learn to play golf from a woman. He'd never hear the end of it if Jimmy and Mitch got wind of that, especially since Whitney would be his instructor. Jimmy didn't belong to the country club, but Mitch did. Could he avoid seeing his cousin there? He could only hope.

On the plus side, Mitch had little use for Whitney after she'd cheated on him while they were engaged. Cheated on him with Jimmy. That was why she'd left town and hadn't come back for eight years until her daddy became very ill.

That whole affair had been the talk of the town for months. Her return a little over a year ago had generated more talk, especially when she'd come to work for Uncle Graham. Her breakup with Mitch, Graham's older son, had angered Graham, and Graham Cunningham was someone a person didn't want to cross. Had Graham let bygones be bygones? It appeared so.

"What do you think, Jeremy?"

His eyebrows raised, Jeremy looked at Graham. Jeremy's mind had taken him down a rabbit hole he couldn't climb out of with ease, and he had no clue what his uncle was talking about. "Sorry, sir, but I didn't hear what you said, because I was thinking about this golf thing."

He wanted to say the game wasn't for him, but that didn't go along with the thoughts he'd had as he'd stepped into this room. *He could tackle any task his uncle put out there.* Even golf.

"Nothing to worry about. The membership and the golf clubs are perks of the job. You don't know how many business deals are negotiated on the golf course."

"Okay. Great." *Or not so great.* How could he negotiate deals with people who would be laughing at his slice or hook or whatever bad shot he'd make? But if they were traveling overseas, maybe he wouldn't have to play that often.

"Now I want to know what you think about having Whitney familiarize you with some foreign phrases that you should know as you prepare for your trip to Europe."

Jeremy suppressed a frown. He couldn't very well say he wasn't interested. What else would push Whitney and him together? "Fine with me."

Graham nodded. "I'll let you two work out your own scheduling to get these things done. I'll meet with you tomorrow, and we'll go over the tentative itinerary for your trip."

"What time tomorrow?" Whitney stood.

"I'm good whenever." Jeremy jumped up to stand beside her. He didn't want to be sitting down while a lady was standing. The good manners his mother had drummed into him while he was young still filled his brain.

"I'll send both of you an email with that information." Graham waved a finger in the air. "And one more thing. Whitney, introduce Jeremy to our new IT guy."

"Certainly." Whitney eyed Jeremy. "Ready?"

"Sure." Jeremy followed Whitney into the hallway.

She stopped so suddenly that he almost plowed into her. She smiled at him. "Sorry about that."

"Good thing I'm quick on my feet, or I'd have knocked you over."

"We'll see how quick you are when I get you out on the tennis court."

Jeremy frowned. "Tennis court? I thought you were going to teach me how to play golf."

"Both."

Jeremy stifled a groan. The country club life. Golf,

tennis, and lunches. Not his thing, but he'd better get used to it. This was his life now.

***

Whitney headed to her office. Working with Jeremy day in and day out would test her mettle. When Graham had told her she would be doing the overseas expansion instead of Alec, she had braced herself for today and all the days going forward. But looking at Jeremy reminded her of Jimmy in too many ways. A pinprick of hurt invaded a tiny corner of her heart when she thought of him.

"So how are things working out with Carla?" Jeremy fell into step beside Whitney.

"Good." Whitney glanced at him, surprised. "Thanks for asking, and thanks for your help with my mom on the Fourth. You were really instrumental in making that all happen."

Jeremy nodded. "I like your mom. Sorry about her difficulties."

"Thanks." Whitney stopped in front of her office door. "Come in, and we'll discuss Graham's requests."

"Sure." Jeremy stepped into her office and stood there as he shifted his weight from foot to foot.

Whitney headed to her desk, while Jeremy stood there looking oh so good in his navy-blue pinstriped suit. "Hey, you don't have to wait for me to sit down. Go ahead and make yourself comfortable."

Jeremy chuckled. "You know my mom would have my hide if she were here and I didn't wait for you to sit first."

Whitney nodded as she went to her desk and sat down. "But she's not here, and I don't care."

"True, but just like saying *yes, sir* and *yes, ma'am* are ingrained in my vocabulary, standing when a woman stands is part of being Mary Cunningham's son."

"As long as you don't *yes, ma'am* me, we'll be fine."

Jeremy laughed as he slid onto the chair next to her desk. "I'm in trouble then because it's sure to come out of my mouth."

"So I'll have to deal with it." She would deal with whatever working with Jeremy brought.

After spending time with him on the Fourth, some of her initial shock of seeing him all grown up had worn off.

Maybe having to reckon daily with Jeremy would force her to face her lost love and move on.

Whitney wanted success for this working partnership with Jeremy, but the way Graham had dumped them together without warning didn't start things out on the best footing. This probably wasn't what Jeremy had expected. The job had been turned upside down on his first day. She couldn't tiptoe around the obvious.

"So what are your thoughts?"

Jeremy stared at her as he rubbed his chin. "You want to know the truth?"

"Truth would be good." She put on her best smile and hoped the truth wouldn't hurt.

"I should've expected the unexpected from my uncle." Jeremy shifted in his chair as he hesitated. First pointing at her, then himself, he waved a finger back and forth. "How do you see this working?"

Whitney gave him credit. He'd turned the question back on her. "Well, if we make this a team effort and not a competition, things should go more smoothly."

Jeremy narrowed his gaze. "I got the distinct

impression that Graham expects you to be my mentor."

"And what do you think of that?" Whitney was happy to turn the question around again.

Jeremy lounged back in his chair as a crooked smile brightened his handsome features. "I think we're going to make a great team. We think alike."

Whitney cocked her head as she met his gaze. "How so?"

Jeremy's smile broadened. "You asked me a question, then I turned it back on you, and vice versa. Maybe like tennis. The ball's on your side of the net. Take a swing."

Whitney laughed out loud as she leaned forward. "Okay. Remember this when we're actually on the court."

"I'll try."

"I'll remind you." Whitney poked a finger in the air. "Do you have a problem with a little mentoring?"

Jeremy remained silent for a few seconds. "I was expecting to get that from Uncle Graham."

"And not me." Whitney wondered if Jeremy was one of those men who resented women in positions of power. Not that she was all that powerful.

Jeremy let out a halfhearted laugh. "You could say that."

Whitney wanted to know where she stood. "So you have a problem with it?"

"No. I'm ready to be a team player, and you have more experience than I do in this arena. After Jimmy took the job here, I ran our daddy's painting business, so I understand some of what it takes to keep customers happy and keep the business in the black." Jeremy released a harsh breath. "But this is a different ball game, and I'm willing to learn no matter who the coach is."

"Even for golf?"

Jeremy laughed with a shake of his head. "I'm not looking forward to golf no matter who's the instructor."

Whitney tried to strangle her laughter without success. "It can't be that bad. Let's wait and see."

"So when do you plan to do this instruction?"

"Let's play on Graham's time this afternoon after lunch."

Jeremy rubbed a hand down his face. "The first day on the job?"

Shrugging, Whitney smirked. "Why not? He told me to sign you up and make a golfer out of you. How can I do that unless we play?"

Jeremy wrinkled his brow. "So Graham is good with us playing golf on company time even when we're not entertaining clients?"

"For now. Yes." Whitney stood. "Let me introduce you to Brandon, then we'll go over the plans Graham has lain out for the international launch. After that, it's lunch and golf."

Jeremy jumped from the chair. "No tennis today?"

Whitney laughed again. At least for now, humor would make this work. "I doubt we can fit it in unless you want to spend the evening with me, too."

Jeremy grinned. "That might depend on how badly you beat me in golf. I might need to salvage my ego with a little tennis, even though I haven't played since the PE course I took my freshman year in college."

"I could always play from the men's tees instead of the ladies'." Whitney raised her eyebrows.

Jeremy shook his head. "Absolutely not. If you beat me from the men's tees, I'd never hear the end of it."

"I'd never tell." Whitney headed for the door.

"Somehow that isn't reassuring." Jeremy joined her as she stepped into the hallway.

"We won't think about golf this morning. Save it for the afternoon." Whitney waved a hand toward the end of the hallway. "The IT department is this way."

"How do you feel about moving out of the IT area?"

Whitney glanced at Jeremy, wondering whether he had any inkling about her interaction with Jimmy while he'd been here. "I've been wearing a lot of hats for a while now. It'll be good to focus on one area."

"You mean IT and sales."

"Marketing and operations, too."

"Wow. That's a lot of hats."

Whitney nodded. "I like the variety, and Graham has taught me a lot about every area of the business. I'm thankful he took a chance on me when I moved back to Pineydale to take care of my dad."

"I'm glad he's taking a chance on me, too."

Whitney stopped in front of the last door on the right side of the hallway as she looked Jeremy in the eye. "You know your uncle is a very generous man. He can be very demanding, but he likes to help people."

"I believe you're right." Jeremy nodded. "Too many people have no idea how much he's done for this town."

"I'm glad to see you understand him better than most people." Whitney smiled as she held up a hand.

Jeremy slapped her hand. "I hope I feel the same way after golf."

Whitney laughed again, then shook her head. "You've got to quit making me laugh."

"How sad would that be? There's nothing like laughter

to make your day."

"Then my day is made because of you." Whitney realized the truth of that statement.

"Who's having too much fun out here in the hallway?"

Jeremy turned toward the doorway where a young African American man stood, a wide grin on his face.

"Brandon, I want you to meet Jeremy Cunningham." Whitney stepped closer to the door and motioned toward Jeremy. "Jeremy, this is Brandon Williams, our new IT guy."

Brandon extended his hand. "Good to meet you, Jeremy. I've heard you're the new man on the job."

"I am. Good to meet you, too." Jeremy shook Brandon's hand.

"Whitney here has me up to speed on everything in the IT department." Brandon nodded toward Whitney. "She has left everything in good order for me, and if you have any IT issues, I'm the man to see."

Jeremy nodded. "I'll remember that."

Brandon turned his attention to Whitney. "When does Alec come on board?"

"Next week. He's getting everything settled over in Johnson City before he starts here. Then we'll have everyone in place." Whitney looked at Jeremy. "So Jeremy and I have to get things settled before Alec arrives."

"Thanks for stopping by. Welcome, Jeremy."

"Thanks. See you around." Jeremy shook Brandon's hand again.

"Let's go to my office and familiarize you with some of what you'll be doing."

"Sure." Jeremy fell into step beside her.

Jeremy had that same confident stride as his brother.

When would she finally look at Jeremy and not think about Jimmy? She hoped it was sooner rather than later.

CHAPTER FOUR

Hot, humid air greeted Jeremy as he left the office. It was too hot for a suit and tie, but no more shorts and T-shirts for work. He probably ought to buy another suit. People would get tired of seeing him in this one. Even though Uncle Graham had said the membership and the golf clubs were perks of the job, Jeremy doubted the golf attire was. And he had to buy luggage for his overseas trips. How much would that set him back? He might have to take out a loan just to outfit himself for his new job.

As Jeremy neared his car, he spied Whitney standing next to hers, a gleaming white Lexus sedan. "You driving?"

"No sense in taking two cars." She opened her door. "Hop in."

"Sure." Jeremy trudged to the passenger side, not sure sharing a ride was the best option. He wouldn't be able to escape. He'd be at her mercy.

While Whitney drove to the country club, she chatted about their plans for the day and for the coming week. His mind filled with golf expectations, he only half listened until he heard her mention Grandfather Mountain Highland Games. His cousin Mitch went every year, but it had been several years since he'd attended, because he often worked on the weekends.

"We're going to the games?"

"Yeah." Whitney glanced his way. "Graham told me last week that he wants us to man our corporate-sponsor booth. We'll be attending every day."

"That ought to be fun." *Or not.* Jeremy couldn't imagine spending the entire time standing in a booth to promote their company. More of Uncle Graham's hoops.

"More like work."

Jeremy chuckled. "That's what I was actually thinking."

Whitney joined in the laughter. "We might manage a little fun if we're lucky."

Jeremy didn't want to ask about running into Mitch and Jimmy at the games. Jeremy was pretty sure he'd heard Jimmy and Mitch talking about spending at least one day there with their wives. Whitney's presence on the Fourth hadn't appeared to create any problems, but Jeremy couldn't help thinking about all the trouble she'd caused between Mitch and Jimmy. Why had she dumped Jimmy for Mitch, then turned around and cheated on Mitch with Jimmy?

She was a smart and attractive woman. It was no wonder the two cousins had fought over her. But when it came to Whitney and romance now, guys didn't want anything to do with her. She didn't have a good track record when it came to relationships.

Every time they were together, the craziness of it all sat in his brain like spoiled milk. It left sour thoughts about her. That couldn't be good for their working relationship.

"You're awfully quiet." Whitney pulled her car into a parking space near the entrance to the country club.

"Just thinking about everything I've got to do for this job." He let out a heavy sigh.

"Sounds serious."

Jeremy narrowed his gaze as he got out of the car. "It is."

"You still worried about getting beat at golf?"

Jeremy looked at Whitney over the top of the car. He didn't want to share his thoughts with this woman. "Nope. I've got bigger things to worry about than that."

"Like what?" Whitney headed for the front door.

"Like what I'm going to eat for lunch. I'm not used to country club food." Jeremy rushed to catch up with her.

Laughing, Whitney shook her head. "No need to worry. The food's good."

"Yeah, maybe for women."

Whitney stopped and put her hands on her hips. "Plenty of men eat here."

Jeremy ran a hand through his hair. "I'm sure the food will be fine. Let's just get this over with."

"Where's your enthusiasm?"

Jeremy stepped around Whitney and opened the door for her. "I think I left it on my desk."

"Just wait and see. I'm going to make you love the game of golf." Whitney stepped into the lobby of the country club.

Jeremy had been here a few times for wedding receptions, most recently for Mitch and Amanda's wedding. Most of his relatives couldn't afford a country club reception. He hadn't paid much attention to the details on his previous visits. He couldn't picture himself as a member of this club.

A round, dark wooden table sported a huge vase filled with colorful summer flowers. A receptionist sat behind a counter on one side of the wide-open space. She stood as

Whitney approached.

"Hi, Whitney. What can I help you with today?"

Whitney motioned his way. "Hi, Maisie, I'm here to get Jeremy signed up for a full membership under Graham Cunningham's account."

"Great." Maisie laid several papers on the counter. "He needs to fill these out. Here's a pen."

"Thanks." Whitney grabbed the papers and turned to Jeremy. "You can do this while we check out things in the pro shop. Follow me."

Grabbing the pen, Jeremy didn't say a word, even though he'd like to give her an earful. He just followed her down the hallway until they reached a dark wooden double door with shiny brass handles. Normally he would've rushed forward and opened the door for her, but her commands bugged him. She was as bad as Uncle Graham, maybe worse. Maybe Jimmy was right. She would be a thorn in his side.

Jeremy stepped into the pro shop. He'd better get used to thorns.

Circular racks of golf apparel filled the room. The paneled perimeter sported one wall of golf clubs of every size and description, and another wall contained shelves filled with more golf-related items.

Whitney sashayed up to the desk at the far end of the pro shop. "Hi, Chad."

"Whitney. What brings you by on a weekday morning?"

"Shopping for Jeremy here." She pointed Jeremy's way. "He needs golf clubs, shoes, etc."

Smiling, Jeremy tried not to look irritated. He felt like he was in elementary school again, and his mother was taking him shopping for new school clothes and supplies.

Chad stepped from behind the counter and approached Jeremy. "Do you have any idea what you're looking for?"

"Not a clue." Jeremy hated feeling like a dunce.

"No worries. That's what I'm here for. To help you out." Chad motioned toward the wall of golf clubs. "Have you played golf before?"

"Not recently." Jeremy wasn't going to tell this guy that he'd played with yard-sale clubs when he was fourteen.

"Then let's give a few different clubs a try." Chad pointed to a smaller room off to one side. "We can go in here to our golf simulator and let you hit a few."

"Sure." As he shrugged out of his suit jacket and laid it on a chair, he wondered whether he would make a complete fool of himself. Removing his tie, he forced a smile.

Chad handed Jeremy a club, then placed a golf ball on the tee. "Let's see what you can do."

Jeremy wanted to turn around in the worst way to see if Whitney was watching, but he didn't dare let her know he cared about her opinion of his nonexistent golf game. He wasn't even sure why he cared about her opinion at all.

Staring at the little white dimpled sphere, he tried to remember the correct stance for addressing the ball. Would this machine really give him any idea about his golf swing? What if he swung and missed? *Relax. That was a joke.* He was wired from the top of his head to the soles of his shoes. He blew out a big breath and took a swing. The ball hit the backdrop with a thud.

Relieved that he hadn't whiffed the ball, Jeremy let the club slide through his hands as he turned to Chad. "So what does it tell you?"

"Not bad for someone who hasn't hit a golf ball in a while." Chad showed Jeremy the readout on the tablet, then discussed the statistics.

Jeremy listened to Chad's explanation with interest. Maybe golf wouldn't be so bad after all. For the next half hour, Jeremy sampled several brands of golf clubs until Chad made a recommendation.

"This set of clubs will serve you well." Chad walked over to a display of golf bags. "Check these out and find one you like. While you do that, I'll get your new clubs for you."

As Jeremy looked over the golf bags, Whitney appeared at his side. "So what do you think?"

"About what?"

Whitney made a disgruntled face. "Why are you playing dumb?"

"Who's playing?"

"Okay, I get it. This isn't your thing, but it's Graham's, so we have to live with it."

Jeremy put himself in Whitney's place. She had to put up with him as he had to put up with her. He shouldn't give her a hard time. "You're right. I have golf clubs. Since you're the golfer, help me pick out a bag."

Whitney's expression brightened, then she looked away as she perused the bags. "This one."

"Whatever you say." Jeremy took the silver-and-black bag to the counter.

Whitney raced after him. "You don't have to take that one if you don't like it."

Jeremy turned to look at her, and his heart did this funny little leap. What was the matter with him? She was the last woman on earth he should take an interest in. She was his coworker. She was six years older than he was. Most important, she was his brother's ex-girlfriend. Three good reasons not to take a second look. And he could probably come up with twice that many reasons.

"This is good. No need to look further."

"You have to get shoes and clothes." Whitney joined him at the counter.

Jeremy wanted to get this over with and get out of here in the worst way. She was an attractive woman. He couldn't deny that. So he'd deal with it. He focused on the business at hand as he rifled through the racks of golf shirts, shorts, and pants. He picked out a few, then found shoes, socks, a cap, and golf gloves.

As Chad rang up Jeremy's purchases, he was thankful for one thing. This all went on Uncle Graham's bill.

Chad handed Jeremy the receipt. "I'll show you the men's locker room and get you set up with a locker."

Whitney followed until they got to the door of the men's locker room. "You want to change now or after lunch?"

"Now." Jeremy hoped a little distance and time would put his thoughts in order.

"Okay. I'll change and meet you in the dining room." She gave a little wave. "See you in a few minutes."

Jeremy nodded, wishing it were a few hours. While he changed and put his new purchases in his locker, he considered his need for a strategy to reckon with this forced togetherness. Because besides today, they would be spending most of next weekend in each other's company.

***

A few golfers and a group of ladies dressed in tennis attire occupied the country club dining room. Whitney made her way to an empty table and wondered how she'd survive a whole afternoon with Jeremy.

Dressed in a dark skirt and white blouse, a young waitress with brunette hair pulled back in a loose bun appeared at the table. "Hi, Whitney. What can I get for you today?"

"Hi, Faith. Jeremy Cunningham, a new member, will be joining me in a few minutes. Just bring us each a glass of water for now."

Faith laid a couple of menus on the table. "I'll be right back with those waters."

As Faith scurried away, Whitney let out a sigh. She couldn't help thinking about the golf outing ahead. She was dreading it as much as Jeremy. Every time she looked at him, she saw Jimmy. Everything from his thick, dark hair to his wide smile made her think of that lost love. Jeremy's speech, his mannerisms, even his laughter made her relive all the mistakes she'd made with Jimmy.

She couldn't let her past define her. Jeremy had no idea his presence made her uncomfortable, sad, and miserable. Letting that continue was insanity. She could rise above those bad feelings and forge ahead.

Faith reappeared and set the glasses of water on the table. "Still waiting on your guest?"

Whitney nodded. "He shouldn't be much longer. Check back in a couple of minutes."

Faith smiled as she left to check on another table. Whitney had the strange sensation that the smile held a bit of pity. Did Faith know about Whitney's history with the

Cunningham family? Probably.

Even though she'd left town within days of her broken engagement to Mitch, Whitney had some so-called friends who'd made sure she knew the whole affair was the talk of the town. Jeremy was a good kid, and he shouldn't suffer because of her misdeeds. Well, he wasn't exactly a kid, but still the baby of his family—a family that obviously cared for him a great deal. Whitney had sensed the protective nature of Janelle's comments on the Fourth.

Whitney wished she'd pressed Graham to consider having Jeremy take lessons from Chad. That might have been the more successful approach, but maybe this was a good test of how she would handle working with Jeremy every day.

While Whitney gave herself a pep talk, Jeremy entered the dining room. When their gazes met, her positive thoughts dripped away like the condensation running down the glasses of water. He smiled as he approached, looking like he'd just walked down the runway of a fashion show for golf apparel.

He slid into the chair on the opposite side of the table and tugged on his shirt. "Got on my new golf duds, and I'm ready to take you on."

"Smack talk. Really?"

"Sure. If I can't play golf, at least I can talk a good game."

Whitney laughed. "Okay. Care to put your money where your mouth is?"

His eyebrows knit. "A wager?"

Before Whitney could lay out the wager, Faith returned. "Ready to order?"

Jeremy picked up the menu and gave it a quick glance,

then laid it down. "Bring me the best thing on your menu."

"What I like best, or what I think you'd like?"

Jeremy grinned up at Faith. "What you think I'd like."

"You got it." Faith turned to Whitney. "Am I going to pick your entrée, too?"

Whitney shook her head. "I'll have the chicken salad."

"Anything else to drink besides water?"

"Sweet tea," Whitney and Jeremy chorused.

Jeremy chuckled. "At least we agree on one thing."

"So you think we don't see eye to eye on much?" Whitney raised her eyebrows as she gazed at Jeremy.

"I don't know that yet, but I do know I'd rather not have to like all this country club stuff."

"What's not to like? Good food. Good sports. Good company." Whitney pressed her lips together to hide a smile as she waited for his response.

"I'll reserve judgment."

"Even on the company."

"Depends on the company." Jeremy had a deadpan expression as he looked back at her.

Whitney returned his gaze, wondering why she cared whether he hated her company. "My company."

Jeremy's mouth curved in a lopsided grin. "You sure like to put a guy on the spot."

"Honesty is important. That's one thing I've learned from my mistakes."

"Okay. Honesty." His grin grew wider. "I'm still trying to figure you out, and so far today the only time I wanted to send you packing was when you treated me like an eight-year-old."

Whitney stomach curdled. "I did that?"

"Yeah. When you marched into the pro shop and

proceeded to tell Chad what I needed." Jeremy smirked. "I thought I was shopping for school clothes with my mother."

"I was trying to be helpful." Whitney shrugged. "Sorry. I had no idea."

"I know you didn't, but you wanted me to be honest."

"Will you always be honest with me?"

Jeremy shook his head. "I can't promise that. I won't pretend to like something if I don't. I can promise that."

Whitney nodded, wondering if she was being honest. She definitely wasn't going to dump her emotional mix-up on him. He didn't need to know her issues unless they related to business. "Good. I'll do the same."

"So what about that wager?"

Whitney laughed again. "Are you hustling me? Pretending to be a neophyte golfer when you really aren't?"

"No. You can set the terms of this wager."

Why had she opened her mouth and put her foot in it? Honesty. She had to go with the honesty they had talked about. She cleared her throat. "I shouldn't have suggested a wager. You don't have a golf handicap."

Jeremy lifted an eyebrow. "So that's going to stop you?"

Whitney held out her hands. "Well, it hardly seems fair for me to go head to head with you, does it?"

Jeremy shrugged. "I don't know. Does it?"

"Okay. Whoever gets the lowest score wins."

"And what do they win?"

What did she want out of this wager? She was sure to win, so she'd better pick wisely.

Just at that moment Faith approached the table with

their orders. She served Whitney, then placed Jeremy's plate in front of him. "Pulled pork barbeque sandwich, fries, and slaw. I hope you like it."

"Looks delicious." Jeremy grinned. "Thanks. Faith, what do you think I should win if I beat Whitney at golf, and what do you think she should win if she beats me?"

Faith chuckled. "Trying to put me on the spot again. I'm good at picking things from the menu but not so good at picking prizes."

Jeremy laced his hands behind his head and leaned back, first looking at Whitney, then at Faith. "You need to help Whitney out. She doesn't know what to wager on our golf game."

Whitney frowned but didn't say a thing. Could he read minds? She hoped not. She certainly didn't want him reading hers.

Faith turned to Whitney. "Do you really want me to say what you should win?"

Whitney waved a hand. "Go for it. You'll probably do a better job than I would."

"Is there a price limit on the prize?" Faith asked.

"A hundred bucks or less." Jeremy brought his hands down to the table.

"Wow! That gives me a lot of choices, but I think it'll make things easy if the winner has to buy dinner at that fancy gourmet restaurant. You know the one I mean, right? I forget the name." Faith gazed at Whitney.

"You mean Holland's Gourmet Grill?" Whitney asked.

"Yeah. That's the one." Faith bobbed her head as she looked between Whitney and Jeremy. "What do you think?"

"Works for me. Makes it easy." Jeremy turned to

Whitney with a grin. "Work for you?"

"Sure. Thanks, Faith." Whitney agreed, but going out to dinner with Jeremy wasn't on her list of things she wanted to do.

"You're welcome. Have fun." Faith trotted away.

"That was easy." Jeremy gazed at Whitney. "Would you like me to give thanks for the food?"

Whitney hadn't even thought about praying before she ate. "Sure."

Jeremy bowed his head, and Whitney followed suit. She hadn't prayed in a restaurant since she couldn't remember when. His simple prayer made her think about her lack of a spiritual life. She'd been going through the motions, at least until her mom started showing signs of dementia. She'd prayed more in the last few weeks than she had in the years since she'd left Pineydale.

Despite her misgivings, maybe Jeremy's presence at work would bring her closer to God. That would be a turn of events she hadn't expected.

"Let's dig in." Jeremy picked up his sandwich and took a big bite.

"Good?"

Jeremy nodded as he took a gulp of his tea.

"I'm glad Faith made a good choice." Whitney picked up her fork. "So now you can say you have good company and good food. The only thing left is to experience good sports."

"Does that mean you're going to let me win?"

Whitney gave him an incredulous look. "Are you kidding me? There is no way I would let you win. You have to beat me fair and square."

"I was afraid of that." He picked up a french fry and

dragged it through a blob of ketchup on his plate. With it poised in the air, he gazed at her. "Working with you will make my life very interesting."

Whitney didn't respond. She didn't know what she would say anyway. She was getting used to him sitting there looking, talking, and laughing like his brother. But no matter how much the brothers resembled each other, Jeremy wasn't Jimmy. So she didn't need to feel awkward around him. She just needed to treat him like any other coworker. Despite another pep talk, she didn't see that happening without a gigantic effort.

***

After lunch Jeremy made his way to the men's locker room to put on his golf shoes and grab his clubs. He hoped he could get through this afternoon without making a complete fool of himself. But he was prepared to keep a positive attitude no matter how terrible he played, and maybe, just maybe it wouldn't turn out to be a complete humiliation.

Jeremy slung his golf bag over his shoulder and traipsed out to the side of the clubhouse, where a dozen golf carts were parked. The bag boy hurried up to Jeremy and took his bag and set it in the nearest cart.

"Thanks." Jeremy handed the kid a tip, then climbed into the driver's side.

While Jeremy sat there studying the score card and layout of the golf course, he remembered how much he'd wanted to caddy or be a bag boy here when he'd been in high school. But he'd been painting houses with his dad and Jimmy every summer. After suddenly losing his dad the summer before his junior year in high school, Jeremy was glad he'd painted houses instead. Otherwise he would've missed that time with his dad.

"I see you're ready to drive."

"I am." Jeremy glanced up at the sound of Whitney's voice.

He swallowed hard as he gazed at her. Sitting across from her while they ate hadn't prepared him for the way she looked in that short golf skirt covered in a splash of red, white, and blue flowers. She smiled as she handed her bag to the bag boy. From the look on the kid's face, Jeremy suspected the teenage boy was as mesmerized by Whitney's tall, slender figure with curves in all the right places as Jeremy was. He had to put his thoughts on another track, or he'd be derailed in a hurry.

"Hop in." Jeremy forced himself not to look at her as she slid onto the seat.

"Sure." Whitney placed her golf ball and tees in the holder.

Jeremy drove the cart forward as he focused his attention on the cart path. He maneuvered the cart to a stop near the first tee box. "Ladies first."

Whitney didn't say a word as she plucked her driver out of her blue-and-white bag. With purpose in her step, she strode to the red tee that matched her sleeveless collared shirt. Bending over, she pushed the tee into the ground. Jeremy tried not to watch, but he couldn't stop himself. She was mighty fine to look at.

This would be a long afternoon if he kept thinking like that.

She took a couple of practice swings, then addressed the ball. With a fluid motion as graceful as a ballerina, she swung at the ball. It sailed into the air in an arc and landed in the middle of the fairway.

"Nice shot. You've already set the bar high."

Her blue eyes twinkled. "Thanks. Your turn."

Jeremy grabbed his driver and trudged to the white tees. "Guess I should start here."

"Unless you want to play from the ladies' tees."

Jeremy eyed her. "Are you saying you think I'm a bad golfer? That I can't outhit you?"

An innocent expression accompanied her smile as she shook her head. "I didn't say what kind of golfer you are. I merely gave you a choice. You can play from whichever tees you'd like. Your golfing expertise is yet to be determined."

Pushing his ego aside, Jeremy stuck his tee into the ground. He would be sorely disappointed if he thought he could beat Whitney. It was okay to lose to a woman. He gave himself the same pep talk he'd used in the simulator, and this time he let the beauty and peacefulness of the golf course soothe his mind. With a relaxed motion that surprised even him, he let the club rip through the air. With a sense of accomplishment, he watched the ball against the blue sky until it started its downward path. It landed just feet away from Whitney's ball.

"Now that's what I call cart golf." Whitney grinned as she sat in the driver's seat. "Nice shot."

"Thanks. I hope it's the first of many." Jeremy settled on the passenger side and looked over at Whitney as she drove ahead. "You like to be in charge?"

She glanced at him, a frown causing a little pucker between her eyebrows. "Why do you ask that?"

"You took over driving."

"Does that bother you?"

Did it bother him? She'd driven to the country club, and he hadn't cared, other than worrying about being stuck with her for the day. "No. Just trying to get a handle on your business style. If we're going to work together, I need to know how you operate."

"I like to get things done in the most efficient way possible. And in this case, my driving now makes for faster play, which is an important aspect when sharing the course with other people." Whitney stopped the cart on the path nearest to where their balls lay.

Jeremy looked toward the first tee as he retrieved his club. "But there's no one playing behind us."

Raising one eyebrow, Whitney plucked a club from her bag. "That doesn't matter. We practice good golf etiquette all the time."

With a grin, Jeremy saluted as he walked toward his ball. "And good golf etiquette says you get to go first because your ball is farther from the hole."

"So it seems." Whitney again took a couple of practice swings, then looked over at him. "I can't let that happen again."

Jeremy's grin turned into laughter. "A little competitive, are we?"

"Hey, there's a dinner riding on this game."

"Oh yeah. I forgot." Jeremy waited for her to hit her ball.

Whitney didn't respond but made her next shot, which landed on the front edge of the green. She smiled with satisfaction. "Can you beat that?"

Jeremy figured the chance of making two goods shots in row was pretty slim. "I'll do my best."

He watched his ball fly into the air. The shot looked good at first, but it wound up in a sand trap on the right side of the green. He had no clue how to hit a ball out of the sand except that he should use a sand wedge. He grabbed it and his putter as he jabbed his fairway wood back into his bag. He held the two clubs on his lap as Whitney propelled the cart toward the green.

Jeremy strode to the sand trap and dropped his putter near the edge of the trap as he stepped onto the sand.

"You know you can't let your club touch the sand in a hazard as you're addressing the ball."

Jeremy turned to find Whitney standing there leaning on her putter. "What happens if I do?"

"Two-stroke penalty."

"Wow! Good thing you told me." Not only was the ball in a trap but his mind was in a trap of his own making. He might as well admit he didn't know what he was doing. "Any pointers?"

"Yeah. Don't touch the sand during your back swing. You should hit behind the ball as you come through."

That sounded too complicated. What if he whiffed the ball? "So I should just take a whack at it and hope for the best?"

Whitney chuckled. "Would you like me to demonstrate?"

"Won't that slow down the pace of play?"

"I'll have to remember that *you* remember everything I say." Whitney narrowed her gaze as she continued to lean on her putter. "As you pointed out, there's no one playing behind us, so I'll have plenty of time to demonstrate. After all, I'm supposed to teach you the game."

Jeremy stepped out of the sand trap and held out his

hand. "Be my guest."

Whitney grabbed a couple of extra balls from her bag and tossed them into the trap. As she stood over one of the balls, she looked over at him. "Watch how I hit behind the ball."

"Sure." Jeremy watched her hit the perfect shot as the ball rolled within a couple of feet of the hole. "And you think I can do that with one try?"

She raised her eyebrows. "I can show you again. Remember, don't take a full swing."

Again she hit a perfect shot, then stepped out of the trap. "Your turn."

"Maybe I should just let you hit my ball."

A wry smile on her lips, she shook her head. "Never do something for someone they can do for themselves."

Jeremy stepped back into the trap. He didn't know why he even cared about this stupid game. He wasn't a golfer. He should just hit the ball and take whatever came. He would get through this round and be done with it. But that wasn't his style. He'd always tried his best, and this was no exception. So he'd labor over each stroke and then probably dream about it in his sleep tonight.

But this was what he wanted. To prove himself. To be his own man and not live in the shadow of his brother. He wanted people to look at him and not see Jimmy. Jeremy was determined to make a success of this job, even if it meant learning how to play golf.

From Whitney.

Staring at the ball, he took a deep breath. He brought the club back and chunked it into the sand behind the ball. He closed his eyes as sand sprayed everywhere. When he opened his eyes, he didn't see his ball anywhere. Had he hit it completely over the green into the sand trap on the other side?

"Where's my ball?"

"In the hole."

Jeremy raced across the green and gazed into the cup, then looked over at Whitney with a grin. "Pure luck or your excellent instructions."

"Has to be my excellent instructions." She stared at him, a hint of a smile on her lips.

Jeremy's heart raced. The excitement of putting the ball in the hole must be the reason. Definitely the reason. Not Whitney.

He plucked his ball from the cup and pulled out the flag in preparation for Whitney's putt. She two putted, and he had won the hole. A good start. Could he finish well, too?

Jeremy drove the cart to the next tee and hopped out. He grabbed his driver from the bag. "Guess I have the honors."

"You do." Whitney stared at him as if she had a secret lurking behind that hint of a smile.

Jeremy couldn't let Whitney get inside his head. Not that his game wasn't suspect anyway, but he couldn't let trying to outdo her make his game worse. He took a couple of practice swings. Tension knotted his muscles. *Breathe deeply. Relax. Focus.*

He addressed the ball and swung. The little white sphere sailed into the blue sky, but what looked like a great shot became a slice that landed in the woods off to the right of the fairway. With a grim expression he jammed his club back into the bag. That shot wouldn't win him any prizes or bets. Whitney would probably hit her ball right down the middle of the fairway. He plopped himself onto the seat behind the steering wheel.

Sure enough Whitney's shot landed right in the center of the fairway. Thankfully, she didn't gloat as he drove the cart toward her ball. She hopped out and grabbed a couple of clubs.

"I'll help you look for your ball. You might want to grab another one in case we can't find it." Whitney headed toward the wooded area.

Jeremy didn't say anything as he followed her. "Did you see where it went?"

She glanced back at him. "Somewhere in this direction."

Shuffling through the underbrush, he didn't have much hope of finding his ball in this mess of overgrown vegetation. Now he remembered why he hated golf. "I don't see it anywhere."

"We'll look for a couple of minutes, and if we don't find it, you can drop a ball and take a penalty stroke."

This whole afternoon was a penalty. His first day on the job already had him dancing to Uncle Graham's tune. Had Jimmy been right? No. This had nothing to do with Jimmy. While Jeremy stewed something white appeared in his vision. He leaned over. A ball. His ball? He looked closer. "I found it."

Whitney stepped closer. "Do you think you can hit it out of there, or do you want to drop and take a penalty?"

Jeremy gazed at the ball nestled in the greenery. He'd seen some pros hit some amazing shots out of crazy places, but he wasn't a pro. Would he be foolish not to take the drop? What difference did it make? Whitney would most likely beat him anyway. He might as well take a chance.

He was taking a chance on this job. What was one more chance?

"Yeah. I'm giving it my best shot."

After a couple of practice swings, he took a whack at the ball. It sprang from his club and sailed toward the green almost as if it had grown wings, landing just short of the green.

"That was a great shot." Whitney peered at him. "Are you sure it's been ten years since you last played golf?"

"Yeah. Must be beginners luck."

"No luck involved there. That was skill."

Jeremy hated to think he was lapping up Whitney's praise, but he was. He had to put a cork in his ego. Letting it run wild was dangerous, especially when it came to women. "I hope my skill doesn't abandon me."

"We'll see."

That statement should put him in his place. One shot didn't make a golf game. He kept that firmly in his thoughts as he drove to the next tee.

Jeremy stopped the cart and looked at Whitney. "When did you take up golf?"

"When I lived in Atlanta." Whitney hopped out of the cart. "Just like you. A business-related activity. Only I was along as an interpreter."

"That must've been interesting." Jeremy grabbed his driver and wished he could interpret his feelings about this whole exercise.

"It was."

"You have the honors." Jeremy motioned toward the forward tees and hoped he wouldn't be hitting second for the rest of the round.

His golf game made for an interesting afternoon. Like

the first two holes, the rest of his game had the markings of Dr. Jekyll and Mr. Hyde. Whitney played steady, finishing with a score of eighty-eight. He came in a close second with a ninety-five. But second meant he had lost their little wager.

He stopped the cart in front of the clubhouse. "Looks like you've won the bet. When do you want to collect your winnings?"

Whitney gazed at him, a smile brimming in her blue eyes. "You name the time."

Jeremy shook his head. "You won. You pick."

Without a word, Whitney jumped out of the cart and went to the back. Jeremy followed as she unzipped a side pocket on her bag and brought out her phone. She tapped the screen and scrolled, most likely looking at her calendar. She finally looked at him. "How about a week from Friday after work? We can go right from the office."

"Sure. Works for me." Jeremy didn't have any plans. He didn't even have a calendar to look at. His nonexistent social life said so much about his life. Work, school, church, and family gatherings had consumed every waking hour for as long as he could remember. He couldn't remember the last time he'd had a date. Of course, this was no date. This was business.

CHAPTER FIVE

....

For once Whitney's childhood home held a welcome as it came into view. Happy the work day had come to an end, Whitney maneuvered her car into the attached garage next to the black sedan her mother didn't drive anymore.

Whitney turned off the engine and sat there gripping the steering wheel as she let the tension drain from her shoulders. From the moment she'd stepped into Graham's office that morning and came face to face with Jeremy, looking so much like Jimmy, the knots in her shoulders had grown knots. Thankfully, her golf game hadn't suffered from all the tightness. She couldn't let Jeremy's presence in the office ruin this job she loved. She would do whatever it took to deal with him.

With a heavy sigh, she trudged into the house. The sound of laughter floated toward her from the kitchen. She walked through the mud room. When she stepped into the kitchen, she saw her mother and Carla working together near the stove.

"You two seem to be having a good time." Whitney moved closer.

Her mother turned, a smile curving her mouth. "Whitney, Carla and I are having the best time. She's showing me how to make something she calls 'rounders.' It's a recipe from her German great-grandmother. Come look."

Glancing at Carla, Whitney smiled. "So what are rounders?"

"Pockets of bread filled with ground beef, cabbage, and onion." Carla held up a baking sheet filled with the round mounds of dough. "These are ready for the oven."

"They look good, and it's so nice not to have to fix supper after I get home from work." Whitney hugged her mom's shoulders. "You and Carla do good work together."

"We do." Eileen hugged Whitney back. "I'm so glad Carla agreed to stay with us."

"Me, too." Whitney sent Carla a conspiratorial smile. "I spent the afternoon on the golf course. Do I have time to take a quick shower?"

"The rounders should be done in about fifteen minutes, and we can eat soon after that," Carla said.

"I'll be ready in fifteen minutes." Whitney hurried toward her room, hoping a hot shower would relieve her tight shoulders.

The smell of freshly baked bread mingled with the aroma of cabbage and onions as Whitney made her way back to the kitchen. She leaned forward to get a better look at the pan Carla plucked from the oven.

"Those smell so delicious." Whitney fluffed her still-damp hair as Carla slid the round puffs of pastry into a basket.

"Wait until you taste them." Carla placed the basket on the table that was set for three. "Let's eat."

Whitney joined her mother and Carla as they gave thanks for their meal. Whitney took in her mother's happy expression with a sense of relief. Having Carla around appeared to be a blessing. Whitney took a bite of her rounder and chewed slowly.

"So what do you think?" Carla raised her eyebrows.

"You're right these are amazing." Whitney nodded, then turned to her mother. "What do you think?"

Eileen smiled as she put the cabbage-filled pouch on her plate. "You have it right. Carla's an amazing cook."

Carla tucked her chin as she smiled. "I can't take all the credit. You helped, too."

Eileen reached over and gave Carla's arm a little squeeze. "Only a little. You should take all the credit."

"It doesn't make any difference who's responsible for these. They taste marvelous." Whitney took another bite.

For the rest of the meal, Whitney mostly listened as Carla told stories about her great-grandmother who had emigrated from Germany at the beginning of the twentieth century and lived in South Dakota. Whitney took in the conversation with a growing sense of joy. Having another person in the house during the day had a positive effect on her mother.

After they finished eating and cleaning up the kitchen, they went into the adjoining family room to watch TV. Whitney didn't care much for game shows, but this evening ritual was something her mother loved. She might not remember the name of their next door neighbor, but she enjoyed her game shows. Whitney feared that would soon end, so she wanted to enjoy these times with her mother as long as she could.

When the game shows ended, Eileen stood. "I know it's still early, but I'm feeling a little tired tonight. I think I'll go to bed and maybe read a little."

Whitney rose from the couch and hugged her mom. "Okay, Mom. See you in the morning."

"Good night." Eileen turned to Carla. "Thanks so much for that wonderful supper."

"You're welcome. Have a good rest."

"I will." Eileen shuffled across the room. "See you in the morning."

As her mother disappeared into the hallway, Whitney stared after her. How long would it be before her mother no longer wanted to read because she couldn't follow a story line? That thought brought a pain to Whitney's heart. She didn't want to think about the future. It hurt too much.

"Are you okay?" Carla's voice shook Whitney from her thoughts.

Whitney turned and tried to smile. "Yeah. It's just hard to think about my mom declining. I think it's good for her to have you here."

Carla nodded. "I enjoyed today."

"I hope you continue to feel that way." Whitney let out a harsh breath. "Especially when I'm gone for nearly three weeks in August."

"Mary said she'd give me a break when she's not working or watching her grandchildren."

"That's so kind of her."

"I know." Carla nodded. "I always loved visiting Mary's family when I was a kid. We had the best time."

Whitney tried to smile as she remembered all the times she'd spent with that family while she'd dated Jimmy. Their family was boisterous and lively and fun. So different from her own. After she'd broken up with Jimmy, she'd missed his family as much as she'd missed him. If only she'd taken a different path, one that she'd wanted, instead of following her parents' wishes.

And now every day at work, Jeremy's presence would

remind her of those decisions.

"Whitney, could I ask you a personal question?"

Judging from the look on Carla's face, Whitney didn't have a good feeling about the other woman's inquiry. "What do you want to know?"

Carla lowered her gaze as she twisted her hands in her lap. When Carla looked up, a little pucker formed between her eyebrows. "Here's the deal. Mary told me about your mom needing help, then had this big meeting with her kids while I was watching the youngsters. After the meeting, she asked me to join them."

"What did she say?" Whitney asked.

"She just said everyone was on board with the plan, but as soon as she left the room, Jimmy and Jeremy started arguing about you."

"What did they say?" Whitney wasn't sure she really wanted to know, but the question was out there to be answered.

Carla made a face. "Maybe I shouldn't have brought this up."

Pretty sure what the brothers had been fighting about, Whitney stared at Carla. "You might as well get it all out in the open, or you will always wonder."

Carla took a deep breath and let it out in a rush of air. "Jimmy told Jeremy you were nothing but trouble and that he should stay as far away from you as possible."

Whitney stifled a sarcastic laugh. She wondered just how much Jeremy knew about her relationship with Jimmy. If Jeremy knew the truth, would he look at her with disdain? Would it ruin the tentative working relationship they'd established? "I wonder if Jeremy was thinking about that warning all day today while we played golf."

"You guys played golf? I thought you were working?"

Whitney lifted one shoulder as she managed a little smile. "It was at Graham's command."

"Oh." Carla looked puzzled.

"Graham thinks it's a good idea to have golf skills. Deals are done on the golf course all the time."

"Oh, so this was business golf." Carla narrowed her gaze. "Were you discussing business deals?"

Whitney finally laughed. "More like discussing the finer points of golf. Jeremy hasn't golfed in a long time."

"So you beat him?"

"I did." Whitney grimaced.

"Good for you."

"Now he owes me dinner."

Shaking her head, Carla frowned. "What will Jimmy have to say about that?"

"Maybe Jeremy won't tell him."

"But that still doesn't explain why Jimmy gave Jeremy that warning."

"No, it doesn't." Whitney sighed. "You might as well know Jimmy and I were high school sweethearts, and it didn't end well."

"What happened, or isn't that any of my business?"

Was confession good for the soul? She supposed in the end that nothing she could say would be worse than what people already said about her in this town. Atlanta had been so easy because she'd been anonymous. Nobody knew her secrets there. The whole town of Pineydale knew her past foibles. "I suppose I should tell you what you want to know."

"You don't have to if you don't want to."

"You might as well know." At least most of the story.

Some parts were still too raw to tell.

"Sure, if you feel like it."

Whitney sighed heavily. "Jimmy got a scholarship to ETSU over in Johnson City. That's where we'd both planned to go to college, but my parents had other ideas. My mom insisted that I go to her alma mater, a women's college near Atlanta. Although I didn't want to, I didn't put up much resistance."

"Is that why you broke up with Jimmy?"

"Let's just say our lives went in different directions after that." Whitney sighed again. "I usually went to summer school, except the year I had an internship with Graham's company the summer before my senior year, so I didn't see much of Jimmy, especially after he joined the army. My parents often came to visit me during breaks. It was almost as if they didn't want me to have anything to do with Jimmy?"

"Why?"

Whitney bit her lower lip. She didn't want to denigrate Jimmy. What did Carla know about his past behavior? "Did you know Jimmy dropped out of college?"

"Yeah, he said something about finally getting his degree. And Kelsey, too."

The mention of Jimmy's wife pricked Whitney's heart. Whitney didn't have any business having feelings for her old beau, but they surfaced all too often. The guilt gnawed at her soul. Although she'd prayed for forgiveness, she didn't feel forgiven. "I'm glad he's found happiness in all aspects of his life, but I wish he didn't have such a low opinion of me."

"I don't understand it."

Whitney smiled halfheartedly. "That's because you

don't know the whole story."

"Are you going to tell me?"

"Yeah." Whitney stared across the room as she looked at the cross stitch that had mocked her the day she'd met with Mary Cunningham. "Jimmy lost his scholarship before the end of his sophomore year and dropped out of school because he decided to party instead of study. He was never like that when we dated."

"Was he trying to fill the void you left behind?"

Whitney shrugged. "I don't know about that, but my parents were the first to inform me. That's when I knew for sure they'd been trying to keep us apart."

"They didn't like him?"

Whitney shook her head. "I don't know about their reasons. I just know they were much happier when I started dating Mitch after Jimmy went into the army."

"You mean Mitch Cunningham?"

"Yeah. We eventually got engaged."

"Wow! You were engaged to Mitch."

"Until I cheated on him with Jimmy."

Carla stared at Whitney, wide eyed. "Now I'm beginning to understand. Do I dare ask why you did that?"

"What had seemed like a perfect match between Mitch and me, especially to my parents, began to fray at the edges. Mitch and I started dating the summer I had that internship, but I soon learned that Mitch only wanted to work on cars. All he talked about was owning his great-uncle's garage and restoring cars. Mitch went to car shows constantly. In the beginning, I went with him, but I didn't care about cars. Those shows were dreadfully boring."

"I can relate. My dad was a big car buff, and I hated going to those shows." Carla gave Whitney a sympathetic look. "So what does this have to do with Jimmy?"

"Well, Mitch went to a car show with his great-uncle Wilbur, and I refused to go. I told Mitch I had things to do for the wedding. That wasn't entirely untrue, since we were getting married in about six weeks. But I had doubts about marrying Mitch."

"Why?"

Whitney twisted her hands in her lap. "Jimmy was back in town after getting out of the army, and I ran into him one day. We exchanged a bit of small talk, and the whole time I was thinking how much I really missed him. Every time our paths crossed, those old feelings resurfaced. I realized I'd been fooling myself, thinking I was in love with Mitch. I was still in love with Jimmy."

"Double wow!" Sympathy radiated from Carla's gaze.

"Yeah." Whitney pressed her lips together. "So I had to figure out some way to break things off with Mitch, and I had no idea how."

"So you decided to take up with Jimmy again and make Mitch angry?"

"Yeah, so *he'd* break it off."

"Guess that worked, huh?"

"It did, but there was a lot of heartache to go around." Whitney shook her head. "My parents insisted I try to smooth things over with Mitch, so I groveled a little. But he wanted nothing more to do with me. I wanted to be with Jimmy, but he didn't want anything to do with me either."

"So what happened then?"

"My parents called up some friend of theirs in Atlanta, who offered me a job. I took it, left town, and didn't come back until my dad got sick."

"And how did you feel about coming back?"

Whitney glanced toward the window, not wanting to meet Carla's gaze. There was nothing good about returning to Pineydale. Whitney wished she could undo those first few months back in town. She'd returned to find Jimmy married, and she'd done an unthinkable thing. Surely Jeremy didn't know about that.

Forcing a smile, Whitney turned back to Carla. "So here I am dealing with my mother's problems and trying to overcome the old gossip."

"You mean after all this time, people still talk about your broken engagement?"

Whitney shook her head. "I don't think they talk about it, but I read the pity in their eyes."

"Maybe they're just sorry about your dad and now your mom."

"Could be, but in a small town, everybody knows your dirty laundry."

"I wouldn't know about that. I've always lived in a big city or its suburbs. We moved a lot because of my dad's job, so I was never in one place long enough for people to know my dirty laundry."

"Lucky you."

Carla shrugged. "I don't know. It might be kind of nice to have a whole town to be close to."

"Stay in Pineydale long enough, and you might change your mind. I loved the years I spent in Atlanta."

"We lived there when I was really little, but I don't remember it much." Carla raised her eyebrows. "I mostly remember Dallas, Kansas City, and St. Louis."

"Which one did you like the best?"

As Carla explained what she liked and didn't like about each city, Whitney breathed a sigh of relief that the conversation had taken a new turn. She didn't want to talk about or think about the mistakes she'd made. Would someone ever love her? Would she find someone to love? Or would she wind up never marrying and living in Pineydale while her mother's mind slowly faded? She didn't have a choice now. Her mother needed help.

***

The door to Graham's office stood open as Jeremy moseyed down the hallway. He'd been on the job for two weeks, and so far everything was going great. He'd spent the first weekend with Whitney manning the company booth at the Grandfather Mountain Highland Games, and despite the awkward meeting with Jimmy and Mitch and their wives, the booth was a success. Last weekend he'd paid off his golf bet by taking Whitney to dinner. She'd been cordial and charming but a little reserved.

He had yet to figure out why Jimmy had warned him about her. Maybe their sorry history created an animosity he couldn't shake. But Jeremy didn't have any reason to doubt her commitment to the company and her job. Her expertise and willingness to help him said only good things about her.

Jeremy had seen nothing out of line from Whitney. Her professional demeanor accompanied her in all circumstances, including golf lessons, engaging customers at the Highland Games, and their dinner conversation the previous weekend. In fact, sometimes he wished he could tell her to lighten up. She was way too serious. But she had a lot of responsibility at home and on the job, so he kept his mouth shut. She didn't need his advice.

As Jeremy drew within feet of the office, his uncle's voice boomed into the hallway. "You can help Jeremy with the marketing aspect of this venture."

"I'm not going to babysit him." Whitney's tone was anything but accommodating.

Jeremy halted. Whitney obviously didn't have any trouble standing up to Graham. Why were they arguing about him? Was he not doing a good job and had to have a watchdog, as in Whitney? Jeremy's heart sank. Maybe Jimmy had been right. No one could please Uncle Graham in this position.

Although Jeremy had been summoned, he wasn't sure he should step into this argument. He stood statue-like, his legs refusing to move.

"I didn't say you should babysit him. He's a grown man, but he's new at this. You can guide him."

"I know he's young and relatively inexperienced. When you hired him, I had my doubts about his abilities to do this job, but from what I've seen so far, he makes good decisions and demonstrates a working knowledge of the position. He's capable of handling this on his own. I'm not going to traipse up to Massachusetts for this event. I'm not signed up for it, and it's way too late to join." Whitney statement rang with conviction.

What would he discover if he stood here long enough? Did he really want to know? At least Whitney thought he could handle the job, but Uncle Graham didn't sound so sure. What did that say about the future?

"No one said you had to join the ride. You just need to be there to make sure everything goes as planned," Graham said.

"No I don't. I need to spend as much time with my

mother as possible since I'm going to be gone for three weeks later in August. Jeremy will do a good job, and he's already involved with the team that's riding. Trust him."

"Okay. On your say so."

Jeremy inched toward the door. Standing to the side, he knocked on the doorframe, then stepped into view. "Did I miss anything?"

Graham glanced at Whitney, then at Jeremy. "Whitney was just telling me she's not going to the PMC. So it looks like you're on your own for this one. Are you ready to take charge?"

"Absolutely." Jeremy wouldn't show any doubt. He wanted to prove he was the man Whitney claimed he was.

"Good. I'll outline my expectations in this meeting, then I'll let you two work out the details.

"Sounds good to me, sir."

Graham motioned toward the chairs in front of his desk. "Have a seat, and we'll get this meeting underway. We have a lot to discuss."

Jeremy waited until Whitney was seated before easing himself into the chair next to her. He prayed this would go well. At least it seemed that Whitney was in his corner.

For the next hour, Graham made clear what he wanted done. Jeremy took it all in as apprehension seeped into the corners of his mind. He couldn't let doubt take over. He could do this. He had something to prove to both his uncle and Jimmy and Whitney, too.

"That's it then." Graham stood as he eyed Jeremy. "I'll expect a good report when you return. I admire you young people, riding for a good cause."

Nodding, Jeremy stood also. "Amanda and Kelsey are quite committed to this ride because of Max, who's a cancer survivor."

"Yes, Amanda mentioned that when she and Mitch came for dinner last weekend." Graham stood in the doorway as Jeremy and Whitney went into the hall. "And, Whitney, you take care of your mom."

"You can count on that." Whitney gave Graham a tentative smile. "Thanks for seeing clear to let me stay here and do that."

"You're welcome." Graham stepped back into his office.

Jeremy stared at Whitney, who seemed lost in thought. "You okay?"

She nodded. "Just thinking about my mom."

"Is she getting worse?"

"Not worse, just not better."

"Sorry to hear that."

"Thanks, but let's not dwell on that. We've got work to do." Whitney motioned down the hallway. "Let's go to my office and finalize everything for your trip to Massachusetts."

"Sure." Jeremy followed Whitney toward her office, taking in the gentle sway of her hips.

He shook his head and wondered what he was thinking. He didn't have any business letting his mind wander into that territory. They were coworkers, and he'd been warned enough times about the trouble Whitney could cause him.

"Are you good with me not going?" Whitney settled behind her desk.

"Sure. Why do you ask?" Jeremy found a seat, then sat forward in his chair. Even though she'd said he could handle this, did she have doubts?

"You just looked suddenly uncomfortable."

Good thing Whitney couldn't read his thoughts. She didn't need to know that he'd been chastising himself for ogling her shapely backside. "I'm a little nervous about flying for the first time."

"I thought y'all were driving."

"Mitch and Jimmy are driving with Amanda and Kelsey and the two babies. Jimmy hates to fly." Jeremy raised his eyebrows. "Don't get me wrong. I love my nephews, but I'm not up for spending hours in a vehicle with crying babies. And they're sure to cry at some point."

Whitney laughed. "So you're flying?"

Jeremy nodded. "First time."

Whitney chuckled. "You need to get into practice. You're going to be on an eight-and-a-half-hour flight over the ocean in a couple of weeks."

"And I'm looking forward to it."

Whitney's eyebrows puckered. "But not the short flight to Boston?"

Jeremy didn't know if he wanted to admit that having Whitney with him would lessen his anxiety about the long flight overseas. He'd be going solo to Boston. "It'll be great to have someone to travel with."

"Nice to know. It's better to have a traveling companion. I've done enough solo traveling to attest to that."

"I hope you're still saying that after three weeks together on the road."

Whitney pushed a piece of her hair behind one ear as she gazed at him. "Yeah. I thought of that, too. I have to admit I've never been on a business trip for that long, not to mention having a coworker with me. Short trips, a few days, but never anything this long."

"Does it worry you?" Jeremy narrowed his gaze.

"Not really. We'll do fine together."

Jeremy hoped she was right, but he couldn't help thinking about Jimmy's warning. It sat in his mind like a piece of moldy cheese, stinking up his thoughts. What was the point in worrying about something nebulous, something he couldn't control? Jeremy couldn't let his brother's worries concern him. "Yeah."

Whitney's eyebrows puckered momentarily. "Do I hear a reservation?"

Jeremy let out a halfhearted laugh. "I'm way more concerned about learning those foreign phrases. I can recognize them when they're written, but they come out of my mouth sounding way different than those recordings I've been listening to."

"Why don't you come over for supper tonight? You can practice on my mom. She knows German, French, Dutch, and Spanish almost as well as I do, because Mom and Dad lived in Europe for several years before I was born."

"Is your mom up to it?"

Whitney nodded. "It would do her good. She does better when she has a lot of interaction with people. That's why having Carla there is such a blessing."

"But I don't want to put you out."

"Believe me. It'll be fine." Whitney reached for her phone. "I'll call Carla just to ease your mind."

"Okay." Jeremy wasn't sure anything would ease his mind when it came to Whitney. Jimmy had said enough unpleasant things about her, and Jeremy couldn't erase them. Going to dinner at her house would only add to his unease, but he would be rude to refuse the invitation, especially if Carla gave the go-ahead.

Whitney looked his way as she held her phone to her ear. "You're in for a treat. Carla's the best cook, and she's making her homemade pizza. What toppings do you like?"

Jeremy had no idea Carla was a super cook, but pizza sounded great. "Pepperoni and sausage. Anything really."

"Even mushroom and olives?"

"Sure. Whatever. I'm easy." But would spending an evening with Whitney and her mother be easy?

CHAPTER SIX

T he sight of Jeremy loping up the front walk of her childhood home made Whitney wonder where her mind was. Would Jeremy's presence remind her mother of Jimmy? Whitney didn't want to find out, but she couldn't rescind the invitation.

He took the steps two at a time and joined her on the front porch. "You beat me here by a mile. You'd better slow down, or you're going to get a speeding ticket. You know you don't live in Atlanta anymore."

Whitney laughed as her worries etched themselves in her mind along with the squeaking of the screen door as she opened it and stepped inside. "Thanks for the warning. I'll try to remember that."

Jeremy held the door as he followed her inside. "You should oil this thing."

"More advice?"

"Yeah, well, old habits die hard. When Jimmy and I worked for my dad in the summers, our job was to make sure the doors in the houses we painted didn't squeak." He gave her a lopsided smile, and her stomach did a nosedive.

"I'll look into it." She took a deep breath and tried to squelch that feeling. She wasn't sure whether her reaction came from talking about Jimmy or looking at Jeremy's smile. Her emotions were a mess. Maybe she could blame it on everything going on with her mother. A poor excuse?

Probably.

"I could always do it for you. I'm handy with a can of WD-40."

"If that's all it takes, I'm pretty sure I can handle it."

"If you ever need help, I'm here to lend a hand."

"Thanks." Whitney was pretty sure she wouldn't be asking for Jeremy's help. She didn't want to involve herself with Jeremy any more than she had to. "Let's see what Carla has prepared. Delicious aromas are floating from the kitchen."

"Sure."

Whitney didn't wait for Jeremy as she hurried through the dining room and prepared herself for whatever her mother would say. Carla was bent over as she retrieved a pizza-laden pan from the oven.

"That looks delicious." Whitney grabbed a cooling rack for Carla.

"Hi, Jeremy, Whitney." Carla smiled as she placed the pan on the cooling rack. "We'll eat in a few minutes. I'll just pop this other pizza in before I cut this one."

"Hey, Carla. Good to see you." Jeremy maneuvered around the kitchen island and gave Carla a hug. "I didn't know you were a gourmet cook."

Carla blushed as she gazed up at Jeremy. "I'm not. This is just pizza."

"She's a marvelous cook." Eileen rubbed her stomach as she waved a hand toward Carla. "She's going to make me fat with all this good food."

"Hello, Ms. Hamilton. Thanks for having me over." Jeremy nodded in her direction.

"My pleasure. It's not every day we get to have a handsome young man over for supper."

Whitney stared at Jeremy. Was he blushing now? Then she glanced at her mother. Why was she flattering him? She'd never had any use for Jimmy, but now she was gushing over his little brother. Whitney had noticed the same thing on the Fourth of July.

Whitney could tell Jeremy wasn't sure how to respond. Should she save him, or would she just make things worse? When in doubt, keep quiet. At least she'd keep quiet about her mother's comment.

"Carla, are we ready to eat?" Whitney asked, hoping to dispel Jeremy's unease.

"We sure are. Grab a plate, and we'll eat right here in the kitchen." Carla motioned toward a stack of plates and the pizza. "This side is pepperoni and sausage, and the other side is just plain cheese."

Jeremy held out a hand. "Ladies first."

Whitney glanced over her shoulder. "Even if we ladies take all the slices with pepperoni and sausage?"

"I'm sure I'll like whichever slice I get." Jeremy stepped back. "Go ahead."

"Jimmy, you are such a gentleman."

Whitney stared at her mother. Was she confused, or was that just a slip of the tongue? Whitney glanced at Jeremy. What was he thinking? That her mother had him confused with his brother? What to do? What to do?

"Eileen, did you mean to say Jeremy?" Carla asked, nodding her head slightly in Jeremy's direction.

Eileen looked confused, but only for a moment, as she tapped her fingers to her lips. "So sorry. I meant Jeremy. It's just that Jimmy often came over when Whitney and he were dating. I know it's been years since then, but you know…"

"I understand, Ms. Hamilton. It's like my mom. She goes through all the names of my siblings before she gets to mine. She even calls me by my sisters' names, so I'm used to it." Jeremy chuckled even as unease settled in his gaze.

Eileen smiled as she plucked a slice of pizza from the pan and headed to the kitchen table. "It's a good thing I only had one child. Only one name to remember."

Placing a slice of pizza on her plate, Whitney took in the exchange. At least it appeared her mother wasn't confused after all. That was a relief, but having the reminder of Jimmy wasn't. Whitney had to accept the fact that her history with Jimmy would pop out and grab her like a snag on a sweater that unraveled one thread at a time. She would have to deal with it as long as she lived in Pineydale.

As Whitney took her seat at the kitchen table, she hoped she could get through this meal without hearing Jimmy's name again. How would she ever succeed in working with Jeremy if the specter of his brother continued to haunt her? At least she didn't have to go to Boston. She should be thankful for that.

When they were all at the table, Eileen held out her hands. "Let's say thanks for this food. Jeremy, would you like to do that for us?"

"Yes, ma'am." Jeremy took Eileen's hand, then held his other one out toward Whitney.

She placed her hand in his, fighting the reaction she feared would come. She lost the battle as little sparks flitted through her midsection. Was this happening because he looked like his brother, or was this just about Jeremy? If it was the latter, she was in trouble. Somehow she had to get a handle on her feelings.

Thankful for the brevity of the prayer, she immediately dropped his hand as he said "amen." She picked up her pizza and took a big bite as she avoided eye contact with him. For a few moments there was silence as they ate. She worked with him every day, so why did his touch affect her? After everything that had happened with Jimmy, any thought of a connection to Jeremy, other than work, was insanity.

Finally Whitney glanced at her mom. "Mom, Jeremy wants to practice his French, German, and Dutch for our trip. Do you think you could do that?"

Eileen smiled. "You are an ambitious young man. Trying to learn three languages at once."

"Just trying to learn a few phrases to get by." Jeremy shook his head as he motioned toward Whitney. "She's the one who will do all the translating. I just want to see if you can understand me when I say something."

"Sure. Give it a try."

Whitney watched and listened as Jeremy mangled several German phrases. She hoped her mother wouldn't be too critical. Jeremy needed encouragement, not criticism.

Her mother tilted her head. "I'm not quite sure what you said. Would you repeat it?"

Jeremy grimaced. "Maybe I'm a hopeless cause when it comes to foreign languages."

Eileen reached over and patted Jeremy's hand. "Oh, no, no, no. You keep trying. You can't expect to get it perfect the first time. Tell me in English what you're trying to say."

Jeremy gave Eileen the English phrase. Then Eileen

prompted him in flawless German, and Jeremy repeated it until he said it to her satisfaction. They went through every phrase in Jeremy's vocabulary. Soon the two were laughing and speaking in German. Eileen's laughter warmed Whitney's heart. She loved that sound, and she hadn't heard it much since her return.

And what could she say about Jeremy? His determination stoked all the good things in her mother. She was more alive tonight than she'd been since the Fourth of July. Maybe Jeremy's presence made all the difference. Too bad there wasn't ample time to do more of this kind of activity before Jeremy left for Massachusetts.

After they finished eating, Whitney stood. "Carla and I will clean up while you two continue with your language practice.

"Sure." Jeremy nodded, then turned back to Eileen. "Time to mangle some French."

Eileen laughed and said a phrase that Jeremy repeated. Whitney took in the conversation between her mother and Jeremy. The evening had turned out much better than Whitney had anticipated.

After Whitney and Carla finished the cleanup, they moseyed into the living room, where Jeremy sat on the couch with Eileen. Jeremy repeated a German phrase. Whitney understood every word he said. He was a quick study.

Whitney stopped near the end of the couch where Jeremy sat. "*Kunt u mij helpenunt?*"

Jeremy looked at her, surprise coloring his features. "*Spreekt u Engels?*"

"*Ja,*" Whitney said.

Carla laughed. "I'm feeling left out of this

conversation."

Eileen got up and cupped Carla's shoulder. "Whitney asked Jeremy if he could help her in Dutch. She switched languages, and Jeremy caught on right away, and he asked her if she speaks English."

"Oh, okay." Carla grinned. "I think I'll stick with English while I go back to my room and give my folks a call."

Jeremy stood and gave Carla a hug. "Thanks for the pizza."

"You're welcome. And thanks for not asking me to say it in Dutch."

"If you'd like to learn, it's *graag gedaan*."

"That's okay." Carla chuckled. "I don't plan on going overseas anytime soon. See y'all later."

"Good night, Carla." Eileen hugged Carla, then turned to Whitney. "I'm going to call it a night, too."

"Are you okay?" Whitney asked.

"Just a little tired."

An uncertain expression clouded Jeremy's face as he glanced around the room. "I hope I didn't wear you out."

"Oh, no." Eileen waved a hand at him. "This is about the time I retire every night. I'm not as young as I used to be."

"Okay. Good night." Jeremy turned toward the door. "I'd better be heading home."

Whitney didn't say anything for a moment as her mother and Carla left the room. Should she ask Jeremy to stay? Would he?

She followed him to the door. "Jeremy, if you don't have to leave right away, can we talk?"

With his hand on the doorknob, he turned to look at

her, curiosity in his gaze. "Did I do something wrong?"

"Oh no." Whitney tried to smile. "I just have something I want to run by you. Can you stay?"

***

Jeremy took in Whitney's forced smile with trepidation. What did she really want? "Sure. I don't have any plans."

"Let's talk out on the front porch."

"Okay." Jeremy opened the door and motioned for Whitney to go ahead of him. "After you."

Whitney went immediately to the porch swing and sat down. Jeremy stood there, wondering whether she expected him to join her on the swing or sit in one of the nearby chairs. The soft glow of light just before darkness highlighted Whitney's blond hair. He wished he were anywhere else. He couldn't forget Jimmy's warning.

"It'll be much easier to talk if you sit down." She patted the space beside her on the swing. "You can sit here."

"Sure." He eyed the spot.

Misgivings dogging his steps, he made his way to the swing. As he sat on the far edge, he grabbed the chain and rested his elbow on the arm of the swing. He almost laughed as an image from his childhood skipped through his mind. He'd been twelve, and his friends had connived to make him sit with Sissy Baker on her front porch swing. It had not turned out well. He'd been the butt of their jokes for weeks.

Whitney wasn't Sissy Baker, but sometimes Whitney gave him that same unsettled feeling in the pit of his stomach. He certainly didn't want that feeling to be anything other than work-related nerves.

"The evening went well, don't you think?"

Whitney's voice brought his thoughts back to the present. "Yeah. Your mom was a tremendous help."

Whitney clasped her hands. "You were a real help to her."

Jeremy shrugged, wondering if this is what Whitney wanted to talk about. "I didn't do anything."

"You helped my mom feel useful again."

"You set it up."

"But I had no idea how it would turn out." Whitney let out a heavy sigh. "This was one of my mom's better days. It helps so much for her to interact with others."

"Glad to be of service." Jeremy shifted so he could look at Whitney without craning his neck. "Is that what you wanted to talk about?"

Whitney pressed her lips together and looked straight ahead rather than at him. "No."

"Then what's on your mind?"

"Our trip."

"Okay. What about the trip?" Jeremy raised his eyebrows. "Are you planning to give me packing advice?"

"No." Whitney hesitated, still not looking his way. "When Jimmy worked for your uncle, we traveled together."

"What does Jimmy have to do with this trip?"

Why was she bringing that up? He thought she'd steer clear of any mention of his brother, but unlike Jimmy, she probably had put that old history behind her. Jimmy, on the other hand, sometimes had a hard time letting go of past hurts. Jeremy pushed that thought away. He hadn't lived through the mess with Whitney as Jimmy had. Judging him wasn't something Jeremy should do.

"Um...I just want to make sure we're good. That my history with your brother won't ruin our working relationship." Finally, she looked his way.

Jeremy's mind whirled with a storm cloud of thoughts, every one of them dark and destructive.

Whitney looked away again as she twisted her hands in her lap. "I probably shouldn't have said anything about it. You were probably too young to remember much."

Jeremy let out a halfhearted laugh. "I remember all too well."

"That's what I was afraid of."

"Why are you bringing this up now? Why didn't you say something right from the start?"

Whitney released a harsh breath, her gaze lowered. "I wanted to, but I didn't think it was appropriate."

"And it's appropriate now?"

"I just decided it had to be discussed. I don't want us working together, traveling together, and the whole time you're thinking I'm this horrible person."

"Whitney, look at me."

"Okay." Her wary gaze met his.

"Where is this coming from? Did Jimmy say something to you?"

Whitney shook her head. "The word around town is Jimmy's advised you that I'm nothing but trouble."

Jimmy had said that more than once. The warning was clear. Jeremy wasn't sure how to admit that or if he should. His opposing thoughts wrestled with each other like he and Jimmy had growing up.

Whitney sighed. "Sorry I brought this up, but—"

"I understand." Jeremy hoped she believed him. "So if Jimmy didn't tell you that, then who did?"

"It doesn't make any difference who said it. It's been said, and I had to know where you stand."

"I form my own opinions, and Jimmy needs to get over the past."

"Thank you." A little smile curved Whitney's lips.

Jeremy wanted to get to the bottom of Whitney's inquiry. "Was Carla the one who told you about the argument between Jimmy and me?"

Whitney's gaze widened, but she didn't say a thing.

Jeremy wished he could take the question back as soon as he said it. But he'd been trying to think about something besides the way this whole thing with Whitney made him uneasy. He wanted to like her but not too much, or he might wind up like his brother. Sorry he'd ever known her. How was he going to keep his thoughts positive while he'd be around her constantly for three weeks? Maybe Jimmy should've warned Whitney about his little brother, instead of the other way around.

"Your silence pretty much gives me the answer."

Concern knit Whitney's brow. "I don't want to get Carla in trouble. She just wanted to know what all the fuss was about."

"And you told her?"

"Yeah. I figured she should hear it from me and not from some gossip in town."

"You're right about that." Jeremy wondered if people were still talking about that. Surely not after all this time, but small towns could be a cesspool of bad memories. And he wondered if he actually knew the whole story. He knew Whitney had cheated on Mitch. But why? Although he would love to know, he wouldn't ask.

"Thanks for not making a big deal out of it." Relief shone in Whitney's eyes. "It was hard coming back here, and I just wanted to make sure you didn't hold any ill will against me."

"We're good." Jeremy stood and headed for the steps. "I'd better get going. I've got to get everything in order before I head to Boston."

Whitney joined him. "I have confidence you'll do great."

"I'm ready." Jeremy hoped that was true, but he couldn't let Whitney think he had any doubts. Even if he did. "Good night."

Jeremy waved as he loped to his car. All the way home, he replayed his visit with Whitney and tried to figure out his reaction to her. Were the Cunningham men doomed to fall for her? No. He wasn't falling for her. He was just aware of a very pretty woman. That was all. At least, he hoped that was all.

***

For Jeremy, the two days biking had been exhilarating and tiring, but the camaraderie and the satisfaction of knowing he'd been riding for a good cause made up for the sore muscles he'd dealt with today while he'd played tourist. Boston Common, all the historic places along the Freedom Trail, the Public Garden, and Fenway Park. Not wanting to miss a thing, Jeremy took in as much as possible during his last day in Boston and snapped photos to preserve the memories of this experience.

Tonight he celebrated the weekend's accomplishments

with his family members as well as the new friends he'd made on this trip. The friends all had connections to cancer. Some happy stories and some sad. He loved the happy story about how Parker Watson had overcome a bitter situation and fell in love with Brittany Gorman, who had been the nanny to his two adopted girls, Rose and Jasmine. That led him to help his former student, Tara Madsen, come to Boston so her little girl, Haley, could receive treatment for a rare cancer. During that time Tara met Caleb Fitzpatrick here in Massachusetts, and the two of them fell in love.

Then there was Heather and Max's love story and how he had overcome cancer. The bonds of friendship had formed through some trying circumstances. Jeremy took in the love of these friends as they sat around the fire pit in the gazebo at the home of Kurt and Molly Jansen.

This trip made him thankful for his health and the ability to ride over a hundred miles on a bicycle. At the end of this week, he'd wing his way across the ocean for a new adventure. Life was good, better than good.

"Did you get all your work-related business taken care of?" Jimmy eyed Jeremy across the fire pit.

Nodding, Jeremy wondered where this conversation was headed. Jimmy had made it quite clear this weekend that he still wasn't on board with Jeremy working for Uncle Graham. "I did. Easy work. I just had to make sure the water bottles got handed out. I had people stationed at the end points of all the routes."

"How did you manage that?" Jimmy looked unconvinced.

"Amanda connected me with Kurt and Molly here, who had people handing out coupons for their bed-and-breakfast. We just put the coupons and the water bottles together. Killed two birds with one stone."

"Good thinking." Jimmy looked surprised. "So are you ready for your big trip to Europe?"

Jeremy grinned. "I'm looking forward to it. It's going to be a lot of work, but I'm excited."

"Are you a white-knuckle flier like Jimmy?" Kelsey looked at her husband, then back at Jeremy.

"Before this weekend, I probably would've said yes, but the trip up here was great. I actually enjoyed the flight, and I sat next to a businessman from Amsterdam on the flight from Charlotte to Boston, so I got to practice my Dutch. He was impressed with what little I know."

Amanda motioned Jeremy's way. "Say something in Dutch."

"What?"

"Anything. Let me see if I can figure out what you're saying."

"*Hoe heet je? Spreekt u Nederlands?*"

Jimmy looked at Jeremy with a blank expression, then laughed. "I need an interpreter."

"What's your name? Do you speak Dutch?" Jeremy grinned.

"Jimmy. And no." Jimmy shook his head. "I've got to hand it to you, little brother. You sound like you know what you're talking about."

"That's until you compare me to a native speaker or Whitney and her mom. Those two are brilliant when it comes to languages. When I get back, Whitney's going to give me some packing tips." Jeremy couldn't help noticing how Jimmy's mouth tightened at the mention of Whitney.

"You mean you can't pack your own suitcase?" Jimmy

frowned.

"I could for a normal trip, but I've got to get three weeks' worth of stuff in a carry-on roller bag and a back pack." Sorry he'd mentioned Whitney, Jeremy stared back at his brother. "Did I hear some kids talking about roasting marshmallows?"

"You did, and here they come." Molly pointed toward the four girls and one boy who trooped across the yard behind her husband, Kurt. "I'm glad Eric has his dad to help balance out the gender ratio there. I think Eric wishes his little brother, Ethan, was old enough to play instead of having to play with Emily, Haley, Rose, and Jasmine.

"At least Ethan won't want for male playmates in a few years, with all these baby boys," Molly said.

"And we'll be adding another one to the group come the beginning of next year." Tara, Molly's good friend, grinned from ear to ear as she squeezed her husband's hand.

Caleb leaned over and kissed Tara on the cheek, then looked back at the group. "We told Haley yesterday. I'm surprised she didn't spill the beans."

Brittany laughed. "I think she told Rose, Jasmine, and Emily, but not Eric. It was the girls' secret. Poor Eric."

"I hope you guys are planning to make this an annual thing." Heather motioned to everyone sitting in the gazebo. "I love getting together with all you guys. The ride wouldn't be the same without you."

"I'd love to do this every year, but we can't make any promises." Amanda smiled. "But we'll be sure to make an effort to come. You guys should make plans to come down to Pineydale for the cancer fundraiser Mitch's mom puts on every year around Labor Day."

"That would definitely be another chance for us to get together," Heather said. "We'll have to see what next year brings."

As the kids roasted their marshmallows over the fire pit, Jeremy wandered off to the side. His earlier feelings of camaraderie flitted away like the sparks shooting up from the fire. Although he enjoyed the fellowship, he was the odd man out with this group. Despite the crowd around him, loneliness encompassed his heart.

But he couldn't help thinking he was the only single in this world of couples and their children. He couldn't remember the last time he'd had a date. He seldom thought about his lack of love life, but tonight seeing all these couples put his singleness squarely in his mind.

"You look lost in thought." Jimmy approached.

In the waning light, Jeremy couldn't read his brother's expression. "Just thinking about my future."

"And what are you thinking about that?"

"That I'm eager to get home and prepare for my trip." *And be away from couples, couples, couples.* Jeremy put on a happy face even though his heart wasn't happy.

"Let me give you a little advice."

Advice? Jeremy wasn't sure he wanted advice from Jimmy that had anything to do with this upcoming work-related trip. "What?"

Jimmy stepped closer. "Watch out for Whitney."

Jeremy shook his head. Was Jimmy ever going to get over his bad history with her? "If you're going to dump on Whitney again, I don't want to listen."

"You need to." Jimmy narrowed his gaze.

"No, I don't." Jeremy turned away.

Jimmy put a hand on Jeremy's shoulder. "Yes, you do.

Believe me."

Jeremy whipped around to face Jimmy. "What is wrong with you? You have a lovely wife, a healthy baby boy, and a successful company. Why are you obsessed with an old girlfriend?"

"This has nothing to do with my former relationship with Whitney," Jimmy said through gritted teeth. "It has everything to do with you and her."

Wrinkling his brow, Jeremy stared at his brother. "Yeah, we work together. So what's the problem?"

"Whitney's out for Whitney. So don't let her convince you that she's there to help you. She's not."

Jeremy took a deep breath. Did he dare defend Whitney? Defending his coworker might be a fruitless endeavor, but he had to try. Jimmy was completely out of line. "I've seen no sign of that."

"Just wait. She sucks you in with her sweet helpfulness, then undercuts you just like that." Jimmy snapped his fingers. "I'm telling you, Jeremy, you can't trust her."

Jeremy shook his head again. "You just have a bad history with her, and you can't get over it. Sure she treated you badly, but that was personal. It had nothing to do with work."

Jimmy let out a heavy sigh. "I can see you aren't convinced."

"No, I'm not. She's been nothing but professional and supportive, going above and beyond to help me learn the ropes. Her assistance has made me look good to Graham."

"It won't last. She's using you like she uses everyone."

"I don't need to listen to you." Jeremy stepped away.

Jimmy followed. "You do whether you want to or not.

Just hear me out. I promise that after tonight I won't say another word about Whitney."

Jeremy let the promise swirl through his mind like the smoke from the fire pit swirling into the night air. "Okay. I'll listen as long as I don't have to hear it again."

"Wise decision."

"Just get on with it."

Jimmy cleared his throat. "Sure. You know that Whitney and I dated all through high school."

"I suppose she used you then."

Jimmy nodded. "Yeah. She did. She wanted to be the head cheerleader and date the star quarterback."

"When she started dating you, you were a nobody freshman."

"I won't argue with you there, but the social pecking order had already been established in middle school."

"So you're saying you were a big somebody in middle school? Just because you were voted best looking in high school doesn't mean that all those years before Whitney was using you because of your good looks."

"That's not what I meant." Jimmy looked toward the heavens, then back at Jeremy. "Don't make this difficult."

Jeremy shrugged. "Just trying to establish the reality of the situation."

"And so am I. So be quiet and listen."

Jeremy released a harsh breath. "Just finish what you've got to say."

"I will if you quit interrupting me."

Jeremy crossed his arms across his midsection and stared at his brother and didn't say a thing. Just waited.

Jimmy lowered his voice. "Some of the things I'm going to tell you are things I've never told anyone, so I hope you'll keep them to yourself. Agreed?"

Jeremy shrugged. "If I don't agree, are you not going to tell me?"

Jimmy rubbed a hand down his face. "I'm only doing this for your own good. If you're going to be nasty about it, maybe I should just let you suffer the consequences of working with a woman who doesn't have your best interest at heart."

Jeremy pressed his lips together in order to keep himself from saying something he would regret. He held out one hand in a sweeping gesture.

"Thanks for letting me finish." Relief registered on Jimmy's face. "When we graduated from high school, the plan was to go to ETSU together, but Whitney had grander plans. She went to that all girls' college in Atlanta."

Jeremy frowned. "So you're saying her choice of colleges put you down and caused you to do all kinds of stupid stuff. Sounds more like you should put the blame on yourself, not her."

"Could you just listen?"

"I'm trying, but the more you say, the more I think you're trying to make Whitney look bad for no good reason."

"After I'm finished, I think you'll have a different opinion." Jimmy raised his eyebrows. "Yeah, I did some stupid stuff, and that's all on me, but Whitney decided, even after I cleaned up my act, that Mitch was a better prospect. More money, more prestige in town."

Jeremy opened his mouth to say something, but Jimmy held up a hand. Jeremy clamped his mouth shut.

"Then when she discovered that Mitch had no interest in his dad's business and instead wanted to run that garage, all of a sudden Mitch didn't seem like such a good catch after all. That's when she decided to pursue me again, and I was dumb enough to fall for it. Now if you want to say something, you can. I deserve it."

Jeremy shook his head. "Don't have a comment."

"This is the part I don't want you to share." Jimmy leaned closer. "While I was working for Uncle Graham, he asked Whitney and me to go to this conference in Denver. I didn't want to go. I was sick of spending time with Whitney, and I wanted to spend time with Kelsey. You know this was before Kelsey and I finally admitted that we loved each other."

Jeremy nodded, wondering where this was headed. Jimmy had married Kelsey so she wouldn't have to tell her family that she was pregnant by her previous boyfriend, and Jimmy had wanted to fulfill Uncle Graham's marriage requirement. Jeremy had always liked Kelsey and was glad their crazy marriage had worked out in the end, but this whole thing with Whitney was another puzzle altogether.

"Anyway, I told Graham that I didn't want to go. He said if I didn't go, I could turn in my resignation."

"Wow! I had no idea."

"It gets worse." Jimmy took a deep breath. "Whitney found out about my possible resignation and came to my office. She tried to convince me that I shouldn't resign and said we should get back together. She was convinced that I wasn't happy with Kelsey. Maybe she knew everything wasn't right with my marriage, but she didn't have any business trying to rekindle a relationship with someone else's husband."

Jeremy was sure his mouth hung open. He didn't want to believe what he'd just heard, and he certainly didn't know what to say.

"Nothing to say now?"

Jeremy shook his head, wishing he didn't know this about Whitney. How was he going to work with her now? Every time he looked at her, he would think of what she'd tried to do.

"I've kept this to myself all this time, but I thought you needed to know now that Whitney might not be your friend." Jimmy sighed. "I don't want to make your working relationship bad, but I just had to warn you about her."

Jimmy's revelation stirred up an array of emotions in Jeremy. Disappointment. Anger. Disgust. And emotions he couldn't name, but they all brought him sorrow. His heart ached for both his brother and Whitney. "All I can say is, I'm sorry."

"Yeah. I never actually wanted to tell anyone about that episode, but I thought I ought to give you a heads-up." Jimmy grimaced. "Do you understand?"

Jeremy nodded. "I don't understand her, but I understand your warning. It's kind of hard to imagine. Even with all the stuff that went on before, I can't figure out why she would do something like that."

"Me neither." Jimmy clapped Jeremy on the back. "But let's put that behind us and go enjoy the rest of our evening."

Producing a halfhearted smile, Jeremy followed Jimmy back to the gazebo, where the kids were consuming the marshmallows they had toasted and were begging for more. Jeremy wanted to capture some of their joy to replace the hurt in his heart. But would anything be the same after learning of Whitney's scheme to steal another woman's husband?

Jeremy accepted Jimmy's reasons for the warning, but that didn't make them any easier to digest. Working with Whitney wouldn't be easy going forward. He had to pray that he could see her through God's eyes and not his own.

CHAPTER SEVEN

Jeremy's office door was closed, and Whitney hadn't seen him all morning. He hadn't stopped by her office to say hello as he usually did when he passed by each morning upon his arrival at work. She'd been expecting him to tell her about his trip to Boston. She almost wondered if he hadn't come to work today.

She raised her hand to knock on the door but hesitated. Maybe he didn't want to be disturbed. Maybe she should send him a text. She traipsed back to her office and plopped onto her chair. She plucked her phone from her desk. Why was she so uncertain about talking to Jeremy?

They were about to depart on a three-week trip together, and she couldn't bring herself to approach him. What had happened to her usually bold demeanor? This was silly. Her doubts. Her trepidation. Her indecision. These weren't the normal feelings of Whitney Hamilton.

As she sat there trying to make sense of her mood, a knock sounded on her door. She looked up. "Good morning, Graham. What can I do for you?"

"Come down to my office, and bring Jeremy with you." Graham stepped back. "We're going to confirm the final plans for your trip."

Whitney stood, still gripping her phone. "Be there in a few minutes."

Graham saluted as he left without another word.

Whitney gathered her folders and headed for Jeremy's office. His closed door greeted her again. Why couldn't Graham have summoned Jeremy instead of sending her on this mission? What was going on this morning? Everything seemed out of sync. She was determined to make sense of her own insecurities today, Jeremy's lack of interaction, and Graham's orders.

Whitney pushed aside her odd feelings of self-doubt and knocked on Jeremy's door. Nothing. Maybe he wasn't here, and Graham didn't know it. That would be awkward. As she raised her hand again to knock, the door eased open.

Jeremy stared at her, an uncertain expression in his blue eyes. "Do you need something?"

"Yeah." Whitney wished the qualms that plagued her this morning would dissipate. "Graham wants to meet with us and go over the final plans for our trip."

Jeremy narrowed his gaze. "And he sent you to get me?"

Whitney shrugged. "Yeah."

Jeremy glanced at the folders and tablet she held. "Let me get my stuff. No need to wait. I'll be down in a minute."

Feeling dismissed, Whitney made her way down the hall toward Graham's office. When she arrived, Graham was on the phone with his back to the door. She knocked lightly, and he turned and waved her into the room. As he continued to listen to the person on the other end of the line, he mouthed, "Where's Jeremy?"

Whitney pointed to the hallway, and Graham nodded. Just as he ended the phone call, Jeremy stepped into the room.

Graham set his phone on his desk. "Good. We're all here. Have a seat."

Whitney scooted into the nearest chair, and Jeremy took the other one without acknowledging her. Something wasn't right, but she had no idea what.

"Okay. Let's get started." Graham settled in his chair, seemingly oblivious to the tension.

Throughout the whole meeting, Jeremy said little. He contributed only when he had to. Graham punched through the agenda in record time and appeared satisfied that everything was in order. The itinerary and the meetings were set, and they had a folder and notes on their tablets for each stop.

Smiling, Graham stood. "I have confidence you two will do a fabulous job. You've got this completely organized. I'm impressed."

"Thank you, sir." Jeremy shook Graham's hand. "I'm looking forward to this."

"I'm glad to hear that, because I want you to take the weekends to have some fun and do some sightseeing. I'm sure Whitney here can lead the way in that adventure, since she's been to Europe numerous times with her previous job."

Whitney nodded as she ventured a glance at Jeremy. "Thanks for the time off while we're there. I can show Jeremy some of the sights."

He nodded in return, but didn't smile. "Sounds great."

"Good. Then that's settled." Graham looked at Jeremy. "I'd like you to stay and give me an update on your trip to Boston. Whitney, you're free to go."

"Okay." Whitney stopped in the doorway. "Jeremy, when you're done here, do you have a moment to stop by my office?"

"Sure." He turned back to Graham without another word.

Jeremy's expressionless response worried Whitney all the way back to her office. What was she to make of this emotionless Jeremy, not the smiling, joking, guy she'd come to know over the past few weeks? Had things gone badly in Boston? Was he worried about the report he'd have to give to Graham, especially after she'd begged off going and told Graham what a good job Jeremy would do?

Whitney paced in her office as she waited for Jeremy to show up. She couldn't concentrate on anything until she found out what was troubling him. They needed to be on the same page for this upcoming trip. They needed a good working relationship, not one of silence and grim looks.

Whitney went to the window and stared out at the parking lot. Heat waves rose off the blacktop. August in east Tennessee brought with it hot and humid weather. Northern Europe would be a welcome change. She would definitely need to pack a jacket. She would have to tell Jeremy to do the same. While she continued to gaze out the window, trying to focus on the positive, a knock sounded on her door. She turned.

Jeremy stood in the doorway, that uncertain look still in his eyes. "What did you want?"

For you to smile. The thought flitted through her mind, but she pressed her lips together to keep from saying it. She motioned to the nearby chair. "Have a seat. I want to find out about your Boston trip."

Reluctance shaded Jeremy's expression as he made no move to sit. "Everything went well. Graham was pleased with the outcome."

"That's good, but I was hoping you'd talk about your ride and meeting Amanda's friends."

"That was good, too."

Whitney let out a halfhearted laugh. "I get the feeling you aren't interested in talking."

Jeremy shrugged. "Got work to do."

"Sure." Whitney manufactured a happy face, even though she didn't feel it. "Before you go, I've got something for you."

"What?"

Whitney reached behind her desk and brought out a large plastic bag. "The backpack you ordered came while you were gone."

"Just in time for the trip."

"Yeah. When would you like those packing tips?"

Jeremy shook his head. "You don't have to bother with that. I'm sure I can figure out how to pack my own suitcase."

"Oh, okay." Something was wrong. Jeremy had been all for help with packing before he'd left for Boston. Did she dare ask what was bothering him? "Then we'll plan to leave Friday morning around eight o'clock?"

"Whatever you think is best." Jeremy shrugged again. "Do you want me to drive?"

"You can if you want."

"I'll drive." Jeremy grabbed the backpack and headed for the door but turned before he stepped into the hall. "I'll pick you up right at eight on Friday."

"If you change your mind about the packing, just let me know. Be sure to pack a jacket. It probably won't be as warm there as here."

"Yeah, I've looked at the weather forecast. Munich is

going to be warm, but Amsterdam will be cooler."

"You're right on top of things."

"I try to be." Jeremy left without another word.

Whitney sat at her desk, but she couldn't concentrate on her work. Her mind kept wandering back to Jeremy. Maybe he was in a panic about this trip but didn't want to admit it. Whatever it was, something wasn't right, and she had to get to the bottom of it. Taking a deep breath, she headed to Jeremy's office.

Again a closed door greeted her. She knocked. No hesitation this time. Within seconds the door opened.

"Did I forget something?"

"No, but may I come in?"

Jeremy stepped aside. "Okay. Is something wrong?"

Whitney folded her arms across the top of the chair sitting in front of Jeremy's desk and stared at him as he still stood near the door. "You tell me."

Jeremy knit his eyebrows. "I don't' know what you're getting at."

"I want to know what's bothering you. You haven't been yourself all morning."

Jeremy held his arms out to his sides, palms up. "I feel like myself." He looked down. "Yep. I'm still Jeremy Cunningham."

Whitney chuckled. "That's the first time today you've acted like the Jeremy Cunningham I know and not some stranger."

"Okay. Now you know it's me. So we're good."

Whitney shook her head. "You're not being honest with me. Something's up, and I want to know what it is."

"You caught me." Jeremy went behind his desk and pulled out one of the drawers. He plucked a gift bag from the drawer and set it on his desk. "I got a little something for you while I was gone."

Whitney reached for the bag as skepticism rifled through her brain. She doubted this gift had anything to do with the way he was acting. She pushed aside the tissue paper and lifted a small tin from the bag. "Boston Tea. I love tea. Thanks."

"You're welcome."

"I appreciate the gift. Now tell me what's really going on."

Jeremy eyed her from the other side of the desk, then dropped his gaze. "Can't I give you a gift?"

"Sure. But we're going to be spending three weeks together, and I don't want anything to mess up our working relationship. So if something's bothering you about this trip, I want to know about it now."

"No problem with the trip."

"Not nervous about flying?"

"Nope. Got my wings on the trip to Boston and back."

Whitney put her hands on her hips and stared at Jeremy. "I'm not leaving this office until you tell me what's wrong."

"Who said anything's wrong?"

"I did." Whitney plopped onto the chair she'd been leaning against earlier. "Spill."

Jeremy sat in his chair, a muscle working in his jaw. He didn't meet her gaze as he laced his fingers behind his head and stared somewhere over her head. His expression told her he was thinking.

"I'm listening." Whitney settled back in the chair and crossed her arms over her torso.

Jeremy suddenly stood and placed his hands on his

desk as he leaned forward and narrowed his gaze. "Why did you try to come between Jimmy and Kelsey?"

Whitney's stomach churned as her head pounded with the terrible memory. "Jimmy told you about that?"

Giving her a laser-beam look, Jeremy nodded as he straightened and rubbed the back of his neck. "He warned me that you're only out for yourself, and I wouldn't believe him because you've been so helpful to me. So he told me how you traded him for Mitch and then cheated on Mitch with Jimmy, then threw him away like last week's trash. Then you come back to town and tried to convince him that the two of you were meant to be together. That's why he quit this job."

"I thought Jimmy had let bygones be bygones. He was downright friendly over at Charlotte's on the Fourth of July."

"That was to please our mom. She instructed us to be nice to you so your mom would ask Carla to stay with you."

"Thanks to your mom." Whitney realized what a jewel Mary Cunningham had always been. "So Jimmy is still harboring some ill feelings toward me."

"That's an understatement." Jeremy stared at her. "Are you going to explain your actions?"

Whitney closed her eyes as she put a hand over her mouth. How could she ever explain her wrongheaded behavior to Jeremy? She pressed her lips together and forced herself not to cry. Her emotions finally under control, she looked at him. "I'm sorry you had to hear that. I'm sorry I messed with so many people's lives. I'm sorry for everything."

Jeremy wrinkled his brow. "If you're so sorry, why did

you come back to town and do the same thing all over again?"

Whitney let out a harsh breath and recounted the whole Mitch and Jimmy thing the same way she'd explained it to Carla. "I really did love your brother."

"Then why on earth didn't you stay with him instead of trying to make up with Mitch."

Whitney stared at the hands she twisted in her lap. "Because my parents insisted, and I didn't have the fortitude to stand up to them. I let them control my life."

"Why would you come back to town and try to start that whole mess again?"

Whitney took a shaky breath as she formulated her answer, praying that Jeremy would understand. "I was told that Jimmy was unhappy in his marriage, that he'd married Kelsey in a rush and realized it was a mistake. I just wanted to let him know I would be there to pick up the pieces or whatever he needed. I knew I'd made a mistake as soon as he looked at me with disbelief and told me he loved his wife."

"I still can't believe you thought it was a good idea to go after another woman's husband no matter what anyone told you." Jeremy shook his head and frowned.

"You're right. I was completely wrong, out of line, despicable. You can call me every name in the book. I deserve it."

Jeremy hung his head. "I'm not out to make you feel horrible. I can see that you're honestly sorry about what you've done. Have you ever thought about apologizing to Jimmy?"

Raising her eyebrows, Whitney stared at Jeremy as she blinked furiously, trying to ward off the tears. Finally she managed to speak. "Are you kidding me? I just want to forget I'd ever done that. I'm not sure he'd even accept an apology from me. I just wanted to stay away from him. Every time I've run into him, I'm reminded of my foolishness."

"Maybe it's time for an apology."

"I can't undo the past."

"But you can tell him you're sorry. Maybe that will help both of you." Jeremy stepped from behind the desk. "He needs to forgive you, and you need to find forgiveness."

Was Jeremy right? Would Jimmy forgive her, or was that wishful thinking? "I wouldn't know how to approach him."

"I can set that up."

"If I do this, will it make things good between us for this trip? I don't want you thinking that I'm out to undermine you. You're an important part of this team, and we need to be able to work together for the good of this company and our jobs." Whitney looked at Jeremy with hope in her heart.

"It'll be a step in the right direction."

Whitney picked up the gift bag, still wondering whether an apology to Jimmy would do any good. She held up the bag. "If you have such a low opinion of me, why did you buy me a gift?"

"I bought it before Jimmy told me about what you'd done." Jeremy sat on the edge of his desk and eyed her.

"So you want to take it back?"

"No, it's yours." He gestured toward the bag. "And I don't have a low opinion of you. I just think you've made some mistakes. We all do. So who am I to judge? I just want you to set things right with Jimmy."

Whitney didn't have a good feeling about Jeremy's request. "I wish I had your confidence that this will be worth the effort."

"You know what? If he doesn't accept your apology, that's his loss. You'll have done your part. That's all you can do." Jeremy pushed away from his desk. "So are you on board?"

Nodding, Whitney released a heavy sigh. "I suppose."

"Okay. I'll figure out a time and a way to meet with Jimmy and let you know when it is."

"You aren't planning to have Kelsey there, are you?" Whitney couldn't imagine having to explain her misguided actions to Jimmy's wife.

"Never in a thousand years." Jeremy shook his head.

Whitney placed a hand over her heart. "Thank you."

"No good could come from that. Jimmy hasn't told anyone about it except me. So that's where it begins and ends."

Whitney clutched the handles of the gift bag as if doing so would make all the bad stuff go away. "Guess I'd better get back to work."

"Sure, and I'll be in touch about that meeting."

"Great." *Maybe.* Whitney left without a backward glance. She didn't want to see any pity in Jeremy's eyes. He knew her terrible secret. Could Jimmy really forgive her? Could Jeremy not think of that incident whenever he looked at her? If only there were do-overs.

She had to remind herself that God couldn't give her a do-over, but He could forgive. She wanted to believe that, but she had a hard time forgiving herself. So how could God forgive her? Forgiveness was all tied up in asking for it. Asking Jimmy and asking God.

***

Whitney's heart pounded as Jeremy parked his car in Jimmy's driveway. She wasn't sure she could get through this apology without crying. But she was strong. She could do this.

After grabbing two drinks from the cup holders, Whitney got out of the car and looked at Jeremy. "You're sure Kelsey's not home?"

"Yeah. I talked to my mom, and Kelsey's watching all the kids over at Mom's today because she has to run errands and didn't want to haul the kids with her. So you don't have to worry about Kelsey."

"Just Jimmy. That's enough." Whitney traipsed across the soft ground in her heels and business suit as she followed behind Jeremy to Jimmy's workshop at the back of his house.

The door to the workshop squeaked as Whitney entered the cavernous space. The smell of freshly cut wood, sawdust, and varnish permeated the air. Her stomach churned as Jimmy looked up from his workbench.

He wiped his hands on a rag and tossed it back on the bench. "What are you doing here?"

Jeremy held up several paper bags. "We brought you lunch."

Jimmy glanced at them. "Why is she here with you?"

"She's here because I invited her." Jeremy set the bags of food and a paper cup on the workbench. "I brought your favorite from the diner."

"And why would you do that?" Jimmy frowned.

"Because I thought you'd enjoy it." Jeremy pulled up a stool to the workbench.

"I'm not talking about the food. I'm talking about her." Jimmy's words came out of his mouth like nails shot from a nail gun.

Shrinking back, Whitney wished she hadn't come. Obviously, Jeremy hadn't told Jimmy that she would be here. This was not going well. How could anything good come from it? Why had she agreed to come? Because Jimmy had been civil to her on the Fourth of July, but his civility had truly been a facade for his mom's benefit just as Jeremy had explained.

"I'll leave." Whitney backed toward the door, drinks still in hand.

"No." Jeremy came after her. "The two of you need to get over the past, and I intend for that to happen today."

Whitney inhaled, her insides quivering with misgivings. Her gaze darted between Jeremy and Jimmy, who looked at her with disgust. *Please, God, let this work.* The silent prayer rambled through her thoughts.

"I'm sorry. I'm so sorry for the pain I caused you. Please forgive me." The words tumbled from Whitney's mouth.

The two brothers looked at each other. They stood in contrast with Jeremy in his navy suit and striped tie and Jimmy in jeans and a T-shirt that read, *Sawdust is man glitter*. Jeremy smiled, but Jimmy still stood there stone faced, and he didn't say anything.

Jeremy raised his eyebrows as he looked at his brother. "Don't you have something to say?"

More silence greeted Jeremy's question.

Whitney wanted to run out of the building and back to

the safety of her office, but her legs wouldn't respond. She wished the floor would open up and swallow her. Why had she let Jeremy convince her that this would be a good thing?

Jeremy got up in Jimmy's face. "I asked you a question, and I expect an answer."

Whitney's pulse raced. She feared the brothers would come to fisticuffs. She tried to step between them. "Please don't fight."

The two men looked at her as if they'd forgotten she was there.

"We're not going to fight." Jeremy stepped back and looked her way, picked up two of the three bags, then turned to Jimmy. "We'll just go. I can see there's no reasoning with you. You'd rather just wallow in your anger. When someone apologizes, the least you can do is accept the apology."

Jeremy took Whitney's elbow and headed for the door. He stepped closer and whispered, "I'm sorry I put you through this. I can't believe my brother's behavior."

Shocked by the whole scene, Whitney followed Jeremy outside, her legs shaky. "It's okay. You tried. I think the hurt goes deep, and I can't undo that."

Before they reached the driveway, Jimmy raced out of his workshop. "Don't go."

Jeremy turned around. "You have something you'd like to say?"

"Yes." Anger still colored Jimmy's expression as he glared at her. "I want to know why you tried to come between me and Kelsey."

Whitney took a deep breath and let it out slowly as she tried to figure out the best way to explain. Maybe there was no best way. She just had to lay it out there and hope Jimmy could find it in his heart to forgive her. She swallowed hard.

"Let's go back inside, eat, and discuss this." His eyebrows raised, Jeremy looked back and forth between Jimmy and her. "Okay?"

Jimmy looked doubtful but nodded. "Sure. No sense in standing out here in this heat."

Whitney glanced at Jeremy as they followed Jimmy, who marched back into the workshop. She leaned closer and whispered, "Do you think he'll really listen and understand?"

Jeremy nodded. "Just tell him what you told me."

Whitney hoped he was right. Her heart was a little lighter because Jeremy seemed to understand. He had a forgiving spirit.

After they entered the workshop, Jimmy immediately brought more stools to the workbench. "Have a seat."

Whitney set the drinks down, then sat on the stool that would put Jeremy between her and Jimmy. Distance would be their friend. Jeremy placed her bag of food in front of her. She opened it and brought out the sandwich and fries. The guys did the same.

"We should give thanks for the food," Jeremy said.

"Okay." In Whitney's estimation, prayers should be said for more than the food, but she wasn't going to pray. She'd let Jeremy do that.

Jimmy didn't say a thing, just nodded.

When Jeremy bowed his head, Whitney did the same. She squeezed her eyes shut tight and clasped her hands in her lap. *Lord, please give me the right words to say to Jimmy.*

"Lord, thank you for this food. Please bless it and our conversation. Amen." Jeremy looked up, his eyebrows raised as he looked at Whitney. "Eat or talk?"

"We can do both." Whitney then proceeded to take a big bite of her sandwich and hoped that would give her enough time to figure out how to start this conversation.

His elbows on the workbench, Jimmy held his burger in front of him but didn't take a bite. He just stared at Whitney. "I'm waiting to hear your explanation."

Whitney swallowed her bite of food and set her sandwich on the wrapper. "Good, because I'm planning to give you one. I hope you'll listen with a forgiving heart."

A muscle worked in Jimmy's jaw. He nodded and took a bite of his burger.

Whitney's heart hammered while her brain wouldn't engage her mouth. She gave herself a mental pep talk. If Jimmy didn't accept her explanation or apology, she had done her part. Jeremy gave her a sympathetic glance as he ate some fries. He was in her corner on this one. That should give her courage.

She took a deep breath and let it out slowly as she tried to smile at Jimmy. "I know we have some bad history between us, but there were some good times, too."

"We don't need to go into any of the stuff between you and Mitch and me. I just want to know why you acted the way you did after you moved back to Pineydale."

"Fair enough." Pressing her lips together to calm her emotions, Whitney nodded. "What I did was wrong, and I apologize and ask for your forgiveness. I know you may never feel like you can be my friend, and I'm sorry for that. And I'm sorry I tried to come between you and Kelsey. I had the misguided notion that you weren't happy in your marriage."

"And why did you think that?" Jimmy asked as a look passed between him and Jeremy.

"Some well-meaning or not-so-well-meaning women in town told me you'd suddenly up and married Kelsey because she was pregnant. You were only being a stand-up guy and taking responsibility, but you weren't happy. You spent most of your time working, not with your wife. But now I see they were wrong, and I was stupid for believing them." Whitney sighed. "All the years I lived in Atlanta, I dated, but none of the guys I met ever lived up to you in my heart. So when I came back, I was sorely disappointed to find out you were married. But then I heard the rumor about the troubles in your marriage, so I thought I'd see what could happen between us. I wish I'd been smarter. Again, I'm asking for your forgiveness."

Jimmy picked up a fry and dragged it through a blob of ketchup on the wrapper. He popped it into his mouth as he stared at her. Wasn't he going to say anything? Did her confession just make her more despicable in his eyes? Was he trying to torture her with his silence? She just wanted to scream at him and then leave, but that would accomplish nothing.

"I've said I'm sorry. I've tried to explain my misguided thoughts and actions. I'm just asking you to forgive me, and we can hopefully move on and let our past mistakes stay in the past."

Without saying a thing, Jimmy walked to the far corner of the workshop. He opened a cupboard and pulled out what looked like a gift box. He carried it over and set it in front of Whitney.

Whitney frowned. "What's this?"

"A peace offering."

Tears threatened as Whitney looked up at him. "So you're forgiving me?"

He nodded, and Whitney pressed her hands to her face as emotions flooded her heart. If she said something now, she could only make a blubbering sound. *Thank you, Lord.*

"Are you going to open it?"

Jimmy's question settled her mind. She took a deep breath and picked up the package as she gave Jimmy a questioning look. "Why would you have a peace offering when you didn't know I was coming?"

"It's something I've had for many years, but it had been forgotten, stuffed in a box. I discovered it a few weeks ago when I was cleaning out my basement. I almost threw it away, but something told me to keep it. So I shoved it in the cupboard out here. God knew this day was coming." Jimmy motioned toward the box. "Open it."

Her hands shaking, Whitney fumbled with the lid on the box, but she finally opened it and wondered what this had to do with God. She stared at the tissue paper obscuring the contents. What could Jimmy possibly be giving her that would serve as a peace offering—one he didn't even know he'd be handing out thirty minutes ago?

Whitney took a deep breath and lifted the tissue paper. She let out a little gasp as she lifted the framed cross stitch. She stared at the words, blurred by her tears.

If we confess our sins, He is faithful and just and will forgive us our sins and purify us from all unrighteousness. 1 John 1:9

The words of the Scripture verse made it very clear why Jimmy had given this to her. The clumsy cross stitch was a pure metaphor for the brokenness God could heal.

As she tamped down her tears, she blinked rapidly, then raised her head to look at Jimmy. "How is it that you have this?"

"Do you remember the summer after our senior year in high school when you were cleaning out your room to get ready to go off to college in Atlanta?"

Whitney nodded, wondering where this topic was going.

"Anyway, you threw that out."

"I did?" Whitney shook her head as she set the cross stitch back in the box. "I don't remember that. I just recognized it as one of my terrible attempts at cross stitch. I certainly don't remember that it had been framed."

Jimmy touched the frame. "It wasn't. I helped you carry out the bags of trash, and when you weren't looking, I rescued that cross stitch. I framed it and saved it with the intention of giving it to you on some special occasion. Birthday. Christmas. Whatever. But you know I got mixed up with the wrong crowd and did some stupid stuff. So I lost you to Mitch, and I tossed it in a box and forgot it."

"And you just found it?" Whitney asked.

"Yeah. Like it was meant to be found at the right time." Jimmy shook his head. "Although I'm sure you aren't interested in keeping it, I thought it would at least show you I've forgiven you."

Relief. Sorrow. Joy. Her heart burst with emotions of every stripe. She picked up the cross stitch again and held it to her chest. "Thank you. Thank you for forgiving me."

"It's about time," Jeremy said as he stared at Jimmy.

Whitney placed the cross stitch back in the box again and put the lid on it, then patted the top. "My mom will love this."

"I'm glad." Jimmy clapped Jeremy on the back. "Thanks, little brother, for making me do this."

"You're welcome." Jeremy grinned. "I was certainly worried for a while there that I'd made a *big* mistake by insisting that you and Whitney make peace."

Jimmy rubbed the back of his neck as he lowered his gaze, then looked up. "I'm just glad I came to my senses." He glanced at Whitney. "All the bad blood between us has been eating away at me for a long time. So it feels pretty good to take a load of bad feelings and get rid of them."

Whitney placed a hand over her heart. "Me, too. I know we probably can't be close friends 'cause Kelsey probably wouldn't appreciate you being chummy with your old girlfriend, but at least we can greet each other without animosity."

Jimmy ran a hand through his hair. "Yeah. I wouldn't want to do anything to mess up the good thing I've got with Kelsey."

"I should've known. I realized the huge mistake I'd made when you looked at me in your office that day and told me you loved Kelsey and that was all I needed to know." Whitney closed her eyes for a moment, then looked back at Jimmy. "I wish I could undo that day, but I'm happy for you and Kelsey."

Jimmy nodded and picked up his sandwich. "I hope our food isn't too cold, but I'm relieved that we've cleared the air."

"Let's eat." Jeremy held up his drink. "Celebrate new beginnings."

"And our upcoming trip." Whitney smiled at Jeremy.

The threesome tapped their paper cups together, then took a drink. Whitney chewed another bite of her sandwich as her mind chewed through the events of the preceding minutes. Sadness still occupied a tiny corner of her mind— sadness that she hadn't fought for Jimmy when she'd had the chance all those years ago. But she had to be satisfied that they weren't meant to be together. She was ready to start a new chapter. Did God have someone else in mind for her? Or was the single life her destiny?

CHAPTER EIGHT

Stationed at the gate ready to take on its passengers, the airliner looked huge, bigger than any plane Jeremy had ever seen. Not that he'd seen a lot of them. He glanced at Whitney as they stood looking out the window in the airline lounge. "That's our plane?"

Whitney nodded. "Impressive, isn't it?"

"Yeah." Jeremy's stomach knotted. "How does that thing ever get off the ground?"

"Aerodynamics." Whitney chuckled. "Getting a little nervous?"

"No. You'll save me if the plane goes down."

Whitney wrinkled her brow. "Don't say stuff like that. You'll make me a nervous flier, and I've never been nervous on a plane."

"Okay. I'll keep any negative thoughts to myself." Jeremy settled in one of the chairs in the lounge. "Except that one time on the golf course, I don't think I've seen you in anything besides a suit since we started working together."

Whitney pulled at the sides of her navy-blue-and-white knit tunic top, then brushed a hand down the knit navy pants. "I told you we should dress comfortably for the flight. I certainly don't plan to sleep in a business suit. Although they do offer pajamas, I don't want to change unless we have to go right from the plane to a meeting."

"Pajamas?" Jeremy didn't want to tell Whitney he hadn't slept in pajamas since he was a kid. He usually slept in a T-shirt and shorts. "I don't need those either. I think my T-shirt and sweatpants will do."

"Yeah. I'm glad you followed my advice about what to wear."

"And the packing. Thanks for the tips."

"I'm glad you let me help you after we resolved the issue with your brother."

Jeremy nodded. "How long before we board?"

Whitney glanced at her phone. "Probably about an hour. First class and business class board first, and someone will make an announcement so we can go to the gate when it's time."

"Okay. Might as well relax."

"Get a drink and something to eat." Whitney motioned to the array of snacks and beverages.

"Sure." Jeremy helped himself to a soft drink and a plate of crackers and cheese. After he found a seat, he grabbed his tablet out of his backpack and logged onto the Wi-Fi. He scrolled through his emails while he munched on his snack.

After he finished his emails, he checked his social media accounts and glanced through his newsfeed. Kelsey had posted a photo of baby Jaime and his cousin Logan, Mitch and Amanda's little boy. At least Jimmy and Mitch were determined not to let their sons continue the rivalry that had separated Jimmy and Mitch for years, until they had married sisters.

Jeremy glanced at Whitney, who had her gaze trained on her phone. He was glad he'd insisted she apologize to Jimmy. It would make this trip a whole lot better.

Even though Whitney and Jimmy had made peace and Jeremy was happy about that, he wished he'd never learned about Whitney's misdeed. He couldn't help thinking about it when he looked at her. He'd been the one who'd taken her side against Jimmy, but what Jeremy had learned still colored his thoughts about her.

Trying to push those unkind thoughts away, Jeremy tried to concentrate on the good things about Whitney. She was super supportive of her mother and had already called to check on her. Whitney was also super supportive of him. She made sure he came off looking good in Graham's eyes when she put in a good word for him at meetings.

Now that he'd started the job, Jeremy realized one big thing. He wasn't prepared for it. He was too young and inexperienced for the position. Sometimes he wondered whether Uncle Graham had hired him just to see him fail, but that was a callous thought. Jeremy needed to rid his mind of those.

With Whitney in his corner, Jeremy believed he could manage his workload. She was smart and did everything she could to mentor him without making him feel incompetent. He was in over his head, but she never let on to his face that she thought so also.

Her belief in him gave him a big boost. He wanted to live up to her expectations as well as Graham's. He prayed every day that she would never know how inadequate he felt at times. He put on a good show. Mr. Confidence with a capital C.

He should concentrate on remembering all those foreign phrases he'd been practicing and not think about his inadequacies.

"Hey, you're lost in thought. Still nervous about

flying?"

"You're the only one who accused me of being nervous." Jeremy was glad she couldn't read minds and actually know what he'd been thinking. "I'm going over the foreign phrases we practiced on the drive over here to Charlotte."

"You did really well with those." Whitney nodded. "You'll be able to order your food and ask for the bill."

"I hope I can do more than that." Jeremy basked in her praise.

Did he depend on her too much? Did he have feelings for her that he shouldn't have? From the very beginning, he'd tamped down any attraction every time it surfaced. The things he'd learned about her recently should cause him even more pause, but her charm and good looks made pushing that attraction away difficult. That was the craziness of it all.

He should remember he didn't have any business thinking about a work colleague in romantic terms, especially Whitney, with her less-than-stellar past. She was off limits in so many ways. But maybe he was like one of those guys who fell for his nurse—in his case, his mentor.

"I'm just happy Graham had us fly over early, so we have the weekend to adjust to the time change and do a little sightseeing." Whitney smiled.

"Any secrets for dealing with jet lag?" Jeremy wrinkled his brow.

"The best thing you can do is try to sleep on the plane. That's why I told you to start going to bed early a month ago."

Jeremy let out a halfhearted laugh. "Not easy when I was up in Massachusetts. I did okay until the ride was over."

"The first day will be rough, but hopefully, we'll adjust quickly. We get there early in the morning. We'll go through customs, then catch a train into Munich. After we get to Munich, we'll find our hotel. We probably won't be able to check in, but we can check our luggage so we can explore."

"Have you been to Munich before?"

Whitney nodded. "Probably six or seven years ago, but I didn't have much time to see anything other than the inside of an office building. It was all business. That's why I'm so appreciative of Graham giving us the opportunity to take in the sights. Your uncle is a great boss."

Jeremy tried to grasp that concept. He couldn't deny what Whitney had said about his uncle, but Jimmy's opinion of Whitney and Uncle Graham had colored Jeremy's thoughts for years. Why had he let his brother define these people? Jeremy made a promise to see Whitney and Graham through his own eyes and not his brother's. Jeremy wanted more than anything to step out from under Jimmy's influence. This trip was a start.

"Are you going over those phrases again? You're always lost in thought." Whitney tilted her head as she gazed at him, curiosity in her eyes.

Jeremy shook his head, wondering if he should admit that he'd never been farther away from home than Nashville and had barely been out of Tennessee until his trip to Boston. "I'm just trying to imagine what it'll be like when we get there. You'll have to put up with this newbie traveler."

Whitney laughed. "I don't mind. Most of what we're going to see is new to me, too. We'll have fun exploring together."

"Do you know what you plan to see?" Jeremy was pretty sure this down time with Whitney would do nothing to help him think of her only as a coworker. Keeping his thoughts in the right channel would be a full-time job.

Whitney patted her tablet. "Got it all right here. I've planned everything to the last detail."

Jeremy had no doubt that she had. She was one of the most organized people he'd ever met. She had already taught him a lot about getting his ducks in a row. Sometimes she was a little more organized than he could handle. His brain froze over when she started throwing charts and spreadsheets at him.

"Would you like to look at the agenda?"

"Sure." Jeremy moved to the seat next to Whitney and wondered whether he'd have a brain freeze if he looked.

She quickly scrolled to a page on her tablet and held it so he could see. "I know most of these names won't mean a thing to you, but here's my plan. We'll do a walking tour of the city, using the info I've downloaded onto my phone. I've got earbuds with splitters so we can both listen."

"How far do you plan to walk?"

Whitney gave him a smile that looked almost like a frown. "This from the guy who rode his bike over a hundred miles?"

He shrugged. "Just curious."

"I'm not sure how far we'll walk, but it's pretty leisurely. A friend from Atlanta recommended doing this. I've got tours for the other cities as well."

"Sounds like you're all set. I'll just tag along."

"If there's something you want to see, just tell me." Whitney gazed at him, a little pucker between her eyebrows. "You don't have to do just what I've planned."

Jeremy grinned again and tried not to think about how his heart did a little twist when she looked at him that way. "I'm sure whatever you have on the agenda will work. I'm glad you've made plans."

As Jeremy finished off the last of his drink, the announcement for their flight crackled over the loud speaker. His pulse quickened. He gathered his things and put his backpack on top of his roller bag. Without saying anything, Jeremy followed Whitney out to the concourse and toward the gate. When they arrived, people were already boarding.

Whitney turned to look at him as they joined the line headed toward the gate agent. "You got your boarding pass and passport?"

"Right here." Jeremy held up the items.

"Good." Whitney turned her attention back to the line ahead of her.

Jeremy wondered if she was excited about this trip or if it was just another trip for her. He showed his boarding pass and his passport to the agent. She waved him on, and he followed Whitney into the Jetway. The wheels of his roller bag whirred along the floor. The sound matched the beat of his heart.

When Jeremy stepped onto the plane, a flight attendant checked his boarding pass and motioned him toward the aisle where his seat was located. He looked at the cubicles along the side of the plane next to the windows and found the one that matched the number on his boarding pass. This would be his home for the next nine hours.

"You can put your bags in the overhead." Whitney's voice shook him from his thoughts.

"Are you right there?" Jeremy pointed to the cubicle behind him.

Whitney nodded. "Make yourself comfortable and check out everything. If you need help, let me know. You can keep some of your smaller electronics in the little drawers."

"Thanks for the advice." Jeremy hefted his roller bag into the overhead bin. "Do you need help getting yours in the overhead?"

She shook her head. "I'm tall enough. I don't need help. I've seen some short women who have problems with these overheads."

Wondering whether he'd insulted Whitney by asking if she needed help, Jeremy dumped his backpack onto the seat and rooted around for his tablet and laptop. After he retrieved those, he put his backpack in the overhead. He settled in his seat and looked over his cubicle. A blanket, a pillow, and a little pouch sat on the shelf opposite him.

As he grabbed the pouch, Whitney appeared beside him. "The flight attendants will be here momentarily with some drinks and probably a little dish of nuts, and they'll take your food order, so be sure to look at your menu. Ask for the water. These planes are really dry, and you'll want to drink as much water as you can."

"Okay." Jeremy knew she was trying to be helpful, but her instructions reminded him of that day in the golf shop when she'd helped him pick out his golf gear. Maybe he should remember she tended to be bossy. That might keep him from liking her too much. Somehow he doubted that. He admired take-charge women. His mom was one of those, and Whitney definitely fit that description.

"Oh, and you'll probably want to wear your glasses

rather than your contacts during the flight because of the dry air."

"How'd you know I wear contacts?"

She tilted her head as she looked at him. "You used to wear glasses when you were a kid, so I just figured you wore contacts now."

"I could've had corrective surgery."

Whitney shrugged. "True, but I saw the case for your glasses while you were getting stuff out of your backpack."

"Why didn't you tell me before I put it up in the overhead?"

"Sorry. I didn't think of it until just now when I was talking about the dry air in the cabin."

"I'll take them out now." Jeremy extracted his backpack from the overhead, then headed for the restroom.

When he opened the door, the size of the space surprised him. He should've known the lavatories in business class would be a little more spacious than the ones in economy class. He made quick work of removing his contacts and putting on his glasses. As he put his things into the backpack, he stared at himself in the mirror. Whitney hadn't seen him in glasses since they'd started working together. What would she think?

The image that gazed back at him said *nerd*. He shouldn't care what she thought of his looks, and he didn't want to examine the reason why he did. Figuring out his feelings for Whitney made him a little crazy. But the day she'd apologized to Jimmy and clutched that cross stitch to her heart had produced a soft spot for her in his own heart. He didn't know what he was planning to do about it. Probably nothing. It was better pushed into a deep corner and never scrutinized.

Even though Whitney had made peace with his brother, Jeremy was quite sure nothing good could come from even the tiniest interest in her. He had to shut down any notion that he could entertain romantic feelings for her.

"Got that?" Jeremy asked his reflection as he unlocked the lavatory door.

When he returned, he had a glass of water and a small dish filled with nuts at his seat. He glanced back at Whitney, who already had on headphones. She appeared to be checking out the TV. "Did you tell the flight attendant what I wanted?"

Nodding, she looked up at him and removed her headphones and waved them in front of her. "Did you find yours?"

"Haven't looked."

"Look in here." She pointed to a compartment near her seat. "I'm checking out the movies, even though I probably won't watch one because I'll try to get some sleep."

"Okay." Jeremy settled in the seat and tried to push thoughts of Whitney aside, but he wasn't having much success. Obviously, she didn't see him as anything other than a coworker and her old boyfriend's younger brother. *Younger* brother. That thought alone should put his thinking on a different course.

But the more he tried not to think about Whitney, the more he thought about her. Three weeks of her constant company wouldn't make it easy to keep his feelings in check. Whatever they were. And he didn't want to spend time trying to figure them out.

After Jeremy finished his snack, he spent time messing out all the gizmos in his cubicle. While he found a space for his belongings, the flight attendants came through the cabin and picked up the glasses and dishes. Seconds later a recorded safety announcement came over the TV. One last time the flight attendants went up and down the aisle as they checked to see that seat belts were fastened and everything was ready for takeoff.

Jeremy's heart raced as the plane back away from the gate. As the plane taxied to the runway, he thought about Whitney, who sat behind him. He had to quit thinking about her. Or maybe he should think about her a lot and get it out of his system. He could imagine gazing into those blue eyes, bluer than a clear autumn sky, running his finger through her flaxen hair, and kissing her tender lips. No. This was crazy. He had to stop thinking about her, or he would go nuts before the trip was over.

He forced himself to concentrate on the scenery out the window. The plane lumbered along until the pilot announced that they were next in line for takeoff. In seconds the plane sped down the runway until the nose lifted, the engines whined, and the plane left the ground.

Jeremy pressed his forehead to the window and stared out as the ground grew farther and farther away. Puffy clouds floated by while they climbed higher. The roads looked like ribbons running through the forested landscape. He glanced at the TV, displaying their flight pattern. It was very similar to the one he'd taken on his trip to Boston. The plane would hug the coastline all the way to Canada before taking off across the Atlantic Ocean.

This was it. His big adventure. One that included Whitney and all her bossiness and her charm.

***

The constant drone of the engines filled Whitney's

ears. She'd eaten dinner, tried to read, and taken another look at her agenda for tomorrow. She should be tired, but she was wide awake. This had never happened to her on an overseas trip before. She had given Jeremy all this advice about how to prepare for the trip and get some sleep, but she was the one who couldn't fall asleep.

She'd gone to the lavatory one more time. When she'd passed by, Jeremy appeared to be dead to the world with his sleeping mask in place. He was covered up with his blanket with the seatbelt buckled over it. He'd taken her advice so the flight attendants wouldn't have to wake him to check seat belts during turbulence. Watching him sleep made her heart trip, something she wished wouldn't happen.

The flat bed that should make sleeping easy on the plane didn't help at all. Whitney punched her pillow and rolled over again. The sleeping mask shut out any light but not the little noises. Even the earplugs didn't help. She prayed for sleep, but it still didn't come. Tomorrow was supposed to be a day of fun, but she wouldn't have much fun if she didn't get some sleep.

Loud noises and screams awakened Whitney from a deep sleep. As she ripped off her sleeping mask and tried to figure out what was happening, the flight attendants raced through the cabin. Whitney sat up and looked around. Turbulence made for a bumpy ride, but it didn't seem bad enough for the screams she'd heard.

She looked at the flight information on the TV screen and checked the time. They were about an hour and a half out from Munich. What was going on? She had finally fallen asleep only to be startled awake by the commotion.

As she was about to unbuckle her seat belt, the

captain's voice sounded over the loudspeaker. Whitney listened as he explained that a sudden drop in altitude had resulted in injuries to some crew members and passengers who hadn't had their seat belts buckled. He cautioned everyone to remain seated with their seat belts buckled until further notice.

Whitney wanted to get up in the worst way and talk to Jeremy. Was he okay? Surely he'd still had his seat belt fastened. She wished they'd taken seats across the aisle from each other rather than having them one behind the other. But when Whitney had chosen the seats, she'd thought they both would enjoy looking out the window on takeoff and landing.

Did she dare call out to him? "Jeremy, are you okay?"

His head appeared around the side of his cubicle. "Yeah. Are you?"

"Are you still buckled in?"

"I am. I was able to loosen it enough to look around. Were you awake when that happened?"

"No, I was sound asleep." Whitney wondered if she had bed head like Jeremy. His hair stuck out in several directions, but it just made him look cute and vulnerable. He'd put on his glasses, and they did the same thing. Oh my!

"Me, too." A little frown wrinkled his brow.

As Jeremy opened his mouth to say something else, the captain asked for everyone's attention. He explained that they were trying to go around a bad weather pattern that would probably cause a delay in reaching their destination.

"That doesn't sound good." Worry radiated from Jeremy's eyes.

"It'll be okay."

Jeremy let out a harsh breath. "I hope you're right."

At that moment, a flight attendant announced that the breakfast service would be delayed until the captain gave them the okay.

Whitney looked at Jeremy, who was still leaning over so she could see him. "I've got some breakfast bars with me. Do you want one?"

"Sure."

Whitney found a couple of bars in her backpack and gave one to Jeremy. Their fingers brushed as he took the bar, and Whitney couldn't deny the little tingle that raced through her midsection as he smiled at her.

"Thanks." Jeremy nodded, then disappeared into his cubicle.

Whitney sat there trying to decipher her feelings. From the first time she'd seen Jeremy on the Fourth of July, she'd felt that initial attraction. She'd attributed it to his resemblance to his brother, but this had nothing to do with Jimmy and everything to do with Jeremy.

Not good for so many reasons!

First, he was Jimmy's little brother. Too young for her. Yes, yes, too young. Secondly, an office romance was completely out of the question. Not good for business. Thirdly, he thought she was old, even if she really didn't think he was too young. Much too old. Fourthly, his family wouldn't look kindly on her interest in Jeremy. Especially Jimmy, even though he'd forgiven her.

The turbulence of her thoughts matched the turbulence of the plane. They jumbled around in her head, keeping her completely off balance. Could she look at him as a coworker and nothing more? She had to for both of their sakes.

Whitney munched on her breakfast bar as she scrolled through the movie selections and finally settled on a documentary about oceans. Entranced with the beauty of the film, she forgot about Jeremy, work, and all of her troubling thoughts. The film reminded her that God made the beauty of the earth and oceans and that He was in control.

Lord, please give us safety as we finish this flight. Help me to deal with Jeremy in a way that would please You. Help us have a successful trip in every way. Amen.

As she finished her prayer, she realized the flight was smooth. The turbulence had subsided. She glanced out the window. Her vision filled with forested land, dotted with villages and roads. A few puffy clouds far below indicated that they had left the storm behind. Were they close to Munich?

As she brought up the flight tracker on the TV, the pilot announced that it looked like smooth flying for the rest of the trip. Although the turbulence had ended, he strongly recommended that they should keep their seat belts buckled. Right after the announcement, a flurry of activities ensued. Several people headed to the lavatories. The flight attendants scurried to serve breakfast and apologized for the truncated meal.

Whitney watched the rest of her documentary while she ate her small quiche and bowl of fruit. She made no attempt to talk to Jeremy. She had to completely clear her mind of romantic thoughts about him before she did that. Was that possible?

"We're almost there, and we've survived so far."

Whitney looked up at the sound of Jeremy's voice. He stood in the aisle next to her cubicle. She managed to smile as she looked up at him. Her heart skipped a beat, and every caution she'd given herself drifted away like the clouds beneath them. "We did, and we'll soon be in Munich. Are you ready for a great day?"

He nodded. "I'm looking forward to it. I've heard I have a top-notch guide."

Whitney couldn't help chuckling. "I hope you won't be disappointed."

"I'm sure I won't. I got a good night's sleep thanks to some advice I heard, and now I'm ready to walk the streets of Munich."

Whitney wished she could say the same. "You'd better put your shoes back on if you intend to do that."

Jeremy glanced down at his slipper-clad feet, then looked back at her with a grin. "Yeah. I'd better do that. I almost forgot I'd taken off my shoes."

Jeremy returned to his seat, and Whitney breathed a sigh of relief that she'd managed not to let Jeremy know how he affected her.

As the plane made its final descent into Munich, folks stowed their items for landing, and the flight attendants retrieved all the breakfast items and checked to make sure everyone had filled out their customs forms and had their seats upright.

A patchwork of farmland, forests, rivers, roads, and tiny villages came into view as the plane approached the airport. As they drew closer, Whitney could see the cars, looking like toys, speeding down a highway. Excitement created a fluttery feeling in the pit of her stomach. Seconds later the plane touched down in what Whitney called a perfect landing.

Whitney prayed as the injured people were transported

off the plane. Praying wasn't something she'd done very frequently while she'd lived in Atlanta. She'd pretty much drifted away from her faith. Spending time with Jeremy and Carla had made Whitney reexamine the need for prayer in her life, especially prayers for her mom. With her troubled past Whitney often doubted that those prayers had any standing with God, but she still prayed.

Finally the rest of the passengers were given the okay to gather their things and exit the plane. Whitney grabbed her bags, and Jeremy did the same.

He glanced at her as they waited in the aisle. "I feel like I've been traveling forever."

"We've still got more traveling to do."

"Why?" Jeremy's brow wrinkled.

"We have a thirty- to forty-minute train ride into Munich."

"Oh. That explains it."

"Explains what?"

"Why I didn't see a city when we landed. I was beginning to think Munich is a little village."

Whitney chuckled. "It's a bustling city with lots to see. I'm excited to share this with you."

"Me, too." Jeremy looked at her with that smile that turned her stomach inside out.

"First we have to go through customs. Thankfully, we don't have to wait on our luggage, since we have it all with us." Whitney nodded as the flight attendants thanked them for traveling with them.

"Now I see one of the reasons you said to take only a carry-on roller bag and a backpack." Jeremy followed close behind as Whitney stepped off the plane and into the Jetway.

Whitney nodded. "I learned a long time ago that the fewer bags you have, the better it is for traveling."

"I'm glad I'm traveling with you."

Me, too. The thought flitted through Whitney's mind, but she didn't say it. She didn't see any end to her mixed-up emotions about Jeremy. "After we go through customs, we'll have to look for the S train. There are lots of signs, so it's pretty easy to find."

Jeremy nodded as he looked around with awe in his expression. "Wow! I'm actually in Germany. A year ago I would never have imagined such a thing. Even a few months ago. This is incredible."

Whitney took in Jeremy's joy with a curling sensation in her midsection. She was going to relish seeing his reaction to everything they would experience today. And she shouldn't worry about her feelings. They were what they were.

CHAPTER NINE

After putting his roller bag and Whitney's on the overhead rack in the train, Jeremy settled in the seat next to her. He tucked his backpack next to him on the seat. Despite his crazy, unwelcome feelings about Whitney, he was grateful every minute for her presence. She had known how to find the train and buy tickets. Without her, he still might be wandering around the airport, wondering where to go.

The train sped by endless fields that contained vegetation he couldn't name. He must have seen the same fields from the air as they had approached the airport. Whitney had her tablet out and appeared to be engrossed in something. She didn't seem interested in talking, and he didn't want to disturb her. Besides, not talking might keep his unwanted attraction to her at bay. *He wished.*

Jeremy turned on his tablet and searched for a book. He read about two pages before he put it away. Why was he reading when he should be taking in the scenery, even if it was only fields and farmhouses?

As the train drew closer to the city, the fields gave way to small towns, then industrial areas, houses, and businesses. Jeremy wondered if he should ask where they would get off the train. Whitney seemed focused on whatever she was studying on her tablet. He didn't want them to miss their stop, but he didn't want to seem clueless either.

What was wrong with him? He stared out the window. He didn't need to ask that question. The answer was Whitney. He tried to pretend she didn't make his pulse skitter when she looked his way, but he knew better. For the sake of their working relationship, he had to get a handle on his feelings and deal with them. He truly was clueless when it came to her. He had to have a laser focus on business, not the woman he would spend the next three weeks with. Was this an impossible task? He was beginning to think so.

Jeremy had to think about what would happen if he fell for Whitney. Even though Jimmy had come to grips with everything that had transpired between him and Whitney, he would have a fit if his little brother suddenly started dating her. Jeremy could see Jimmy's head explode over that one.

Jeremy gave himself a mental shake. That scenario was so impossible. Whitney had no interest in him. That should be enough to keep his attraction in check, but for some reason his brain and his heart weren't on the same wave length. They were battling each other over his feelings for his coworker. Not good. Not good. Not good.

"Better pack up your stuff. The train's almost at the station."

Jeremy glanced at Whitney, glad she didn't have an inkling about his thoughts. "Oh good. I was wondering when we would get there."

"The route ends at the central station. Our hotel isn't far from there."

"That's good." He motioned toward his feet. "I wouldn't want to wear these out before we get started today."

Whitney shook her head as she gave him a quizzical smile. "I think you're in good enough shape to handle whatever we'll do today."

Minutes later the train pulled into the München Hauptbahnhof. Jeremy followed Whitney off the train along with a crowd of passengers like lemmings headed for who knows where. A dozen other trains sat at the platforms. People scurried everywhere. He just stood there for a minute and took it all in. Food kiosks of every description were scattered throughout the cavernous space. Coffee, sandwiches, pizza, and heart-shaped gingerbread were just a few of the food items in his line of vision.

A cacophony of foreign languages assaulted his ears. He listened intently to the people around him and tried to see if he could recognize what language they were speaking. Could he recognize any foreign phrases or decipher any of the signs in the huge hall? The many signs in English surprised him.

"Well, what do you think?"

Jeremy glanced at Whitney, and her smile made his heart skip a beat. Guess he'd better get used to that. He couldn't suppress his reaction to her, so he might as well learn to live with it, just like living with a chronic illness. The only cure was not being around her, and that was not going to happen until they got back home.

"Well, are you so stunned that you can't say anything?"

Jeremy eyed her. "You're certainly impatient. Give a guy a chance to take it all in."

"Okay, but I'm going to start walking." Whitney took off, pushing her roller bag ahead of her.

Racing to catch up, Jeremy pulled his bag behind him. He found it faster to pull it rather than push. He joined Whitney on the sidewalk outside the station. "Wow, this is a busy intersection."

"We can go to the crosswalk. Our hotel is just across the street."

Jeremy laughed. "You could've told me that."

"I said it was close."

"You did, but not how close." He looked down at his feet. "You made me think I'd be walking a ways."

"You just surmised, and I didn't correct you."

"Please correct me from now on."

She gave him a sideways glance. "Are you sure?"

"Absolutely. I want to know which way is up."

Whitney pointed a finger to the sky. "Does that help?"

Jeremy laughed again. "You're quite funny."

"Thanks." She wrinkled her nose as she pointed to the crosswalk signal. "We can walk."

"I got that figured out." Jeremy tried to tamp down his reaction to the little face she'd made. An exercise in futility for sure.

"Make sure you have your earbuds and a cap before you stow your bags."

"So we're wearing what we've got on?"

"I am." Whitney plucked a ball cap out of a side pocket in her backpack. "You have a problem with that."

"I guess not. I just feel like I've been wearing these clothes forever."

"It's really been less than twenty-four hours."

"Sure seems longer than that."

"It's going to be warm today, so we'll just change and shower when we get back to the hotel for check-in."

"Anything else I need besides my earbuds, phone, wallet, and passport?"

Whitney shook her head. "I've got sunscreen. Sounds like you have everything else you need."

After grabbing his Atlanta Braves ball cap from his backpack, Jeremy again raced to keep up with her. In minutes they entered the hotel lobby. Whitney went right to the check-in desk and asked about storing their bags until the rooms were ready. The young woman behind the counter quickly tagged their bags and stowed them in an area behind the desk.

Whitney turned to Jeremy. "I'll get directions to the Marienplatz, a central square in the old part of Munich where we want to start our walking tour."

"Sure. You're the lady with the plan."

Jeremy listened as the young woman behind the desk, who spoke English almost better than he did, as she used a map to give Whitney directions.

After the woman finished with her instructions, they thanked her and headed outside.

Whitney pulled her hair back in a ponytail and poked it through the back of her pink ball cap with an Atlanta Falcons logo on it as she placed it on her head. "Ready for our daily adventure?"

"Ready as you are." Jeremy slapped his ball cap on his head as they strode down the sidewalk. "Looks like we share a city but not a team."

"If I'd known you were going to bring your Braves cap, I would've brought mine. Next time we'll have to coordinate better." Whitney chuckled.

She headed toward the corner. "It's about a mile and a half walk to the Marienplatz. There's a glockenspiel that plays about fifteen minutes of music while figurines move all about. I'm told it's a definite must-see, but it only plays at eleven in the morning, noon, and five in the evening."

"Surely we can make one of those times." Jeremy fell into step with Whitney as they passed businesses of every sort along a wide pedestrian-only street. Most of the stores weren't open yet. Folks, who were probably headed to work, hurried along the wide walkway. Others, who appeared to be tourists like Whitney and him, walked at a less frantic pace.

Whitney glanced at her phone. "Yeah, it's a little past nine right now, and this walking tour takes about two and a half hours, so we might be back in time for the one at noon. If not, we can catch it at five o'clock."

"Whatever." For the first time, Jeremy wished he'd taken the time to learn more about the places they planned to visit rather than letting Whitney do all the planning. He'd rationalized that he'd been gone on the bike trip to Massachusetts and she'd had the time to plan.

"You sound unhappy."

"Oh, no." He definitely needed a better attitude. Maybe fighting his attraction to Whitney was coloring his whole perspective about everything.

"Okay. I hope you won't be disappointed in my plans."

"I'm sure I won't." Jeremy motioned to the stores lining the walkway. "Wow! Footlocker, Tommy Hilfiger, Disney Store. I never expected to see those here."

Whitney nodded. "It's a small world these days."

"If you say so." As far as Jeremy was concerned, it was a big, big world. One he'd never seen, and this was his chance to take in as much of it as possible.

"You don't sound convinced." Whitney raised her

eyebrows.

"I get what you mean, but this is all a new adventure for me." He was embarrassed to admit he felt like a kindergartener on his first field trip.

"Me, too. Really. And I'm excited to share this with you."

Jeremy wondered whether that was personal or just a general statement. He was failing miserably at keeping his personal emotions in check. For his job, for his family, for Whitney's sake, he had to rein in his thoughts, tie them up, and shove them deep inside his mind and heart, never to resurface. *Good luck with that.*

As they entered the Marienplatz, modern civilization gave way to century-old buildings. "Another wow! I don't know what I expected, but this is impressive."

Whitney nodded, her gaze directed upward as she turned in a circle. "Impressive doesn't say the half of it."

"So where do we start?"

"Right here." Whitney pulled her phone from her purse. "Sorry I don't have a newer phone so we could use wireless earbuds, but this will have to do."

"My phone doesn't have the wireless ones either. I'm sure what we've got will be fine."

Whitney shrugged. "We might feel a bit tethered. I hope you don't mind."

Jeremy stared in dismay as Whitney plugged a splitter into the jack on her phone, then plugged her earbuds into one side of the splitter and offered the other side to him. "You didn't exaggerate when you said we'd be tethered."

She gave him an apologetic smile. "Maybe I should've had you download the audio to your phone, but my friend from Atlanta said it was easier for both people to listen to the same audio. Otherwise, you get out of sync with each other."

"Let's get started." Jeremy pushed the earbuds into his ears and hoped for the best. He was out of sync all right. Whitney's presence put him on high alert for unwanted feelings. And this arrangement wouldn't do anything to help him not be completely aware of Whitney's every move. Surviving the day and keeping his emotions in check had turned into a monumental challenge.

"Since I have the audio on my phone, will you take photos with yours? Then you can share the photos with me." She raised her eyebrows as she gazed at him.

Nodding, he gave her a wry smile. "You're going to trust me to take photos for you? You might be sorry."

She gave him an indulgent smile. "I think you're just as good at point and shoot as I am."

"If you say so."

"I do." Whitney tapped her phone. "There's an introduction. Then the tour starts. Do you hear it okay?"

Jeremy nodded again as the male voice turned to a chipmunk sound. Whitney slowed the sound to its regular speed, and the guide described the new town hall that flanked one whole side of the square.

Whitney paused the recording and looked at him as she motioned toward the towers. "The glockenspiel I was telling you about. Do you see the figures in the middle of the square?"

Jeremy nodded as Whitney unpaused the audio. He took in the information about the story told through the glockenspiel figures. After learning about the statue built in 1590 to honor the Virgin Mary, they were instructed to look at the old town hall and remember that many of the buildings were heavily bombed during World War II, then restored. Next they headed to St. Peter's church, built in 1368. The antiquity made Jeremy wish he'd paid more attention in history class.

Then they came to the Viktualienmarkt, a marketplace filled with food, flowers, spices, and a beer garden. They took a moment to learn about the symbols on the colorful maypole, which represented the trades and craftsmen from the time when most of the population was still illiterate and used the pole for information. All this history made Jeremy realize he had a lot of things to learn. Travel was definitely expanding his horizons.

For the rest of the morning, they toured three more churches, the famous beer hall Hofbräuhaus, and a modern food market, where Whitney bought some chocolate. Jeremy tried not to examine why he noted her love for chocolate. They also visited the Residenz, the palace of the rulers of Bavaria, where they saw jeweled crowns and other treasures, and later walked down the street where Hitler had led his band of Nazis in the 1930s.

When the tour ended in the garden near the Residenz, Whitney unplugged her earbuds. "Did you enjoy that?"

Jeremy removed his earbuds as he nodded. "I learned a lot. Thanks for thinking of this."

Whitney shrugged. "Don't thank me. My friend told me about the audio tour, and it sounded like a good way to see the city."

"Thanks to your friend then." Jeremy wound the cords on his earbuds in a neat circle so he could shove them into his pocket. He felt cut loose from Whitney. He didn't have an excuse to be near her anymore. He should be happy about that, but he wasn't. This was only day one, and nothing he tried took his focus off her.

Hadn't he told himself to just go with it? The more he tried to suppress his thoughts and feelings for her, the more they came to the surface. So why fight it?

Jeremy could answer that in one word. *Jimmy*.

Whitney glanced at her phone. "I think it's too late to get back to see the glockenspiel at noon. We should grab a bite to eat and then head to the Nymphenburg Palace."

Once again Jeremy didn't have a clue about this place. "Is that different than the place we saw this morning?"

"Yes, it's the summer home of the Bavarian rulers who lived in the Residenz. When the Nymphenburg Palace was built, it was outside the city surrounded by countryside. Now it's part of the city just a few miles from here."

"Are we walking there?"

Shaking her head, Whitney tapped her phone. "We could, but I prefer to take the tram. I don't want to waste an hour walking when we can get there in fifteen or twenty minutes using the tram. I've got instructions right here."

"You're the guide." Jeremy fell into step beside Whitney as she headed down the street.

"We take tram seventeen from Karlsplatz to the palace. We can get tickets right where we catch the tram."

"How far?"

"About half a mile."

"I'm still not used to calculating kilometers into miles."

"I just estimate. Five kilometers is about three miles. Close enough."

Jeremy laughed. "Math was never my thing. In fact, I can't think of a subject that was my thing. I wasn't the best student. I managed to get through school on my charm."

Laughing in return, Whitney frowned at him. "You got your college degree, so you must not have been that bad in school."

"Why do you suppose it took me six years to get my degree?"

"I figured it was because you were working full time. That's an accomplishment in itself."

Jeremy couldn't help basking in Whitney's praise. She made it very hard to ignore the zing in his pulse when she looked at him, even with a frown. "Thanks, but—"

"No buts. I've seen how hard you've worked at this job. And I know from hearing others talk about your work ethic, that you're not the terrible student you pretend to be."

Jeremy knew the truth, but if she wanted to believe he was all that she said he was, he wouldn't argue with her. Her praise did nothing to help him conquer the feelings he'd been fighting all day.

As they made their way toward Karlsplatz, Whitney studied her phone. Jeremy trudged along beside her. He wished he knew what to say. Maybe he should try out some of his German?

"*Ich habe Hunger.*"

With a smile tugging at the corners of her mouth, Whitney looked up from her phone. "*Ich auch.*"

"You said 'me too,' right? And you understood me. Great!"

Whitney nodded. "*Sehr gut.*"

"Well, I don't know that my German is very good, as you say, but at least you knew what I said."

Whitney waved her phone in the air. "I've been looking for a good place to eat near where we catch the tram. I think I found a fast-food German place."

"Really. They have fast food that isn't American? I saw a few American fast-food places on our walk this morning."

"You probably won't find any burgers at the German place, but you might find sausages and meatballs." Whitney tapped her phone again. "We want to experience the local culture, not imported American food."

"That works for me."

They spied the restaurant Whitney had found in her search. They ordered and found a place to sit in the square near the fountain, with a number of other people enjoying the sunny day.

Jeremy glanced at Whitney, whose blond hair, sticking out from beneath her cap, gleamed in the sunlight. His pulse raced as he watched her pop the last bite of her bratwurst into her mouth.

"That was good. Did you enjoy yours?" She licked her lips.

Nodding, Jeremy tried not to stare. When he'd accepted this job, he never dreamed he'd be having romantic thoughts about Whitney. She wasn't the thorn in his side that Jimmy had imagined. She was something Jeremy had never pictured—a thorn in his heart.

Whitney hopped up from the spot where she sat. "Ready for the next leg of our adventure?"

Jeremy held out a hand. "Lead the way."

After they purchased their tickets, they waited with several other people for the tram. While they stood at the tram stop, Whitney started a conversation with a woman standing nearby. The woman smiled as Whitney conversed in German. Jeremy tried to follow along, but they were talking too fast for him to catch it all. He understood a few phrases here and there.

Once they were on the tram headed to the Nymphenburg Palace, Jeremy settled on the seat beside Whitney, who was still talking to the woman she had met at the tram stop. Finally, Whitney turned to him and introduced him to the lady, whose name was Angelika.

Jeremy breathed a sigh of relief after he managed to greet the woman and sound halfway coherent. He was happy when the two women excluded him from the conversation. He stared out the window at the passing buildings as the tram rumbled along the tracks.

The woman got off the train at the fourth stop, and Whitney turned her attention to Jeremy. "Angelika was impressed that we could speak German. You did well."

Jeremy grinned, his heart thumping. "Thanks."

"Angelika was telling me about the carriage museum. She says if we don't see anything else at Nymphenburg Palace, we must go to the museum."

"Whatever floats your boat." Jeremy leaned back and laced his fingers behind his head as he read the excitement in Whitney's expression. For just a moment she looked like a schoolgirl, thrilled about an upcoming school activity. He might as well admit that he enjoyed every minute of being with her, even though he wasn't crazy about museums.

She narrowed her gaze as she looked at him. "Are you making fun of me?"

"Oh, no. I'm just happy you're happy." Jeremy straightened in his seat. That was the honest truth. Wow! He had it bad.

"Well, I'm happy."

Jeremy wasn't so sure that was true. And she didn't

seem convinced he was happy. Maybe it was best just to keep his mouth shut until they reached their destination. He glanced at the time on his phone. They should arrive in less than ten minutes.

"Two more stops. Then we get off."

With a nod, Jeremy remained silent. Walking a tightrope would be easier than walking through the land mine of his feelings. Thankfulness filled his heart when they finally arrived at their stop.

"Looks like a palace straight ahead."

Whitney turned to him with an annoyed expression. "Really? I thought it was the local tavern."

Jeremy stopped in the middle of the pathway. "Are you upset with me?"

"No, but I thought maybe you are upset with me for dragging you out here."

"Like I said before, I'm happy if you're happy." Jeremy chuckled.

"That's just it. I can't be happy unless you're happy."

"I'm happy." Jeremy produced a big cheesy grin. "See."

"That isn't real."

"Sure it is." Jeremy held up his phone and stood beside her in an attempt to take a selfie. "Let me see how happy you are."

Whitney knit her eyebrows, barely visible beneath the brim of her ball cap. "What are you doing?"

"Taking pictures like you suggested." He punched the button on his phone. "Let's see that smile. We wouldn't want the folks back home to think you're not having a good time."

Whitney tried to frown, but a smile escaped, and

Jeremy's heart did a little dance. He was hopeless. *Embrace it. Don't fight it.*

For the rest of the afternoon, Jeremy tagged along with Whitney as she oohed and aahed about every room of the palace. When they went to the side building where the carriages were displayed, she just stood there as Jeremy snapped photos of her awestruck expression. Carriages and sleighs with ornate golden carvings filled every space.

"These are amazing, aren't they?" Whitney motioned to one of the sleighs.

Jeremy nodded, thinking that Whitney was amazing. He was seeing an entirely different side of her, a less serious Whitney. She had always seemed so businesslike, even when they'd been playing golf his first day on the job. Her mother's problems probably made for a life filled with stress and worry. Yet Whitney had time to mentor a wet-behind-the-ears coworker, as she had called him.

As they left the carriage museum, Whitney let out a heavy sigh. "That was amazing."

"I have to agree. When you first mentioned it, I wasn't all that excited to see it. But it surpassed all my expectations."

Whitney stopped and put her hands on her hips as she frowned. "So you're finally admitting that you weren't happy about this excursion."

Jeremy grinned. "I'm not admitting anything."

"Okay." Whitney shrugged. "I'll let it pass this time. Let's head back. We can check into our rooms when we get back."

"I'm ready for a shower." Jeremy tugged on his shirt.

"You're not tired?"

"You've kept me too busy to be tired."

"That's good, but don't be surprised if you wake up in the middle of the night and you aren't able to go back to sleep."

"So I'll get to experience jet lag for the first time?"

Whitney laughed. "I've never heard anyone who seemed excited about jet lag."

"Not excited, just accepting reality." Jeremy shrugged. "I usually don't have much trouble sleeping. Anywhere. Anytime."

"Good for you. What's your secret?"

"Just lucky, I guess."

"We'll see. I've never traveled overseas with anyone who didn't have some jet lag."

"You want me to knock on your door if I do?"

Shaking her head, she let out a halfhearted laugh. "No thanks."

Jeremy glanced at his phone. "Do you plan to stop and listen to the glockenspiel before we head to the hotel?"

"What do you think?"

"So you're rethinking checking into the hotel when we get back?"

Whitney nodded. "I don't think we'll have time to check in, shower, and then come back to catch the glockenspiel." Whitney raised her eyebrows as she stared at him.

"It's up to you."

"Are you sure? Because I think we should listen to the glockenspiel at five, then grab a bite to eat. Afterward we can head to the hotel and crash."

"I'll let you call the shots."

"Great." Whitney pointed toward the tram stop. "There's our tram. Run so we can catch it."

Jeremy resisted the temptation to grab Whitney's hand as they sprinted toward the stop. They managed to jump on the tram just before it left. Laughing, they plopped onto the nearby seats. As Jeremy sat there, his eyelids grew heavy. For the first time all day, the fact that it was nearing bedtime at home hit him. He blinked rapidly to keep from falling asleep. He glanced at Whitney. She didn't look tired at all. He had to say something or he might nod off.

"What did you like best about today?"

Whitney jerked her head. "Wow! I was about ready to fall asleep. I guess the swaying of the tram is like being rocked to sleep."

Jeremy laughed. "I was just asking the question to keep myself awake. I didn't think you looked tired."

"The busy day is catching up with me."

"I hope I don't fall asleep in my supper."

Whitney nodded. "That would be embarrassing. What do I need to do to keep you awake?"

Kiss me. The phrase came unbidden to his mind. Was sleep deprivation causing crazy thoughts to take over his mind? He'd been having foolish thoughts all day about her, but this one was worse than all the others.

He'd had hand-me-downs from Jimmy his whole life. Clothes, ball gloves, bikes, jobs. He didn't want a hand-me-down girlfriend. But here he was thinking about kissing Whitney.

"Nothing. I'm suddenly very wide awake." Man, was he!

"Good. Once we start walking again, we won't feel so sleepy."

Whitney was absolutely correct. After they got off the tram and headed for Marienplatz to listen to the glockenspiel, Jeremy was wide awake. He could never act on the folly running through his brain. He'd never be able to explain it to Jimmy or the rest of his family, and he certainly didn't want to act inappropriately toward a coworker. That should keep his mind on the straight and narrow when it came to Whitney.

"You're certainly quiet. Are you still tired?"

Whitney's question shook him from his troubling deliberations. "I'm good." *He wished.* "Ready to hear the glockenspiel."

"Me too." Whitney glanced at her phone. "We have ten minutes to get there. So we should make it."

When they arrived, hundreds of people filled the square, most of them with their faces turned upward as they anticipated the beginning of the show. Moments after Jeremy and Whitney found a spot to take in the spectacle, the music started and the figurines began to tell the story of the royal wedding of Duke Wilhelm V and Renata of Lorraine from 1568, including a jousting tournament and ritualistic dance.

As the music played, Jeremy took photos and a few minutes of video. After he finished, he glanced over at Whitney, who had her chin tilted skyward, her mouth slightly open as she stared in wonder at the figurines while they made their passes. He had the urge to put an arm around her shoulders and pull her close, but he took more photos instead to keep from acting on the idea.

When the show was over, Whitney looked at him. "That was cool!"

"It was. Now I think we should indulge in another selfie with the glockenspiel in the background."

"How about if we do that when the place isn't so

crowded?"

"And when would that be?" Jeremy gestured toward the crowd all around them.

"How about early tomorrow morning?" She smiled. "We'll probably be wide awake then."

"If you say so, but I'm not sure about that." Jeremy eyed her with skepticism.

"When you get up in the morning, come knock on my door. We'll see how early that is."

"Whenever I wake up, even two or three in the morning?"

Whitney shook her head. "After the sun is up."

"Oh. Okay. Glad you clarified. I sure would hate for you to lose any beauty sleep."

Whitney flashed him an annoyed frown. "I don't want you to miss yours either."

"But you need it worse than me because you're older."

Whitney crossed her arms over her midsection and glared at him. "Is that any way to treat your elders, reminding me that I'm older than you?"

"Touché. I won't do it again." Jeremy grinned. "I've learned my lesson."

"Let's hope so." Whitney chuckled.

Jeremy hoped he hadn't upset her with the age remark. She seemed to take it as the joke he'd intended. Their age difference didn't bother him, but he was sure she saw him as Jimmy's little brother. That was a good thing. It would help him remember not to do something foolish like kissing her. "What's next?"

"Food. I've found a restaurant near here that is supposed to have fabulous schnitzel." Whitney motioned down the street. "You have to taste that while you're in

Germany."

"Looking forward to it. Lead the way." Jeremy tried to squelch the idea of tasting Whitney's sweet lips. Why did everything she said make his mind go off on a tangent that would get him in all kinds of trouble? Maybe it was sleep deprivation that had him constantly thinking things he shouldn't.

For the rest of the evening, Jeremy did the best he could to keep his thoughts channeled in the right direction. The scrumptious schnitzel was everything Whitney had promised, and he thought he might have it every night while in Germany. Maybe that was overkill, but when would he have a chance to do it again?

As they walked back to the hotel, the pedestrian street, lined with retail stores of every description, lit up the night. And people of every description moseyed along the walkway, everyone from tourists like them to locals. Jeremy was especially fascinated by the Muslim women dressed from head to toe in black with only their eyes showing through the slit in their head garb.

This trip opened up a whole new world of experiences. He realized he'd led a sheltered life in a small southern town. He liked his roots, but he wanted to expand his horizons. This job would give him that opportunity, so he'd better not mess up. And not messing up meant keeping his interest in Whitney under wraps.

This definitely fit under the category of stepping out from under Jimmy's shadow. Jeremy would have experiences that his brother would probably never have.

After they got to the hotel, they checked in and retrieved their bags. While they rode the elevator to the floor where their rooms were located, Jeremy leaned against the side. He was certainly ready for a shower and bed.

"You've been awfully quiet since supper."

Jeremy glanced at Whitney, who had her gaze fixed on the lighted numbers that indicated which floor they were passing. "Just ready to hit the sack."

Whitney tapped the fitness tracker she wore on her left arm. "Did you know that we walked nearly ten miles today?"

Jeremy smiled wryly as he shook his head. "I knew you were trying to wear me out."

"Not so." Whitney laughed. "I hope I didn't bore you today dragging you around to all the places I wanted to see. You were a good sport about that."

"I wasn't bored in the least. The day was super." *I loved every minute of being with you.* The words sat on the tip of his tongue, but he couldn't say them. He shouldn't say them.

Thankfully, the elevator came to a stop and the door whooshed open. Pushing her bag ahead of her, Whitney laid a hand on her chest as she stepped into the hallway. "That's a relief. I was sure you'd had a terrible time today."

Jeremy shook his head as they made their way down the hall. "I don't know why you think I didn't enjoy the day."

"You seemed a little withdrawn tonight." She stopped in front of a door. "Here's my room. Yours is the next one down the hall."

Wouldn't she love to know why he'd been withdrawn? No she wouldn't. "Just tired. I'll be the life of the party tomorrow."

"Maybe you'd like to plan the day."

"Don't you already have plans?"

She shook her head. "Nothing set in stone, except that selfie early in the morning."

Jeremy smiled. "Okay. After the selfie, a short run or walk. Do you know of a good place to do that?"

Whitney nodded. "As a matter of fact I do. I know the perfect place."

"Great. I'll let you plan that part."

"Then what?"

"How about a trip to the site of the 1972 Olympics?"

"Great minds think alike. That's something I want to do, too."

"After we go there, I'd like to go over our meeting plans for the rest of the week." Did he dare let her know he was nervous about them? Or should he just blunder his way through?

"Sure, we can do that. I know you'll do a great job with your presentation. If Graham approved it, you know it's top notch. He doesn't approve second rate anything."

"That's good to know." Feeling better, Jeremy turned toward his room, then stopped and looked back at Whitney. "*Gute Nacht und träum was schönes!*"

Whitney laughed as she stopped in the doorway to her room. "*Sehr gut.* I hope your wish comes true and both of us have a good night and sweet dreams."

Jeremy nodded as he pushed his key card into the slot. The little green light blinked at him, and he pushed the door handle down. "See you bright and early in the morning for that selfie."

"Not too bright and early."

Jeremy watched Whitney slip into her room, knowing

his dreams would be filled with images of her. He had lost the battle on that front.

CHAPTER TEN

Whitney awakened with a start. She peered into the darkness, then remembered she was in Munich and had promised Jeremy a selfie at the glockenspiel.

What time was it? She glanced at the fitness tracker on her arm. Three thirty in the morning. She punched the pillow and rolled over, hoping she'd go back to sleep.

A half hour later she was still wide awake. She shouldn't be awake now, even if she'd warned Jeremy about waking up in the night and not being able to go back to sleep. She was still tired. So why was she wide awake?

Jeremy.

He was the reason.

Whitney punched at her pillow again, as if doing so would rid her mind of any thoughts about him. Was she doomed to fall for a Cunningham man? Surely not Jeremy. She was six years older than he was, besides the fact that he was her ex-boyfriend's brother. She'd already told herself not to have an interest in Jeremy, but her heart wasn't listening. Treacherous heart.

Never during all the times she'd traveled for business with a single male coworker had she had an interest in or even considered a relationship with him. Jeremy was making it hard to abide by her own rule in that regard. He was funny and charming, and she couldn't forget the way he'd stood up for her when he'd confronted his brother.

Jeremy melted her heart with his kindness, especially the way he looked out for her mother.

But any thought of romance with Jeremy was doomed from the start. He was off limits in so many ways. As she recounted all the reasons to keep Jeremy at arm's length, she dozed off.

A knock at the door made her sit straight up in bed. She looked at her fitness tracker. Five forty-five. It had to be Jeremy. She scurried to the door and looked out the peephole. A distorted image of the man who made her pulse quicken stared back at her. Her heart skipped a beat as she opened the door a crack. "Hi."

"Did I wake you?"

"You did, but it's time to get up. I'll be ready in a few minutes." Whitney's heart continued to thud as she peered at him. "If you don't mind waiting until I get dressed, we should be able to get breakfast when we go down."

"Works for me. Just knock on my door when you're ready."

"Okay. See you in a few."

Whitney hurried into the bathroom and stared at herself in the mirror. She had bags under her eyes. Surely washing her face would wake her up. Thankfully, her hair wasn't sticking out in several directions.

After washing her face in cold water, she looked in the mirror again. She felt a little more awake. Worrying about what she looked like accomplished nothing. She should go out without a care about what Jeremy thought of her appearance. That was her objective. *Don't fret about him or his view of me.*

Minutes later she stood in front of Jeremy's door and braced herself to follow through with the goal not to worry about Jeremy and to keep her feelings about him under wraps. She took a deep breath and knocked.

The door opened, and a grinning Jeremy looked her over from head to toe as he gave her a salute. "You're pretty quick. I was expecting to wait a lot longer."

"I can get ready quickly when I want to." Whitney smiled as she observed his T-shirt and shorts. "I see you're dressed for our run."

Jeremy stepped into the hallway. "Did you say run?"

"Yes. Run. I do recall you said something about a short run or walk after the selfie."

"I must've been half asleep when I said that." He looked downward. "These legs weren't made for running."

Whitney shrugged as she chuckled. "Then we can walk."

"Sounds more my speed."

"Okay, but dare I say you're an old man in a young man's body?"

Jeremy laughed out loud. "You can say whatever you'd like."

"Then I say you'd better grab a jacket. Even though it's going to be a warm day, it's cool this morning."

"Gotcha." He gave her another salute before going back into his room and returning with a light jacket. "Will this do?"

"Looks good to me." Whitney turned toward the elevator. "Let's grab breakfast."

After they reached the main floor, they headed toward the room where breakfast was served. The place was almost empty, with only one other couple sitting in the far corner. Whitney found a table and put her jacket on the back of one of the chairs. Jeremy did the same, and then they went to the buffet along one side of the room.

Jeremy picked up a plate, then turned back to Whitney. "No bacon, eggs, or toast?"

Whitney nodded. "Yeah, you won't find the typical American breakfasts here, but the breads are usually amazing. Try them with the cheese and salami. And you can have a hardboiled egg."

Jeremy knit his eyebrows. "Sure."

Whitney hid her amusement over Jeremy's lack of enthusiasm for the offerings on the breakfast buffet. She helped herself to a crusty roll, several slices of cheese, a cup of yogurt, and coffee. She settled at the table and waited to eat until Jeremy joined her.

She looked at his overflowing plate. "I guess you must be hungry."

"I have to figure out what I like and don't like."

Again she hid a smile. "That's good."

He gazed at her. "Would you like me to give thanks for the food?"

"Sure." Whitney watched as Jeremy bowed his head.

Whitney barely bowed hers as she listened to his prayer. She wasn't good about praying in public, but she had learned one thing about Jeremy in the time they had worked together. He had no trouble expressing his faith. She barely had faith and added this to her list of reasons why they didn't suit each other.

In no time Jeremy had eaten almost everything he'd taken from the buffet. He left the yogurt and one slice of meat. "I'm finished. What about you?"

"I'm done. Looks like you found a lot to like on that buffet."

Jeremy leaned back and patted his lean stomach. "I

have to admit that almost everything was delicious. You were right about the bread, but this yogurt is nasty stuff."

"Do you usually like yogurt?"

"Not really." He wrinkled his nose.

Whitney laughed. "Then why did you take it?"

"I thought German yogurt might be better."

"Well, now you know." Whitney stood. "Ready for that selfie?"

Jeremy picked up his jacket and pulled his phone from the pocket. "I am."

"Let's go."

Jeremy hurried to open the door for her as they left the hotel. "Do you care if I listen to music while we walk?"

"Go ahead." Whitney pulled her phone and earbuds from her pocket. "I can do the same."

"Thanks." Jeremy pushed his earbuds into his ears as he walked down the street. "I didn't want to be rude."

"You can't be rude this early in the morning. Sometimes it takes me a while to feel human in the mornings. I'm not a morning person." Even though she didn't care that he wanted to listen to music, she wondered if he really didn't want to talk to her. That should work in her favor. His lack of interest in her should certainly be a sign to squash her interest in him.

Jeremy gave her a sideways glance. "You could've fooled me. You always look very put together in the mornings."

"Thank you, but you do notice unless Graham calls an early morning meeting that I kind of hibernate in my office until midmorning."

Jeremy gave her a lopsided smile. "You're right. Now that I think about it."

"So what are you listening to?"

"Since it's Sunday, some contemporary Christian stuff."

She should've known that would be Jeremy's choice in music. Did she dare admit she didn't have even one Christian song in her playlist? He might as well know she was practically a heathen when it came to her music. "I can't say I've listened to much contemporary Christian music. My mom has lots of old hymns in her collection."

"I'll have to recommend some and bring you into the twenty-first century of Christian music."

"I guess you will." She smiled at him. He was so nice. He wasn't judgmental. That just made it harder not to like him more than she should.

"What are *you* listening to?"

"Something classical."

"Highbrow stuff."

Whitney let out a laugh. "If you say so."

"Yeah. Classical is highbrow to me." Jeremy raised his eyebrows as he gazed at her with those intense blue eyes. "I have an eclectic playlist. My mom likes country, my dad liked rock, and I took a page from both of them."

"That's probably a pretty good way to go. Listen to a little bit of everything." Whitney swallowed hard as her heart tripped. "Let's just listen and walk."

"Sure." Jeremy nodded.

A few people meandered along the quiet street, but the area was much different than the evening before when throngs of people had been shopping or listening to street performers. The peacefulness of the silent city did little to bring peace to Whitney's troubled thoughts about Jeremy. Sometimes she thought he was too good to be true. Too nice for the likes of her. She had to remember that every time he smiled and made her heart thunder.

She let the strains of Beethoven's *Fifth Symphony* fill her mind with the beauty of the music rather than her worries. In no time they reached Marienplatz and the glockenspiel. Like the streets, the square was almost empty. The sun peeked over the buildings and cast long shadows across the space.

Whitney pulled out her earbuds and looked at Jeremy. "Well, we're here. Time for the selfie."

Jeremy stopped and surveyed the area. "Where should we stand for this selfie?"

"Let's take several and see which ones we like."

Whitney took a deep breath and prepared for that sinking sensation that hit her stomach every time she was near Jeremy. "Okay."

"Over here." He pointed to the column in the center of the square. "Let's see how much we can get in the picture if we stand here."

Whitney joined him and stood as close as she dared as they looked into the camera on his phone. "What do you think?

"Smile, and we'll see." Jeremy snapped several photos. "Now let's look."

Whitney stepped away, her pulse racing. She hoped these would be enough. *Too close for comfort* was her only thought as Jeremy scrolled through the photos.

"Any you like?"

"I like them all. Let's see what they look like on a tablet or computer when we get back to the hotel. We can tell better when they're bigger."

Jeremy nodded as he stuffed the phone into his pocket.

"Good idea."

"Can we start out jogging?"

"You know jogging is bad for the knees, especially for someone as old as you." Jeremy wrinkled his brow as he stared at her, then grinned.

Whitney held her head high as she stared back. "Starting out with insults so early in the morning? After all, I did say you were an old man in a young man's body. So afraid of a little running."

His eyes opened wide. "You knew I was kidding, right?"

Whitney doubled over with laughter. "You're easy to tease. Of course I knew you were kidding. I hardly think thirty is old."

"Me neither. Actually, I don't think you're old at all."

"Jeremy, it's all right. I don't care if you think I'm old." *That was a lie.* She shouldn't be telling lies on Sunday, or any other day for that matter. She hated that he kept reminding her of the difference in their ages. But that was good. It was also a reminder that she had no business entertaining romantic thoughts about him.

"Bad for my knees or not, I'm headed out running. You can follow if you want." Whitney pushed in her earbuds and turned on her music, then raced out of the square without looking to see if Jeremy had followed.

In seconds Jeremy was running beside her, and her traitorous heart pounded in double time to her footfalls slapping against the ground. She tried to ignore him and listen to the music, but he matched her stride for stride until they reached the Isar River, where they took a bridge across the expanse of water. She slowed her pace to a jog and noticed that Jeremy didn't miss a beat.

They jogged along the river bank for a good ways, neither saying a word. A few other joggers traversed the same path. Eventually, Whitney slowed to a walk and waited for Jeremy to say something, but he just matched her speed without breaking stride. Maybe he was ignoring her, lost in his music. That should teach her not to care.

As she slowed down more, Whitney pulled her earbuds out. "How you doing over there?"

"I'm doing fine. How about you? I noticed that you keep getting slower and slower. Is the old lady getting tired?" He grinned.

"No. I thought maybe you were, and I didn't want to wear you out."

"I'm good. Got my music." Still grinning, he tapped his ears. "Couldn't be better."

"Glad to hear it."

He held up a finger. "Question."

"Go for it."

"This is a nice area, and since it's Sunday, I thought we could stop for a little Bible reading and prayer."

Leave it to Jeremy to think of that, but her plans for the morning fit right in with his thoughts. "If you wait a little bit, there's a place up ahead that'll be perfect for that."

"Sure. Lead the way."

About twenty minutes later, Whitney pointed off to the side. "Right over there is a little grove with a chapel in it. You can't go into the chapel, but it's a secluded area where we can sit for a while. Okay?"

Jeremy nodded. "I'll follow you."

Whitney walked down the walkway until the The Marienklause Chapel made of wood and stone came into view. She stopped and looked at him. "See it?"

"Yeah." He gazed at her. "You say we can't go inside?"

"Right, but we can sit on the steps, if you want."

"That sounds good to me."

Cool air greeted them under the shade of the trees surrounding the little chapel built into the hillside. They traversed the dirt path that led to the stairway.

Whitney stopped on the path. "Do you want to look inside, even though we can't go in?"

"We're here. We might as well." Jeremy took the stairs two at a time, then waited for her at the top.

"You're a speedy one."

"That's because I'm so much younger than you." His eyes twinkled as he clearly tried to stifle a smile.

"Hmmm. I think the teasing goes both ways."

He nodded. "How did you know about this place?"

"Research. I was looking up stuff to see here on our free days."

"Good thinking."

Whitney shrugged as she held her hands in front of her. "What did you expect from someone as organized as I am?"

Jeremy laughed. "And I'm afraid you're trying to organize me."

"Have I succeeded?"

"Keep trying." Shaking his head, Jeremy laughed some more. "Tell me what you've learned about this place."

"The roman numerals tell you when the chapel was built."

"You expect me to remember roman numerals from school?" Jeremy squinted at the building's facade with large roman numerals splayed across the front.

"You're younger than me. It's been fewer years since you've been in school."

"A lot of help that is. I told you before I wasn't the best of students."

"If I tell you sometime in the mid-eighteen hundreds, can you figure it out from there?"

Jeremy gazed at the building, then turned to her. "Eighteen sixty-six."

Smiling, Whitney nodded. "You're smarter than you let on."

"If you say so." Jeremy laughed. "Let's look inside."

"Sure." Whitney led the way. "Even though we can't go into the small space, there's a button we can press to turn on a light that illuminates the interior."

After they reached the opening, they peered inside. An altar at the front contained candles, flowers, pictures, and figurines perched on the crevices in the rocky backdrop of the altar.

With one hand, Whitney motioned around the area. "I don't remember the name of the guy who built it. He was a supervisor of one of the locks on the river, and he erected the chapel to give thanks for being saved from the floods."

"Thanks for bringing me here. It reminds me that we should remember to give thanks for the good things in our lives."

"And what are you thankful for?" Whitney didn't know why she'd asked him that question. Just standing there with him muddled her thoughts.

"Wow! So much." He stared at her. "I can't name just one thing. My life is blessed beyond all expectations. Family, friends, job, this trip."

Whitney nodded, hoping he wouldn't ask what she was

thankful for. She had a lot of good things in her life, but the bad things weighed her down. "Let's sit, and we can have that Bible reading and prayer."

"Sure." Jeremy held out his hand, indicating she should go first. "We can sit right here on the top step. We've got the place to ourselves."

Whitney settled on the step with her legs bent. She placed her elbows on her knees as she cupped her chin in her hands while she stared straight ahead at the pathway. She tried not to react as Jeremy sat beside her, but she couldn't control the pounding of her heart. She reminded herself that even though he said he was teasing, she was pretty sure he thought she was old.

As he took his phone from his pocket, he looked her way. "Do you have a favorite Scripture?"

Her stomach sank, and an uncomfortable feeling stole across her mind. A favorite Scripture? She searched her mind. Could she remember one of the verses on those old cross stitches? Her mind buzzed, but she couldn't focus. "Too many to choose from. You can just read some, can't you?"

"Yeah." He tapped the screen on his phone several times, then scrolled. "I'll just share my daily Bible reading."

"That sounds good." *Daily Bible reading*. When was the last time she'd done anything like that? Maybe Jeremy's presence on this trip would make her feel guiltier than ever.

"Follow along while I read." He held the phone out for her to see.

While he read, she let the deep timbre of his voice touch her heart while the words of the eighth chapter of

Romans came to life.

The message of the verses that talked about life in the Spirit, being heirs with Christ, the Christian's future glory, and God's everlasting love gave her a peace she hadn't expected. Although some of the verses brought to light her failings, most of the passage gave her hope—hope in God, who gave His Son as a sin offering. The lesson of the Scripture gave her something to live for and live up to with the help of God's Spirit.

Jeremy looked up from his phone. "There's an excellent message in those verses. What would you say is your favorite part?"

Whitney's stomach curdled as she looked down at her feet. What would he say if she told him how weak her faith was? He probably wouldn't be surprised, given the things she had done. But did she out and out confess it? "You're right. I think the best parts are those assurances, like in verse one." Whitney leaned over and scrolled back to the first verse. "'Therefore, there is now no condemnation for those who are in Christ Jesus.'"

Jeremy nodded and scrolled to another part of the chapter. "I've always liked these verses. 'No, in all these things we are more than conquerors through him who loved us. For I am convinced that neither death nor life, neither angels nor demons, neither the present nor the future, nor any powers, neither height nor depth, nor anything else in all creation, will be able to separate us from the love of God that is in Christ Jesus our Lord.'"

"Even when we mess up badly?" Whitney wrinkled her brow as she looked at Jeremy.

"Even then, as long as we ask for forgiveness."

Whitney summoned her courage to admit her doubts.

"I suppose it won't be much of a surprise to you that my faith is pretty weak. I've been an anemic Christian for years, just kind of going through the motions without much conviction. I was an Easter and Christmas Christian while I lived in Atlanta. And since I've been back in Pineydale, I've attended church because my mother expected it. How have you managed to maintain such a strong faith?"

Saying nothing, Jeremy stared at her. Whitney swallowed the lump in her throat. Why had she admitted her failings? Was she driving a wedge between them so her unexplained attraction would never amount to anything?

When Jeremy still didn't say anything, Whitney shook her head. "Sorry. I didn't mean to put you on the spot."

"You didn't do anything wrong. You've just made me think."

"I did? I just thought I embarrassed us both by—"

"You didn't embarrass anyone. You were honest, and I like that."

Relief flooded Whitney's heart. The traitorous heart that wanted Jeremy to like her. "Oh good. I've done a lot of things I regret."

"We all have, but you can't keep reliving them. You've asked for forgiveness, and you have to move forward knowing God has forgiven you."

Whitney gave Jeremy a sad little smile. "But I have a hard time feeling forgiven."

"That's a common problem for everyone."

"You, too?"

Jeremy nodded. "I wasn't sure how to answer your question about my faith. I've had some doubts from time to time, but in the big picture, I always see how God works things out. Like verse twenty-eight. 'And we know that in all things God works for the good of those who love him, who have been called according to his purpose.'"

"But I don't always see that." Whitney folded her arms across her knees and put her head down on her arms. Her heart ached for the loss of her dad and for her mom's problems. Whitney wished she hadn't opened up, but she'd thrown it all out there. Her foibles and her doubts.

"Are you okay?" Jeremy's voice came out in a whisper.

Straightening, Whitney nodded. "Sorry. I was just thinking about my parents."

"Yeah. That's tough."

Whitney turned to Jeremy. "Did you question God when your dad died?"

A thoughtful expression painted Jeremy's features. "I can't say that I did. It was a terribly sad time for our family, especially for Jimmy, who was on his way home from Afghanistan and never got to say goodbye when Dad died. Our faith sustained us and drew us closer to God rather than making us doubt. I know my mom would never have gotten through the experience without her faith and the help of the church members who gave us so much support."

"You're right about the support of the church. They were a real help to my mom and me when my dad died." Whitney sighed. "But I still don't understand why my mom has to suffer with the loss of her memory. How does all this fit into God's plan?"

"I can't answer that. We don't always see what God sees. There's a verse in second Corinthians that talks about that. Let's see if I can find it." Jeremy scrolled through his Bible app. "Yeah, right here in chapter five, verse seven, it says, 'For we live by faith, not by sight.'"

Whitney gazed at him. "Do you study the Bible all the time so you know all this?"

He shrugged. "I have a reading plan I start every year. This year I'm reading through the New Testament. Last year I read through the chronological Bible."

"You read through the whole Bible in a year?"

He nodded. "One of the guys who worked with me when I ran the painting company challenged me to do it."

"Guess I should get one of those reading plans."

"We could do a challenge with each other."

"But it's past the middle of the year."

"You don't think you can catch up?"

Whitney raised her eyebrows as she looked at him. "You're challenging me to read twice as much as you?"

"Don't think you can do it?"

"Do you really think it's a good idea to trash talk about reading the Bible?"

Jeremy laughed out loud. "That's not trash talk. Just a challenge. There's a program to read the New Testament in twenty-four weeks."

"Twenty-four weeks?"

Jeremy glanced at his phone. "Let's see. There are twenty weeks left in the year. If you doubled up a couple of weeks, you could be finished by the end of the year."

Whitney narrowed her gaze. "I hardly think that's fair."

"I didn't say anything about being fair." Jeremy shook his head. "I'm just issuing you a challenge to read the New Testament."

Jeremy had backed her into a corner. He knew exactly what he was doing. She was afraid to accept the challenge because she wasn't sure whether she was doing this for herself or to impress him. She should do it for herself. Maybe this would jump start her spiritual life. This was another step in setting her life in order, now that she'd apologized to Jimmy.

"Okay. I accept your challenge."

A smile broke out on Jeremy's face. "You won't be sorry."

Whitney hoped that was true. With each passing hour, Jeremy was pulling her under his influence. He was good for her in so many ways but so bad in a lot of others. She would have to pray for wisdom. "So I just start at the beginning and read through to the end?"

"Yeah." He held out his phone. "See this website? It has the plan. You click on it each day, and the chapters you are supposed to read will come up. Simple as that."

"Now I just have to do it every day."

"It might be hard to remember in the beginning, but pretty soon you've developed a habit. It's just part of your daily routine."

Whitney nodded. "Guess I'd better get started today if I'm going to catch up."

"You'll do it. I have confidence in you."

"Thanks." Whitney's heart did a little jog around her chest. When he said stuff like that, she wanted so badly to tell him she had feelings for him. But it shouldn't be done. It couldn't be done on this business trip or probably any other time for that matter. Their working relationship would be ruined, especially if he didn't share those feelings.

"Would you like to pray about our meetings this week?"

"Sure. Would you say the prayer?" Whitney didn't want to pray out loud.

"I'd be glad to." Jeremy bowed his head. "Lord God, thank You for the wonderful world You have created, and thank You that You've given us the opportunity to explore some places we haven't seen before. Thank You for Your word and its message that we shared today. We come before You asking that You bless our efforts this week as we speak to businesses here in Munich about working together. May our meetings be productive, and give us wisdom in our negotiations. We ask for safety as we travel, and bless our time here. In the name of Jesus I pray. Amen."

"Amen." Whitney smiled at him as their eyes met, and her pulse quickened. "Thanks for praying."

"You're welcome. What's next on your agenda?" Standing, Jeremy stretched his arms above his head and went down a couple of steps as he shook out his legs. "Feels good to stand."

Whitney joined him as he went down the stairs. "We'll head back to the city center, and if we see a place along the way, we can grab a bite to eat if you're hungry."

Jeremy grinned. "I'll be hungry after all this running, jogging, and walking."

Shaking her head, Whitney couldn't help smiling. "You didn't eat enough at breakfast?"

"I did, but all this exercise has made me hungry again." He widened his grin. "Are we going back the same way?"

"No. There's a bridge a little ways from here that takes us to the other side of the river. We'll go back on that side and see something new."

Jeremy gave her a quizzical glance. "No running this

time?"

Whitney laughed as they fell into step beside each other. "No running, just walking. Trying to save my knees, as you suggested."

Jeremy laughed. "Glad you're taking my advice."

As they neared the bridge, Jeremy squinted and pointed ahead. "What's that stuff all over the bridge guard railing?"

Whitney glanced at him. "You'll see when we get there."

"Why can't you tell me now?"

"I want to see your reaction." Whitney jogged ahead and wondered whether this was something Jeremy had never seen before. She had never seen it until she'd been to Europe.

"Hey, I thought you weren't going to run." Jeremy caught up to her as she stepped onto the bridge.

"Just getting here a little faster so you could see what's on the railing."

Jeremy stopped. "Padlocks? Why are they here?"

"Love locks." She peered at him. "I guess you've never heard of them."

"No. Why are they called love locks?"

"The padlocks usually symbolize the love of a couple. They put their names or initials and a date on the padlock. Lock it to a place like this, then toss the key away. Here they toss it into the river."

Jeremy went over to one of the padlocks and lifted it. "Renate and Franz. August 10, 2009." Jeremy looked at her. "This appears to be their anniversary. I wonder if Renate and Franz are still together."

"We should hope so." Whitney couldn't help thinking about her name and Jeremy's on one of those padlocks.

The crazy thought flowed through her mind like the water flowing under the bridge. This foolish thinking would put her under the bridge and down a stream of trouble for sure.

"I have to take a photo. People back home have never seen something like this."

"You want me to take a photo of you in front of the railing?" Whitney held out a hand for his phone.

"Let's do a selfie." Jeremy motioned for her to come closer.

Whitney smiled. Just what she didn't need, getting close to Jeremy again. "Okay."

She stood beside him as they smiled into the camera. As he took the photo, an older couple moseyed by and stopped. They smiled. Whitney smiled back.

The woman motioned to Whitney and spoke in English with a thick German accent. "Would you like me to take your photo?"

Whitney didn't want to be unkind, so she nodded. They probably thought she and Jeremy were a couple. Jeremy handed the woman his phone, and she held it up.

The woman lowered the phone and waved her hands together. "Closer."

Jeremy put an arm around Whitney's shoulders, and the woman grinned and nodded as she held up the phone again and took several photos. After she finished, she handed the phone back to Jeremy.

"*Danke.*"

"*Gern gescheh'n!*" The woman said as she waved and moved on with the man who hadn't said a word.

"That was nice of her." Jeremy glanced at Whitney. "I hope you didn't mind my putting an arm around your shoulders. I don't want to get into any trouble by overstepping my bounds with a coworker. Maybe I should've asked first. Can't be too careful these days."

"It's okay, Jeremy. I understood we were playing for the camera. The woman obviously thought we were a couple." Whitney's heart bumped against her rib cage as she took in his worried expression.

"You're sure about that?"

She nodded. "Yes. If I wasn't, I would have said so."

"Okay. I don't want to be out of line."

"You're worried about that?"

"Yeah, I've never spent three weeks with a woman who wasn't related to me."

"I won't bite."

"I know, but I don't want to do that wrong thing or say the wrong thing."

"Why are you so concerned?"

"When I was in college, I took this class, and one of the units had diversity and sensitivity training. That part of being on the job makes me more nervous than anything else."

"Let's make an agreement. If either of us feels the other one is out of line or not being honest, we should confront each other. Just like our discussion after you got back from Massachusetts. Being truthful about what's happening will be best." Even as Whitney said the words, she knew she wasn't being truthful about her growing feelings for Jeremy. But those were better left unsaid for so many reasons.

Jeremy held out his hand. "Yeah. So let's shake on that."

"Here's to a good working relationship." Whitney smiled as she slipped her hand into his. The contact made her heart skitter.

If only he knew what she'd been thinking while they'd stood there together. She'd been wishing it were all real. She was silly for even imagining that. What an emotional mess! He was worried about crossing a line with a coworker, and she wished she could really be honest. That wasn't going to happen. Time to move on in more ways than one.

"Let's find a place to eat lunch." Whitney forced a smile.

"Sure." Jeremy pocketed his phone. "Thanks for a great morning."

"*Gern gescheh'n*!" Whitney grinned at him. "Then after lunch we can visit the Olympic Park."

While they ate, Whitney berated herself for falling into a pit of her own making. Why was she falling for another Cunningham male? Maybe it was all an illusion or a bad dream. She'd wake up tomorrow and find she thought of Jeremy almost as a little brother, a coworker who needed her guidance and nothing more. If only that were true.

CHAPTER ELEVEN

T he conference room contained a long table surrounded by chairs and looked like any office back home, with windows looking out on the street below. But this wasn't just any meeting room. This was Jeremy's first big presentation. He tried to tell himself he wasn't nervous about this occasion, but that wouldn't be honest. This opportunity would show not only Graham and Whitney that Jeremy had what it took to do this job, it would show himself.

He summoned his confidence and found a seat next to Whitney. He placed his computer in front of him. Beate and Harald Huber, a couple probably in their mid-forties, were the ones who would be the final judge of his presentation. They would decide whether Jeremy had convinced them to form a partnership with Graham's company.

"Beate and Harald are getting the necessary equipment for your presentation, so I think you can go ahead and set up your computer."

Jeremy summoned his confident expression. The Hubers seemed like nice people, and they shouldn't make him nervous. "Good idea."

"I'll be here if there's anything that needs translating, but having spoken with Beate and Harald several times, you may not need me. They have a good grasp of English."

"Great." Oh, he was going to need Whitney. She didn't have any idea how much. She was his cheerleader, sounding board, and mentor. They had gone over everything in detail last night after their trip to the Olympic Park. He was better prepared for this than anything else he'd ever done. So he should be calm, cool, and collected.

Beate and Harald returned with the necessary equipment. Beate, who was tall and slender with curly blond hair that just reached her shoulders, assisted her husband, a stout man with light-brown hair. As they finished the setup, Jeremy said a silent prayer for a good outcome.

Within the first minute of his presentation, he had their complete attention. He gained more confidence as he spoke. Whitney's smile told him it was going well, and he sent up a silent prayer of thanks.

After showcasing what GCPineydale Enterprises could do for Beate and Harald's company, Jeremy smiled. "Do you have any questions?"

Harald stood and extended his hand to Jeremy. "Thanks for that information. I see a lot of potential for working with your company. We would like to talk over a proposal, but first I'd like for you to see our operation."

"That sounds wonderful." Whitney shook hands with both Harald and Beate. "When would you like to give us a tour?"

"We would like you to join us for the midday meal, and after we eat, we will show you our operation." Harald glanced from Whitney to Jeremy. "Do you agree?"

Jeremy nodded. "*Das ist wunderbar.*"

"Wonderful indeed." Whitney gave Jeremy a knowing smile.

"We have a favorite place we like to eat. We will call ahead and let them know we are coming," Harald said. "I hope you don't mind walking there. It's not far. You can wait here while I make that call."

"We're used to walking. We've done a lot since we've been in Munich," Jeremy said."

"*Großartig.*" Beate smiled.

Jeremy nodded, not quite sure of what Beate had said. The word she had used was unfamiliar to him. He hoped he hadn't made a mistake by nodding.

"Great, for sure," Whitney chimed in, as she glanced at Jeremy.

Jeremy surmised that Whitney wanted to make sure he knew what Beate had said. He had guessed at the correct translation, but Whitney's quick response gave him a sense of relief.

Before anyone could say anything else, Harald returned. "We have a table waiting for us. We can go now."

Harald and Beate led the way as they traversed the cobblestone streets. Beate and Whitney talked with each other in German. Whitney appeared to enjoy the chance to use her German language skills, which she hadn't needed in the meeting. Jeremy loved the way she connected with all the people she met. She was a different person here than she was back in Pineydale. It was almost as if she belonged here.

Jeremy glanced over at Harald. "I'm sorry I know so little German. I only learned a few phrases for the trip."

Harald nodded. "I understand. I like to practice my English anyway. So it is good to talk to you in English."

Jeremy chuckled. "That's nice to know. I've been

surprised by how many people we've met who know English."

"Many students take English in school here, and they most often start around the age of nine. More and more people are learning English. Many schools require students to take another language as well."

"Wow! I wish our education system taught languages earlier. I took a couple of years of Spanish when I was in high school, but I didn't know anyone who spoke Spanish, so I never used it. I remember very little of what I learned."

Harald poked a finger in the air. "Ah, yes. That is a problem for you in the US. Here we have many languages spoken in countries not far away, so we have an opportunity to use the languages we've learned."

"There are some places in the US where many people speak Spanish, but not close to where I live. The big cities in Tennessee have many more Spanish-speaking people than the small towns similar to where we live."

Harald stopped and motioned toward an eating establishment with a few tables out front under an awning. "We are here."

After they were seated at their table near the window, the waiter quickly handed them menus and took their drink orders. Jeremy looked over the offerings and noticed the schnitzel.

"You should try the goulash. It is excellent here." Beate laid her menu aside.

"That sounds delicious." Whitney nodded.

As the waiter brought their drinks, Harald seconded Beate's choice. Disappointment dogged Jeremy's thoughts at not having the chance to have schnitzel again. But he should consider this a chance to experience something new. Wasn't that one of the reasons he'd looked forward to this trip? He should take advantage of every opportunity presented to him.

"What about you, Jeremy?" Whitney raised her eyebrows.

"Sure. I'm game for something new." His heart did one of those little twists. She was getting to him again, even in this business setting. He'd made it through the morning only thinking of her in a work-related way, but without warning his attraction to her jumped out and grabbed him.

"*Gut*." Harald lifted his glass. "Let's toast to a productive day."

When the goulash arrived, Jeremy looked at the stew-like dish with big chunks of meat smothered in a thick reddish-brown sauce. It looked good. He hoped it tasted good, because he didn't want to offend Beate. Even if it didn't taste as good as it looked, he would have to force it down with a smile.

Jeremy didn't have to force himself to eat the dish. He had to keep himself from gobbling it down. *Good* hardly began to describe the tasty meal. When he was finished, he patted his stomach as he looked around the table. "*Sehr gut*."

"I agree. Very good. I should learn how to make goulash. My mother would so enjoy it. My parents lived in Germany before I was born."

"Where did they live?"

"In Berlin. They taught at one of the universities there."

"Do you know which one?" Harald asked.

Whitney shook her head. "I'm sure my mother told me at some time, but it wasn't something I put in my memory bank."

Jeremy noticed the sad expression in Whitney's eyes. Was she thinking her mother might not remember either? Whitney had seemed happy the previous two days, more carefree than she'd been back home, even when checking in with her mom made for a difficult conversation when Eileen became confused.

"There are many fine universities in Germany," Beate replied, then turned her attention to Jeremy. "I am so happy that you enjoyed the goulash. I will give Whitney a recipe, and she can make it for both you and her mother."

"*Danke.*" Jeremy grinned as he looked at Whitney. "I think that's an excellent idea."

"Maybe I'll have Carla make it for all of us." Whitney raised her eyebrows as she smiled at him, then turned to Beate. "Carla is the young woman who is caring for my mother, since her health has declined."

"So sorry to hear that," Beate said.

"It's hard to be away, but I'm thankful I have Carla to look after my mom." Whitney ate the last bite of her goulash, then set her napkin aside. "Thanks again for this treat."

"You're welcome." Harald glanced around the table. "If we're ready, I'll pay the bill and we can make our way over to our shop."

"*Danke.*" Whitney nodded. "I'm looking forward to it."

Jeremy echoed that sentiment. When the ladies stood, Jeremy followed suit. The morning had taught him that all his preparation had paid off, and he had Whitney to thank. She had coached him and given him the opportunity to prove himself, and she had taken a backseat, even though she could have made the presentation herself. He owed her a lot, and he didn't want to ruin their working relationship by acting on the romantic thoughts he had about her. How could he purge those thoughts from his mind?

***

The smell of freshly cut wood, paint, and varnish filled the air as Whitney followed Harald and Beate into the large warehouse-like building that housed their operation. The smells reminded Whitney of the day Jeremy had taken her to Jimmy's workshop. That day had made her appreciate Jeremy for the kind and thoughtful man he was. He helped her be a better person. That alone made her like him way too much for her own good, or his either.

Harald ushered them down an aisle where workers operated big machines that cut pieces of wood into numerous shapes. The noise from the machines echoed through the space. The sound made talking difficult, and Harald walked through the area without saying much of anything, just pointing out the different items being made. After they walked through the machine area, Harald led them into a room where dozens of people sorted and stacked the pieces of wood.

Harald stopped in one of the aisles between the tables where the wooden shapes awaited a custom paint job. "Many years ago my grandfather employed people who made these items by hand. I know many people want to have something handmade, but we've found it efficient to machine cut the pieces and then have them assembled and painted by hand. So we label our products hand painted rather than handmade."

"So your company has been handed down through the generations?" Jeremy asked.

"Yes, we take pride in our longevity. My great-grandfather started this company and passed it on to his son, my grandfather, who is in his nineties and comes to visit the factory once a week. He still enjoys painting one of the Christmas ornaments and signing his name on the back. They are special."

"I'm sure they are." Whitney placed a hand over her heart. "Do you have any that you can show us?"

"We offer tours to school groups and tourists who make arrangements ahead of time. When we finish here, it leads into one of our retail stores. I will show you some of the ornaments my grandfather has made. We have them in a special collection."

Whitney pointed to an area on the far side of the room. "What are they making over there?"

"They are making weather houses. They are little houses that predict weather, sometimes better than the weather forecasters." Beate chuckled as she motioned to Jeremy and Whitney. "Come, and I will show you."

"This is fascinating." Whitney fell into step beside Jeremy. Would he feel weird if she mentioned Jimmy's workshop? She leaned closer to him. "This reminds me a little of Jimmy's shop, but on a much bigger scale."

Jeremy nodded. "The products are smaller, but the operation is much bigger."

"You should mention your brother's work."

Jeremy shrugged. "You think so?"

"Why not? You might form a bond with Harald that would make a business partnership more appealing." Whitney hoped Jeremy wasn't thinking she was bossy. She should stop worrying about what he thought and think about the success of their business venture.

"You're probably right," Jeremy turned to the other man. "Harald, I find the story of your great-grandfather and grandfather very interesting because my grandfather's grandfather was the one who started the company Whitney and I work for."

Surprise colored Harald's expression. "Tell me more."

"He established a small variety store in our town, and it served the community for several generations. Eventually it was passed down to my dad and his brother. My dad had no interest in a dying variety store and let my uncle have it. My uncle saw an opportunity that my dad didn't. He took the company and built it into what it is today. He's done well for himself and helped a lot of other people along the way."

"You and Harald have similar stories." Beate smiled. "And I've been privileged to be part of Harald's legacy."

"After working for our uncle for several months, my brother chose a different path, but his work is similar to yours. He makes custom-made furniture and cabinets. Much like you, he has machines that cut the wood needed for his furniture and cabinets, but he finishes the rest of it by hand. He has quite a thriving business, too."

Harald nodded. "I am an only son. My two sisters chose to go into other occupations."

Jeremy nodded. "And my uncle has two sons. One chose to go into business on his own, while the other son works for the company."

As they toured the rest of the operation, Whitney wished she could tell Jeremy what a good job he'd done today. There had never been any down time in which to do so. She'd tried to convey her thoughts with a smile, but she couldn't tell whether he had gotten the message. He had connected well with the Hubers, especially Harald.

"Let me show you where we paint the ornaments and nativity scenes." Harald wrinkled his brow as he looked at Whitney and Jeremy. "Is that how you say it?"

"Nativity scenes?" Whitney asked. "Yes."

Harald nodded. "I wasn't sure of the English word."

"You got it right." Jeremy smiled. "Much better than I am with my German."

"Let's take a look." Harald led them into another room.

Workers meticulously painted the wooden ornaments with the perfect colors. Whitney took in the dozens of Christmas decorations shaped like bells, stars, elves, Christmas trees, Santas, reindeer, sleighs, among other holiday related items.

"Wow! They're gorgeous and every one unique." Whitney had to make sure she bought some of these to take back home. Her mother loved to decorate for Christmas. She would be delighted with these treasures.

"*Danke*. We pride ourselves in every production." Beate motioned toward a nearby door. "Would you like to go into the shop now?"

"That would be great." Jeremy indicated Whitney should go ahead of him as Harald opened the door.

"We'll let you explore, and we'll be back in a little while," Harald said.

As Harald and Beate went back into the workshop, Jeremy turned to Whitney. "Do you suppose they're going to talk things over about our proposal?"

"I think so." Whitney gazed around the shop. "I do think these items would be an excellent addition to our offerings."

"I agree." Jeremy raised his eyebrows. "When Harald and Beate return, we should talk to them about our offer."

Whitney nodded. "I'll let you do the talking."

"Are you sure?"

"Yes, totally. You had them in the palm of your hand this morning."

Jeremy gave her a smile that morphed into a serious look. "Thanks for your confidence. I can present the contract, but in the end, it will come down to the lawyers."

"I think you really connected with Harald with the story of Graham's company and how it was handed down from your great-great-grandfather. You did a wonderful job this morning."

Jeremy's smile returned. "Thanks. I'm happy to hear that. And if you think it's best for me to handle the negotiations, I'll do it."

"I do. Now I'm going to check out the things in this shop."

Glad that she'd been able to tell Jeremy how well he'd done this morning, Whitney explored the entire place, stopping to examine every different ornament and nativity set. She couldn't help wondering whether Graham would consider opening a Christmas store in Pineydale just for these items. The tourists who came to town to camp, fish, hike, and look at the fall colors would certainly find some treasures in a Christmas store. She would have to run her idea by Jeremy to see what he thought.

Jeremy came up beside her. "I'm impressed. What about you?"

"Absolutely. I hope we can come to an agreement to do business with them."

Jeremy nodded. "My thoughts exactly."

"I'd like to purchase a few things to take back home." Whitney picked up an angel ornament and held it by the string. "My mom would love this."

"I should buy some things for my mom, sisters, and Jimmy, too." Jeremy surveyed the items on the shelf. "It'll be hard to pick from all of these."

"I know my mom loves angels. So that makes mine easy."

After Whitney and Jeremy wandered around the shop and finally decided on several items, they went to pay for them. As they finished the checkout procedure, Harald and Beate returned.

"I see you've found some things you like," Harald said.

"We did." Whitney held up the bag containing her purchases.

"You have so many fabulous things that it was hard to decide which to buy." Jeremy picked up his bag from the counter.

"We hope you have room for a couple more items." Harald stepped forward and held out two ornaments. "We want you to have these. They are from my grandfather's collection."

"You are too kind." Whitney fingered the two delicately painted Christmas trees.

"One for each of you." Beate smiled.

"Thanks so much." Jeremy took one and added it to his bag. "Now I hope you have time to look over our offer and discuss it."

Harald and Beate glanced at each other, then Harald stepped closer. "We will be glad to review it now, but we can't discuss it or make any decisions until we look everything over thoroughly."

Jeremy shifted his shoulder bag for easy access to the zipper pocket. "I have a copy of the contract right here, and you're welcome to take whatever time you need to look it over. If you have questions, feel free to call. My phone number and Whitney's number are at the beginning of the contract. We leave Friday morning for Brussels, so we can find time to meet in person again, if you'd like."

Harald took the packet that Jeremy offered. "Thank you. We will go over this thoroughly and get back to you as soon as we've made our decision. We appreciate all the information you have provided for us today. We are eager to find a partner in the United States."

Jeremy closed the zipper and looked from Beate to Harald. "We enjoyed meeting you today and spending time learning about you and your business. We look forward to hearing from you."

Jeremy and Whitney shook hands with the Hubers, then left the shop.

Jeremy turned to Whitney as soon as they were outside. "Did I blow that? They put us off like they were letting us down easily."

Whitney shrugged, a feeling of unease settling in her gut. "I don't know. I usually have a sense of how things are going, but their sudden standoffishness really threw me. I thought you handled that well. I just don't know what to say."

Jeremy sighed. "I think you should handle tomorrow's meeting."

Whitney sensed Jeremy's deflation. "Believe me. Their reaction had nothing to do with what you said or did. Maybe they are just very cautious people. They want to let their lawyers look at it before they say anything."

"I wish I knew that for sure." A muscle worked in Jeremy's jaw, disappointment radiating from his eyes. "I still want you to handle things tomorrow."

"Okay, I can, but you shouldn't have expected them to make a decision today."

Jeremy shook his head. "I didn't, but I had expected to talk things over with them and see what they thought about what our company can do for them. You said they were very receptive to what I presented, but their reaction this afternoon feels less than enthusiastic."

"Well, we can hope for the best." Whitney forced a smile in hopes of putting a positive spin on the day. "We have meetings with two more groups here, so let's get ready for those."

Jeremy glanced at his phone. "Guess we should find someplace to eat on the way back to the hotel."

"We can do that. Then we can go over our plans for tomorrow."

"I'm up for schnitzel. What about you?"

"You really like that stuff, don't you?" Whitney laughed, feeling better already. Jeremy made her smile, but that was a problem in itself. An interest in Jeremy was dangerous, unprofessional, and foolish, but her heart was telling her not to listen to reason. Was she fighting a losing battle?

***

The following evening Jeremy sat across from Whitney as he stabbed a piece of his schnitzel and popped it into his mouth. So far the best part of this trip was the schnitzel.

Today's meeting had been another disappointment.

"What do you think we're doing wrong in our presentation?" Jeremy took a forkful of spätzle.

"I don't think we did anything wrong. Today's meeting just confirmed that this company isn't compatible with our business plan. It had nothing to do with the presentation."

Jeremy shook his head and wished he could look brilliant in Whitney's eyes. Did he dare admit to her that his confidence bordered on zero? She'd convinced him to do the presentation again, and he'd failed to close another deal. "Doesn't seem that way to me. I'm zip for two."

"You don't know that about the Hubers. Who knows how long it will take their lawyers to dissect the contract. At least they took the contract to look over."

Jeremy sighed. "I suppose you're right."

"I know I'm right. We can't expect to close every deal."

"I know that, but I'd at least like to hear some positive news." Jeremy took a big gulp of his drink and wished his thoughts were entirely on the business ventures and not on how much he wanted to impress Whitney.

The more time he spent with her the more he liked her, but that thought brought with it trouble—trouble he couldn't ignore.

"So what's our plan for tomorrow?"

"The same."

"You're going to trust me to do the presentation again after the results of the last two days?

"Absolutely. You know the material inside and out. You've got it down pat. Why would we change?"

"If that's what you think we should do."

"I do. I have confidence in you."

"Thanks."

Jeremy's heart did that little twist he'd been living with ever since he'd witnessed Whitney and Jimmy forgiving each other. A tender spot for her in his thoughts had sprouted and grown ever since she'd clutched that old cross stitch to her heart. He couldn't forget the look on her face, a look of peace and happiness, and he had helped make it happen. Why did that scene haunt him?

"You know all about tomorrow's company, more than you knew about the Hubers' operation, right?"

"Yeah, but that doesn't mean much. I knew a lot about today's company, too."

"What do I have to do to get you on a more positive train of thought?"

Jeremy let out a halfhearted laugh. "You're right. I need a better attitude."

"So what will it take to get you there?"

"I don't know." Jeremy shrugged.

He didn't want to think about that question. It might make him think about Whitney in a way that had nothing to do with business and everything to do with romance. Not good. He didn't know how to change that any more than he knew how to change the results of the meetings of the last two days.

"Let's just relax tonight. Get some ice cream, then wander down the pedestrian walkway and listen to the street performers. What do you think?"

"Sure. If that's what you want to do." Jeremy didn't think that would help him with either of his problems, but he didn't want to go back to the hotel and sit around by himself.

"Great. I know just the place."

"Then let's pay the bill and get out of here." Jeremy signaled to the waiter, who promptly came to the table. "*Kann ich bitte die Rechnung, haben?*"

Whitney smiled. "You are getting quite proficient with your German."

Jeremy gave her a lopsided grin. "It's not that hard to ask for the bill. A phrase here and a phrase there doesn't exactly make me proficient in German."

"Better than most."

Jeremy wanted to tell her she was good for him, but that wasn't entirely true. Her praise lifted him up when he felt down, but she also made for a big distraction that could derail everything good about this job. He had to find a balance for his warring thoughts. He just had to get through this trip. Then their forced togetherness would end. He could do it.

CHAPTER TWELVE

Two days later Whitney pushed her suitcase through the train station in Brussels as she followed Jeremy. She hoped the new city would give them better results in their efforts to gain international business partners. Jeremy had said very little on the train ride from Munich. He'd had his nose buried in the presentations they would make this week in Belgium.

His somber mood was evident in his demeanor and his manic compulsion to read his files over and over. She wanted to lighten his mood, but she wasn't sure how to do that. She feared the only way to change his disposition encompassed some good coming out of their meetings in Munich. She didn't have much hope for that.

As they emerged from the station into the bright sunshine, Whitney glanced back at Jeremy, who studied his phone. For a moment they stood where five streets converged. People scurried right and left, while cars buzzed through the busy intersection.

"Do you want to get a ride or walk to the hotel?" Whitney asked.

He looked up. "How far?"

"About a mile."

"Do you know how to get there?"

Whitney held up her phone. "Got the directions right here."

Jeremy grinned. "Since you're determined to make sure I get my exercise, we might as well walk, as long as you know where you're going."

"This way." Whitney pointed across the street.

After crossing, they walked along the sidewalk next to office buildings, shops, and impressive buildings behind iron gates with armed guards. Whitney had to keep her emotions under guard as well. She feared at any moment they would race out from behind the barriers she had erected and make her do something foolish, like throw her arms around Jeremy and kiss him.

She liked him. He'd been kind and understanding. Still, he was Jimmy's little brother, and she feared her old feelings for Jimmy were mixed up in there somewhere, not to mention her misguided engagement to Mitch. Her past romantic messes made her wary, very wary. She didn't want misplaced feelings to lead her down the wrong path again.

"How much farther?"

She glanced at her phone. "It says we should arrive in five minutes. So maybe three or four blocks. Are you getting tired already?"

Jeremy laughed. "No, but I just wanted to be sure you were paying attention to where we were going. You seemed lost in thought. Worried about the upcoming week?"

"No." Thankful he had no idea what she was thinking, Whitney motioned toward the corner. "We turn here."

"Have you thought about our plans for the week ahead?"

"I'm thinking about our plans for the weekend. What we're going to see."

"Maybe we should spend our weekend getting ready for meetings so we have better results than we had last week."

Whitney stopped and placed a hand on one hip. "Jeremy, more planning isn't going to change the results. How many times do I have to tell you that you made excellent presentations? More preparation wasn't going to make it better. It is what it is, and we have to accept that."

"But will Graham accept it?"

"Are you worried about your job?"

Jeremy didn't answer right away. He stared back at her, concern in his eyes. "I don't know. Maybe."

"Don't be. Do you think every venture Graham entered into was a success?"

"I've never thought about it."

Whitney grabbed hold of her suitcase again and pushed it forward. "I'll remind you again. Not every business deal goes through."

"I know that, but I wanted us to have at least one success."

"I understand, but at least we have a collection of Christmas-related items we can share with our relatives." Whitney gave him a sympathetic smile.

"For sure." Jeremy sighed.

"Just think. This coming week we can collect boxes of chocolates to share with them as well." Whitney hoped for Jeremy's peace of mind that they would find success in the days ahead.

Jeremy smiled wryly "Thanks for pressing me to look on the bright side. I'm usually not such a pessimist. So what do you have planned for the weekend?"

"We're going to Ghent and maybe Brugge."

"Aren't we going to Brugge on Monday for a meeting?"

Whitney nodded. "That's why I said maybe."

"Since we have a meeting there on Monday, I wasn't sure whether we should go there. What do you think?"

"Definitely go because we won't have time for touring while we're there on business. That will give us a little familiarity with the city when we speak with these prospective business partners."

"Good idea." Whitney nodded. "So we can take the train to Brugge in the morning and stop in Ghent on our return."

"Do you have tours planned like you did in Munich?"

Whitney touched the side of her head. "You know I've forgotten what I've downloaded. I'll check when we get to the hotel."

"Plans for dinner?"

"Do you like Indian food?"

Uncertainty showed in Jeremy's expression. "I've never had Indian food."

"Then I think you should try it."

"You mean there's no special Belgium food I should try?

"Chocolate."

Jeremy laughed. "What if I told you I don't actually like chocolate?"

Whitney was sure the incredulity on her face flashed like a beacon. "Seriously?"

"I eat it, but I'm not a big fan of sweets."

"So that's why I had to practically drag you to the ice cream place in Munich."

Jeremy shrugged. "I went, didn't I?"

"Yeah, but did you enjoy it?"

"I didn't say I hated sweets, just that I can go without them."

"I'll remember that when we're tasting all those chocolates this week." Whitney eyed him. "You'd better summon your sweet tooth rather than practicing your presentation."

Jeremy let out a snicker. "Maybe."

Whitney shook her head as they crossed the street. "I can't believe you don't like chocolate. Maybe Belgian chocolate will change your mind."

"We'll see."

"We turn here." Whitney wheeled her suitcase around the corner. "This is the street. The hotel should be in the middle of this block."

"It sure doesn't look like there's a hotel here. It looks like a row of office or apartment buildings."

Whitney slowed her pace as she gazed at the numbers on the buildings. "Many European hotels are quite different than those in the States. They often have a small number of rooms."

"The place we stayed in Munich was much like an American hotel."

Whitney nodded. "It was rather new and one of the well-known chains popular in Europe as well as in the US. This place caters to business travelers like us."

"So you're saying the place is old?"

"Old, but nice. You'll see." Whitney stopped in front of a set of five steps leading up to a wooden double door with glass insets that gave a view into the lobby and the check-in desk.

Jeremy reached for her suitcase as she lowered the

handle. "I'll carry that up the stairs for you."

She glanced at him with a smile. She was perfectly capable of carrying her bags up the steps, but she wasn't going to squash his desire to be a gentleman. "Thanks. I can carry my backpack."

"Okay." Jeremy hefted his backpack over his shoulder, then picked up their roller bags and carried them up the steps.

Whitney opened the door. "Our home for the next several days."

"I hope it's as nice as the last place."

"Graham wouldn't book us here unless it is."

"If the lobby is any indication, the place should be good." Jeremy set the bags in front of the desk as if he was resigned to whatever the hotel provided.

After they checked in, they wheeled their bags to the elevator. When the doors opened, Whitney stepped in beside Jeremy and hit the button for the sixth floor. "Nice that we have rooms on the same floor. I was a little worried that we might be on different floors because this place is so small."

"Easier to have meetings to solidify our plans." The elevator doors opened, and Jeremy indicated she should get out first.

"True." Whitney couldn't shake the feeling that Jeremy was still worried about the week to come.

Jeremy wheeled his suitcase into the small hallway and looked around. "Just five rooms on this floor, and two of them are ours."

"Here's mine." Whitney placed the key card in front of the sensor. When the light blinked, she opened the door and turned to Jeremy, who stood in front of his room directly across the hall. "After you get settled, come over and we'll make our plans for the evening."

Jeremy nodded, then entered his room without a word or a backward glance.

As Whitney unpacked, she didn't know what to make of Jeremy's silence. This whole day she'd been trying to bring him out of his funk without much luck. Would taking him to eat Indian food make him feel better or worse? Was he thinking she was bossing him around again?

She was torturing herself over nothing. But against her better judgment, she wanted him to like her, and not just in a working relationship. She couldn't shake the misguided emotions. She was probably spinning her wheels anyway. He treated her like his older sisters, teasing, cajoling, and, encouraging her to have a stronger faith. He saw her as his brother's old girlfriend, a woman six years his senior, a coworker, and nothing more. She needed to stamp those facts into her brain and hoped they seeped down to her heart, where all her crazy feelings resided.

As she hung up the last of her clothes, a knock sounded on her door. Jeremy. Her heart took a little leap. Not good. Not good at all. She took a deep breath and looked through the peephole just to make sure, and her heart did another funny little turn as she recognized Jeremy's distorted figure.

She took another calming breath and opened the door. "Hi. All settled?"

"Your room looks the same as mine. Bed, sitting area, desk." After glancing around, he turned to her. "Did you know we would have kitchenettes in our rooms?"

"No. Are you planning to fix me breakfast in the morning?"

Laughing, Jeremy pointed to himself. "Me cook?"

"I thought that's why you were asking." Whitney managed to keep a straight face.

"Not if you want to eat breakfast. I confess I'm not a cook." He wrinkled his brow. "I eat a lot of takeout and stuff from my mom. And I have a handy jar of peanut butter and bread in my cupboard."

"No jelly?" Whitney delighted in learning something new about him. She had a hopeless case of something when it came to Jeremy. She wasn't sure what it was, but it struck her almost every time she saw him and made her weak in the knees, or maybe weak in the brain.

He gave her a lopsided smile. "I told you I don't care for sweets, and jelly is sweet."

"Oh yeah. I forgot." She waved a finger at him. "You really do need to find your sweet tooth before Monday."

"And how do you suggest I find it?" His smile morphed into a grin.

Whitney's heart raced in double time. She turned toward the window to gain her equilibrium. "Maybe you can work on it tomorrow on our trip to Brugge."

"Sure thing." He joined her at the window.

Whitney took a shaky breath as her heart rate slowed to a steady thud. She looked out over the old buildings that characterized the city. "Beautiful view."

"It sure is." He gazed at her.

His gaze made her pulse quicken. Surely he wasn't talking about her. That was just wishful thinking. "Should we search out that Indian restaurant?"

"Sure." Jeremy waved toward the window. "I'm eager to see more of these old buildings up close. This has been fascinating and a trip of a lifetime for me."

And a trip of a lifetime for her in an unexpected way. She'd never dreamed she would develop an interest in Jeremy that went beyond their working relationship. She should have recognized the warning signs from the beginning, but she'd thought her reaction to him had to do with her regrets regarding Jimmy and Mitch and nothing to do with Jeremy himself. Now she finally realized the reality of her feelings.

Whitney picked up her jacket from the bed. "I'm taking my jacket. You might want one, too. Once the sun goes down, it'll be cooler."

"Okay. I'll get mine and meet you in the hallway." Jeremy hurried from the room.

Whitney closed her eyes and embraced the emotions she'd been fighting all day. She liked Jeremy way more than was good for either of them, but she didn't want to let those feelings go, even though she knew she should. What would he say if she told him? She shook her head. She couldn't do that. It would ruin this whole trip. Things might turn awkward.

Whitney shrugged into her jacket and picked up her purse. She would enjoy the Indian food, the company, and keep her feelings to herself. With that caution zinging through her mind, she stepped into the hallway, letting the door close behind her.

Jeremy stood there waiting for her. "How do you know about this Indian restaurant?"

"Graham." Whitney punched the elevator button.

"And how does he know about it?" Jeremy indicated she should go first into the elevator.

"He told me about it when we were making last-minute preparations for this trip while you were in Massachusetts.

He came here on vacation a few years ago and stayed in this hotel and ate at that restaurant."

"Then I guess we have a good recommendation." An undefined expression crossed Jeremy's face. "I hope this trip turns out like Graham hopes it will and we don't go home empty handed."

"We won't." Whitney promised herself she'd do whatever it took to move Jeremy into a more positive thought process. "We're going to find just the right people to partner with us."

"I need your attitude."

"I'll be glad to share." Whitney nodded as the elevator doors opened to the lobby. She hated to admit that she wanted to share more than her attitude with Jeremy.

"I can hope some of your positive thinking will rub off on me." Jeremy held the door open for her.

Whitney shrugged as she stepped outside. "It's all up to you."

Jeremy stopped at the bottom of the steps. "I just want you to know I couldn't have a better business partner than you. I'm glad you've put all that stuff with Jimmy behind you. I wanted to say again that all's good and I don't hold anything against you."

"Thanks. I appreciate your telling me that." Whitney wasn't sure where this was all coming from, but it was a good reminder that Jeremy was all about this job. She should have the same thoughts. "Now let's get to that restaurant. It's not far. We can walk."

"Why doesn't that surprise me? You're determined to make me healthier." Jeremy chuckled.

"Don't you exercise when you're at home?"

Jeremy shook his head. "I haven't worked out since I

quit playing sports in high school. I worked long hours painting and even longer hours when I ran the company after Jimmy went to work for Graham. The last thing I wanted to do when I got done for the day was exercise."

"Oh." Whitney took in this newest bit of information about this man, who made her heart and mind a jumble of opposing emotions.

"I suppose you're one of those people who gets up early and does a workout before going to the office." Jeremy opened the door.

Whitney zipped her jacket to ward off the cool early evening air. "At the country club."

"One of those happy, early morning people."

"If you say so." Whitney's heart sank. He didn't remember what she'd said about not being a morning person. That should show her how much attention he paid to what she said about her personal likes and dislikes. She exercised early in the morning even though she hated it, but she wasn't going to say so. Jeremy didn't care.

"I'm trying to figure you out." Jeremy gave her a sideways glance.

"What do you mean?"

"You seem to be a health nut in regard to exercise, but you indulge in sweets."

Whitney laughed despite the knot of disappointment in the pit of her stomach. She wanted to think he was trying to figure her out because he had an interest, but that wasn't true. "Sweets in moderation."

"I want to see that when you hit the chocolate shops."

Whitney stared at him. "One piece per shop."

"Yeah, you wouldn't want to overdo it." Jeremy grinned. "How many shops can you hit in an hour?"

Whitney shook her head. "You think you're funny, but I don't think you have anything to talk about. Schnitzel every night while we were in Munich?"

"You can get chocolate anywhere, but not schnitzel."

"Okay. I'll grant you that." Whitney glanced down at her phone. "We turn here, and the restaurant is in the next block."

"Great. My first taste of Indian food, but not in India, in Belgium." Jeremy smiled at her. "You're making my life interesting."

"Glad I can be of service." Whitney took a little bow.

As they went into the restaurant, Whitney wished she made Jeremy's life interesting not because of Indian food but because he loved being with her. How messed up were her thoughts?

Could she manage two more weeks of this charade? How long could she pretend that he didn't make her heart flutter or jumble her thoughts until she couldn't think straight? She enjoyed being with him, but at the same time, it was torture not to act on her feelings.

***

"I can hardly believe we're starting our second week of business meetings. I hope it goes better than the last." Jeremy said as he and Whitney stepped off the train in Brugge. "And thanks for another great weekend, but it ended too soon. There's so much to see."

"Time flies when you're having fun, and the trip will be over before we know it." Whitney pulled some papers from her satchel.

"It does." The weekend with Whitney had been more

than fun. It solidified Jeremy's feelings for her, but that only complicated his life. Sometimes he wished it were only the two of them without business or family to deal with. Those were the thoughts of a man in deep, deep trouble when it came to emotional well-being. He had to think of his job. "I hope the meetings this week go better than the ones last week.

"I promise this week will be better."

"How can you promise that? You have no idea how people will respond to our proposals."

Whitney turned and stared at him. "I'm choosing to think we'll have a better week. And besides, it involves chocolate."

Jeremy laughed even as Whitney's words chastised him. How could anything improve if he went around with a negative-Nellie attitude? He used to have an optimistic outlook. What had happened to him?

"Point taken, but didn't you have enough chocolate over the weekend?"

"There's never enough chocolate in my opinion."

"You did a good job as tour guide."

"Thank you, kind sir." Whitney waved a hand at the cobblestone streets and historic buildings. "And this looks very familiar. Thanks for suggesting we tour here before our meeting."

"All the thanks goes to you for finding the interesting places to go."

"What was your favorite?" Whitney forged ahead as they neared the central part of the town, where many of the chocolate shops were located and the one in particular they planned to visit today.

"I know what your favorite was. The chocolate shops."

Jeremy loped along beside her.

Whitney chuckled, then gave him a serious look. "I did like the peacefulness of the Begijnhof. It seems as though I was stepping back in time there. I could almost imagine those women from the seventeenth century walking through the grounds."

"Yeah, I know what you mean. I think the whole town feels like we're stepping back in time."

"And you still haven't told me your favorite part."

"I have to pick?" During their tours each day, Jeremy had been disappointed that they hadn't been forced into close proximity by an audio tour like they'd had in Munich. But it was probably for the best. Being too close to Whitney for an extended period of time could have been his undoing.

"You do."

"The canals."

"Wait till you see the canals in Amsterdam. You'll love those, too."

"And the architecture. The pointy buildings, the church tower, all of it. I liked this place even better than Munich."

"Better than Brussels?"

Jeremy shrugged. "Brussels is amazing, especially the Grand Place. Those guild halls were cool, but it's a big city, and I'm a small-town boy, and Brugge has a small-town feel."

"But you are enjoying your big-city adventures, right?"

"For sure. I told my family before I left that I was going to see the world on Uncle Graham's dime. Don't you dare tell him that." Jeremy grinned. "It could get me in trouble."

Shaking her head, Whitney smiled. "Your uncle is a

very generous man. I don't think he'd mind. After all, he did tell us to use the weekends to play tourist."

Jeremy gave Whitney a sideways look as they crossed one of the canals. The smooth water reflected the morning sun and the nearby brick buildings. The beauty of the peaceful scene made him think about the upcoming meeting and how they needed to make it a matter of prayer. He tapped Whitney on the shoulder. She turned, a question on her face.

"This place is so peaceful, I'd like to stop here and say a prayer for our meeting. Maybe things didn't go so well last week because we didn't pray before our meetings."

Whitney wrinkled her brow. "But we did pray. We prayed last Sunday, and we prayed yesterday when we had our prayer time and Bible reading here in the park."

Jeremy nodded. "But we didn't pray right before we went into the meeting, and I think we should do that today."

"Sure."

"You look unconvinced."

Whitney glanced around. "Where do you want to do this?"

"We can do it right here."

"Okay." Whitney's expression displayed her discomfort. "We're just going to stop here and pray?"

Jeremy nodded. "I hope that's all right."

"It is." Whitney smiled, but tension marked her mouth. "You can say the prayer."

Jeremy bowed his head as he placed his hands on the brick railing. "Lord, thanks for this beautiful day and the grandness of Your creation. We pray You will guide us today in our presentation. We pray those we meet will be receptive to our proposals. We give You the glory. In Jesus's name we pray. Amen."

Whitney touched his arm. "Thank you."

Jeremy swallowed hard as he looked at her, his heart racing. He had to think about business and not about her. "Do we want to go over any last-minute details?"

"We're good." Whitney patted her satchel, then tapped the side of her head. "Got it all right here, computer, brain. And besides, you just prayed, and this is all in God's hands now."

Jeremy's tangled emotions calmed as he looked at her. Her last statement put everything into perspective. Their meeting today and his feelings about her. They were all in God's hands. "I'm thinking good thoughts about today's meeting because of our prayer and your positive outlook."

"Great! We've got this."

Jeremy nodded, glad their meeting today was casual. No need for a suit and a tie, because right now he feared a tie would have him feeling strangled. Despite his prayer and his positive thoughts, he couldn't squash his anxiety. Even though Whitney had appeared to be uncomfortable with the idea of prayer in public, she was the one who showed confidence that God could do what they had asked. Ask, believing. That was what a Christian was supposed to do.

"We'd better get going. Our meeting will start soon."

Whitney smiled again as she glanced at her fitness tracker. "Yes, but we have plenty of time to get there, so let's enjoy our morning walk."

"You mean we don't have to run?"

Whitney laughed. "No. Today you get to indulge in chocolate and more chocolate. No exercise required."

"Didn't we do enough of that on Saturday? And then Belgian waffles yesterday. My sweet tooth has had a workout."

Whitney gazed at him. "You make me smile."

"Better than making you cry." Jeremy wished he could make her do more than smile. A mental *aargh* shot through his brain. What could he do to keep his thoughts on the business at hand? "What's the name of the women we're meeting with today?"

"Inne Bruneel and her daughter, Justine Verdonk."

"And they make the chocolates right there on the premises?"

"Yes, and I can hardly wait to taste them." Whitney licked her lips.

Jeremy tried not to notice, but he couldn't. "I'll let you do most of the tasting."

"If you say so." Whitney chuckled. "Inne and Justine speak very good English, but I'll be there for translation if we need it."

"Just like in Munich."

Whitney nodded. "But we'll be using Dutch instead of German."

"Not French."

"No, especially here. We can use French in Brussels, but it's Dutch in this area. Actually there are more Dutch speakers in Brussels as well, but French is widely used, too."

"Maybe I should've practiced my Dutch. I'm still thinking in German. The mix of languages here must get confusing." Jeremy wrinkled his brow.

"I don't know, but thankfully everyone we'll be working with on this trip speaks English." Whitney pointed ahead. "Here we go. The shop is in the middle of this block."

Jeremy said another silent prayer as he followed Whitney, and he tried to recall a few of the Dutch phrases he'd learned. When they reached the shop, he opened the door and let Whitney precede him. Delightful smells wafted through the air as a bell rang, signaling their entrance.

A woman, dressed in navy pants and a royal-blue smock, scurried to the counter. She smoothed her short, light-brown hair. "*Goedemorgen.*"

"*Goedemorgen,*" Whitney said. "I'm Whitney Hamilton, and this is my colleague, Jeremy Cunningham. We're looking for Inne Bruneel."

The woman's face broke into a smile. "I am Inne. You are the Americans. *Welkom.*"

"*Dank u wel.*" Jeremy hoped she understood his thanks.

Her smile broadened. "We are pleased you are here. We are eager to begin our discussions."

"How would you like to proceed?" Whitney asked.

"First you should sample some of our chocolates." Inne reached into the case and brought out a small tray filled with a variety of candies. "This is a good sample of our chocolates and other confections."

"I would love to sample." Whitney took the tray. "Where would you like us to do this?"

Inne raised a finger as she peered toward the back of the store. "I can take you to a place in the back, but let me introduce you to my daughter."

"Okay." Whitney nodded as she held the tray while Inne disappeared through a door behind the counter.

"You're eyeing those chocolates like you can hardly wait." Jeremy gave her a wry smile.

"That's no lie."

As a group of customers entered, and Inne returned with a young woman, who also wore a royal-blue smock. "Whitney and Jeremy, this is my daughter, Justine. She is working in the kitchen. She will take you there while I wait on these customers."

Justine motioned for them to follow her as her mother hurried to greet the newcomers. "*Welkom*. I hope you can understand my English."

"You speak very well." Whitney pointed to the tray. "I am eager to try these treats."

"We make very delicious chocolate." Justine smiled. "Come. Sit at the table and enjoy."

Jeremy glanced around the kitchen as Whitney set the tray on the table. Gleaming stainless steel was everywhere, from the bowls to the appliances. Molds and spatulas sat on the immaculately clean counter. "Are you working on something now?"

Justine shook her head. "We saved the morning to meet with you."

"Oh, I was hoping we could see you make some chocolates," Whitney said.

Justine glanced toward the front of the shop. "When my mother returns, we'll see what she has to say, but I'm pretty sure we could give you a demonstration."

Whitney clasped her hands. "That would be wonderful. Now I'm going to taste some of these."

Jeremy watched as Whitney looked over the samples and finally chose one. She held out the tray to him, but he shook his head. "I'll let you go first."

Stepping closer to the table, Justine looked at him. "You must also try."

Whitney laughed as she held a piece of chocolate. "Can you believe he doesn't really like chocolate?"

Unbelief registered on Justine's face as she gazed at Jeremy. "Tell me it isn't so."

Jeremy sighed as he grimaced. "I'm afraid it's true, but I'm sure your chocolates are wonderful."

Justine shook a finger at him. "Still, you must try some."

"I will, but I'll let Whitney have the first honors." Jeremy nodded in Whitney's direction.

She gave him an impish smiled as she lifted a dark chocolate morsel to her mouth. She took a small bite and closed her eyes as she breathed deeply. She opened her eyes. "Oh, that was so good. Oh my. The best I've tasted since we've been here."

Justine looked at him. "She thinks it is good. You should not resist."

"Okay." Jeremy picked up a piece and popped it into his mouth as he tried to forget the image of Whitney enjoying that chocolate. An explosion of flavors hit his tongue, and he savored the chocolate as it melted. He turned to Whitney. "You're right. That was beyond delicious."

Justine put her hands together in a prayerful pose. "It is so good to hear you like it."

"Not like. Love! But I'm not going to take mine all in one bite like Jeremy. I'm going to relish mine, not gulp it like a starving man." Whitney took another bite of the candy.

Jeremy laughed. "I'll try to control myself with this

next piece."

"So you're going to try another? I guess you've found your sweet tooth." Whitney lifted her chin as she gave him a questioning look.

Grinning, Jeremy shrugged. "Maybe."

Inne entered the room as Jeremy enjoyed another chocolate. Justine rushed over to her mother and said something in Dutch. He wondered what that was all about. He hoped it was good. He glanced at Whitney to see her reaction. She didn't seem bothered by what Justine had said, whatever it was.

Inne motioned to the front of the shop as she and Justine approached the table. "Sophia, one of my nieces, has come to wait on customers while we have our meeting."

"Wonderful." Whitney stood. "Where would you like to start?"

"Justine tells me you would like to see how we make our chocolates. Yes?"

Whitney nodded. "That would be wonderful if it's not too much trouble."

"We can't show you the whole process. It takes several days, but I can explain a few things and put some chocolate in molds."

"I don't want you to go to any trouble." Whitney's gaze flitted between Inne and Justine.

"I will just show you how we temper the chocolate before we put it into the molds." Inne led them over to a table with a white marble top. "This is where we get the chocolate ready for the molds."

"Thank you for showing us this." Whitney stepped closer.

"We are happy to do it. If you had days to spend with us, we could show you the whole process."

"What happens before this?"

Inne put her hands to her cheeks. "So much. Let me explain."

Jeremy took in the awe on Whitney's face. She was like a teenager learning she'd been given a brand-new sports car. Every day of this trip opened a new window into this complicated woman, who was stealing his heart little by little. Could he grab it back before it was too late?

"To make our chocolate, we start with the finest beans that we get directly from cocoa farmer cooperatives. That way we have a say in how the beans are treated and make sure the farmers get good prices for their beans, because many are from very poor regions of the world." Inne smiled as she nodded.

"That is wonderful to know. Thank you for sharing that." Whitney placed a hand over her heart. "What comes next?"

Inne smiled, her excitement matching Whitney's. "The beans are fermented, turned, and dried before they get to us. Then we receive the beans and roast them. Once the beans are roasted, we must crack them open and remove the thin, papery shell around them. The remains are called nibs."

"Wow! I had no idea there was so much involved in chocolate making," Jeremy said.

"There is much more." Inne's voice held a hint of awe. "We grind the nibs until they become a paste we call cocoa liquor. This is the unrefined form of chocolate, and it contains cocoa solids and cocoa butter. We use a hydraulic press to extract the cocoa butter. Then we can add extra cocoa butter to give the chocolate a smoother, glossier texture."

"Is that the end of the process?" Whitney asked.

"Oh, no. There is more." Inne made several animated hand motions.

"We put the cocoa mass into a conch. It is a machine that refines the chocolate into very small particles. During this refining process we add the sugar, milk powder, and other flavorings. This part can take hours or days to complete. This is a very important part and has a lot to do with the flavor of the finished chocolate. And this is where the skill of the chocolatier comes in." Inne pointed to a space behind them to a metal cylinder that contained two wheel-like structures. "That machine is the conch."

Jeremy gave Whitney a sideways glance as she went over to examine the machine more closely. Her interest in the chocolate-making process made him think she would be sorely disappointed if they didn't make a deal with Inne and her daughter. After all of this, he felt more pressure to make this meeting a success.

"Now we come to the part I'm going to show you." Inne's statement shook Jeremy from his thoughts. "Tempering the chocolate."

Whitney stepped closer as Inne set the implements on the marble top. "Why do you temper the chocolate?

"Great chocolate is shiny and snaps when you break off a piece, like this." Inne took a small bar of chocolate and held it up and broke it in half. "Did you hear the snap?"

"Yes, I've never thought about that before," Whitney said.

"Cocoa butter is composed of three or four glycerides

of fatty acids. Each of these solidifies at a different temperature. When you melt chocolate, the fatty-acid crystals separate. Tempering melted chocolate gets the fatty-acid crystals of cocoa butter back into one stable form." Inne glanced from Jeremy to Whitney. "I hope I am not getting too technical."

"Oh, no. I love learning about this." Whitney smiled.

"We temper the chocolate by raising, lowering, and raising the temperature of the chocolate to form exactly the right kind of crystals. The chocolate will be soft and crumbly and not melt evenly on the tongue if we don't temper it. Well-tempered chocolate is resistant to developing chocolate bloom, the whitish film, streaks, or spots of cocoa butter that form on the surface of chocolate." Looking at Whitney, Inne held up a palette knife and a metal scraper. "We do the tempering by hand, but large chocolate manufacturers have machines for that. Would you like to help with the process?"

"Do you trust me not to ruin it?"

"I will guide you." Inne nodded. "First I will demonstrate, and you will enjoy."

Whitney glanced at Jeremy as she gritted her teeth in a nervous grimace. "Okay."

Jeremy loved watching her. She brought another dimension to this whole process. He might give the presentation, but she connected with Inne and Justine in a personal way. He remembered how she'd told him to talk to the Hubers about his uncle's company and how that had made a connection with them. She was definitely a people person. He was sorry that whole business with Mitch and Jimmy had made her a pariah in her own hometown. It shouldn't be that way.

Inne looked over at her daughter. "Justine will monitor the temperature for us. We'll be working with some dark chocolate this morning. The melted temperature should be between forty-six and forty-eight degrees."

"That's Celsius, right?" Whitney peered at the thermometer Inne picked up from the counter.

"Yes. I think that is somewhere around one hundred fifteen degrees Fahrenheit." Inne wrinkled her brow. "I'm never quite sure of the conversions."

Whitney chuckled. "Me neither."

"You use lower temperatures for milk chocolate and white chocolate, but we won't deal with those since we are doing dark chocolate today." Inne motioned toward the bowl of melted chocolate that Justine had extracted from the conch machine. "What's the temperature?"

"Forty-six. Perfect." Justine handed the bowl to her mother.

"I'm going to pour a little over half of this onto the slab." Inne held the bowl over the marble slab and poured, then held up two tools, one in each hand. "I will demonstrate how to use the palette knife and metal scraper to temper the chocolate. Then you can try."

Jeremy watched with awe as Inne moved the melted chocolate back and forth across the marble, scraping the dark-brown liquid from the marble, then pushing it off the scraper with the palette knife. She repeated the motions several times.

Inne looked at Whitney and held up her utensils. "Your turn."

An uncertain look radiated from Whitney's eyes as she took the palette knife and scraper. "I hope I do this right."

"Just do what I was doing." Inne nodded.

Whitney mimicked Inne's motions. "Am I doing it right?"

"Excellent." Inne smiled. "You see how the chocolate is getting thicker?"

Whitney nodded. "Yes. Should I keep going?"

Inne picked up the bowl. "Let's put that chocolate on the slab back into the bowl."

The two women worked together to return the tempered chocolate to the bowl. Then Inne stirred the chocolate. "See how it is thicker and smoother?"

Jeremy joined Whitney as they gazed at the contents of the bowl.

"What happens next?" Jeremy asked.

"I'm going to do a little test." Inne took a small piece of paper from Justine and dipped it into the chocolate. The chocolate solidified on the paper. "See how it has a glossy sheen? And hear it snap when I bend the paper?"

Jeremy nodded. "So is that it?"

"Now we put it into the molds." Justine placed several plastic molds on the table.

Inne poured the chocolate into the molds and agitated them as she tapped them on the table. "We do that to get rid of air bubbles. After it solidifies, I will let you taste it."

"I can hardly wait." Whitney licked a dollop of chocolate off one of her fingers. "This tastes delicious just like that."

Jeremy narrowed his gaze, again trying not to let the image of Whitney licking the sweetness off her fingers make him think of kissing her sweet lips. "How do you make all the different shapes and get fillings into them?"

"We have other molds, but before we use them, we have to temper the chocolate again. These pieces just make the chocolate we'll use for our specialty candies."

"This is amazing. Thank you so much for showing us this process."

"You are welcome. Now should we get on with the real reason for your visit?" Inne indicated a small table at the back of the kitchen near a window.

Jeremy picked up his computer bag from the floor. "It'll take me a few minutes to set up my presentation."

"While you do that, I'll show Whitney some of the special molds we use for our candies." Inne led Whitney to another part of the kitchen.

As Jeremy set up his equipment, he said another prayer. Surely the camaraderie they had experienced today with Inne would lead to an agreement and a working relationship. Even though he had prayed, doubts slipped into his thoughts as easily as the liquid chocolate had slid into the molds. He wanted a good outcome for himself, but he wanted it for Whitney especially. After all the things she'd been through lately, she deserved some good things in her life. Could he make that happen?

CHAPTER THIRTEEN

An overcast sky greeted Whitney as she emerged from the train station in Amsterdam. Leaden clouds symbolized her mood. They had come away from Belgium with nothing concrete to show for their efforts. An optimistic attitude eluded her, even though she tried to show a bright side to Jeremy, who was definitely depressed about the failure of their efforts. She'd been so sure that Inne and her daughter wanted to do business, but even after a follow-up call, nothing. The other meetings in Brussels had been cordial, but just as in Munich, it was evident from the meetings that nothing would come from them.

Whitney surveyed the area. A large cruise ship was docked across the way. Cars, buses, and bicycles filled the streets. Sometimes it appeared that there were more bicycles than cars. She glanced over at Jeremy, who gazed around in amazement. She loved his excitement over each new adventure. How could she translate that into a good last week?

"Wow! Do you see that? A parking garage for bicycles." Jeremy waved a hand toward the structure.

Whitney nodded. "You'll see a lot of people riding bicycles. In fact, you have to watch out for the bicycles more than the cars when you cross the street."

"Are we walking to the hotel?"

"Of course. We have to get our exercise after sitting on a train for several hours."

Jeremy chuckled. "That was a stupid question."

"Never any stupid questions."

"Here's one." He raised his eyebrows as he looked at her. "Are we ever going to have any success on this trip?"

Whitney sighed. "I wish I could answer that. I still have hope."

"You are a cheerleader for sure."

"Yeah, I did that in high school." Whitney didn't know why she brought that up. It would only serve to remind Jeremy of the difference in their ages. She'd been long gone from the cheering squad by the time he'd arrived at Pineydale High School.

"Which way to our bed-and-breakfast?"

"Cross the street, then we turn left."

They walked several blocks and then made another left turn that took them down a cobblestone street. Their suitcases rumbled across the uneven surface.

"I'm not so sure it was a good idea to walk. Pulling our suitcases across this rough ground is jarring my teeth." Whitney stopped. "I hope I'm not losing a wheel."

Jeremy stopped beside her. "Is your suitcase okay?"

"Yeah, but I can't push it. I have to drag it."

"How much farther?" Jeremy asked.

"Not far." Whitney waved a hand to the right. "We turn at the end of the block. Maybe we'll get rid of these cobblestones."

After they turned, the roadway became smooth again as they crossed a bridge over one of the many canals in Amsterdam.

Jeremy glanced heavenward. "Do you feel raindrops?"

Whitney held out a hand. "Not really."

"My imagination." Jeremy stopped on the bridge and stood near the railing. "Boats parked in the canal and cars parked beside the canal. Cool!"

"It is an interesting city.

"Do you have plans for our weekend?"

"Of course." Whitney grinned, then grimaced as she gazed skyward. "You weren't imagining things. It's beginning to sprinkle. Hopefully, we can get to our destination before it begins raining hard. Looks like we're going to need that umbrella I brought."

"You brought an umbrella?"

"Sure. I told you to bring one, too, but you went all guy on me and insisted you didn't need one." Whitney quickened her steps as the rain came a little harder.

Matching her pace, Jeremy gave her a wry smile. "You don't need to say 'I told you so.'"

Whitney feigned innocence. "I would never say anything like that. Our B and B is in the middle of this block. I hope we don't get too wet before we get inside. We have to put a code into the pad at the door."

"Got the code ready?" Jeremy asked.

"Right here on my phone." Whitney pointed to the nearby door. "This is it. Six, seven, one, three."

As they huddled closer to the building, Jeremy punched in the code, then turned the knob. The door opened, and they scrambled into the entrance. Pushing her hair back, Whitney wiped the rain from her face, then looked up. Jeremy stood there staring at her, a look in his eyes she couldn't decipher. Her heart pounded. Her brain froze. They stood so close that for a moment she thought he would lean over and kiss her.

She shook the crazy thought away. She was most certainly the only one thinking about a kiss. Whatever Jeremy was thinking, that was so not going to happen. That was probably the last thing on his mind. He was probably just glad to get out of the rain.

Turning, she looked into the room at the right of the entrance. A dark wooden desk filled with papers and a computer monitor sat in the middle of the space. A tall, thin man with light-brown shaggy hair emerged through a door on the right side of the room.

Whitney stepped forward. "*Hallo. We hebben een reservering.* Whitney Hamilton and Jeremy Cunningham."

The man smiled as he held out his hand to Whitney. "Welcome. I speak English, so there is no need for you to speak Dutch unless you want to."

"I guess you can tell by my accent that Dutch is not my first language." Whitney smiled.

"*Ja.* I am Hendrik Melgers. I am happy to meet you." Hendrik shook hands with Jeremy, then went to his desk. "I will find your reservation and take you to your room."

Whitney heard the word *room* and hoped he meant *rooms*. She glanced at Jeremy to see if he had any reaction to what Hendrik had said, but Jeremy was looking at something on his phone.

"Here it is." Hendrik looked up from the monitor. "I'll get your keys."

Keys. He'd said keys. That was a relief. He pulled out a drawer and selected two keys from a board inserted into the drawer. "I hope you don't mind climbing the stairs."

"We don't." Whitney grabbed the handle of her suitcase.

"Follow me," Hendrik said.

Whitney trudged up the stairs behind Hendrik, while Jeremy brought up the rear. When they reached the landing, Hendrik pointed to his left. "This is the sitting room. There is a television and tour books for you to use. Around the corner is where we serve breakfast between six and nine."

Hendrik led them down a short hallway until they came to a white six-panel door. He opened it using one of the keys. As the door swung open, he stepped inside. A queen-sized bed with a white comforter took up most of the space in the room. A dresser sat along one wall near the large window that looked out on a courtyard with a huge tree in the middle. The view was beautiful and peaceful.

As Whitney opened her mouth to ask about their other room, Hendrik handed each of them a key and smiled. "Here we are. If you have any questions, let me know. Have a good evening."

Whitney's stomach did a somersault as she looked over at Jeremy, who stood there with a blank expression as his mouth hung open. "Hendrik, we were supposed to have a reservation for two rooms."

"Two rooms?" Hendrik's brow wrinkled.

Whitney nodded and extracted her phone from the front pouch of her shoulder bag. She quickly punched at the screen and scrolled. "I'll show you the reservation."

Hendrik took the phone Whitney offered to him and gazed at it for several seconds. "Yes, I see." Then he looked up. "I am sorry for the mistake, but I am afraid this is the only room I have available."

Whitney let out a harsh breath as she turned to Jeremy, who still stood there with the same expression. "What should we do?"

Jeremy rubbed the back of his neck. "Good question. Wish I had an answer."

Hendrik motioned in a circle with one hand. "I have…aah, what you call it? Push bed."

"Rollaway bed?" Whitney asked.

Hendrik nodded. "I can bring that into the room, if that will work?"

Whitney ran a hand through her hair, then rubbed her temples. How could that work with the thoughts she'd been having about Jeremy from day one of this trip? "Is there any possibility we could find rooms somewhere else?"

Hendrik shook his head as he shrugged. He bowed slightly and handed the phone back to Whitney. "August is our busiest time. I could try to call around for you, but I do not have much hope for finding something."

Whitney sighed as he gazed at Jeremy. "What do you think?"

"Let him call, and if he doesn't find something, we can manage with the rollaway bed. I'll sleep on that. At least we aren't sleeping on the street."

Whitney sighed again as she glanced down at her phone. "It's nearly time for dinner. We can leave our bags here, and hopefully when we return, we might have other accommodations."

"I will do my best." Hendrik grimaced. "You might like to try the nearby pub for your evening meal. Go to the end of the block and turn right. It is three doors down from the corner."

"*Bedankt*." Whitney unzipped her backpack and extracted an umbrella and held it up. "Just in case it's still raining."

"It has stopped, but it is good to take it with you."

Hendrik motioned toward the window. "I apologize again for the mistake. This does not usually happen."

"I'm sure." Whitney tried to smile, but all she could think about was sharing a room with Jeremy. "We'll see you after we eat."

The threesome went down the stairs, and Hendrik hurried into his office. Whitney and Jeremy opened the door and went out. As soon as the door closed behind them, she turned to Jeremy. "This is a disaster."

Jeremy gave her a wry smile. "Like I said, we should be glad the whole reservation wasn't lost. We have a roof over our heads and beds to sleep in."

Whitney didn't know what to make of Jeremy's optimistic attitude. He obviously had no idea that his traveling companion had been thinking of him in romantic terms for too many days, and this situation wouldn't make things better, only worse. What would Graham say? He was the one who had made the reservations here because he and Donna had stayed here on one of their trips.

"I'll hope for the best." But Whitney didn't know what was for the best.

"Good. Now let's get something to eat. I'm starved."

They walked to the end of the block in silence. Daylight lingered, but the cloud cover dimmed their surroundings and Whitney's attitude. The rain had left behind a dampness that chilled Whitney despite her jacket. Or maybe the thought of sharing a room with Jeremy was what sent a chill through her body. She had to get over it, because that was a distinct possibility for their future. They turned the corner, and a group of young people stood on steps underneath a lighted sign for the pub.

"That looks like the place," Jeremy said. "Since those

people are standing outside, do you suppose we'll have to wait for a table?"

Whitney held up her umbrella. "If we have to wait, at least I have this."

Jeremy looked overhead. "It's gray, but no rain at the moment. Let's go inside and see if we can get a table."

Jeremy hurried up the steps and opened the door for Whitney. She stepped inside. A crowd stood or sat at a long bar that occupied most of the place. A few tables sat along one wall, and others were scattered in the space at the back. Near the door a small table for two was empty.

Jeremy glanced at her. "Should we claim it?"

Whitney surveyed the area. "Sure. It looks like there's another empty table for four near the back. So this appears to be free. Let's take it."

Jeremy pulled out a chair for Whitney. She looked up at him with a smile as she sat down. He was such a gentleman and so easy to like. These kinds of thoughts wouldn't help. They should talk about the weekend ahead and their plans for this week's meetings. That should take her mind off the room problems. Maybe.

As soon as Jeremy settled in the chair across from her, he picked up the menu. "Good. They have the listing in both English and Dutch. Do you see anything you like?"

"I'm going for the cheese plate."

"That looks good to me, too."

Whitney narrowed her gaze. "I thought you said you were hungry. That doesn't seem like a lot of food to me."

"When I'm done, if I'm still hungry, I'll order something else or another one of those." Jeremy shrugged.

After a young man came to the table and took their order, Whitney sighed. "Okay. We can't ignore the problem with our lodging."

"You don't know there's a problem yet. He may find a place for us, or at least one of us."

Whitney shook her head. "He didn't sound optimistic, and for good reason. A lot of Europeans take August vacations, and everything is booked."

"So what's your plan?"

Whitney drummed her fingers on the table. "I wish I had one."

"Let's make one. Just to ease your mind. I sleep in a T-shirt and workout shorts. I can go to the sitting area while you get ready for bed. You can text me when you're in bed. Then I can use the bathroom. Same thing in the morning. I'll wait out there until you're ready. It's not the end of the world." He gave her a lopsided smile.

"Yeah. I guess we can make it work. It's just very inconvenient." *Very inconvenient.*

As Jeremy said, it wasn't the end of the world. It wasn't even the worst thing that had ever happened in her life, but it definitely didn't make this trip any easier. The prospect of a whole week sleeping in the same room with Jeremy made her uneasy. This wasn't about him but her own emotions about him. And she would definitely have to find something to wear to bed other than her usual attire, something that covered more skin.

The food came, and they ate in silence while the laughter and conversation of the other patrons swirled around them. She had to come to grips with her growing attraction to Jeremy. Nothing she did diminished her feelings for him.

When he'd told her that he was a small-town boy who preferred smaller towns, she'd almost told him he was a small-town boy with a big heart. She feared she wouldn't be able to keep her feelings to herself for much longer. Maybe when she got home and back into a regular routine, all these crazy feelings would disappear. She could only hope being back in Pineydale would put everything into perspective. Their hometown and all the people there would help her realize a relationship with Jeremy was improbable, unfeasible, and basically insane. If she told herself that enough times, she might believe it.

***

While Jeremy punched the code into the keypad, he prayed he and Whitney would make the best of whatever the future held on this trip. The rain hadn't returned, and they had walked back to the bed-and-breakfast with the moon trying to peek through the cloud cover. His thoughts were clouded with the realization that his feelings for Whitney only complicated this fiasco with the room. He might not get any sleep.

As soon as they opened the door, Hendrik appeared in the entrance to his office. "I don't have good news for you. I called and had friends call, but no one was able to come up with another room."

Whitney shrugged one shoulder. "I thought that would be the outcome."

"I have already put the extra bed in the room," Hendrik said.

"Thanks." Whitney's sad little smile said so much.

"We'll make do." Jeremy tried to think in a positive vein.

"Be sure to come to breakfast before nine in the

morning. That's when we quit serving."

"We'll be there early. We have big plans for tomorrow." Whitney started up the stairs, shoulders slumped.

Awkward didn't begin to describe their situation. Was there anything he could do to make it better? Not much. Maybe stay out of her way as much as possible. That meant spending most of his non-sleeping time in the sitting area.

When they reached the room, Whitney unlocked the door. "Do you want to go over our plans for the week?"

"Sure." With their lack of success in the preceding weeks, he felt as though these plans were an exercise in futility.

"Okay. I'll get our folders." Whitney rummaged in her backpack and brought out a folder for each company they would meet with. "You can sit at the desk with your laptop if you want."

A chair and the small desk occupied one corner, but with the rollaway bed sitting there, getting to the desk was a challenge. Jeremy managed to scoot through the small space between the beds. "What files do you want me to open?"

"Bring up the PowerPoint files."

Jeremy's fingers tapped on the laptop keyboard as he tried not to think about how close Whitney was as she sat on the edge of the nearby bed. "They're up."

"Let's look through them and see if we need to tweak them."

For the next couple of hours, they worked on refining their presentations. Finally Whitney flung herself back on the bed, her legs hanging over the side. She didn't say a thing. Jeremy wasn't sure what to do. Was she thinking they would never get it right, or was she just tired?

"Are you okay? Are you ready to call it a night?" Jeremy held his breath.

She sat up like a jack-in-the-box and looked at him, her blue eyes swimming with tears. "I don't know. This is just too weird."

Jeremy glanced around. "You mean sharing the room?"

Whitney blinked rapidly as she stared at him, but she didn't answer. She pressed her lips together, and he wondered what had her so upset. So upset that she couldn't manage to talk about it.

"Talk to me." He hated to see her this way. Jeremy resisted the urge to sit beside her and put an arm around her shoulders to comfort her. Her reaction reminded him of the day he had confronted her about trying to come between Jimmy and Kelsey. Jeremy didn't want to make her feel bad, but what was he supposed to do? He couldn't manufacture a room out of nothing.

Her lips quivering, she stood and walked over to the window. For the longest time she stood there with her arms folded across her torso. Jeremy joined her, not saying a thing. He would give her time. He hoped she wasn't afraid of him.

Please talk to me, Whitney. Let me know what you're thinking.

The sky had cleared, and moonlight filtered through the tree branches and cast long shadows across the courtyard. The idyllic scene made him think about taking Whitney in his arms and dancing in the moonlight. Not good. Not good at all. He needed to send his mind in another direction, but she turned to him, her lips parted as if she wanted to say something but was afraid to speak.

Very kissable lips. The phrase flitted through Jeremy's mind. Most of the evening he'd been trying to think about something besides kissing Whitney, but he wanted to do just that because he cared about her. He shut down that thought. That was the last thing he should be thinking in this situation.

Maybe he was kidding himself, and Jimmy was right. Whitney was trouble, not because of anything that had to do with what Jimmy had said but because Jeremy couldn't forget she was an attractive woman. But it was more than that. So much more. He feared he was falling in love with her. And here they were sharing a room. Wouldn't the folks back home find this more than interesting?

Finally she shook her head. "I'm sorry. I'm working to get a handle on my spent emotions. This trip has been so disappointing. I've been trying to keep a positive attitude, but today just brought all the bad stuff to the fore. I don't mean to bring you down with me."

"You aren't bringing me down. Let's just consider this a camping trip, and we're in our own tents on the same campground."

Whitney let out a sad little laugh as she gazed at him. "Thanks for trying to cheer me up. I don't mean to be a downer."

"You're not being a downer." Jeremy used all of his willpower not to pull Whitney into his arms, hold her close, and kiss away her sorrow. Those actions would probably earn him a good slap. "You want to talk about our plans for the weekend? That might cheer us up."

Whitney's sad face morphed into a smile. "Sure."

"What do you have planned?"

She picked up her phone and waved it. "I have audio for Amsterdam."

"Good." Jeremy smiled, knowing that meant having an excuse to be close to her. "So what's on the agenda?"

Whitney sat on the bed again. "There are three tours. The city tour, the Jordaam tour, and the red-light district tour."

"You're going to take me to the red-light district?" Jeremy resumed his seat on the chair at the desk.

"I'm not pawning you off to any ladies of the night, if that's what you're afraid of."

Whitney laughed, and the sound made Jeremy's heart skitter. Hearing her laugh was so much better than seeing the tears in her eyes.

Jeremy shrugged. "Doesn't sound like a place I really want to go. Have you been there?"

Whitney nodded. "When I was here before, I went. It's full of tourists, and I didn't go down the street where the ladies are on display. I've heard they don't even let tourists go down that street anymore. The rest of the place has pot shops, but since pot is legal in lots of places in the US now, it's not much of a novelty anymore. We don't have to do that tour. We can decide later."

"Are you planning to do a tour each day, or are you going to do them both on one day?"

"I think we can do them on the same day. One in the morning and the other in the afternoon. I hope you don't mind that I bought tickets to the van Gogh museum. We have a scheduled time tomorrow morning."

Museums seemed to be her thing, and Jeremy had learned they weren't all bad. He wanted her to enjoy their time here, and if going to a museum made her happy, he would be happy to go, too. Yeah, he was in deep trouble. Instead of trying to figure out how not to fall in love with Whitney, maybe he should be figuring out how to tell her and his family.

Wasn't that getting way ahead of things? Whitney probably didn't share his feelings. How was he supposed to figure that out? Just out and out tell her, but not until this trip was over. When they were back in Pineydale and things were back to normal, then he'd tell her how he felt and let whatever happened happen. He couldn't go around suppressing his emotions forever without feeling as though he would explode.

"You don't look as if you're really excited about the museum." Whitney tilted her head as she gazed at him.

Jeremy wrinkled his nose. "I have to admit I'm not a museum kind of guy, but I'll give it a try."

"Yeah, you might like it."

He would definitely like being with her, and that was all he needed. "True."

Whitney's expression brightened. "And we'll take a boat ride on the canals and a bus ride to a little town near here where there is a bunch of working windmills."

"And we have to have more cheese."

Whitney laughed again. "Remember, one of our business meetings involves cheese."

"Oh yeah. Like the chocolate." Jeremy shook his head. "I still can't believe we didn't make a deal with Inne. Her chocolate is amazing. And that's a lot said from a guy who doesn't care for chocolate."

"I know." Whitney's shoulders sagged. "I thought we'd made a great connection with Inne. I'm beginning to think I've lost my touch with people."

Jeremy wished he could tell her she hadn't, especially with him, but this wasn't the right time. "We did the best we could."

Whitney sighed as she motioned toward the clock on the little nightstand. "If you don't mind, I'm going to get ready for bed."

"Sure." Jeremy stood, then climbed through the narrow space. He grabbed his phone from where it lay on the rollaway bed. "I'll be waiting in the sitting area for your text."

"Okay." She smiled, but the nervous look in her eyes said so much more.

Thankfully, the sitting area was empty. He didn't feel like having a conversation with anyone. In fact, he hadn't seen any other guests at all. He plopped onto the faux-leather couch and picked up a tour book from the table. As he thumbed through it, he read about some of the things Whitney had planned for their weekend. They would have to take a photo on one of the bridges that crossed the many canals in Amsterdam. He doubted they could get a good photo with a selfie. Maybe he could persuade a passerby to take a photo of him and Whitney together, like they'd done in Munich.

Whitney and him together. The thought skipped through his mind like all the other thoughts about her, threatening to stay even as he tried to push them away. Why did he keep torturing himself with this? He feared the unknown or maybe the known reaction of his family and friends if he started a relationship with her. Then there was the reality of this whole thing. She probably didn't have any interest in him. This was all in his own mind.

What a mess he had created in his mind and heart.

Jeremy sat there for the longest time paging mindlessly through the tour books. He made note of the photos of the lighted bridges throughout Amsterdam. That was something they would have to see. Of course, Whitney had already visited here and experienced the city. She had way more experiences in life than he had. Did she look at him as a kid rather than a man? After all, she had told him he was still "wet behind the ears."

Jeremy's phone buzzed as it sat on the coffee table in front of the couch. This had to be Whitney. She'd called instead of sending a text. He was happy to hear her voice. "Hey, are you ready for bed?"

"Yeah. The bathroom's all yours."

"Okay. I'll be there in a minute. *Zoete dromen.*"

Whitney's laugh sounded over the phone. "So you know how to say sweet dreams in Dutch, too."

"I looked it up."

"You do the same. Good night."

Jeremy ended the phone call feeling as though he wouldn't have any dreams, sweet or otherwise. He feared he wouldn't get any sleep at all. Instead, he'd lie awake thinking about Whitney and her proximity to him.

In the room, darkness filled the space except a dim light coming from the bathroom. He closed the door behind him. Whitney lay in the bed with her back to him. Obviously she didn't want to talk. She'd said her good-night on the phone.

After changing and brushing his teeth, he flipped off the light and used his phone flashlight to find his way to his bed. He plugged his phone into the charger before turning off the flashlight. Quiet surrounded him as he pulled back the covers and climbed in. He lay there for a moment and drank in the quiet.

Jeremy lifted a prayer into the night. His prayers included his thankfulness for this job and the opportunity to see the beauty of God's world, even in its fallen condition. He prayed for a successful week, and he prayed for the people back home, that God would bless their lives. Finally he prayed for Whitney and that he would be whatever God wanted him to be in her life. Whether that meant only a friend who had helped her find peace with Jimmy or something more. Jeremy whispered amen into the moonlit room. He was ready for whatever the morning would bring.

CHAPTER FOURTEEN

The plane touched down on the runway as Whitney pressed her forehead to the window. After a layover in London, she was finally home, or at least back in the United States. Despite the less-than-successful trip, a feeling of contentment filled her heart. She had survived all the ups and downs of this adventure.

Eager to get off the plane, she gathered as many of her belongings from the cubbies near her seat as she could without unbuckling her seat belt. She didn't want a flight attendant to reprimand her for unbuckling too soon. She took her phone off of airplane mode and stuck it into her purse.

Her heart tripped as Jeremy looked around his seat. "You ready to get off this plane and back to Pineydale?"

Before she could answer, her phone dinged like crazy. She retrieved it from her purse and stared at the number of missed messages and phone calls. What was going on? She poked at the screen and brought up the first message, from Carla.

Whitney, I don't know when you'll get this message, but your mom has been taken to the hospital over in Johnson City. I'll send another text as soon as I know more.

Whitney's stomach sank, and her heart raced. She couldn't think clearly. She couldn't speak.

"What's wrong?" Jeremy asked.

Whitney handed him the phone.

"Did you read the other messages?" Jeremy held out the phone to her.

Still stunned, Whitney shook her head. "You read them and tell me what they say."

"Okay?" Jeremy looked back at the phone. "You've got a couple of voicemails as well. Do you want to listen to them, or should I?"

Whitney closed her eyes, fearing the worst. She didn't want to hear the bad news. Her emotions were on overload, and she was afraid to speak for fear her voice would come out in a blubbery sound he couldn't understand anyway. She just waved her hand at him.

"I'm guessing that means you want me to listen to them."

Whitney nodded.

Jeremy punched the screen. "The messages have been transcribed. Are you sure you don't want to read them."

Whitney shook her head again. Why did something more have to happen to her mother after almost everything had gone wrong on their business trip? Was this God's punishment for her past bad behavior?

The plane reached the gate, and the passengers around them retrieved their bags from the overhead compartments. People all around them were eager to disembark. Jeremy sat sideways in his seat and scrolled through the messages.

Finally, he glanced up. "They believe your mother has had a stroke. She's in the hospital, and she is stable and resting. Let's get off so we can get you to the hospital."

Like an automaton, Whitney gathered her things. Thankfully, they had Global Entry and would be expedited through customs and didn't have to wait for bags. Everything passed in a blur as Jeremy guided her through the airport and outside to catch the shuttle to the long-term parking. Numb with fear, Whitney didn't know what to say as she sat next to Jeremy on the shuttle bus. He was a rock in her stormy sea of worry.

"Are you okay?" Jeremy knit his brow as he gazed at her.

Whitney shrugged. Nothing seemed real. Maybe this was all a dream, and she would wake up and find out they'd closed a half dozen deals while they were gone and that her mother hadn't had a stroke. Blinking back the tears, she looked into Jeremy's kind blue eyes. Why was she thinking about him when she should be thinking about her mother? The answer was all too plain. She'd let herself fall in love with him, but she couldn't deal with that now. She had her mother to think about.

"Whitney, please talk to me."

The kindness in his voice melted Whitney's heart. No one had cared about her feelings in such a long time. Maybe that was all it was, not love, just the joy of having someone care about her and not think bad things about her. Being in Pineydale had hurt until Jeremy came into her life, but she couldn't tell him that.

The bus pulled into the long-term parking lot, and people scrambled to file off. This offered Whitney a reprieve from having to talk to Jeremy. But the nearly three-hour ride to Johnson City would be another matter.

Jeremy unlocked his SUV and put the suitcases in the back. "Do you need anything from your bags?"

Whitney shook her head. She had her purse and phone. Glad Jeremy was driving, she slid into the passenger seat and closed the door. Jeremy drove out to the highway leading out of town without saying a thing.

Finally when they left Charlotte behind, he turned to her. "Do you mind if I turn on the radio?"

"That's fine."

A crooked smile curved his mouth. "She speaks."

"Yeah. I don't feel like talking."

"I understand." He reached toward the radio, then stopped. "Before I turn on the radio, let's pray for your mom."

Whitney nodded. "Thanks. I'd appreciate that, but how will you pray while you're driving?"

Jeremy gave her a sideways glance. "I can talk to you while I drive, so I can talk to God while I drive. Prayer is just talking to God."

"Okay. I just didn't want you to close your eyes while you were driving."

Jeremy let out a little laugh. "No worries. I do this a lot. You can bow your head and close *your* eyes if you want to."

"I'll follow your lead."

"Okay." Jeremy looked straight ahead. "Dear Lord, we want to thank You for giving us a safe flight today. Lord, we ask that You be with Eileen and heal her body. I pray for Whitney, that You would give her strength and comfort as her mother recovers. Please help them to know that they can lean on You. Please give us continued safety as we head to Johnson City. We ask these things in the name of Jesus. Amen."

"Thank you." Whitney contemplated Jeremy's prayer with a sense that he was good for her spiritual life. He had a real relationship with God, and he had helped her see she needed that, too. Every Sunday of their trip, he'd taken time to find a spot where they could take in nature and spend some time in Bible reading and prayer.

They had spent their last Sunday morning in Zaanse Schans and toured the working windmills there. They had found a bench in a peaceful little garden where they were mostly undisturbed while they shared that time together. Jeremy's unabashed faith and willingness to pray or read the Bible anywhere made Whitney see someone who didn't just talk about faith but lived it.

As Jeremy turned on the radio, Whitney leaned her head back against the headrest and closed her eyes. She prayed. *Lord, You know I haven't been very faithful to You over the years. Please forgive me. Please help my mom, and help me to help her. Give me wisdom and strength to deal with this situation. And, Lord, help me know how I should deal with my feelings for Jeremy. I don't want to mess up our friendship or make things difficult for him. Amen.*

Whitney sat straight up and looked around, then at Jeremy, as he pulled the car to a stop in the hospital parking lot. "We're here. Did I fall asleep?"

Jeremy smiled. "You did. After all, it's bedtime in Amsterdam."

"I'm sorry. I should've kept you company, although I fear I'm not very good company."

"Don't worry about that." Jeremy opened the door. "Let's go see your mom."

As they entered the hospital, Whitney pulled out her phone. "Carla told me what floor my mom's on."

"Where are the elevators?"

Whitney pointed ahead. "Over there."

The smell of medicine and disinfectant filled the air as they stepped off the elevators onto the floor where her mother was. Whitney hurried to find the room but hesitated before she entered. She looked across the room to the bed where her mother lay hooked up to machines. Her eyes closed, she looked pale and small, not the strong, intelligent woman Whitney had known all her life. Sadness gripped her heart.

Whitney moved slowly into the room. "Mom?"

Eileen's eyes fluttered open. "Whitney."

Whitney rushed to her mother's side. "I got here as soon as I could. How are you doing?"

Eileen didn't say anything for a few seconds. She appeared to be grasping for words. "A mini-stroke."

"Is that better than a regular stroke?"

Eileen nodded and looked toward the door. "Who's that?"

Whitney turned. She'd forgotten all about Jeremy. He'd understand. She returned her attention to her mother. "That's Jeremy."

Eileen nodded and blinked several times. "Where have you been?"

"Mom, did you forget that I've been traveling in Europe for my job?"

A blank stare colored Eileen's expression. Finally she nodded. "Oh yes, I forgot. You came home today."

"Yes, I talked to you on the phone while we had our layover in London."

Eileen shook her head. "It's all so confusing. I didn't want to come to the hospital, but Carla insisted."

"And Carla was right." Whitney would have to thank Carla. "Where is she?"

Eileen shook her head. "I don't know."

"Hello, Mrs. Hamilton." Jeremy stepped closer to the bed. "I saw Carla talking on the phone out in the hallway."

Eileen wrinkled her brow. "I'm sorry I didn't recognize you. I've been a bit confused."

"I understand." Jeremy briefly placed his hand over Eileen's where it rested on top of the covers.

Eileen smiled. "You are such a nice young man."

Whitney could agree with her mother on that. Whitney wished she could slip into Jeremy's arms and find comfort there, but that wasn't going to happen. It didn't need to happen. Her mind was so messed up. She had to concentrate on her mother and not on these foolish emotions revolving around Jeremy.

Other than the confusion, her mother didn't seem to have suffered any other effects from the stroke. Whitney wished she could talk to a doctor. Did she have to have the medical power of attorney to do that? "Mom, can you tell me what the doctors have done?"

"A bunch of tests. I'm not sure what kind." Eileen closed her eyes as she lay back on the pillow.

"When did you last see the doctor?"

"I'm not sure." Eileen shook her head. "I'm tired."

"Okay, Mom. We'll go and leave you alone for a little while." Whitney leaned over and kissed her mother's cheek.

"Good evening, Mrs. Hamilton. I hope you're feeling better soon." Jeremy gave a little nod as he backed away.

Her insides a twisted knot, Whitney stepped out of the room and looked up and down the hall, then turned to Jeremy. "Where did you see Carla?"

Jeremy pointed to his right. "I noticed her over there

right before I came into the room."

"I need to find her and thank her for insisting my mom come to the hospital, and I'd really like to talk to a nurse or doctor to see what the prognosis is." Whitney sighed. "But I'm not sure they'll tell me anything with all these health privacy laws in place today."

"Won't your mom give permission for you to talk to the doctor?"

Whitney shrugged. "I would think so, but she's confused. I have a medical power of attorney, but it's at home."

"Would you like me to go get it for you?" Jeremy raised his eyebrows as he gazed at her.

Whitney swallowed a lump in her throat, then shook her head. "I'm pretty sure I'll get to talk to the doctor without it. Let's see if we can find Carla."

Whitney moseyed down the hall until she came to another hallway that turned off to the right. She looked around the corner and discovered Carla sitting on a chair while she still talked on the phone. Whitney approached and gave a little wave. Carla waved back but continued to talk. Whitney sat in a chair nearby and waited for Carla to finish her conversation.

As soon as Carla ended her phone call, she stood. "I see you got my message."

"I did." Whitney rushed over to the other woman and gave her a hug. "Thanks so much for taking care of my mom. You're a lifesaver."

Carla smiled wryly. "I had to use all my powers of persuasion to get her to go to the hospital."

"Thankfully, you prevailed. Can you tell me anything?" Whitney pressed her lips together as she tried to push away her feelings of uncertainty.

Carla shrugged. "Just what I learned from your mom. They ran a bunch of tests, but of course, the doctors didn't talk to me, just to your mom. I asked her about them. Some things she understood, but others confused her."

"Yeah, that's pretty much what she told me. She mentioned being confused a couple of times while we were talking to her."

"Anyway, we do know she had a mini-stroke. It doesn't seem to have affected her all that much. Just the same confusion she's always had. But back at the house, she was acting even more unstable than usual and complained of a terrible headache. Then I noticed one side of her face drooping. That happened to my grandmother when she had her stroke. That's what clued me in."

"I can't begin to tell you how grateful I am to you."

"I'm glad I was there to help." Carla glanced down at the phone in her hand, then looked up with worry in her expression. "I have bad news of my own."

"Oh no, what is it?" Whitney asked.

Carla held up her phone. "I was talking with Mary about my plans."

Whitney frowned. "Plans?"

"Yeah. I got a call earlier today from my grandfather. My grandmother had another stroke. They need me back at home because my parents got a fabulous deal on a trip to Australia. They left three days ago and won't be back for a month. I need to stay with my grandparents."

"Then you should go. My mom will be here for a few days probably. I'll have to look for some kind of assisted living facility for her."

Carla sighed. "I hate that this has happened and that I

have to leave, especially now."

Whitney shook her head. "Don't worry about it. You take care of your grandmother. She's blessed to have you."

"Thank you." Carla blinked rapidly. "I really loved taking care of your mom. This has been a wonderful job, and I will miss y'all."

"We'll miss you, too. When do you plan to leave?"

"That's why I was talking with Mary just now. She has booked me a flight for tomorrow. So just like that I'll be gone."

Whitney hugged Carla. "So soon. Be sure to let us know how your grandmother is doing."

"I'll check in with you to see how Eileen is, and we can share." Carla glanced between Whitney and Jeremy. "I need to go back to your house and pack."

"Do whatever you need to do." Whitney nodded. "Do you have a ride to the airport?"

Carla nodded. "Jimmy's going to take me."

"Good." The mention of Jimmy's name made Whitney remember that her feelings for Jeremy had to be sorted out at some point. Too many things to think about.

"Will I see you before I go?" Carla asked.

"I don't know. Let's say our goodbyes here, and if I see you tomorrow, we can say goodbye then, too." Whitney hugged Carla again.

Carla waved as she headed to the elevators. Whitney stood there feeling lost. What was she going to do now? She'd said she'd find an assisted living facility for her mom, but where to start was a major issue. Whitney didn't know what she'd do with the house. She had a premonition that her mother would never be able to return to her home.

"What are your plans?" Jeremy asked.

Whitney let out a harsh breath. "I wish I knew. I need to know my mom's prognosis before I can do anything, but I doubt I'll be able to leave her alone."

"I'm sorry for all your trouble." Jeremy looked at her, that ever-present kindness in his eyes. "Maybe my mom can—"

"No, I already asked your mom to do what Carla's been doing."

"I wasn't going to say that. I thought my mom might be able to help you find a place for your mom. She knows a lot of stuff like that."

Whitney shook her head. "I'm sorry I didn't let you finish. My mind is whirling, and I've got jet lag. And you've been so wonderful to bring me here."

"It's nearly suppertime. Do you want to grab a bite to eat, or do you just want to stay here with your mom?" Jeremy raised his eyebrows.

Whitney glanced in the direction of her mother's room. "Let me check on her, and then I'll decide."

She and Jeremy traipsed back to the room. Having him by her side gave her a sense of peace and at the same time a sense of agitation. She glanced his way. "Thanks for your support."

"You're welcome." Jeremy stood in the doorway.

Whitney went to her mother's bed. She was sleeping, the machines beeping. The scene tore at Whitney's heart. First her dad, now her mom. Whitney closed her eyes and prayed. *Lord, please heal my mom. I don't want to lose her, too. Amen.* She turned back to Jeremy. "She's sleeping, so I think it's okay to slip away for a little bit."

"Where do you want to eat?"

"What are our options?"

Jeremy shoved his phone in her direction. "There are a few fast-food places not far from the hospital. What do you think?"

"This one. I like their food." Whitney pointed at a spot on the phone's screen.

"Suits me."

Whitney followed Jeremy to the elevators and rode in silence to the main floor. The walk to the parking lot and the ride to the restaurant were equally quiet. She didn't know what to say. Their three weeks together were over. Would everything at work go back to normal? Would there ever be anything normal about her life again?

***

Jeremy parked his car in the lot of the restaurant, and they went inside without saying a word. He couldn't believe they'd just spent three weeks together. Three weeks in which they had spent every waking hour together, and the last week even their sleeping hours. Thankfully, that had all worked out despite their first awkward night. They'd fallen into a routine the rest of the week and hadn't blinked an eye when they'd bumped into each other in the mornings.

Now they didn't know what to say to each other.

The restaurant hummed with activity. The smell of french fries and grilled meat wafted through the air.

Whitney went immediately to the counter and stood in line. Jeremy stood behind her, wishing he could comfort her and take away her worry. When her turn came, she ordered her food and drink. The young man behind the counter handed her a drink.

Jeremy stepped up beside her. "I'm paying for hers and mine."

Whitney glanced at him but didn't argue. "Thanks. I'll find a table."

"Okay, I'll join you in a minute."

As soon as Jeremy paid, he took his drink and went in search of Whitney. When he spied her sitting in a corner booth at the back of the restaurant, his heart skipped a beat. Would this continue happening once they got back to work? They definitely wouldn't spend as much time together. Maybe she wouldn't be at work for a while because of her mother. That would give him time to get his mind straight, push away all those romantic notions.

Jeremy put a sign on the table to indicate their order, then sat down. "Are you doing okay?"

Whitney shrugged. "I don't know. I'm not sure about anything. I wish I could talk with a doctor."

"Maybe you should seek out one of the nurses."

"I still want to talk to a doctor."

Jeremy nodded. "Yeah, but maybe a nurse can at least reassure you about the situation."

"Maybe. I'm not sure what will happen. That's the worst part."

Jeremy had never felt so helpless. He wanted to make everything good for her, but he couldn't. "I wish I could help somehow."

"You can."

"How?" Jeremy frowned.

"You can give Graham the final report on our unsuccessful trip. I don't think I'll be in the office this coming week."

"So I get to take the brunt of his displeasure." Jeremy

grinned and hoped he could get Whitney to smile.

"Who knows what he'll say." Whitney took a sip of her drink.

"Have you ever had a business trip go so badly before?"

"No."

"That doesn't make me very confident."

"Just give him the report. We did our best, and we came up empty handed. We can't sugarcoat it."

"Maybe I can give him a box of chocolates."

"That might not go over so well." Whitney giggled, then covered her mouth.

Jeremy's heart tripped at the sound. That was something he'd never heard before. A giggle from Whitney. "Cheese?"

Whitney's giggle turned into full-blown laughter. "Jeremy, I'm so glad you were the one to make that trip with me. You make me smile and laugh and feel so much better."

"Whatever I can do. I'm at your service." If only she knew how much her statement meant to him. He wanted to tell her how much he cared for her and that he'd do whatever he could for her. But with all this stuff going on with her mom, it just wasn't the right time. Would there ever be a right time?

"Maybe you can be my sounding board. I need to throw some ideas out there."

"Sure. I'm all ears."

"I'm trying to imagine you as one big ear." Whitney smiled.

Jeremy laughed. "I'm glad you're feeling good enough to joke and a little less worried, or at least your smile tells me you're doing better."

Whitney nodded. "It's good to know my mom isn't paralyzed or something like that."

"Yeah, for sure." Jeremy folded his hands on the table. "Now what would you like to say?"

Before Whitney could say anything, a young woman placed a tray on their table and whisked away the sign. "Enjoy your meal."

"Should we pray?" Jeremy held out a hand across the table. He hated to admit this was an excuse to hold her hand. He really was intending to give thanks for the meal, but he wasn't above using the moment.

"Okay." She put her hand in his and bowed her head.

"Lord, thank You for this food. Thank You that Eileen appears to be recovering. Please guide Whitney and Eileen as they make decisions for the future. Amen."

As soon as the prayer was over, Whitney extracted her hand from his and took off the lid on her salad. He chastised himself for his foolish thoughts about holding Whitney's hand. He was acting like a middle school boy instead of a man.

Jeremy unwrapped his sandwich. "What did you want to talk about?"

"You said your mom could probably give me advice on finding a place for my mom."

"Yeah. She can. You could call her."

Whitney shook her head. "Not yet. I'm just throwing stuff out there to clear my mind of the clutter and try to get some direction."

"Sure. Tell me everything you're thinking."

Whitney looked at him as if he had two heads. "I'm sure I don't want to tell you everything I'm thinking."

Jeremy gave her a lopsided smile. "You know I didn't mean that literally."

"Yeah, but for some reason I'm taking everything that way tonight. I think it's jet lag or something." She took a bite of her salad.

"Do we get to blame everything on jet lag for a few days?"

Whitney laughed. "I am."

"Then me, too." Jeremy leaned forward. "So I'm waiting to hear what you have to say."

Whitney set her fork down. "I'm thinking about an assisted living facility for my mom, but I'm not sure she'll be on board with that. She was doing so well with Carla."

"Do you think the doctor will order rehab for her?"

Whitney shrugged. "That's why I need to talk to someone to see what the recommendations are. Mom doesn't seem to have any disability, but I'm just seeing her lying in bed. But whatever her issues, I can't leave her home alone for any amount of time no matter how short."

Jeremy nodded. "I'm with you. Without Carla there, things could be bad."

"Then I was thinking about putting the house up for sale."

Jeremy raised his eyebrows. "Your mom definitely wouldn't go for that."

"I don't know. She might. The house is bigger than we need. More to take care of than we need."

"But where would you go?" Jeremy took a bite of his sandwich.

"I could live in one of those apartments on the edge of town. They're nice."

Jeremy set his sandwich on the wrapper. "But won't

you be sad to sell your childhood home?"

Whitney stabbed at her salad and took a big bite, as if she didn't want to answer that question. Finally she set her fork on her plate. "That house doesn't mean much to me. To be honest, Pineydale is just a web of bad memories for me. The only reason I'm here is to help my mom. Otherwise, I'd probably still be back in Atlanta."

Jeremy's stomach sank. That should tell him everything he needed to know. He was part of Pineydale, and she didn't want anything to do with it. "But you love your job."

Whitney gave him a sad little smile. "I do, and that's about the only good part. I could move my mom someplace else."

"But wouldn't she miss her friends?"

Whitney nodded. "And that's the one reason why I would stay."

"That's a good reason." Jeremy wanted to be the reason she wanted to stay. Was there any chance he could change her mind about the hometown he loved? *Foolish, foolish heart.* There was no denying he'd fallen in love with Whitney. When the time was right, would he be brave enough to tell her?

"I'm just throwing this stuff out there so I can figure out my plans for the future. If I sell the house, I won't have any ties to Pineydale except my mom, and when she's gone, I'll be gone."

"I'd miss you." Sadness formed a lump in Jeremy's throat.

"You're about the only one."

Jeremy couldn't ignore Whitney's sardonic tone. "You're wrong."

"Name one other person."

"Graham."

Whitney sat back in her seat and crossed her arms. "Maybe. He likes what I bring to his company, but I'm not sure he really likes me. After all, you've forgotten what I did to Mitch."

Jeremy hadn't forgotten anything Whitney had done, but it didn't matter. It was all in the past. He wished she would forgive herself. He'd thought when she and Jimmy had talked, she had done that, but apparently not. She was still carrying around the guilt.

"Mitch is happy with Amanda. Jimmy's happy with Kelsey. You and Jimmy have made peace. Don't keep carrying around your guilt."

Whitney nodded. "I know you're right, but I don't feel good enough for forgiveness."

As Jeremy took the last bite of his sandwich, he prayed he would have the right words to say to Whitney. "We can never be good enough on our own. That's why God gave us His grace."

Whitney reached across the table and took his hand. "You're just the person I need in my life right now. You've helped me so much to see God during the time we were gone."

"Don't put me on a pedestal. You'll be disappointed. We're all sinners."

"Some of us just bigger ones than others." Whitney's shoulders slumped.

"See, there you go again, putting yourself down. Live forgiven."

Whitney smiled, a thoughtful look on her face. "I like that expression. You'll remind me to do that, right?"

"I will." *You could be happy with me.* Another foolish thought popped into his mind, one he had to banish like all the others. She wasn't talking anything romantic. All this was about her spiritual life, not her love life. He had to pound that into his brain.

Whitney let out a harsh breath. "I have a lot of decisions to make."

"You do, and your mom could be around for a long time. You need to learn to love Pineydale." *And me.* There was another foolish thought clamoring to be spoken. He gritted his teeth to keep from saying it.

"True." Whitney took the final bite of her salad and then a gulp of her drink. "We'd better get back to the hospital. Thanks for listening."

"Anytime, and I mean that."

Whitney stood as she slung her purse over her shoulder. "I know you do. You're a bright spot in my life. I can't tell you that often enough."

"Are you going back home tonight?" Jeremy opened the door for Whitney to go out.

"No. I've got my bags from the trip. I have everything I need to spend the night. I want to be here in the morning so I can talk to the doctor." Whitney hurried across the parking lot.

Jeremy paused and looked over the top of the car at Whitney. "That's a good idea. I'll help you take your bags up when we get to the hospital."

"No need for that."

"Sure there is." Jeremy wanted to spend as much time with Whitney as he could.

When they reached the hospital, Jeremy unloaded Whitney's bags from the trunk. He pulled her roller bag while she carried her backpack. The sun rode the treetops, casting long shadows across the parking lot as they made their way to the hospital entrance.

Whitney glanced at him as they entered the elevator. "You really didn't have to do this. After all, I did manage to wheel my suitcase through several cities in Europe."

"I know, but you needed a treat."

"You mean chocolate isn't enough?" Whitney grinned.

"You're planning to eat your chocolate tonight?"

"Why should I wait?"

Jeremy returned her grin. "I'm glad I hid my chocolate from you, or you might have eaten it all before we got back."

"But you don't like chocolate."

"Gifts. My boxes of chocolate will make my mother and sisters very happy."

"Certainly, but I can't believe you think I'd eat your chocolate. I only ate my own box. Yours are safe from me."

Jeremy titled his head. "I don't know. You devoured a lot of chocolate while we were in Belgium."

"Chocolate is good for you. Didn't you know that?"

"I'm glad you're feeling good enough to joke."

Whitney let out a contented sigh. "I can't stay unhappy when you're around."

"I'm glad I'm good for something." Jeremy wished all this joking meant she actually cared for him, and not just as a friend, but he would take what he could get for now.

"You're good for a lot of things. Don't sell yourself short, especially since you'll be talking to Graham about the trip."

"Yeah. Any advice on that?"

"I told you before—just lay it all out there. We can't change what happened."

Jeremy blew out a big puff of air as the elevator doors opened. "I hope he can come to grips with all the money he spent for nothing."

Whitney stopped in the hallway just outside her mother's room. "It wasn't for nothing. We laid some groundwork. You never know what the future might hold."

Jeremy knew one thing he'd like the future to hold. A date with Whitney. A kiss. A future with her. He used all his willpower to keep from pulling her into his arms and kissing her. He peered into Eileen's room. "Looks like your mom's still asleep. Call me in the morning to let me know what you've found out. Promise?"

"Promise. Good night, Jeremy. Thanks for all you've done." Whitney leaned in and gave him a kiss on the cheek.

"You're welcome. Anytime. I'll be waiting to hear from you. Good night." Jeremy hurried toward the elevators for fear he would turn back and do what he'd been thinking about all evening. Kissing her. Kissing her for real. The sisterly peck she'd given him on the cheek wasn't nearly enough.

CHAPTER FIFTEEN

T he moment of truth had come. Graham had requested Jeremy's presence in his office. The Labor Day weekend had passed, and things were back to normal, if anything could be normal without Whitney there. All morning into the afternoon he'd been waiting with dread for this summons. The day was almost over, and Jeremy thought Graham might not want to hear the dismal report. He'd known from their brief conversations and emails throughout the trip that things weren't going as hoped.

Jeremy picked up his laptop, portfolio, and a gift bag, then trudged down the hall. Walking to the gallows might be easier. Whitney had tried to cheer him when he'd talked with her earlier, but even the thrill of hearing her voice couldn't take away his trepidation.

Jeremy paused outside of Graham's office. *Lord, give me wisdom, and may Graham accept the effort that Whitney and I made for this company, despite the unsatisfactory results. Amen.* Jeremy knocked on the doorframe and waited.

"Come in." Graham sat behind his desk with his elbows resting on the arms of his chair and his fingers steepled. He nodded as Jeremy entered the room. "Glad to have you back, and I'm eager to hear your final report. I'm sorry Whitney can't be here to share in this with you, but

I'm glad her mother is progressing well."

Jeremy nodded as he took a seat in the chair on the other side of the desk. "It seems that it's mostly good news for Eileen, but she will have to do some rehab."

"Yes, Whitney told me the doctor has recommended a facility where she can get the help she needs. That seemed to be a big relief for Whitney."

Jeremy set his files on the desk. "She was definitely worried about that, and I'm happy that's resolved."

Graham leaned forward and eyed Jeremy. "So what do you have to report? Whitney said you'd give me the full rundown."

"Yes, sir." Jeremy wasn't sure whether to start with the bad news or give him the really bad news. He grabbed the files and opened them. First the meeting with the Hubers. Might as well start at the top and go down the list of failures. "I wish I had better news to report, but hopefully this will be the beginning of some future international ventures."

"We can't expect everyone to jump on board. We dipped our toes into the international waters, and that's good."

Jeremy wasn't sure what to make of Graham's Pollyanna attitude, but he shouldn't dismiss his boss's positive mindset. Jeremy spent the next hour going over all their meetings, the discussions, and the businesses that had had enough interest to look over their contracts.

After he finished making his report, Jeremy picked up the gift bag. "Whitney and I got a couple of gifts for you and Donna."

Graham took the bag and brought out its contents and set them on the desk. "Chocolate and a Christmas ornament. Donna and I will enjoy these. Thanks."

"I wish we'd been able to bring you some business instead of just gifts."

Graham leaned forward and pressed the button on his intercom. "Lisa, has that package arrived?"

"Yes, sir. I've just finished putting it all together."

"Bring it in when you're ready."

In a few minutes, Lisa entered the office and handed Graham a blue folder. As she left the room, Graham leaned forward and held it out to Jeremy. "You might be interested in this."

"What is it?" Jeremy wrinkled his brow as he took the folder.

"Open it." Graham leaned back and laced his fingers as they lay across his midsection.

Jeremy's heart raced. Maybe this was his severance package, even though he'd only been on the job a couple of months. After all, his uncle Graham was a hard taskmaster, and he liked to see results. No. Uncle Graham wasn't that hardhearted. Jeremy made himself generate a more positive outlook. Whitney had shared in this trip, and Uncle Graham certainly wasn't going to let her go.

Every nerve zinging, Jeremy opened the cover. His gaze darted across the heading. The contract with the Hubers. He rifled through the papers until he reached the last page. Signed. Wow! Signed. They did get a contract after all. He wished Whitney had been here to share in the good news.

Jeremy looked up. Graham sat there with a big grin on his face. Why had Graham made Jeremy go through that whole mess of reports and then given this to him?

"Why didn't you show me this to begin with?"

"Because I've been waiting for the signed documents all morning. When you came into the office, we still were waiting on their final signatures. I had a verbal agreement, but I wanted to wait on the signed documents before I told you the good news. Good job!"

"You should probably thank the lawyers."

Nodding, Graham grinned. "Yeah, this international stuff requires a lot more when it comes to lawyers. They have to make sure we dot all our i's and cross all our t's. Lots of international trade laws to consider, but it's done."

Jeremy couldn't quit grinning. He wanted to share this with Whitney. She should've been here to share in this success. "I'd like to call Whitney and let her know."

Graham picked up his phone. "I'll do that right now."

Disappointment filled Jeremy's heart. He should be the one to give her the good news, but he wasn't going to override his boss. Jeremy listened, wishing he'd at least asked to have the conversation put on speaker. He was a coward. He was afraid to confront his boss and afraid to tell Whitney his true feelings for her. He was afraid that would put his job in jeopardy if she didn't share his feelings.

"How's your mother doing?" Graham paused to listen. "Glad to hear that. When will she move to the rehab facility?"

Jeremy listened to the one-sided conversation. He wanted to know what was going on with Eileen. He'd have to call Whitney privately as soon as he could.

"Besides calling to find out about your mom, I called to give you some news…" Graham paused.

Jeremy wished he could see Whitney's expression when she heard the news. He wished he were there in person, but maybe he should be grateful that he wasn't. He might forget himself and hug her.

"I wanted to let you know that thanks to you and Jeremy, we have a signed contract with the Hubers' company." Graham grinned, then laughed at something. "He is. Would you like to talk to him?"

Graham held out the phone to Jeremy. "Whitney wants to talk to you."

Jeremy took the phone as he tried to calm his pounding heart. "Hey. Everything set with your mom?"

"Yes. Jeremy, how can you be so calm about this exciting news? I'm ready to jump up and down and scream, but I can't because I'm in a hospital. Will you jump up and down for me?"

Jeremy laughed. If only she knew he wasn't the least bit calm inside. "Sorry. That's not going to happen. You can do that on your own."

"Jeremy, you're no fun."

"That's not what you told me when we were in Europe."

"I must've been mistaken."

Jeremy had the feeling Whitney was actually flirting with him. Must be his wishful imagination. "I think you got it right the first time. Congratulations."

"Congratulations to you, too. That must've made your report to Graham a lot easier."

"Not so much."

"Really?"

"Yeah. I'll give you a full report later."

"Okay." Understanding sounded in Whitney's voice.

"Let me talk to Whitney." Graham held his hand out.

"Graham wants to talk to you again." Jeremy handed

the phone to his uncle.

Graham took the phone. "I'll put this on speaker."

Jeremy gritted his teeth. *Now Graham decides to put on the speaker?* Why couldn't he have done that from the beginning?

"Whitney, do you think you can get away for a little while so we can have a celebratory dinner? We can head over your way to make it more convenient. I'll ask Donna to join us. What do you say?"

"I would love to do that, but let me see how things are with my mom. I'll give you a call right back, okay?"

"That'll be fine. Again, good work, and congratulations."

"Thanks. I'll talk to you in a few minutes."

Jeremy said goodbye just before Graham ended the call. Although it was super of Graham to take them out to dinner, Jeremy wished he could do the celebrating alone with Whitney. But maybe this was for the best.

"So do you think we've got a chance with the chocolate company?" Graham's question made Jeremy sit up.

"It could happen just like this contract." Jeremy tapped the folder lying on the desk. "Whitney kept telling me that we had laid the groundwork."

"That's why I sent you over there. Now we have feelers out with several companies." Graham nodded his head. "I have a good feeling about all of this."

Jeremy didn't want to get too hopeful. Just like he wouldn't let himself get hopeful about anything developing with Whitney.

The phone rang. Graham answered. "Great. We'll pick you up in about half an hour."

"We're on for dinner?" Jeremy asked.

"You got it. I have to say it again. Nice work." Graham stood and offered Jeremy his hand "I'll drive, and we can swing by and get Donna."

"Great! I'll put these things in my office and meet you in the parking lot."

On the ride to Johnson City, Graham talked with Donna about the success of her Labor Day concert fundraiser for cancer that was held the day Whitney and Jeremy had arrived home. Graham and Donna's daughter-in-law Amanda, Mitch's wife, was one of the headliners along with her mentor Willow Childs, star of gospel and country music. Amanda wrote some of Willow's songs. Jeremy couldn't quite get over the fact that his family knew an actual country music star.

Lots of folks from Pineydale had gone to see Amanda sing at the Ryman in Nashville the year before she and Mitch were married. Jeremy still remembered the song Amanda sang that night for Mitch. "Kiss Me Once, Kiss Me Twice." He'd like to sing that to Whitney, but he couldn't carry a tune, and it was the last thing he should do if he wanted to keep his job.

"I'm sorry Whitney and I had to miss it." Jeremy had hoped they would arrive home in time to attend the concert. It would've been the perfect excuse to take Whitney without it being an actual date. But that had all fallen apart when they'd learned of Eileen's stroke.

Donna turned to look at Jeremy. "That's completely understandable. Poor Whitney. It's been one thing after another for her. First her dad, now her mom."

Jeremy wished Whitney were here to see that neither Donna nor Graham held any animosity toward her.

Whitney still couldn't let go of the guilt she had over what happened with Mitch and Jimmy. What would it take to free her? He wished he could do it, but she had to let it go herself.

Maybe she thought everyone still looked at her through the same lens as before. Some people obviously did—otherwise they never would've told Whitney she should pursue Jimmy when she came back. Mean girls. Were there actually thirty-year-old mean girls? He guessed so. Whitney's supposed friends were probably just jealous that Whitney had gone off to the big city and had a successful career while they were stuck in Pineydale with little to show for their lives. So they wanted to make someone else's life miserable. That was the only explanation he could think of for their mean-spirited act in telling Whitney that Jimmy wasn't happy in his marriage.

When they arrived at the hospital, Whitney was waiting outside the entrance for them. She hopped into the backseat with Jeremy.

"I can't get over the fantastic news." Whitney held up a hand to give Jeremy a high five.

Jeremy slapped hands with Whitney. The sight of her brightened his day. "It sure is, and I'm glad we can celebrate. Is your mom doing okay now?"

"She's resting, and tomorrow they're going to move her to the rehab facility where they have assisted living. I hope she likes it. I think it will meet all her needs. I checked it out, and she can get a nice little apartment there. And it's not too far away, so her friends and I can visit often. And it'll give her some interaction during the day."

Jeremy didn't say anything, but it sounded as though Whitney was trying to convince herself that she was doing the right thing. "Did you mention selling the house?"

"I did, and surprisingly enough, she said she'd consider it. I think she wants to see how she likes the assisted living first."

"That's reasonable."

"I really think she'll like it there. I talked to your mom today, and she put in a good word for the place with my mom. I think that helped a lot." Whitney smiled, but Jeremy read the anxiety in her expression.

"Mom would know about that for sure. It's great she was able to give you a recommendation." Jeremy wished he could put Whitney's mind at ease, but the best he could do was support her decisions.

"We're here." Graham pulled into the parking lot. "This place has a wide variety of food. So everyone should find something."

The hostess seated them at a table in the well-appointed restaurant with its dark wooden paneling and soft lighting. Jeremy joined Whitney on one side of the high-back booth with black leather-looking upholstery. Shortly a waitress came to take their drink orders while they studied their menus in silence. Muted conversation and laughter surrounded them.

After the waitress brought their drinks and took their food orders, Graham laid his menu aside and lifted his glass. "Let's toast to Whitney and Jeremy's success and many more like it."

The group cheered as they clinked their glasses, then took a sip of their drinks.

"I'm so proud of you two. I remember y'all when you were youngsters. And now look at y'all grown up and successful business people." Donna set her glass on the table. "Jeremy, you were the youngest of the cousins. Didn't Whitney used to babysit for you?"

Thanks, Aunt Donna, for that reminder. Jeremy nodded and wished he could stuff those words back into his aunt's mouth. Just what he didn't need, Aunt Donna reminding Whitney of the difference in their ages. Oh well, she probably hadn't forgotten that either. Too bad he was hung up on an older woman. "Not very often. Mostly my older siblings got that privilege."

Donna laughed. "You were such a sweet little boy."

Jeremy wrinkled his brow, trying to figure out how he could change the topic. "I'm still sweet."

"Even though he doesn't like chocolate." Whitney grinned at him.

"Seriously?" Donna looked at him with incredulity on her face. "How can anyone not like chocolate?"

Graham turned to Donna. "Jeremy and Whitney brought us some Belgian chocolates, but I forgot and left it in the office."

Donna wagged a finger at Graham. "You'd better not eat it all."

"I wouldn't have mentioned it if I'd planned to do that."

Before anyone could say anything else, the servers brought the food, and Graham asked Jeremy to give thanks for the meal.

After Jeremy prayed, he picked up his fork. "I'm glad to have experienced food from other cultures, but I like being back home."

"But you're going to miss those schnitzels." Whitney laughed as she looked at Graham and Donna. "He ate them every day while we were in Munich."

"He's a man who knows what he wants." Graham chuckled, then took a bite of his steak.

Yeah, Jeremy knew what he wanted all right. Whitney.

***

The quiet house did nothing to ease Whitney's mind. She had spent most of the day cleaning and getting rid of some of the clutter, including her terrible cross stitches, as she went through her mother's things. She would let her mom keep those in her apartment.

Thankfully, Graham had told Whitney she should take as much time as she needed to get her mother's things in order. If they wanted to put the house up for sale, the place needed to be decluttered and painted. With Pineydale becoming a bedroom community for Johnson City, she hoped for a quick sale.

Her mother was a collector, so going through the house would be a major project. After a serious discussion with her doctor, Eileen had agreed to give Whitney power of attorney. The doctor had explained that a mini-stroke often led to a major stroke within a year, but he hoped the preventive measures he put in place for her rehab would lessen that possibility. He also said most likely her mother's dementia was the result of repeated mini-strokes she may have had and didn't even know it. Whitney couldn't thank Carla enough for recognizing the signs.

Whitney pulled a large box from the shelf in the closet of her mother's bedroom. *Important papers* was written on the side. She set the box on the nearby bed and lifted the lid. She wondered why these papers weren't part of those she'd retrieved from the safe deposit box at the bank. She had yet to go through them. She'd just grabbed the contents of the box and dumped it in the big paper bag that now sat on the bed. She would sort through them together and put them in order of importance.

When Whitney plucked one of the large envelopes from the box, she recognized her parents' tax return from fifteen years ago. She quickly rifled through the other envelopes and discovered tax returns for the last fifteen years. Only the last seven years needed to be saved. She would have to shred the rest. Maybe her best option was to go through the safe deposit box stuff first, then she could get the shredder out.

She moved the box aside to make room for what was in the bag. One by one she pulled out the contents. This was like a grab-bag prize. She didn't know what she would find. The first envelope contained the title to her mother's car. Next came the deed to the house. She placed it in the folder for return to the safe deposit box.

Certificates of authentication of artwork throughout the house, birth certificates, social security cards, stock certificates, and a collection of old coins came from the bag. So far all of this needed to go back. Maybe she should've gone through this at the bank, but she didn't want to stand in one of those little cubicles. She wanted to search through these papers and make an inventory of everything.

Another large envelope lay at the bottom of the bag. Whitney opened it and pulled out the contents. As she held the papers, a photograph fluttered onto the bed. She set the other papers aside and picked up the faded color photo. Her parents, who were much younger in the photo, stood with an even younger couple, who looked like teenagers, but

Whitney wasn't sure. Who were these people? She turned the photo over. The date and the names were scribbled on the back. The photo was taken the year before she was born, and the names read Eileen, Melissa, Niels, and Donald.

Whitney frowned and realization dawned. Was this Melissa the reason her mother sometimes mistakenly called her by that name?

Whitney studied the photo. This had to have been taken when her parents lived in Europe. An old brick facade stood behind them in the picture, and she wondered where they were when the photo was taken. Why had her mother saved this photo in their safe deposit box? Maybe it had been stuck with some of the other papers and put there by mistake. As Whitney shuffled through the papers, her heart raced and her stomach did a nosedive. She couldn't believe what she was seeing.

She sank to the bed and stared at the last piece of paper. She read it over and over again. She didn't want to believe what she saw. No, it couldn't be, but here was the evidence. Pressing her lips together, she closed her eyes in an effort to waylay the tears that threatened. Her whole life had been a lie.

One big lie.

The clock radio on the nightstand read five-thirty. Would Jeremy still be in the office, or had he gone home? She had to talk to someone. Jeremy was the only person in Pineydale who really cared about her. She'd shared more with him in the past few weeks than she'd shared with anyone in a long time.

Taking a deep breath, she tapped his name.

The phone rang several times. If she had to leave a

voicemail, how long would it be before Jeremy listened to it? *Please answer.*

No answer.

Tears flooded her eyes. She couldn't deal with this all by herself. She needed Jeremy. She needed him so much. She was about to leave a voicemail, when her phone beeped. Jeremy. Her heart leaped.

"Hello."

"You need something?"

You. "Yeah. Are you free to come over? I need to talk to you about something."

"Sure. You want me to bring something to eat?"

"Okay." Whitney was sure he was hungry, but she didn't think she could eat a thing.

While Whitney waited for Jeremy, she paced, cried, and paced some more. She stood by the front window and breathed deeply, trying to pull herself together before he got there. He didn't want to deal with a blubbering mess. She was strong. She just wanted answers, and she was afraid her mother wouldn't be able to provide them.

As Jeremy loped up the front walk, Whitney's heart fluttered as she swallowed hard and opened the door. "Hi. Thanks for coming."

"Hi." He held up a bag from the Pineydale Café. "I remembered what you liked from that day we talked to Jimmy."

"You're sweet to remember." Whitney took the bag.

Jeremy grinned. "That's what my aunt Donna tells me. Sweet as they come."

Whitney laughed despite the ache in her heart. "You are."

"Do you want to talk while we eat?"

"Okay." Whitney's stomach churned.

"Do you want to eat in the kitchen?"

"Okay."

Jeremy stared at her. "Are you all right? You seem out of sorts."

Whitney stared back. "I am. That's why I called you over to talk."

Jeremy placed a hand on her elbow and guided her back to the kitchen, then set his bag on the table. "Has something more happened with your mom?"

"You might say that."

"Might?" Jeremy took Whitney's bag and set it on the table next to his. "Sit and tell me what's going on."

"I have to get something first. You can go ahead and start eating. I'm not that hungry." Without waiting for Jeremy's response, Whitney raced back to the bedroom and grabbed the papers and the photo.

When Whitney returned, Jeremy was sitting at the table, already eating. He looked up. She didn't know where she should begin. Maybe with the photo. She set it on the table. "Do recognize anyone in that photo?"

A puzzled expression on his face, Jeremy set down his sandwich and picked up the picture. He studied it for a few moments, then he looked at her, his head tilted. "This looks like an old photo of your parents. This young woman could be you, but your parents are too young for this to be you. And I have no clue about the young man. Who are they?"

"I…I think." Whitney let out a sob as her voice cracked.

"Whitney." Jeremy jumped up and came to her side. "Tell me what's wrong."

Unable to speak, Whitney shoved the papers at him. He

took them and laid them out on the table. He studied each one, his brow knitting in concern.

Finally he looked up. "Does this mean what I think it means?"

Whitney wasn't sure she could speak without blubbering. She closed her eyes and took a deep breath. "I think so."

"You're adopted."

Nodding, Whitney swallowed hard and picked up two of the papers. "My original birth certificate and the birth certificate I've always seen, the one where Eileen and Donald Hamilton are my parents."

Jeremy nodded. "Who is the Melissa Hamilton listed as your mother on your original birth certificate?"

"The girl in the photo?" Whitney picked up the picture. "I don't know."

"You look very much like her. Do you have the high school yearbook from your senior year?"

"Somewhere. Why?"

"I want to see your senior picture."

"We don't have to find the yearbook. My mom has that photo framed and on the wall in the spare bedroom." Whitney headed for that bedroom.

Jeremy joined her in the room with the cherry bedroom set and blue-and-white comforter on the bed. He took the photo and held it up next to the portrait. "You see the resemblance?"

Whitney nodded. Was this young woman her mother? A mother who hadn't wanted her? Why had Eileen and Donald never revealed the truth? What had prompted them to keep the adoption secret? Whitney's heart ached as she looked at Jeremy. "Should I confront my mother?"

Jeremy sighed as he handed Whitney the photo. "Do you think you'll get an answer from her? How is her state of mind?"

"She gets confused from time to time, but she has understood everything we've discussed in recent days." Whitney grimaced. "I'm fearful this could derail her recovery."

"I don't see how you can let this go. You have to ask her."

Whitney closed her eyes as she tried to control her emotions. She wasn't sure what she was feeling. Anger, sadness, betrayal, and so much more. The emotions swirled around in her head. This revelation erased all the good feelings over their contract with the Hubers.

Photo in hand, Whitney headed toward the hallway. "I wonder who else knows about this. My parents were both only children, so I never had any cousins, aunts, or uncles growing up. I'm pretty sure my parents never shared this with anyone. That's why I've always loved your family, because it was big, fun, and boisterous."

Jeremy smiled. "I never thought of my family that way, but I guess you're right. But sometimes they can be overwhelming."

Whitney shrugged. "Not really. I loved coming to your house. I think that's half the reason I dated your brother."

"Let's go eat."

Whitney wondered why Jeremy had abruptly cut off the conversation about his family. Maybe he didn't want to think about how she'd tried to be a homewrecker by pursuing Jimmy when he was married. Could she ever live that down?

Whitney trailed after Jeremy. "I'm still not sure I feel

like eating."

He turned to her. "You should eat. Then we'll visit your mom and get some answers."

As she sat at the kitchen table, the thought of confronting her mother made Whitney's stomach curdle. How could she even think of eating? "I'm sorry. Your food is probably cold."

Jeremy smiled and picked up his sandwich. "It's okay. I just want you to eat something."

"I'll try." Whitney nibbled on her sandwich as she looked at Jeremy. What would she do without him? He was here to help her pick up the pieces of her shattered life.

"Not eating won't help you."

"I know." Whitney tapped the photo. "Do you suppose this young man is my father? There was no father listed on the original birth certificate."

"Could be." Jeremy eyed her. "That's why you have to talk to your mom. She has the answers."

Whitney had told herself over and over again that she was brave, but deep inside her a coward lurked. She was definitely a coward when it came to Jeremy. She wanted in the worst way to tell him how much he meant to her, how much she cared for him, how much his presence in her life brightened every moment. Maybe when this whole adoption thing was settled, she would find the courage to tell him.

CHAPTER SIXTEEN

T he tile in the hallway of the assisted living facility gleamed in the sunlight coming through the windows as Whitney led the way to her mother's apartment. On the drive over, Whitney had said very little, and thankfully, Jeremy hadn't pressed her to talk.

Anger bubbled up inside, but anger wouldn't get her mother to talk. Who were her parents? Maybe the couple in the photo. Why had they given her away? Why hadn't they wanted her?

Jeremy had been so supportive. He was a prize among men. It was all she could do not to throw herself into his arms and seek comfort there.

When they reached the door to Eileen's apartment, Jeremy paused and touched Whitney's arm. "Let's pray before we go in."

Whitney gave him a sad little smile. "I can always count on you to think of doing that. Thanks."

Jeremy held out his hands to her, and without hesitation she gladly placed her hands in his. This felt so right, but this wasn't the time to think about it. This was a time to ask their God to grant her favor in this quest.

Jeremy bowed his head. "Lord, thank You for this facility where Whitney's mom can live and recover. We pray she will recover quickly and have a good quality of life here. Lord, You know what's on Whitney's heart. She wants to get answers regarding her parentage. We pray she will get the answers she needs without upsetting Eileen. Grant us wisdom. We pray in the name of Jesus. Amen."

Her heart hammering, Whitney squeezed his hands. "Thank you. I don't know what I'd do without your help."

He gazed at her, sympathy in his eyes. "You can call on me anytime. I'll be there. I'll be your backup today while you talk to your mom."

"I can't thank you enough." Whitney took a deep breath as she knocked. "Here we go."

Eileen opened the door. "Whitney. Jeremy. How good to see you. Come in."

"How are you doing, Mom?" Whitney clutched the bag containing the documents and the framed cross stitches she'd taken from the house. "Is everything going well here?"

"It is." Eileen smiled and hugged Whitney. "Thank you for finding this place."

"I'm glad you like it."

"It takes a little getting used to, but everyone here is very nice." Eileen motioned to the gray tweed couch in her little living room. "Come sit down."

"Have you been eating in the dining room with the other residents, or are you fixing your own meals?"

"I get my own breakfast, but I eat in the dining room for my other meals. I don't feel like fixing lunch and dinner, and the food is good."

"I'm glad to hear that."

Jeremy joined Whitney on the couch while Eileen sat in the nearby chair. Whitney continued to engage her mom in conversation as she tried to determine her mother's state of mind. She seemed quite coherent.

"Mom, I've been going through the house. The real estate agent said we need to declutter and paint."

Jeremy sat forward in his seat and grinned. "You know I can recommend an excellent and very reliable painting company."

Whitney turned to him with a smile. "Are they booked way out?"

"I don't know about that, but I believe I have some pull and can get you in right away."

"You aren't just saying that, are you?" Whitney asked.

"I'll talk to Janelle if you want."

"Yes, please do." Whitney turned back to her mom. "I'm going to start bringing some things over, and I want you to decide what you're going to do with them."

"What do you mean?" A puzzled look crossed Eileen's face.

"You can't keep everything from the house. Some things you'll want to bring here, and other things we should donate or just toss."

Eileen clasped and unclasped her hands. "But I don't want to get rid of my things."

"Some of those things you haven't used in forever, and if we sell the house, you won't have room for them here. There is no sense in keeping them."

Leaning back in her chair, Eileen crossed her arms. Her lips formed a grim line, and she didn't say anything, just stared at Whitney.

"It won't be as bad as you think. Some of those things you've probably forgotten."

Eileen frowned. "Just because my memory isn't what it used to be doesn't mean I should get rid of my things."

Whitney said a silent prayer that this disagreement

wouldn't escalate. If it did, she feared bringing up the adoption would make things worse. She took one of the cross stitches from the bag sitting by her feet and held it out to her mom. "See what I brought you."

Eileen smiled. "I'm not getting rid of this."

"I brought it so you could put it up on one of your walls." Whitney reached into the bag again. "And I brought two others."

"Thank you. I've always treasured these." Eileen pressed the cross stitch to her chest.

Whitney couldn't help remembering how she had done much the same that day in Jimmy's workshop. And she also remembered how instrumental Jeremy had been in arranging that meeting and giving her and Jimmy the opportunity to forgive each other. She owed Jeremy a debt of gratitude for so many things.

"Next week I'm going to start working half days and spend the afternoons getting the house ready to put on the market."

Eileen let out a heavy sigh. "Do you suppose I can see the place again before it's sold?"

Whitney reached over and patted her mother's arm. "For sure. I want you to see it after we get it all fixed up. We'll sit on the front porch swing and have some sweet tea."

Eileen smiled. "That sounds lovely."

"Mom." Whitney scooted forward on the couch as she pulled a folder from the bag, then glanced over at Jeremy before returning her gaze to Eileen. "While I was going through your things, I found these. Adoption papers."

The color drained from Eileen's face as she twisted her hands in her lap. Her expression told Whitney that her mother remembered, but she didn't say a thing.

"Would you like to explain?"

Eileen's eyes filled with tears, and still she remained silent. Whitney sat there and waited for her mother to respond, but she sat statue-like, staring straight ahead.

Jeremy touched Whitney's arm, then took the photo from the folder. "Mrs. Hamilton, could you tell us about this photo?"

Eileen's lips quivered as she took the photo. A tear trickled down one cheek. She wiped it away as she looked at Whitney. "I'm so sorry."

"Mom." Whitney knelt in front of her mother. "What are you sorry about?"

"That we never told you…" Eileen burst into tears and covered her face with her hands.

"Mom, it's okay. Just tell me now." Whitney grasped her mother's hands. "I want to know."

Eileen lowered her hands and wiped away the tears. Misery painted her features. "We were going to tell you when you were old enough to understand, but the years went by, and we just couldn't find a way. We were all so happy. I feared telling you would change everything."

Whitney pointed to the photo. "Are these my parents?"

Eileen licked her lips as she looked at Whitney with uncertainty. "The young lady is your mother. I'm not sure about your father."

"Then why is he in the picture?"

"First I need to tell you who the young woman is."

"Melissa. Is she a relative?" Whitney remembered how Jeremy pointed out the resemblance between her and the woman in the photo.

Eileen took a shaky breath. "She was our daughter."

"Your daughter? My mother was your daughter? You're really my grandmother?" Whitney's brow wrinkled. "I don't understand."

Eileen hung her head. She remained silent for what seemed like days instead of minutes. Finally she looked up. "This is a hard thing for me to talk about. It seems like it happened yesterday instead of thirty years ago."

"I'll give you as much time as you need to tell it." Whitney tamped down the anger again. She couldn't let that emotion ruin the chance to find out what had happened. Taking a calming breath, she pulled a chair from the table in the kitchenette and put it next to her mother. As she sat down, she rubbed her mother's arm as much to comfort herself as to comfort her mom. "Tell me about Melissa."

Eileen blinked rapidly, looking confused for a moment, but a determined look crossed her face. "You're so much like her. It's like having her with me all over again. She was bright, funny, full of life and cheer. She wanted to experience everything. We lived in Europe before you were born. Your mother was a first-year student at the university in Berlin, where we were professors."

"Was that when the photo was taken?"

Eileen nodded. "Niels was a student there, and Melissa dated him."

"But you still don't know whether he's my father?"

"Melissa wouldn't tell us." Eileen slowly shook her head. "We had already returned to the States when she told us she was pregnant. We tried to get her to tell us who the father was, but she would never confirm that Niels was the one."

"Why?"

"I don't know for sure, but they had a falling out at the end of the school year, and Niels went back home to Amsterdam. Melissa wouldn't talk about him or what happened between them."

"What happened to my mother? Where is she?"

Eileen's eyes filled with tears again. "She died. The day after you were born, she suddenly had excessive bleeding. The doctors couldn't save her."

Whitney closed her eyes. She had never known her mother, but an uncontrollable sorrow inundated Whitney. How could she grieve for a mother she had never known? How could she sort out her feelings?

"Did you ever try to contact Niels?"

Eileen hung her head again. "We were grieving, and we weren't going to go on a wild goose chase after a young man we didn't even know that well. Melissa never named him as the father, so we had nothing to go on. No father made the adoption process much easier."

A blind fury made Whitney want to yell and lash out at her mother…not her mother, her grandmother. It was hard to understand how this woman she had believed to be her mother for all of these years had kept her from knowing about her real mother and maybe her real father. Cheated. Deprived. Deceived. She felt all those things. How could she ever look at this woman the same again?

Forgiveness. That was how. Jeremy had taught her how important it was to forgive. She looked over at him. She loved him. Could he ever love her? Would this mess make him look at her differently?

"What is Niels's last name?" Whitney asked.

Eileen's face registered confusion again. Did she not remember? Whitney feared she would never know the man responsible for giving her life. Did it matter? Yes. She wanted to know her parents.

"Do you remember?"

"Lindemann. Niels Lindemann."

"Thank you." Whitney let the name run through her mind. "I want to know about my mother, your daughter."

Eileen stared into space, and Whitney feared her mother was drifting away into her own little world. Eileen shook her head, as if to make sense of what Whitney had asked. "There are two big plastic bins under my bed. They're full of photos and your mother's things. You can look through them."

"Thank you."

Tears in her eyes again, Eileen touched Whitney's shoulder. "You're a lot like your mother. She loved languages, too. She could speak a half dozen of them. I wish you could've known her."

Whitney just nodded. She feared if she spoke, the anger she'd been suppressing would spew forth. She should've known about her mother as a child, not discovered her by accident as an adult. But Whitney determined to put aside her anger and to love her grandmother and learn about her mother now. But she wanted to know about her father, too.

Was Niels Lindemann her father or just a young man who had dated her mother? Could she find out? Was that even possible? Maybe she should take this one step at a time. Learn about her mother, then try to find her father. Whitney decided not to press her mother any more today. At least Whitney knew the truth of her adoption. The rest could come later.

***

The whole time Jeremy had sat there and watched Whitney talking with her mother, he'd wanted to take her in his arms and just hold her. Did she suddenly feel unloved because her grandparents had essentially lied to her for years, kept her from knowing the truth about her parents?

He knew one thing. He loved Whitney and wanted to tell her. He had to quit second-guessing himself. If he kept putting it off because it didn't seem like the right time, that time would never come.

When they got back to her place, he would tell her.

The street light on the corner lit up the block as Jeremy parked his car in front of Whitney's house. Now that they were here, his courage slipped away just as the moon slipped behind the clouds. It had all seemed so right when they'd walked out of Eileen's apartment. Now his plans seemed all wrong.

Lord, if this is the right time and the right woman for me, give me a sign. As that prayer winged its way to heaven, Jeremy glanced at Whitney, her expression hidden in the dim light. "Do you want to talk about it?"

Silence filled the car. Jeremy's heart sank. Not the answer he'd been hoping for. What was he thinking anyway? She'd just learned some life-changing news, and he wanted to plop something else in her lap? Not smart. *Thanks, Lord, for setting me straight.*

"I guess you don't. I understand."

"But I do." Whitney touched his arm. "I just don't know where to begin."

"I'll be glad to listen." Jeremy's pulse raced at her

touch. "Do you want to talk here?"

"No. Let's go inside." Whitney got out and hurried to the front porch.

Jeremy wasn't sure what the Lord was trying to tell him, but for sure he was meant to help Whitney through this. Every nerve zinged as he waited for her to unlock the door. She flipped on the light as soon as she stepped inside.

The small lamp that sat in the corner near the couch projected a soft glow throughout the room. Whitney's blond hair shimmered in the light. Jeremy's heart thudded against his rib cage.

Whitney turned to him. "I want to go through those bins my mother told us about."

"Sure."

Jeremy stood by as she hunched down on her hands and knees, lifted the bed skirt, and pulled out a long plastic container and then another one. Looking girlish in her blue jeans and pale-knit shirt, she sat cross-legged on the floor and took the lid off one bin.

Before she touched anything, she gazed up at him. "You can join me."

Happy for the invitation, Jeremy sat beside her on the floor. "Are you just going to go through this one piece at a time?"

Whitney nodded. "There doesn't appear to be any organization. It's just a jumble of papers, photo albums, and folders."

"This looks like a baby book." Jeremy pointed to a pink rectangular shape.

Nodding, Whitney picked it up and held it for a moment. She took a deep breath and opened it. The first page contained a photo of a baby wrapped in a simple blanket. Melissa Elizabeth Hamilton was written under the photo. Then a page of birth statistics, weight, length, hair, and eye color.

"Your mom had blond hair and blue eyes just like you." Jeremy touched the photo.

"I think she was bald just like me when I was a baby." Whitney chuckled. "I don't see much hair there. I didn't really have much hair until I was two."

Her amusement made Jeremy happy, but he had to resist touching her hair as they sat so close. He followed along as Whitney leafed through the rest of the book that told the story of birthdays, Christmases, and school years.

For the next couple of hours, Whitney took every paper, photo, and piece of memorabilia out of the bins. She read her mother's school papers and looked at the awards and accolades her mother had received.

Whitney laughed at some of the photos in which her mother had a big toothless grin. The photos showed a transformation of a gangly preteen into a beautiful and poised young woman who had embraced living abroad with her professor parents. Did Whitney see the resemblance to herself in those photos?

"This one looks a lot like you. Do you see it?"

Whitney looked up at him. "I suppose. You were the one who thought my senior photo looked like the photo I found with the adoption papers."

"You don't agree?"

"I see it a little." Whitney shrugged. "I keep thinking about my father's contribution to who I am."

"Could you search for him?"

"I really would like to do that. But how?"

"You were the IT person. You should know."

Whitney frowned. "An IT person helps people when they have computer issues, not search for long-lost relatives."

Jeremy grimaced. "I just thought you could do some kind of computer search."

"Possible, but unless Niels Lindemann is a well-known person, he might be hard to find. And how many Niels Lindemanns are there in the world? And when it all comes down to it, he might not be my father."

"True, but I think you should try to find him."

Whitney smiled. "Thank you for standing with me in that."

Jeremy wanted to stand with Whitney through whatever happened. He'd been waiting all evening for the perfect time to let her know how much he cared for her, but the time never seemed right, even now.

Whitney returned her attention to the remaining items in the last bin. She picked up a manila envelope and dumped the contents on the floor. Photos and a hospital band lay there. She scooped up the hospital band and looked at it. Tears filled her eyes as she closed her hand around it. "This was mine when I was born."

Jeremy nodded but didn't say anything to disturb Whitney.

With her other hand she spread the photos. She let out a sound that was half gasp, half sob as she picked up one of the photos. She stood and turned away from the scene before her. She walked toward the window and pressed the photo to her chest as sobs wracked her body.

Jeremy looked at the other photos lying on the floor. Melissa Hamilton, smiling and holding her newborn daughter, Whitney. Jeremy's heart hurt for Whitney as he jumped up and raced to Whitney's side. He put an arm around her shoulders. In an instant she turned into his arms as she wept on his shoulder. He held her close and let her cry as she let the photo fall to the floor. He wanted to take away her hurt.

When her tears subsided, she stepped away and picked up the photo, embarrassment on her face. "I'm so sorry."

"Don't be sorry." Jeremy took a deep breath, his heart in his throat. "I told you I would be here for you no matter what."

She smiled through her tears. "And you are. Thank you."

Jeremy stepped closer. "Whitney, I'm not sure this is the right time, but I have something to tell you."

Whitney stared at him wide eyed. "Tell me what?"

Jeremy's pulse pounded in every inch of his body. *Just spit it out*. He couldn't make his mouth form the words.

"Are you trying to tell me something terrible?" Whitney's brow wrinkled. "Tell me. Just tell me. I can take it. I've had so much bad news, what's a little more?"

"I hope what I have to say isn't terrible or bad news."

"Just tell me."

"Whitney, *ich liebe dich. Je t'aime. Ik hou van je*."

Whitney laughed and cried at the same time, then flung her arms around him. "You learned how to say 'I love you' in three languages?"

Jeremy held her tight. Did this mean she shared his feelings? "Yeah, I would've learned more, but I wasn't sure I could remember more than three, because I'm plenty nervous right now."

"Why?" Whitney stepped out of his arms.

"I didn't know if you felt the same way. After all, you

were my brother's girlfriend, and I'm six years younger than you. I thought you might still look at me like the kid you used to babysit." Jeremy clamped his mouth shut. He was rambling.

She looked into his eyes. "Jeremy, I don't care about any of that. I care for you a lot. I've got a terrible track record when it comes to love, so I'm not sure what I'm feeling. I just know when I'm with you everything seems right with the world, even the bad stuff. So if that's love, I'm in."

Jeremy pulled her into his arms again. "We'll figure it out. But our biggest challenge is work and family."

"What will Jimmy say?" The words came out of their mouths at the same time.

They laughed as they stepped away from each other.

Jeremy took a deep breath. "I kept telling myself a relationship with you would never work because of him."

"I know. I kept thinking you just looked at me as your brother's old girlfriend. And *old* was the thorny part of that equation."

Jeremy shook his head. "Most of the time I don't think about your age, only when I wondered whether you thought I was too young for you."

"We obviously have no problem with our ages, but we could have a problem that's work related." Whitney's mouth formed a grim line.

"You mean Graham won't approve?"

Whitney shook her head. "I doubt that Graham cares. I dated and got engaged to Mitch when we both worked for Graham. The problem came when we broke up. It can cause all kinds of problems. That's the issue."

"So we won't let that happen." Jeremy knew that was a

crazy statement. He couldn't predict the future. He held his breath as he waited for Whitney's response.

"I'd like to believe we could do that."

"I sense a *but*." Jeremy raised his eyebrows.

"We can't know the future, and if we want a relationship, we just have to go for it."

Jeremy put his arms around Whitney's waist. "I'm going to kiss you unless you tell me no."

Whitney lifted her face to his. "And why would I want to do that?"

"I have no idea." Jeremy's lips met Whitney's, and his world exploded into a kaleidoscope of colors. She melted into him, and he pulled her closer. He wanted to shut out the world around them. They needed to make this work, because he never wanted to let her go.

When the kiss ended, they stood in each other's arms, their foreheads pressed together.

"How do you want to handle this?" Whitney gave him a little peck on the lips, then stepped away.

"As in, how do we tell people we're dating?" Jeremy gave her a wry smile.

Whitney nodded. "Let's not."

"You mean you want to keep our relationship a secret?" Jeremy wasn't sure about that idea.

Whitney bit her lower lip and nodded. "Are you ready to tell your family?"

Letting out a heavy sigh, Jeremy let the question roll through his mind. He didn't know what his family, especially Jimmy, would say. Was this a sticking point that had already put a dart into this relationship? "I'll have to figure that out."

"Okay. Then in the meantime, we don't have to tell

anyone."

"So we just don't tell anyone right now, and I'll have to figure out how to tell my family. I don't know how they'll react."

"So you're saying your family doesn't like me?"

"No. That's not it. You know the history. You're part of it."

"Maybe this is going to be an issue we can't overcome."

Jeremy grabbed her hands. "No. I won't let that stand between us."

"I'm sorry. I shouldn't have said that. I understand your reluctance to announce this to your relatives." Whitney put a hand to her mouth.

"Are we already having our first fight?" Jeremy grinned.

Whitney laughed and hugged him. "No, because I can't stay mad at you long enough to have a fight. So what's your plan?"

"We'll work on our projects together. Go out to dinner together as part of work. We can meet over in Johnson City when we visit your mom. And eventually we'll figure out how to break the news to the people around us."

Whitney smiled. "You're a man with a plan, and I like it."

"And I like kissing you."

Whitney didn't wait for him to kiss her. She put her arms around his neck and pressed her lips to his. He hoped he wasn't dreaming. Whitney Hamilton was kissing him, and they were dating. In secret.

CHAPTER SEVENTEEN

D ust motes floated in the late afternoon sunshine on a Friday as Whitney dusted the coffee table. How could it be so dusty when she had just dusted? Keeping a house tidy in case someone wanted to look at the place made her feel as though she couldn't live in her own home. She was constantly cleaning and making sure nothing was out of place. The house had been for sale for a few weeks, but no buyers had emerged.

Whitney couldn't believe it was already the beginning of November. September and October had come and gone in a whirlwind of work, fixing up the house, and Jeremy. He made everything about her life brighter.

November had ushered in much-cooler weather, but nothing had cooled Whitney's feelings for Jeremy. Their clandestine relationship brought fun and excitement to her life. They shared a secret. They left love notes on each other's desks, written on official stationery in official envelopes so no one would suspect what was inside.

In the beginning, Sunday afternoons were reserved for a visit with Eileen and dinner afterward in Johnson City. The only issue came when Jeremy's mom wondered why he was always missing the family supper on Sunday night. This prompted a change to Saturday visits and dinners so Jeremy wouldn't have to continually make up excuses for his absence.

When Janelle could only fit painting the outside of the house into their schedule, Jeremy had spent evenings with her painting the inside until it was ready to show. As promised, Whitney had brought Eileen to the house, and she had insisted Jeremy join them. His weekly visits brought so much joy to her mom.

Even though things between Jeremy and her seemed almost perfect, some days Whitney wished she hadn't suggested the secrecy. Jeremy never made any move to tell his family about their relationship, and she wanted to tell her mom in the worst way.

Whitney had let little doubts niggle at her mind. Maybe Jeremy couldn't bring himself to share this with his family. Maybe he didn't love her enough. While he'd been all in, telling her from his first confession about his feelings for her that he loved her, she'd been the one not sure of her feelings. Now she was head over heels in love with him and wanted to shout it to the world. Had Jeremy found the opposite to be true?

In all of the crazy emotions swirling around her, Whitney had come to grips with the secret her grandparents had kept for so many years. She would never have known her mother, but she would have known of her mother and might have come to know her father. She still had trouble adjusting to the thought of the mother she'd known her whole life actually being her grandmother.

Not a day went by that Whitney didn't think about Niels Lindemann. She and Jeremy had done some research. A few of Whitney's friends from Atlanta had also joined in the search, but it had resulted in frustration. There were plenty of Niels Lindemanns in the world. How did you decide which one to pursue? She had looked for clues that might indicate one of them had a connection to Melissa Hamilton, but Whitney had come up empty.

As Whitney finished dusting the tables in the living room again, her phone rang. She plucked it from the small table sitting near the front door and looked at the number. Her real estate agent. "Hi, Alicia."

"Whitney, I have a couple who would like to look at your house."

"Great. When?"

"As soon as possible."

"Oh, wow! I think everything's in place. I've just finished dusting. I'll do one last check and disappear."

Alicia laughed. "Okay. I'll give you fifteen minutes. Is that good?"

"Absolutely. Talk to you later."

Whitney raced through each room, making sure nothing was out of place. She turned on the lights everywhere, then grabbed her purse and went out to the garage. As she slid into the driver's seat, she grabbed her phone. She tapped Jeremy's name in her contacts.

"Hello, Ms. Hamilton, is there something I can do for you?" Jeremy's deep voice sounded in her ear.

Whitney almost giggled. "Would you like some company?"

"Isn't that breaking the rules? And didn't we just leave the office? Do you miss me that much?"

"Maybe, but I need someplace to go while the Realtor shows the house."

"That's good news. A showing. Sure, you can come over, but we have to have a cover story if someone should discover you're at my place."

Whitney couldn't help smiling. "Jeremy, I think we

have a built-in cover story. We work together."

"Oh, I forgot about that. Hmmm. We work together. Good cover."

"You always make me smile."

"I can hardly wait to see that smile. I'll be waiting for you."

"Be there in five minutes." Whitney ended the call, eager to see the man she loved.

Maybe it was time to put an end to their secret.

Wearing blue jeans and a heather-blue crewneck sweater, Jeremy stood on the front porch of his white clapboard bungalow when Whitney arrived. As soon as she opened the car door, he loped down the sidewalk to meet her.

His blue eyes twinkled with their secret as he escorted her onto his front porch. "*Du siehst schön aus*!"

"*Danke*. So you don't want your neighbors to know you think I'm beautiful?" Whitney resisted the urge to kiss him while they stood on the porch. "Are you sure none of them speak German?"

Jeremy grinned. "If they do, our secret's out. Let's go inside so I can give you a proper greeting."

Jeremy ushered Whitney into the house. As soon as the door was shut behind him, he took her in his arms and kissed her. Whitney didn't think she could ever get enough of his kisses, but she tempered her desire. She didn't want to lead them down the path of no return, a path they would both regret.

She stepped out of his arms. "That was quite a greeting. What have you been up to since you got home?"

"I'm doing research for you."

Whitney wrinkled her brow. "My father?"

Jeremy nodded. "Come in here, and I'll show you what I've been doing."

Whitney followed him to the spare bedroom he had set up as an office. A laptop sat on a computer desk occupying a space under the lone window. Bookshelves lined the opposite wall. Books, framed photographs, and knickknacks his nieces and nephews had made filled the shelves. She'd been in this room only twice before they had started dating and not again until now. They had tried to keep their contact outside of work to a minimum in case someone should get suspicious.

"Okay. Show me what you've been doing."

"I'm cyber stalking all the Niels Lindemanns on the social media sites."

"And just how is that going to help?"

"You know a lot of people post memories, old photos, or they might mention something from the past." Jeremy shrugged as he sat at the desk. "See what I mean."

Whitney stood behind the chair as Jeremy brought up a list of Lindemanns. "Are you looking at all of those?"

Jeremy shook his head. "No. Just the ones who might be the right age. That eliminates a lot."

"Isn't it hard to see what they post when you don't have a connection with them?"

Jeremy sighed. "Yeah, but there are a few who don't have any restrictions on who sees their posts. So I've started scrolling through those."

"Interesting. Show me more." Whitney leaned over Jeremy's shoulder.

"The big problem is not being able to understand what they're saying. Can you translate?" Jeremy stood and indicated she should sit.

Whitney slipped onto the chair. "Yeah, but tell me what you're looking for."

"A connection of some kind to your mother."

Whitney looked back at him over her shoulder. "That was over thirty years ago. How are we going to find something like that?"

"Prayer."

Whitney should've known Jeremy would say that. Eventually she hoped his trust in God would rub off on her. But in the end, she had to embrace her own faith and her own trust that God would lead her to her father if that was His plan. Jeremy helped point the way for her to find that trust despite all the disappointments she'd experienced, some of her own making.

"Then we should pray right now. Will you?"

Jeremy nodded. "Heavenly Father, thank You for the ability to connect with people all over the world. Please grant Whitney success in finding her father. Guide us in our search. Amen."

"Thank you."

"This should be our daily prayer."

Whitney nodded. "You know I'm still working on getting my spiritual life in order."

"That's a work in progress for all of us, not just you."

Whitney read through several of the posts on the page of one Niels Lindemann. Nothing of significance for her search. She moved on to another one and another and another. She rubbed the back of her neck and rolled her shoulders.

"Are you getting tired of sitting there?" Jeremy stepped closer and rubbed her shoulders.

"Oh, that feels so good. You can keep that up all day."

Jeremy laughed. "My hands would wear out."

"That's okay. My brain is wearing out. I haven't read this much Dutch in years."

"How do you keep it all straight?"

Whitney shrugged. "I've always had a knack for languages. They just came easily to me."

"Maybe Dutch is easy because your father is Dutch."

"It's so strange to think of that. I wish I knew. I wish I could've known my mom." Whitney sighed and bit her lower lip.

"I wish I could be of more help."

"You've helped a lot."

"Are you planning to visit your mom tomorrow as usual?"

Whitney shook her head. "I talked to her earlier today, and she wants me to get her Sunday morning and bring her to church in Pineydale. She misses coming to church here."

"Is she up for that? Is she allowed to leave the facility?"

"Yes, I can check her out for a few hours."

"Sounds like she's a library book." Jeremy grimaced.

"Only you would think that. That's why I love you." Whitney chuckled as she jumped up and gave him a kiss.

As they stood there in each other's arms, Whitney's phone rang. She scrambled to get it out of her purse. "Hello, Alicia."

"Whitney, you have an offer on the house. Asking price."

"Oh wow! I can't believe this. What do I need to do?"

"You have some papers to sign. I'll wait at the house for you."

"I'll be right over." Whitney ended the phone call and

flung her arms around Jeremy. "Jimmy, I've sold the house."

Jeremy was out of her arms in a flash. "Jimmy?"

Whitney clamped a hand over her mouth. The expression on Jeremy's face could freeze a molten volcano. How could she undo one misstated word? "Jeremy, I'm sorry. An old habit."

"From how long ago? Seems to me in eight years you would've gotten over that habit unless Jimmy's still on your mind. Jimmy's still in your heart. Jimmy's still the one you love and not me. Have I just been a substitute for him all this time?"

"No. No. I love you." Whitney's heart hurt because she feared he didn't believe her. She had such a rotten reputation when it came to her relationships. "It was just a mistake. I misspoke."

"I guess you did. Now I understand why you wanted to keep our relationship a secret. It was just fun and games for you, using me to placate yourself over your loss of Jimmy."

"That's not true." Whitney closed her eyes as misery welled up inside her. She wanted to wake up and find out this was all a bad dream. "Why can't you believe me? How could you just throw away everything from the last few months?"

"Because it's all been a lie. I've always lived in Jimmy's shadow. So this is nothing new." Jeremy's eyes radiated hurt. "You need to go sell your house, Whitney. Goodbye."

Whitney stared back. She couldn't believe this was happening. Jeremy's wounded expression curdled Whitney's insides. She fought back the tears as she grabbed her purse and fled.

When she reached her car, the tears came. She slid into the driver's seat and grasped the steering wheel and laid her head on it. Her heart ached so much she thought she would burst from the pain. Why was she so terrible at love? Why had her mother had to die? Why had her grandparents kept the truth from her? An avalanche of sorrow and regret inundated her.

Finally, she gathered herself and drove away. Had Jeremy been watching? Probably not. He was done with her. That thought was like a sword piercing her heart. She managed to keep from crying as she drove back home.

After parking her car in the driveway, she checked her reflection in the visor mirror. Thankfully, she didn't look as horrible as she felt. She would get through this.

Whitney pasted a smile on her face as she greeted Alicia. Somehow Whitney managed to keep a mask of delight on her face as she went over the paperwork and signed in the appropriate places. A closing date at the end of November would give her little time to find a new place and empty this house.

Still holding a smile in place, Whitney watched Alicia drive away. Whitney stood on the front porch and gazed at the swing where she and Jeremy had sat and talked about her bad history with Jimmy. Why couldn't Jeremy believe that was all behind her?

Work would be a problem going forward. How ironic that she'd mentioned the issue when they'd first started dating, and Jeremy had said they wouldn't let a breakup happen. He said he'd be here for her no matter what. How could he change his mind so quickly? He must not have loved her after all.

She would have to talk to Graham about working out of the office in Johnson City. She would find a place to live there. She would be closer to her mom and wouldn't have to see Jeremy on a daily basis. He'd probably be happy about that, too.

Their secret relationship was a welcome thing now. She wouldn't have to explain to anyone why she'd ended another relationship with a Cunningham man. But probably in the end, it was what had spelled disaster for them. Secrets were never good.

***

The doorbell rang, and Jeremy hurried to answer the door. Who was visiting him the day before Thanksgiving? He had mostly kept to himself since he and Whitney had broken up. Even though he didn't have to explain the breakup to anyone, he was out of sorts and didn't feel like socializing. He couldn't deny that he missed Whitney. He even missed his visits with Eileen. He still loved Whitney, but she was hung up on his brother. She might deny it, but she had called him by his brother's name.

Jeremy opened the door. "Janelle, what are you doing here?"

"I just came to check on my little brother, and Mom wants to know why you didn't respond to her text about inviting Whitney and her mother to Thanksgiving dinner." Janelle stepped into the house.

"I've been busy with work." That wasn't a lie, and Jeremy didn't want to explain why it would be a bad idea to invite Whitney.

"You could take two minutes to respond." Janelle

poked a finger at his chest.

Jeremy backed away. "I don't know. Do you really think that's a good idea?"

"Mom obviously does. Things were good on the Fourth of July."

"That was months ago, and we were outside at an event, not sitting around a dinner table."

Janelle frowned. "What's your problem? Jimmy told me you were the one who helped Jimmy and Whitney put the past behind them."

"Yeah, so?" Jeremy turned away, fearing Janelle would read the despair in his eyes, because talking about Whitney hurt. "What does that have to do with Thanksgiving dinner?"

"Since that whole debacle is behind them, Mom thought it would be nice to ask them. After all, you work with Whitney, and you've been to visit Eileen numerous times."

"We don't work together anymore."

"Is that all it is?"

"Yeah."

"Jeremy Cunningham, you're not a very good liar."

"That's the truth. We don't work together now."

Janelle raised her eyebrows as she gave him a laser-beam look. "But that's not all the truth, is it? I saw you and Whitney together. What happened?"

Jeremy swallowed hard. What had Janelle seen? "What are you talking about?"

"Something is or was going on between you two."

"Why do you say that?"

"One night over in Johnson City, I was waiting at that steak place not too far from the hospital for some of my friends for a girls' night out, when I saw you and Whitney in the parking lot. I thought you must've had a business meeting, and I started to come over to say hello. Before I got there, you two were kissing. Seconds later, you got in separate cars and drove away."

Jeremy knew he couldn't explain that away. They'd been caught. "Yeah, we dated for a while, but it's over. That's why it won't be a good idea to invite Whitney and her mother to Thanksgiving dinner."

"So are you going to tell Mom, or should I?"

"Neither. Whitney and her mom probably already have plans."

"But you don't know that, do you?"

"No, but I'm not inviting them. If they come, I won't be there."

Janelle plunked down on his couch and crossed her arms. "I'm not leaving until you tell me what's going on."

Jeremy stared out the front window at the gray sky that matched his mood. Explaining anything about Whitney gave him a headache, but he wouldn't get rid of Janelle until he did. "Okay, here's the short version. I fell for her. Jimmy warned me that she was trouble, but I was too dumb to listen."

Janelle rubbed a hand across her forehead as she appeared to hide a smile. "I don't want the short story. I want the whole novel. If you tell me, it won't go any further, and I'll run interference for you with Mom."

Could he trust his sister not to divulge this fiasco? "If you promise not to tell anyone, especially Jimmy. He'd never let me live it down."

"I promise. You can count on me to keep this to myself."

"If I find out otherwise, I'll never forgive you."

Janelle tilted her head. "That doesn't sound like you at all."

Jeremy hung his head. "I know. This thing has made me pretty angry at myself for falling for her line."

"Tell me what happened."

Jeremy didn't want to tell Janelle anything, but he was a prisoner of his own stupidity. "I don't know what to say?"

"Why didn't you tell anyone you were dating?"

"It was Whitney's idea, and isn't it obvious?

"You mean because of Jimmy?"

"Yes, Jimmy and work. And I went along with it. Now I know it was all about Jimmy."

"Why?" Frowning, Janelle shook her head.

"She's still not over Jimmy."

Janelle's frown deepened. "I don't believe that."

"Believe it. The day the Realtor called to tell her she had an offer on her house, as soon as she ended the call, she threw her arms around me and called me Jimmy."

Janelle stood and put her hands on her hips. "And you broke up with her over that?"

"Isn't that enough?" Annoyed, Jeremy wondered why Janelle was suddenly sticking up for Whitney.

Janelle shook her head. "I can't believe you. How many times has Mom called you Jimmy?

"That's different. She's my mom, not my girlfriend who used to date my brother." Jeremy turned away, not wanting to endure Janelle's scrutiny.

"Jeremy, if you still care about her, you need to apologize, grovel, or whatever you need to do to win her back."

"Why are you on her side?"

"I'm on your side."

"Seriously?"

"Yes, up until a couple of weeks ago, you've been happier than I've seen you in years. At first I thought it was the new job, but then I saw how you helped Whitney paint the inside of her house. The thing that sealed my suspicions about you and Whitney was seeing you kiss her." Janelle shook her head. "I didn't tell anyone. I kept that to myself."

"Thanks for that much."

"So what are you going to do about it?"

"About what?"

"Getting her back. It's obvious you still care about her, or you wouldn't be moping around."

Jeremy let out a heavy sigh. Would Whitney welcome his apology? "I wouldn't know how."

"If you can't figure that out, you're sad case, little brother." Janelle pressed her lips together in a grim line. "You've let yourself live in your brother's shadow, the good and bad. It's time you quit doing that."

Wasn't that what he'd promised himself he'd do? But he'd done the opposite. He'd let Jimmy fill his mind with doubts about Whitney. Jeremy paced, then turned to his sister. "First I'm going to talk to Mom and tell her the whole thing."

"You don't want me to do it?"

"No, I made the mess. I'll deal with it. Mom. Whitney. Everything. I have to figure it all out before Whitney will be invited to any family dinners."

"Okay." Janelle headed for the door. "I'm going to trust you to do that. See you tomorrow."

Jeremy hugged his sister. "Thanks for setting me

straight."

"That's what big sisters are for." Janelle smiled. "I'll be praying for you."

"Thanks. I'll need it." Jeremy stood on the porch as Janelle hurried to her car.

He rubbed the back of his neck. What did groveling entail? He had a lot of thinking and praying to do.

***

The noise and commotion of the Amsterdam Schiphol airport greeted Whitney as she entered the arrival hall. Anticipation, Anxiety. Exhilaration. The emotions overwhelmed her. She was going to meet her father. She had buried her sorrow over losing Jeremy by doubling down on the search for the man she'd wondered about ever since she'd learned she was adopted.

The search had led her to Niels Lindemann, a fifty-year-old software engineer. Whitney had come across an old photo a friend had tagged him in on one of his social media platforms. The photo of a group of friends included a young woman who looked so much like the photo Whitney had of Melissa Hamilton. That led her to find a way to contact Niels Lindemann. She'd been able to enlist the help of a friend in Atlanta, who had found a phone number.

After she had talked with Niels, he had offered to let her post her photo on his page. Once he'd seen the photo, he'd agreed to take the DNA test. When the DNA test had confirmed his paternity, he was eager to meet her. He'd made arrangements for her to fly to Amsterdam the day after Thanksgiving.

Whitney looked forward to also meeting her teenage half sister, still at home, and two half brothers who were attending university. They were coming home just to meet her. She prayed they would like her and she them. After being an only lonely child for years, she had a family, and she wanted them to be marvelous people. Just the fact that her father had invited her to visit buoyed her spirits. Their invitation gave her hope that her new family would be all she had hoped for.

The only thing missing was Jeremy.

She shouldn't be thinking about him, but her heart still ached from his rejection. How come he couldn't understand? She'd thought she'd pleaded her case, but he didn't want to listen. He'd simply turned her away. That sad thought had filled her mind during her every waking hour.

Now that Whitney was back in Amsterdam, she couldn't help thinking of the time she'd spent here with Jeremy. She wished he were here to share this experience with her since his research had prompted her quest on social media. It had brought her to this moment.

Whitney scanned the area for the man whose photo she had studied on the flight. He was thirty-one years older than the photo Eileen had saved, but he looked very much the same. The most significant differences were a few wrinkles and the gray mixed with the straw-colored closely cropped hair, unlike the longer, more unruly hair of his youth.

Finally, Whitney spied Niels holding a sign with her name on it while he stood under the sign where they had agreed to meet. Her heart raced, and she waved timidly as she approached him.

Smiling, Niels returned her wave and strode toward her. "Whitney?"

She nodded, the threat of tears all too real. She wasn't sure how to greet this man. Hug? Handshake? Nothing? What to call him? Niels? Father? Dad? She'd never thought this meeting through. "Hello."

Niels nodded. "You look like your mother. You take me back thirty years."

"Thank you for meeting me." Whitney knew that was a lame response, but she didn't know what else to say."

"I am glad you found me. I cannot tell you how much it means to me to meet you, the daughter of my youth." Niels shifted his weight from one foot to another. "I am excited to get to know you. My wife is readying a meal for us. I hope they did not feed you too much on the plane."

Whitney laughed. "They always feed you too much, but I'm excited to get to know you and your family. This is a treat."

Niels shook his head. "I can hear your mother's laugh."

Whitney smiled and wondered why her mother and Niels ended their relationship and why her mother never named Niels as the father of her child. But Whitney would never know her mother's reasons.

On the ride to Niels's home, Whitney commented on the sights while she really wished to find out the answers to questions she'd been thinking about since she'd found out about her adoption.

"Niels, do you mind answering some questions about you and my mother?"

Niels gripped the steering wheel until his knuckles turned white. He kept his gaze focused on the road ahead. "I will try."

"Thank you. Why do you suppose my mother never identified you as my father?"

"That is a tough one. We cannot know for sure."

"Any guesses?"

Niels sighed heavily as he glanced Whitney's way. "We had a terrible disagreement, and it is difficult for me to discuss it even these many years later. Do you mind if I write this in a letter that you can read?"

Whitney nodded. "That will work. I know it must've been a shock for you to learn of my existence."

"Yes, but a pleasant shock." Niels smiled. "We are almost there. I will work on that letter and make sure you have it before you go."

"Thank you."

"Danique will get to meet you when she comes home from school today. Timo and Ruben plan to come on Sunday. They are all eager to meet you. We will attend church together."

"I would like that." Whitney recognized the change of subject, and she wondered what this letter would contain. Would it answer any questions or just make for more?

CHAPTER EIGHTEEN

Sunshine reflected off the glass in the doors of the assisted living center. Jeremy strode down the hallway toward Eileen's apartment. He had to talk to Whitney.

She wasn't answering her phone. He hoped she wasn't refusing to answer because she didn't want to talk to him. He would talk to her in person, but he didn't know where she lived now that she'd move to Johnson City, and he certainly couldn't confront her at the office. He prayed that Eileen would have the answers.

After Jeremy knocked on the door, Eileen answered with a smile, looking much better than the last time he'd seen her. "Hello, Jimmy."

Jeremy smiled. How ironic that Eileen had greeted him this way. "Eileen, it's me, Jeremy, Jimmy's younger brother."

Eileen put a hand to her mouth as she shook her head, much the way Whitney had done that day. "Please forgive me. You and your brother look so much alike, and I am so forgetful these days."

"No problem, Eileen. You're not the only one who gets us confused." A reminder from God. Jeremy wished he could undo his foolish response to Whitney's mistake. He hoped this meeting would get him on a path to make amends.

Eileen motioned toward her little sitting area. "Please

come in."

Jeremy took a seat. He wanted to see Whitney, but he should spend some time visiting with Eileen instead of getting the information he wanted and hurrying off. "How are you doing, Eileen?"

"I am doing much better. I like it here. I'm so glad Whitney found this for me, and it's a relief not to have to worry about the house. And now Whitney is close by, and she can stop to see me every day after she gets off work. We often eat supper together."

"That's good. I'm happy for you. How is Whitney doing since she moved here?"

Eileen shook her head. "She seemed so sad when she moved here, and I didn't understand why because she was the one who suggested we sell the house, but now she is so happy. She found that man."

Jeremy's heart plummeted. Had Whitney already found someone else? "What man?"

"Her father. She's visiting him now in a…that city." Eileen shook her head. "I can't remember, but she's coming home tomorrow. She told me I wouldn't be able to call her, but she gave the nurse the information should I need to talk to her."

"Is she driving or flying home?" Relief washing over him, Jeremy hoped Eileen could tell him.

"Flying."

"Into Tri-Cities?"

"I don't remember." Eileen reached for a little notebook on the end table. "It might be in here."

Jeremy took the notebook and opened it. He recognized Whitney's neat script. *Amsterdam to London. London to Charlotte. Arrive 4:40PM.* Tomorrow. He had to meet her at the airport. That meant asking Graham for time off and a talk with Jimmy.

Jeremy stood. "It was good to see you, Eileen. I hope to make my visits more frequent from now on, but I need to get going today."

"That would be lovely."

"No need to see me to the door. Thanks for telling me the good news about Whitney finding her father."

Eileen nodded. "You're welcome. I look forward to seeing you again."

Jeremy hurried to his car. First stop, Jimmy's.

Jeremy stepped into Jimmy's workshop. The familiar scent of wood and stain filled his nostrils. The sound of a saw filled the space.

Jeremy waited until the noise stopped. "Jimmy!"

Jimmy turned at the sound. Flipping off his safety goggles, he smiled. "Hey, little brother. What brings you by?"

"I've got something to tell you and a favor to ask."

"Go for it."

Jeremy took a deep breath and prepared for Jimmy's disapproval. "I hope you can accept what I'm about to tell you with an open mind."

"I'll try."

Praying for the best, Jeremy launched into an account of his relationship with Whitney. He left out the information about her adoption because he wasn't sure she wanted that to be common knowledge. He would let her make that announcement. As he continued the story, he couldn't read Jimmy's reaction. "I know you might not approve, but will you drive me to Charlotte tomorrow so I can ride home with Whitney, if she'll accept my apology?"

Jimmy's expression remained unreadable. "So you want me to hang around until you know for sure she won't reject your remorse?"

Jeremy nodded.

"I told you she was trouble." Jimmy slowly shook his head.

Jeremy's shoulders slumped. "Are you going to help me or not?"

Jimmy grinned and clapped Jeremy on the back. "Yeah, I'll help you. Whitney was bound to snag one of the Cunningham men. Don't blow it."

***

Whitney breezed through customs and headed toward the spot where she would catch the shuttle to long-term parking. She was still pinching herself. The trip had seemed like a dream. Her new family was everything she had hoped for, and on the flight back, she'd read her father's letter over and over again. He had loved her mother, and losing her had resulted in a change in his life. The regret in the missive made her see she had to do something to win Jeremy's good favor again.

Her father's experience told her she didn't want to repeat his mistakes in letting a love go too easily. The issues that had torn her parents apart weren't the same as hers and Jeremy's, but they were a lesson in not giving up on love. She loved Jeremy, and she wanted him in her life forever. Could she make that happen?

As she wheeled her suitcase toward the exit where she would catch the shuttle, her heart jumped into her throat. Jeremy stood near the door as he held a bouquet of roses.

She approached with caution, a lump in her throat.

"Whitney." Uncertainty in his voice, Jeremy stepped toward her. "Hi."

Whitney released the breath she'd been holding. "Hi. Are those for me?"

Jeremy's face broke into a slow smile, and he held the roses out to her. "Yes. A peace offering. Will you forgive me for my knuckleheaded reaction to your slip of the tongue?"

Without taking the roses, Whitney wrapped her arms around him and held him close. "Jeremy, you don't have any idea how happy this makes me. I've been praying you'd forgive me."

Jeremy hugged her tighter. "Thank you for forgiving me and giving me another chance. I was wrong, very wrong. I want you in my life. I've missed you so much."

Whitney stepped out of his arms and took the roses. She held them up to her face and took a deep breath. "These are beautiful, and they smell marvelous. Thank you."

As they walked to the shuttle stop, Jeremy grabbed his phone from the pocket of his jacket. "I have to call Jimmy and let him know we're good and he can go, as long as you're willing to give me a ride home."

"Jimmy knows about us?"

Jeremy gave her a lopsided smile. "Yeah. And it's all good."

Whitney returned his smile. "Glad for that. Let's get to the shuttle. I'm eager to get home and talk to my mom."

"You mean your grandmother?"

Whitney looked over at him as the shuttle stopped at the curb. "Even though I know she's my grandmother, she'll always be Mom to me."

"I'm glad. I think that's good for you and her. I saw her yesterday, and that's how I knew when your flight arrived." As they boarded the shuttle, Jeremy placed his phone to his ear and gave Jimmy the okay to head home. After he ended the call, Jeremy looked at Whitney. "He told me to tell you to treat me well."

Whitney laughed, and it felt so good, as if a huge stone had been lifted from her heart. "I plan on it. While we drive home, I'll tell you all about my trip."

"I want to know all about it. How did you find your father?" Jeremy asked as they left the shuttle.

Whitney sighed. "When you broke up with me, I poured all my hurt into the search for him."

"I'm sorry I hurt you. I wish I could undo that day."

"But without that hurt I may not have searched as diligently. I'm choosing to look on the bright side of it."

"Thankfully for me." Jeremy put an arm around her shoulders and pulled her close

Whitney unlocked the car, and Jeremy put her suitcase in the trunk while she laid the roses and her backpack in the backseat. "Let's get on the road."

"So how did you find your dad?"

While Whitney drove to the highway that led out of town, she told Jeremy about the photo she'd seen on social media and what had transpired from there. "I connected with all of them immediately. It was like we've known each other forever, and yet I was only there a few days. They want to come visit me sometime next year. I can hardly wait."

"Whitney, I'm so happy this has all worked out for you."

"If you get into my backpack, there's an envelope in there. It contains a letter from my father. I want you to read it aloud to me."

"Isn't it private?"

"It is, but I want you to know, and I don't think Niels would mind. I told him about you and how his experience with my mother was prompting me not to let our love go. Even if you hadn't come to meet me today, I was going after you when I got home."

"I love you, Whitney, and I don't want anything to come between us again." Jeremy pulled out the envelope and opened the letter.

"I feel the same way." Whitney glanced over at him. "Please read it."

Jeremy's deep voice sounded above the hum of the motor and the sound of the tires against the road.

"'Dearest Whitney,

"'This letter is difficult to write because it brings back some painful memories. But I have learned that painful things in our lives can sometimes bring about good. You are one of those good things in my life. I am grateful to God that He allowed me to learn of your existence. Meeting you has enriched my life more than I can tell you. I ask your forgiveness that I wasn't there for your mother, that my selfishness led to my missing thirty years of your life.

"'You want to know what happened between your mother and me. This is a difficult thing for me to talk about, but I must be honest with you. I loved your mother, but I was leading a degrading life and bringing her down with me. One day she stood up to me and told me she could no longer be with me if I chose to do drugs and spend my time drinking instead of going to class and studying. She said I was wasting my talents and told me that we could no longer be intimate. It was wrong outside of marriage. I laughed at her and told her to find a choirboy to hang with. I regret those words.

"'We never saw each other again, but her words came back to me months later when one of my friends died of a drug overdose. It was a wake-up call. I tried to find Melissa, but I soon discovered she and her parents had returned to the States. I had no idea where they had gone. Maybe I could have found her if I had had the tools back then that you had to find me now. But losing Melissa made me change my life, and it brought me into contact with my wife, Anneke, who is a Christian. She helped me give my life to the Lord. Our country is very secular, and Christians are in a minority. It makes me happy that you are a Christian also. This is one more thing we can share.

"'You asked why your mother never named me as your father. I don't know for certain, but from what I have already told you, you can see that she would not consider me good father material. And since we were separated by an ocean, I believe she thought it better not to include me in what must have been a difficult time for her and her parents. You have told me of your struggle to understand how your grandparents could have kept your parentage from you, but I think they did what they thought was best. I am glad you have chosen to forgive them. Forgiveness frees us.

"'I will pray for you, my dear daughter, as you seek to reconcile with this young man you love. Please let me know how it all turns out. I look forward to our next meeting. God be with you until we meet again.

"'Your loving father,

"'Niels'"

Silence filled the car as Jeremy placed the letter back in the envelope. Whitney gripped the steering wheel tighter as she waited for Jeremy's response.

"Whitney, that was an incredible letter." Jeremy's voice sounded husky.

"I know. It touches my heart every time I read it. I'm so blessed. I have you, and I have my new family."

"Are you tired? I could drive if you want."

"That would be great. We can grab a bite to eat in the next little town and switch drivers then."

"Good idea."

After they picked up some fast food, Jeremy drove, and Whitney tried not to fall asleep. But her eyelids drooped. "I hope you don't mind, but I'm afraid I can barely keep my eyes open."

"That's okay. Get some rest."

"Thanks." Whitney closed her eyes, her heart content for now.

So why did she worry that something would go wrong? She had seemed to have everything a girl could want when she'd been in high school, but since that time, everything she'd touched had turned to fool's gold. Had things changed, or would something unexpected go wrong just when she thought everything was perfect?

She had to quit worrying and put her trust in God. He would guide her through the good times and the bad. Wasn't that what she'd learned over the last few months? Jeremy had helped her see that, and he was back in her life again. That should give her joy, not worry. She drifted off to sleep with thoughts of Jeremy's love filling her mind.

***

The headlights of Whitney's car illuminated the drive at Jeremy's house. Jeremy glanced over at Whitney, who still dozed in the passenger seat. He hated to disturb her, but he had something he wanted to show her and something more important that he wanted to say. She had forgiven him. She loved him. So wasn't this the perfect time to ask her to marry him?

Doubts joggled his mind. Was it too soon after their reconciliation? Not for him, but maybe for her. Without a doubt he wanted to make her his wife, and there was only one way to find out if she wanted the same thing.

"Whitney, we're back in Pineydale."

Whitney's eyes fluttered open, and she straightened in her seat. She looked around. "Pineydale? What are we doing here? Did you forget I don't live here anymore?"

Jeremy turned to face her, one arm resting on the top of the steering wheel. "I brought you here because I have something I want to show you."

"What?"

"Come with me." Jeremy got out of the car and went around to open the door for her.

Whitney followed him as he made his way up the front walk. "How can I see anything when it's dark?

"Just wait right here." Jeremy took the steps to the porch two at a time and leaned over. "Watch."

In an instant the front of his house was flooded with colorful lights. The tree in the yard sparkled with tiny snowflake lights. Lighted candy canes lined the walk. A large star lit the nativity scene on one side of the yard.

"Wow! You've already decorated for Christmas."

Jeremy grinned. "Yeah. I remembered from when I was a kid how much you loved looking at Christmas lights. I wanted to surprise you."

Whitney raced up the steps and hugged him. He pulled her into his arms and kissed her. He'd missed her kisses. He'd missed her bossy attitude. He'd missed her laughter. He didn't want to live without those things in his life ever again.

When the kiss ended, he held her at arm's length. "I've got one more thing to show you, but it's in the backyard. Come with me."

They traipsed through the house to the back door. Jeremy motioned for Whitney to go ahead of him out onto the deck. She turned and looked at him. "More Christmas lights out here?"

"Wait right here and you'll see." Jeremy plugged in a cord, and just like the front yard, the backyard became a fairyland of Christmas lights.

"Jeremy, you've outdone yourself. When did you have time to do all of this?"

"When I was trying to figure out how to win you back." Jeremy put an arm around her shoulders. "Janelle knows about us."

"So does Jimmy. What about the rest of your family?"

Jeremy shook his head. "They don't know, but Janelle knows because she saw us together over in Johnson City one night. She's the one who told me I should apologize and grovel in order to win you back."

"She did?"

"Yeah. Did I grovel enough?"

Whitney laughed. "You didn't need to grovel, but I like

the Christmas lights."

"Good. I've got one more little surprise." Jeremy flipped one more switch. On the far end of the property that backed up to a wooded area, multicolored lights glowed in the darkness.

"What's lit up way back there?"

Jeremy grabbed one of her hands. "There's a creek back here and an old footbridge. I didn't know it was there until I started decorating and cleared brush away from the creek. So I decided to decorate it, too."

"Is it safe to walk on?"

"Absolutely. Let's take a closer look." Hand in hand, they raced together to the bridge.

"I'd like to see this in the daylight, too."

"You'll get to do that." Jeremy reached into his jacket pocket and fingered the padlock and key that he'd purchased yesterday. "I have something else to show you."

"More lights?"

"No, this." Jeremy held the padlock in the open palm of his hand and put it under one of the lights on the bridge railing. "See what's written on it?"

Whitney looked down. "Whitney and Jeremy." She looked up at him, a question in her eyes.

"Should we put a date on this, lock it to the bridge, and throw the key in the creek?" Jeremy's heart hammered as he gazed into her eyes reflecting the Christmas lights.

"Does this mean what I think it means?"

"If you're thinking I want to marry you, then yes."

"And I want to marry you."

Jeremy pulled her into his arms and kissed her. A thousand Christmas lights exploded in his head, and bells rang in his ears as they stood in each other's arms.

When the kiss ended, Whitney stepped back. "You're my dream come true."

As they stood on the bridge, the lights twinkling around them, Jeremy got down on one knee. "Whitney Hamilton, I love you. I want to spend the rest of my life with you. Will you marry me?"

"Yes, but I don't want to wait very long to get married. I want to get married as soon as possible so my mom will know what's happening."

"We'll get married on whatever day you want."

Jeremy stood and took a little box out of his pocket and popped it open. A diamond ring reflected the colorful lights like a rainbow. He plucked it from the box and placed it on Whitney's finger. "Now just one more thing. The love lock. And some day we can tell our children why this padlock is hooked to the bridge."

Together Jeremy and Whitney wrote the date on the lock and tossed the key into the night. It landed with a splash in the creek. Then they attached the lock to the railing and snapped it shut. Jeremy pulled Whitney close for one more kiss, a kiss filled with promise for their future.

EPILOGUE

February the following year

Candles flickered in each of the windows of the church where Cunninghams had been getting married for decades. The myriad colors of the stained glass glowed in the candlelight, giving a rainbow effect to the sanctuary. Whitney stood at the back of the church, her arm through her father's. She smoothed the skirt of her white satin gown covered in filmy lace. Smiling, she looked up to him, so happy she had found him.

Niels returned her smile as the first strains of the bridal march, played by three men on bagpipes, sounded through the air. "Ready?"

Whitney nodded and gripped his arm. As she walked down the aisle, she looked straight ahead at Jeremy. He stood beside his best man, Jimmy, both men dressed in the Cunningham black-and-red tartan and black jackets. Jimmy leaned over and said something to Jeremy, and the two men smiled. The acrimony of past years was gone, and love and respect had taken its place. Jeremy was the reason. He was the reason for love. He was the reason for so much good in her life.

As Whitney and her father reached the front of the church, he kissed her on the cheek and placed her hand in

Jeremy's. With the other hand she gave her bouquet of red roses to Danique, who wore a chiffon bridesmaid dress with a flowing black skirt and a bodice of swirled black and red to match the colors of the tartans.

Jeremy squeezed Whitney's hands as she turned to face him. Whitney couldn't believe this day had come. She had found a new family in the Lindemanns, and now she would join the Cunningham family. The lonely only child had found what she had dreamed of forever.

A big family.

Jeremy and Whitney repeated the traditional vows with strong voices that sounded over the church's sound system. They exchanged rings and had their own unique unity ceremony as they hooked together two padlocks through a ring on the closure of a treasure box filled with love letters and memorabilia from their wedding and trip to Europe. They made a promise to open and share it with their children when they were old enough to understand. They dropped the keys into a little cloth bag made of the Cunningham tartan.

As Whitney and Jeremy shared the final kiss of the ceremony, the congregation applauded. Hand in hand, the smiling couple hurried down the aisle and then stood ready to greet their guests, along with the best man, maid of honor, and parents.

Whitney glanced at her mom as she said hello to Charlotte. Today was a good day for her mom, and Whitney thanked God that she and Jeremy had decided not to wait to get married. They'd managed to plan the wedding in two months, and it was everything she'd hoped it would be.

As Charlotte wrapped her gnarled fingers around

Whitney's hand, she smiled, moisture in her eyes. "You are a beautiful bride, and I'm happy to see you finally grabbed one of those Cunningham boys. They're good men."

"They are, especially this one." Whitney leaned over and kissed Jeremy's cheek.

Laughter and joking ensued as the gang from the PMC ride, kids and all, filed through the reception line. Jeremy introduced Whitney to all the couples and children he had met on last year's ride.

Heather hugged Whitney. "I'm so glad you two have decided to join us this summer for the PMC ride. Poor Jeremy was a little lonely this last year, but now he has you. It'll make the ride that much better."

Whitney nodded. "I'm looking forward to it. Thanks so much for joining us on our special day."

Heather turned to Amanda, who stood next in line. "Amanda here has given us a connection to Pineydale, and we're so glad. Wait until you see what Max, Mitch, and Caleb have cooked up for you guys."

"If my cousin Mitch is involved, I'm sure it'll be interesting." Jeremy chuckled.

After the last of the guests had gone through the line, the photographer gathered the wedding party and parents for pictures. The guests made their way to the country club for the reception, while Whitney and Jeremy posed with family, then by themselves for photos.

After the photos were completed, Whitney and Jeremy emerged from the church and stood at the top of the stairs. The sun shone brightly and warmed the late afternoon of a winter day to above normal temperatures, as if God had reached down and given Whitney a perfect day for her wedding.

Jeremy laughed out loud as an unbelievable contraption rounded the corner and parked at the curb. "Heather said those three guys had cooked something up, but I never would've guessed at something like this."

Whitney wrinkled her nose. "Do you think it's safe?"

"I don't know." Jeremy raised his eyebrows.

"Come on, y'all. Your chariot awaits." Grinning, Mitch motioned for them to get into the strange-looking vehicle. "I made it myself, and I guarantee its safety."

Jeremy took Whitney's hand and led her down the steps. "I'm counting on that guarantee."

"Mitchell Cunningham, this better not fall apart while we're riding in it." With Jeremy's assistance, Whitney stepped into the rickshaw-like contraption attached to three bicycles and sat down.

"If it came out of my garage, you know it can't be beat." Mitch grinned. "I thought this was the perfect touch for one of our PMC riders."

With a salute, Mitch joined Max and Caleb as they got on the bikes and propelled the vehicle through town toward the country club for the reception.

Whitney laughed and gave Jeremy a kiss on the cheek. "This is marvelous."

Jeremy put an arm around Whitney's shoulders and pulled her close. "I love you."

Whitney snuggled up to Jeremy. "I love you, too. And you've taught me one important thing."

"What's that?"

"Ever since I left Pineydale after high school, this place has never held any welcome for me, but I found you, the love of my life right here."

"I think that calls for a kiss." Jeremy leaned over and

thoroughly kissed his wife.

With a contented sigh, Whitney leaned into him and drank in the sweetness of his kiss and the sweetness of their life to come filled with all the love she could ever want. She had found family, faith, and happiness in this tiny town called Pineydale, a place to find love.

Dear Readers,

Thank you for reading *A Place to Find Love*. I hope Whitney and Jeremy's story touched your heart and brought you a lesson about God's forgiveness and how important it is to forgive others and treat them with compassion. I hope you enjoyed the glimpse of some foreign settings as my characters traveled to Europe.

I would love for you to let other readers know what you think about *A Place to Find Love*. You can do so by posting an honest review wherever you purchased this book and also on Goodreads or Book Bub. Please consider mentioning *A Place to Find Love* on your social media sites, especially where you talk about reading! Word of mouth is the number one reason people pick up unfamiliar books. Every review and mention helps.

This is the last book in the Front Porch Promises series. I've had so much fun writing these stories. If you haven't read the other books in the series, I hope you'll look for them. Although each book can be read without having read the others, I enjoyed connecting each book with the others through characters and settings. Please check out the other books in the Front Porch Promises series, *A Match to Call Ours*, *A Place to Call Home*, *A Love to Call Mine*, *A Family to Call Ours*, *A Song to Call Ours*, and *A Baby to Call Ours*.

If you would like to get information on my upcoming books, please sign up for my newsletter on my website.

Merrillee Whren

ABOUT THE AUTHOR

Merrillee Whren is an award-winning and a *USA Today* bestselling author who writes inspirational romance. She is the winner of the 2003 Golden Heart Award for best inspirational romance manuscript presented by Romance Writers of America. She has also been the recipient of the RT Reviewers' Choice Award and the Inspirational Reader's Choice Award. She is married to her own personal hero, her husband of forty plus years, and has two grown daughters. She has lived in Atlanta, Boston, Dallas, Chicago and Florida but now makes her home in the Arizona desert. She spends her free time playing tennis or walking while she does the plotting for her novels. Please visit her website, www.merrilleewhren.com or connect with her on social media sites.

https://twitter.com/MerrilleeWhren
https://www.facebook.com/MerrilleeWhren.Author/

Other Books by Merrillee Whren

Dalton Brothers Series
Four Little Blessings
Country Blessings
Homecoming Blessings

Kellersburg Series
Hometown Promise
Hometown Proposal
Hometown Dad
Hometown Cowboy

Front Porch Promises Series
A Match to Call Ours
A Place to Call Home
A Love to Call Mine
A Family to Call Ours
A Song to Call Ours
A Baby to Call Ours
A Place to Find Love

Pinecrest
Second Chance Love
Second Chance Gift
Second Chance Forgiveness

Novellas
Puppy Love and Mistletoe

Puppy Love and Jingle Bells
Puppy Love and Christmas Cookies

Other Books
Miracle Baby
Second Chance Christmas

Village of Hope
Annie's Hope
Kirsten's Mission
Melanie's Resolve